3, 2,

"I wish for wealth..." Haroun began.

"Granted. I mean, hearkening and obedience," said Khalid the genie. A bag of gold the size of a yearling lion cub fell from the ceiling, nearly smashing Haroun's foot.

"I wish you'd be more careful," Haroun snapped, then clapped his hand over his mouth.

"Too late," Khalid's smile was meaner than a hungry hyena's. The bag of gold jerked itself back up to the ceiling and floated down as carefully as possible.

"I don't think that was fair," Haroun protested.

"I don't have to be fair, I just have to be your slave until you've used up your three wishes. Whining won't change anything. Rules are rules. Stop dawdling and try wishing for something useful this time."

Haroun licked his lip. "I've decided—"

"Yes, yes, yes—?"

"More wishes. As many wishes as there are stars in the heavens and grains of sand on the shore."

"You can't do that!" Khalid exploded. "You agreed to the terms. Three wishes, no more, and you can't use any of them to wish for more wishes."

"You never said anything about that, about not wishing for more wishes." Haroun straightened his shoulders, pleased with himself.

"The *However* clause!" Khalid cried. "I forgot the *However* clause!"

It was Haroun's turn to smile. "Careless of you."

"You wouldn't make me grant all those wishes, will you? It wouldn't be fair."

"I don't have to be fair," said Haroun.

"But my forgetting the *However* clause—that was only an accident; a slip of the tongue! Surely I shouldn't be punished for that?"

"Whining won't change anything," Haroun said. "Rules are rules. Don't make such a fuss." He picked up the genie's lamp. "This is going to be *fun*."

BAEN BOOKS by ESTHER FRIESNER

The Sherwood Game
Wishing Season
Chicks in Chainmail, editor

WISHING SEASON

ESTHER FRIESNER

BAEN

WISHING SEASON

This is a work of fiction. All the characters and events portrayed in this book are fictional, and any resemblance to real people or incidents is purely coincidental.

A Baen Book. This edition is reprinted by arrangement with Atheneum Publishers, Inc., an imprint of Macmillan Publishing Company, a division of Macmillan, Inc.

Baen Publishing Enterprises
P.O. Box 1403
Riverdale, N.Y. 10471

ISBN: 0-671-87702-X

Cover art by Darrell K. Sweet

First Baen printing, January 1996

Distributed by
SIMON & SCHUSTER
1230 Avenue of the Americas
New York, N.Y. 10020

Printed in the United States of America

To all my cats, past and present:
Benny, Cutesella I and II,
Paddington, Oliver James, and Nero.

CHAPTER ONE

Horrible in power, terrifying in face and form, mightier than all the armies of the earth, the genie Ishmael streamed from the gem of King Solomon's ring and hung the sky behind his awful person with curtains of fire and lightning. Twin scimitars gleamed in his mighty fists, blue smoke poured from his wide nostrils, and when he opened his mouth the tremendous roar of his battle cry struck the eagle from the sky and chased the lion back into his den as if he were a pussycat.

On the plains before the high city of Jerusalem, the great army of Unbelievers saw and trembled. Their swords were as many as the hairs of a young man's head, their spears keener than a fishwife's tongue, their chariots swifter than the changing of a young girl's desires or the passing of an old man's days. They had come in their uncounted ranks to pull down the shining walls of King Solomon's city. Now they were having second thoughts about the entire enterprise.

In the rear of the enemy host their king turned to one of his generals and said, "A fiend incarnate! You never told me Solomon had a fiend incarnate on his side, Nahash."

The general stroked his artistically curled beard and replied, "Mmmmmno. I don't think that is a fiend incarnate, Your Glorious Majesty. Our spies would have told us if Solomon had any of those lurking around the palace. I think it's an ogre unleashed."

The king was not used to being contradicted. "I wasn't born yesterday, General. I know a fiend incarnate when I see one."

"Ever-Living Lord of All You Possess or Covet, much as I dislike arguing with Your Supreme Omnipotence, I really must point out that the fiends incarnate never carry weapons. I have an uncle who is an evil sorcerer with whom I used to spend the weekend, so I know about such things."

"Do you." The king's eyes narrowed and a nasty light glinted in their depths. "Well, any fool with or without uncles knows that ogres are eaters of human flesh. *I* say it's *not* an ogre. And I further say that *you* shall go forth to the very front rank of my invincible army to confront the creature. If it eats you, it is an ogre, and I shall admit that you were right all along. If it only tears you limb from limb you will *have* to acknowledge that it is a fiend incarnate, just as I said, and you owe me an apology."

General Nahash paled and began to shake. "Majesty, I—I think it may indeed be a fiend incarnate, as you have so wisely observed. There's really no need to delay our attack over silly little experiments which are quite unnecessary to—"

"It's a genie," said the general's personal slave. He was a bright young man, an Israelite captured during a minor skirmish while the invincible army was making its way to Jerusalem from the seacoast. Now he leaned at his ease on the general's second-best shield, shaded his eyes against the sun, and studied the monster a little longer before adding, "Yes, I'm not mistaken; a genie. My lord King Solomon is master of many such fabulous creatures. Everyone who is anyone knows that."

"A genie, you say?" The slave spoke with such easy

confidence that the king had to believe him. "And—ah—do you also perhaps know anything about the—er—habits of genies? As compared to ogres unleashed and fiends incarnate, I mean."

"Well, genies never eat human flesh—"

"Oh, good."

"—or rend you limb from limb—"

"Much better."

"—when it's so much simpler for them to reach down and pluck your head right off your neck before you can say boo, just like a girl picking oranges."

The king swallowed hard and placed both hands lovingly around his own neck. The general did the same. The slave continued to observe the genie, who was now stalking back and forth before the first rank of the invincible army, bloody foam frothing from his lips and huge sparks of green fire coming out of his ears. He had grown a second set of arms, the better to display a pair of matched javelins which had appeared out of thin air. When he twirled them, the sky filled with an eerie wailing sound, as if ten thousand widows were weeping for the soon-to-die.

The general's voice was suddenly very dry and brittle. It broke easily when at last he asked, "If—if that's how genies like to do their killing—plucking your head off, like you said—then why—why is *that* one making such a spectacle of himself with those swords and javelins?"

"Showing off," the slave replied, cool as northern snow. "All genies, you see, are the slaves of my lord King Solomon. Some he keeps imprisoned in boxes, some in lamps, some in mystic talismans. That one there looks like the jewelry kind: magical rings, bracelets, ear-hoops, whatever you fancy. If you spent centuries inside a diamond or ruby big as a pigeon's egg, you'd be inclined to do things a little gaudily yourself. Besides, the greater a show he makes of your inevitable deaths, the more likely he is to impress my lord King Solomon and the more likely my lord King Solomon is to free him in gratitude. It's been known to happen."

The king had not absorbed everything that the slave had said. "Deaths?" he repeated. "Our *inevitable* deaths?"

"Sure as taxes," said the slave. He jerked his thumb at the genie, who had begun to growl. "Hear that? You're making him angry. When he plucks your head off your shoulders, he'll do it *slowly*."

"In all the gods' names, how am I making him angry?" the king cried out in anguish.

With yet another don't-you-know-*anything?* look, the slave explained: "It's the army that's doing it. And it's *your* army, Majesty. They're not retreating."

"Nor should they!" The general struck a proud pose. "We have trained all who serve in Your Uncontested Magnificence's army to stand their ground, no matter what. Death is but for a moment, they are taught, but the wrath of their beloved and adored king can be made to last several months. They will not run, no matter how frightened they are."

"That's the problem," the slave said. "It would look *much* better for the genie if his appearance alone were enough to scare off the enemies of my lord King Solomon. Why, he'd be guaranteed his freedom if he did that! But if he has to put himself out to the point of actually *killing* all of you, one by one—well! It just isn't half as likely to impress his royal master."

One royal master was impressed. "Call them off!" the king shouted, his fingers digging into the eyes of the two carved gryphons that were the armrests of his portable throne. "Sound the trumpets! Give the word! Retreat, retreat, immediate retreat!"

The king's orders sent the general into a sputtering tizzy. "But—but—but, Your Peerless Splendor, what about the battle? What about the plundering of King Solomon's riches? What about the songs of praise that the court poets and musicians will write about us—I mean, you—when we return in triumph?"

A new growl from the genie's throat sounded like blackest thunder across the heavens. "Hear that?" asked the slave, studying his fingernails. "Now he's getting *madder.*"

"To the utmost pit with the battle, the plunder and *the praise-songs, you fool!"* the king screamed, seizing the general by his beard and yanking out half the curls. "I said we must get out of here!"

And so they did, although in the confusion of retreat the general misplaced his third-best sword, his second-best shield, and one newly acquired Israelite slave. That lucky slave was only the first to begin the plunder of the abandoned enemy camp.

A great cheer went up from the walls of Jerusalem when the people saw the invincible army fleeing for their lives. The great gates opened and the people raced out to join the slave in tearing apart the deserted tents, looking for valuables. To reach the camp, they had to run between the legs of the genie, but not even the youngest among them showed any fear of passing so close to so great a monster. Like the newly freed slave, they knew that Ishmael was under the absolute control of their king and so was not to be feared while Solomon lived.

Finally, to the sound of trumpets, Solomon himself emerged from the city. He was carried on an ivory throne by eight princes. Four more carried upright silver poles that held a rich canopy of purple, crimson, and gold above the king's head. The throne, the poles, the canopy, and the princes were all liberally decorated with fabulous gems. As for the king, he wore no jewels except for a single ring whose giant ruby seemed dark and lifeless, as if the soul had escaped from it.

Then Solomon raised his hands to his mouth and called: "Ishmael! Ishmael, my servant!"

The genie heard, and immediately began to shrink. Smaller and smaller he grew until he was only a little more than man-size. He no longer smoked or flamed, and his weapons had vanished along with that extra set of arms. He bowed before the king and said, "Behold, Your Majesty, how I have fulfilled your command." His voice was deep and rumbly, but nowhere near the bloodthirsty roar of earlier.

"You have, Ishmael." Solomon smiled. "And fulfilled it admirably. You have my thanks. Now, to celebrate this victory, I wish for you to bring here a royal banquet. Let there be tables of gold and silver covered with silk. Let there be meat and drink of every kind. Let there be enough so that every citizen of Jerusalem may come and be satisfied and come again when next he is hungry and—"

"No," said the genie.

King Solomon frowned. " 'No'?" He repeated the word as if pretending he'd misheard it would change it.

Ishmael spread his powerfully muscled hands. "If Your Majesty will recall, when you first acquired me you wished for me to help with the construction of the Temple. Then you wished for me to fetch a suitable gift for the Queen of Sheba as a souvenir of her visit to Jerusalem. Last of all, there was today's wish. That's three. And that's all."

King Solomon began to turn the color of his canopy, but Ishmael remained firm. "I told you the rules when you first called me out of the ring: Three wishes, and *no* using one of those three to wish for more wishes. You agreed, you wished, I complied, and now I am free."

King Solomon drummed his fingers on the arm of his ivory throne. "Even knowing that I possess powers to command the Armies of the Air to destroy you where you stand, you refuse me?"

The genie folded his arms. "You knew the terms. Fair is fair. And since you *do* have more than your share of magical beings to serve you, I think it would be selfish of you to fight over so small a thing as my freedom."

King Solomon considered this. "Fair is fair," he agreed. "And truth is truth. Behold! You value your freedom more than your existence, yet you value what is *fair* more than your freedom. Is it so?"

"Precisely, O Wisest of Earthly Monarchs." Ishmael bowed more elaborately this time.

"Oh," said King Solomon. He pulled the ruby ring from his finger. "You'll be wanting this back, I suppose."

"If it is not too great an inconvenience, Majesty."

"No, no, not at all." He flipped the ring high into the air and remarked, "Catch."

The ring spun in the sunlight, a blur of blood-red and gold. As it tumbled against the bright blue sky, it slowed in its flight, climbing and climbing, never reaching the top of its arc, never beginning the fall back to earth. Its outline became fuzzy. Small glints of ruby-colored light broke away from the great jewel, filling the sky with free-falling flakes of brilliance. The lights multiplied until all that could be seen was a blizzard of scarlet brightness. King Solomon disappeared behind the sparkling veil, the towers of Jerusalem vanished, and the whole world was swallowed in a scarlet haze.

"Teacher! Teacher! I can't see what King Solomon is doing!"

Ishmael turned from the fading vision of past glory

that he had conjured up for his students and sighed. Really, this new generation of genies was quite without any appreciation for a really *artistic* ending.

With infinite patience he answered, "There is nothing more to see, Gamal. The vision has made my point. And what do you think that point is?" He raised his bushy gray eyebrows and regarded his unpromising pupil hopefully.

Gamal shifted uncomfortably on his flying carpet, making it buck and dip in mid-air. Although genies could change their looks, they could not change them *entirely*. An ugly genie could transform himself into a horse, but it would be an ugly horse. Gamal would make a *very* ugly horse. He was big and beefy, with a flat, sallow face that always seemed to be frozen in a sulky frown. He mumbled something which was not the correct answer.

There was a ripple of laughter from the other young genies in the classroom. It stopped abruptly when Gamal glared at them. He had a reputation as a cheater of mortals, a liar, and a brat, but mostly as a bully.

Only one of the assembled genies did not stop laughing at Gamal. This was because he had never started. He lay comfortably on a lush blue-and-green carpet that hovered in the corner of the classroom nearest to the garden window. Clearly he held himself to be above these petty schoolday squabbles. A little leather-bound book of poetry was in his hand. Without bothering to look up from it he said:

"Your point, O Teacher, is that no matter how high and mighty the mortal master we serve, our first duty is loyalty to the rules that limit our magic. Even if it means putting ourselves in danger." He raised his handsome face from the book and his honey-colored eyes twinkled with a smile. "After all, fair is fair."

"Well said, Khalid!" Ishmael could not hide the

pride he felt for this, his best student. The lad was—what?—no more than a century and a half old, yet he had easily mastered every lesson of Advanced Hearkening and Obedience, lessons it took other genies half a millennium to complete.

If only he did not know *how smart he is,* Ishmael thought. *Ah, well! I suppose he has good reason to be so vain.* A teasing voice whispered in the elder genie's ear, *Pride goeth before destruction, and a haughty spirit before a fall.* "Oh, shut up, Majesty," he muttered to King Solomon's ghost.

A hand shot up in the back of the classroom and a sweet, musical voice said, "O Revered Teacher, the vision likewise shows us that no matter how high and mighty the mortal master we find, we must always be certain to state that he or she is entitled to three wishes, three wishes only, and none of these may be used to wish for more wishes."

Khalid sniffed. "I didn't think I needed to mention something so obvious, so . . . *elementary.*" He went back to his poems.

Ishmael clapped his hands together and, to punish his uncalled-for sneering, Khalid's book vanished in a blaze of blue fire. After the necessary reprimanding frown at a startled Khalid, the teacher's smiles were all for the pretty genie maiden, Tamar. The lass was often Khalid's equal in the classroom, yet modest where he was smug. "You are right, Tamar," Ishmael said. "What is vital is often elementary. It was careless to have forgotten mentioning the *However* clause." He looked at Khalid meaningfully.

"I did not forget it," Khalid maintained. "I simply didn't think—"

"*That's* for sure." Gamal snickered nastily.

"At least Khalid didn't say that the point of our teacher's lesson was how to pluck the heads off mortals," Tamar snapped. Her flying carpet rose with her temper until her dark curls nearly brushed the domed ceiling.

So much fire, Ishmael mused as he observed Tamar's heated defense of Khalid. *Beauty and brains to match.* He clicked his tongue. *I wonder how many centuries will pass before she realizes that Khalid notices none of it?*

It was all very depressing, and Ishmael had one time-proven cure for sorrow. "For tomorrow, practice making blue smoke come out of your nostrils, bloody foam from your mouths, and green fire from your ears. Class dismissed!"

The young genies leaped from their carpets and bowed the moment that their feet touched the tiled floor. "HEARKENING AND OBEDIENCE," they all cried as one, and vanished. This time only five of them neglected to make their hats disappear too.

Ishmael chuckled over the forgetfulness of youth as he gathered up the castoff turbans and veils. A snap of his fingers sent them flying back to their owners. Then he went out into the garden to sit beside the fountain pool, feed tidbits to the goldfish, and forget the quirks and failings of his students.

"They will learn better once they have cut their teeth on the real world," he told the fat fish. They rolled their goggly black eyes at him, opening and shutting their mouths, saying nothing. "I only hope it comes in time for Khalid. If his head gets any bigger, soon he won't be able to get it through the classroom door. He's certainly bright enough to enter the wishing business—an even chance whether he or Tamar will be the first to graduate, in fact. Once out there, he'll find out that book-learning doesn't give you all the answers for dealing with humans. Yes, after the first encounter with a mortal, everything falls right into perspective."

Ishmael grew suddenly thoughtful. A notion had

lodged itself in his mind, and the longer it stayed, the more attractive it became. "Yes," he said to himself. "Yes, of course, that might be just what he needs. Khalid!"

"You summoned me, O Teacher?" Khalid was seated beside the older genie almost before Ishmael had finished shouting his name into the air. He looked as cool as if he had been there all along.

Ishmael beamed and patted his best student on the shoulder. "Khalid, my lad, I have good news for you. . . ."

CHAPTER TWO

"—Into a *lamp*? Oh, Khalid, that's wonderful!" Tamar clapped her hands together and gazed at him with undisguised admiration. As Ishmael had already observed, Khalid remained entirely unaware of the genie maiden's affection.

"Yes, isn't it?" he replied, basking in the congratulations of his fellow students. Ishmael's pupils had gathered at their usual after-school spot to sip sweet sherbet drinks and watch the unicorn races. Ever since Khalid's announcement, however, no one paid any attention to the race. "He said it's the custom to assign new genies to rings, but because I show such promise, he's lending me his very own lamp for a trial run. If I succeed in correctly granting wishes to one human being, I go straight into a lamp of my own."

"Straight into a stewpot's where *you* belong," Gamal grumbled. The big genie's face darkened with hate as he saw how Tamar still hung onto that obnoxious Khalid's every word. *Brains aren't everything,* he thought bitterly. *In a fair battle of magics I could take that pretty little rosebud Khalid and snap his stem in two. And in a battle of magics the way* I *like them, there'd be nothing left of him but a few worm-eaten petals and a gooey black smudge.*

Tamar sighed. "I wonder how long it'll be before I earn my own lamp? I've heard those rings can be so crowded, hardly any storage space, and no room at all to raise a family . . ." She let her voice drift off suggestively, her eyes on Khalid.

"Oh, I'm sure Master Ishmael thinks you're bright enough to be assigned to a brass bottle, not a ring," Khalid said, missing any and all hints Tamar might send his way. "Well, I must be off. The lamp awaits." He made the briefest of bows to his classmates and began to dematerialize.

"I hope your first master's kind!" Tamar called after him.

"Why shouldn't he be?" Khalid responded. "All mortals are pretty much alike."

"What? All mortals *alike*?" Tamar's eyes were wide. "Not by a long shot! Weren't you in class when we studied—? That's right, you weren't. Khalid, wait, you really ought to know! Why, there's males and females, tall and short, clean-faced and whiskered, bald and hairy, hair curled or straight, hair, eyes, *and* skin in so very many colors you can't begin to count them, some whose eyes cannot see, some whose ears are incapable of hearing, some who run, some who cannot even crawl—"

"Yes, yes, I *know* all that." Khalid's body was mist from the waist down. The vanishing effect climbed swiftly up until his last words before it reached his mouth were, "You'd think I wouldn't know a mortal when I saw one!"

Khalid lay scrunched up within Ishmael's lamp and wondered how his teacher had managed to squeeze into a ring. It was not only cramped in the lamp, it was boring. The worst part was not knowing how long his captivity might last. Senior genies did not have to inhabit their lamps at all times. Only junior-grade genies had to stay within the objects containing them, until they had proved themselves to their elders. They could not afford to take the chance of being so far away that they missed a summons. Experienced genies like Ishmael had senses so trained that they might fly to their proper places the moment some lucky mortal found the lamp and rubbed it. Until then, they were free to enjoy the gardens, orchards, palaces, and ten thousand other pleasures of the genie homeland.

The result of this arrangement was that no senior genie knew where in the mortal world his lamp was. For all Ishmael could tell, this lamp he'd sent Khalid to inhabit was at the bottom of the sea, or buried in the ruins of an earthquake. On the other hand, it might be sitting in some merchant's shop, or already in the possession of the mortal destined to rub it and get the surprise of his life.

"May it be so," Khalid muttered to himself. He squirmed against the cold metal walls. "Master Ishmael is a great teacher, but I don't care for his taste in furnishing a lamp. When I get one of my own, I shall ask for something a little more cushiony and comfortable." He worked a bad cramp out of his right arm. "*If* I ever get this stupid assignment done and get my own lamp, that is."

All at once, a prickly, electric buzzing ran up Khalid's spine. His eyes flashed. A joyful grin spread itself wide across his face. There was no mistaking what was happening. Even though the elder genies claimed they could not put the feeling into words, no genie since the dawn of time ever mistook *that* sensation for anything but what it was: Someone was rubbing the lamp.

Khalid straightened his turban, tugged a wrinkle out of his silk trousers, decided he would come out in a puff of blue smoke, then changed his mind and made it orange. The tug of a magical summons drew him from the lamp before he could switch smoke colors a third time. Surrounded by orange clouds, he soared upward. Sunlight from the lamp's spout dazzled his eyes. He burst out into the fresh air with a happy shout, accompanying his big entrance with a modest thunderclap.

The scrawny, brown-striped alley cat stared up at him and sneezed.

"Hail, O master!" Khalid made his fanciest bow, eyes lowered all the way. It was only good manners. "Name your wish, for I will grant it. Yes, three wishes and no more I will grant you. *However!* not one of these may ask for more wishes. If these terms please you, then by them I am your slave." The last words were uttered in Khalid's deepest voice, for they were the most potent of spells and bound the genie utterly to his newfound master.

The alley cat sneezed again from all the smoke, then rubbed its mangy chin against the lamp again.

Hearing no word from his new master, Khalid looked up. He saw that he was in a dark, smelly, very cluttered place. There were no alleys in the genies' world, nor rubbish heaps, nor cats. The smallest animal Khalid had ever seen was an infant dragon, and that was almost as big as he.

Ah, he thought. *It seems that Tamar was quite right. These mortals* do *come in a bewildering lot of shapes and sizes. This one is a lot smaller than those Master Ishmael showed us in his visions. His whiskers are not as tidy as that General Nahash's, and—What is that long thing curled around his feet?*

Khalid squatted down and repeated his offer of three wishes to the cat. He still got no answer and became worried. *Perhaps I should have listened more carefully to what Tamar told me of mortals,* he thought. *The week that Master Ishmael taught about them, I missed class. I vanished so fast during disappearing practice that I made a draft and caught cold from it. I meant to ask Tamar for the lessons, but—*

The alley cat had no idea of the thoughts passing through the young genie's mind. His own mind was full enough, although his stomach was not. He was not a fighter, and he did not find life in the alleys pleasant. Although he could not speak, his heart and mind yearned strongly and constantly for some food, some time to give his fur a proper washing, and a home with someone to love him. He couldn't tell a genie from a human any more than Khalid could tell a human from a cat. Heart full of hope, he went up to Khalid and rubbed against his hands, skinny body shaking with purrs.

"Master?" The genie was bewildered.

"Meow," said the cat.

" 'Meow'," Khalid repeated thoughtfully. "I know I was in class when we learned all the tongues of mortals. That word sounds *almost* Chinese, but the accent is wrong. Hmm. Perhaps this human is like one of those Tamar mentioned—having eyes but unable to see. He cannot speak! And see how he is so weak, he must support himself on all fours, like a unicorn. Oh, Master, Master, if you cannot speak, how can you ever make your wishes? And since I have already bound myself to serving you, how can *I* ever grant them and get out of here?" Feeling very sorry for himself, Khalid sat down cross-legged in the dirty alley while his new master rubbed against him, purring madly.

Without thinking, Khalid let his hand stray to scratch the cat's ears. The purring grew louder and more ecstatic. When the gloomy genie began tickling the cat under his chin while still scratching his ears, something happened.

"Gooooood."

"What did you say, Master?" Khalid dropped his hands and stared.

"More! Don't stop! Grrraaahhh, *more*!"

The demand was inside Khalid's head. The genie laughed, realizing what it meant. "Master, what a fool I am! If you cannot speak with your mouth, I can at least hear your desires with my mind. They teach us that trick when we are babies. Nothing is easier, as long as you *allow* me to read your thoughts. May I—?"

"Scratch under my chin some more before I bite you!"

"At once, O Master." Khalid was his old, smug self again. "I will not even count this as one of your wishes. Speaking of which, what *do* you wish for, Master?"

The thoughts were there almost before Khalid finished the question: "Food. Clean fur. Loving home."

"Hearkening and obedience," said Khalid, doing his best to keep scratching his master's chin. What he wanted to do was leap up and dance with joy. *Three wishes, all so easy, and all made at once! Oh, I'll be in a lamp of my own before another sunset!*

Khalid gestured, and a small banquet was laid before the alley cat. He had read the creature's thoughts and knew what foods would please it most, then he had improved on the order. On a piece of white silk with gold embroidery lay a blue dish filled with tender chicken, skinned and boned, cooked to perfection. Beside it was a red glass bowl of creamy milk, a platter of flaked fish, and some delicately cooked minced beef. There were also six live mice, but they ran off as soon as Khalid materialized them. Face deep in chicken, whiskers dripping milk, the happy cat never missed them.

While the cat ate, Khalid's magic removed all dirt from his fur, mended the patches torn off in fights, cured him of the mange. This done, Khalid searched the neighborhood for the loving home that would fulfill the third wish.

A few blocks away, in the Street of the Fuel Sellers, a young man was walking along very sadly. He was in good health, and neither poor nor ugly, but he was alone. In the same way that the cat's wishes had found their willing way to Khalid's mind, this young man's thoughts were loud and clear for anyone with the power to hear them:

"I'm so lonesome. I wish I had someone—anyone!—to share my home, my life with me."

The young man kicked a piece of broken pottery in the Street of the Fuel Sellers, and before his foot came back to earth he was in the alley. He looked around in confusion, but all he saw was a sleek, pretty cat and some empty dishes on a square of now-dirty white silk. The cat saw his big chance and rushed over to the young man, butting his legs and purring most persuasively.

The lonely young man smiled and picked the cat up. "Well, and what's such a fine-looking fellow like you doing here? You deserve a better home. Would you like to try mine?" The cat almost split himself purring and mewed eagerly. "Fine! It's settled. And these shall be your estate"—he crammed the empty dishes and the silk into the big leather pouch he carried—"for Heaven witness, it's not a rich man's household you're joining."

As he was carrying his new friend from the alley, the young man stumbled over something. Staggering to keep on his feet, he cursed the obstacle until he saw what it was. Still holding the cat, he knelt to pick up the lamp.

"It looks like someone around here has the habit of throwing out pretty things," he told the cat. "A lamp like this and a cat of such beauty in this filthy alleyway . . . It's like something out of those old stories. I wonder—?" The lamp quickly joined the other items in the young man's pouch and he continued to wonder all the way home.

Khalid presented himself before Master Ishmael to make his report.

"So quickly back?" The elder genie sounded pleased, surprised, and doubtful, all at the same time.

"I was fortunate, O Teacher, to find a mortal master whose wishes were simple."

"Truly? Then mortals have changed since my more active days. He did not demand to rule the world? To wed a princess? To wallow in gold?"

"Not at all." Khalid felt only a momentary pang of guilt when he stretched the truth thin by adding, "I believe that the dramatic way I chose to come out of the lamp may have shocked him into keeping his wishes modest."

"My boy!" Ishmael embraced his prize pupil, then invited him to sit down and share some mint tea. "You must tell me the details, and then I shall call the elders together so that we may arrange the ceremony for presenting you with your own lamp."

Khalid sipped his tea and spoke to his teacher as if they were now equals. "I did not have a long time with my first master, but it was still an interesting time. The most difficult part was discovering his wishes."

"So shy? I hope you didn't scare him."

"It was not fear. Poor man, he could not speak. The only sound I heard him make was a queer, rumbly noise, like distant thunder." Khalid tried to mimic a purr.

Ishmael frowned. "Was that—that sound all he could voice?"

"No. There was one other. Very strange it was, and almost like true speech."

"Strange?" The older genie was apprehensive. "How so?"

"I will do my best to imitate it, O Teacher. Bear with me." Khalid concentrated, cleared his throat, and proudly uttered: "Meow."

Ishmael buried his face in his hands and laughed until he cried.

CHAPTER THREE

"I don't see why I have to go through *this* if Master Ishmael thought the whole thing was so cursed funny!" Khalid hunched himself into a new position within his teacher's lamp, but it was just as uncomfortable as the old one. If he had had a hard time finding elbow room in the lamp before, now it was worse. Now he had that awful *book* in there with him.

For what felt like the hundredth time, Khalid slammed the book's cover shut and glared at it furiously. *Yazid's Guide to Better-Known Mortal Animals.* "A child's book, that's what my great and wise teacher, Master Ishmael, gives me to read! 'Study it well,' he says! 'I may choose to give you an examination on your return.' I have never been so insulted. All I needed was for Tamar to find out, or that wooden-headed bully Gamal. A maiden as smart as she is would never want to speak to me again, if she knew what a foolish mistake I made. As for Gamal, he'd laugh himself sick, then run and make sure Tamar heard all about it."

A crick in his neck made Khalid wriggle. One corner of the book jabbed him in the cheek. "Ow!" Grumbling and wishing the book to the eternal fires. Khalid went back to memorizing the chapter on cats while he waited for a second chance at earning a lamp of his own. He was annoyed with his teacher, he was fed up with the world, and he was angry with himself.

Worst of all, he was impatient to find a *real* master, grant some wishes, and put the whole unpleasant incident of the cat behind him.

"Pick me up, for pity's sake," he muttered, gazing up at the hole at the end of the lamp's spout. "Come on, come on, *find* me, rub me, let me out of here and I'll give you your heart's desire before you can say 'I want it.' Somebody, *any*body, find me! I want to get this stupid test over with so badly, I can taste it. Come on . . ."

He did not understand the dangers of being *too* impatient.

"Well, Boabdil, what do you think? Should I do it?"

The young man looked from the lamp in his hands to the cat at his feet. The cat did not bother to respond. He had been given a nice bowl of milk to drink, a battered old pillow to sleep on, and the freedom to do whatever he liked in his new human's home. He was satisfied, and a satisfied cat never troubles himself about other people's problems. Like all cats, he was a bit of a philosopher. He preferred to think over a problem for a long, long time before doing anything about it. If you thought about some problems long enough, they went away.

"You're not being any help, you know," the young man said, rubbing the cat's neck with his bare toe. He returned his attention to the lamp, took a deep breath, let it out slowly, and said, "At least there's no one but you in the house to see me acting like an idiot, Boabdil."

The cat raised his nose ever so slightly as if to say, *Yes, but cats remember.* It was wasted.

"You know, in the stories, it's always a poor boy who finds the magical lamp and releases the genie," the young man continued. He pushed a lock of straight black hair out of his eyes and rearranged his long, skinny legs on the floor cushion. "Yes, a poor boy or a shipwrecked sailor. Usually the genie who is the Slave of the Lamp brings his master wealth and fame and a beautiful bride. I'd say it was worth the risk of looking like an idiot for the chance of such rewards." He balanced the lamp on the palm of one hand and raised the other, as if about to begin rubbing.

He paused, hit by a second thought. "Sometimes, though, the genie is savage. A monster! No sooner does he emerge from the lamp than he tried to kill the man who freed him." He put the lamp down on the floor beside him and rested his chin in his hand, considering this unhappy possibility.

Now used to regular feedings, the cat Boabdil decided that it was about time for another. His loud meow was supposed to mean "Feed me! NOW!" It wasn't his fault if his human chose to take it for a mystical sign.

"Aha! You are right, Boabdil! In those tales where the genie tried to destroy his master, the man always found a way to trick the creature back into its lamp and toss it to the bottom of the sea. They are remarkably stupid, genies are. I've read all the tales; I know the trick for getting an evil genie to shut himself up in his own lamp. I can control whatever may come out of this one." Full of confidence, he picked up the lamp.

This time he got as far as having his rubbing hand touch its brassy side before he put it down again.

"Do you think *this* genie may have read the same tales I have and be too smart to fall for that old trick, Boabdil?"

Boabdil meowed once more, louder. Having a roof over his head—even such a modest one—had spoiled him already. His life in the alley was not even a bad memory. He knew that as a cat he was entitled to better service than this from his human.

"What is it, Boabdil? Are you angry at me for being a coward?"

"*Mrowrooowwww!*" Frustrated with human stupidity, Boabdil butted his human's hand, hoping the thickheaded two-legs would take the hint and use that hand to fetch an honest cat a nice piece of chicken.

"Ah!" The young man was awestruck. "Behold, a dumb animal pushes my hand closer to the lamp. This is truly a sign from heaven."

Boabdil had his own opinion about who was the dumb one. With nothing but dignity in his stomach, he stalked out of the room. His human did not see him go; he was too busy rubbing the lamp.

Nothing happened, at first. The young man's face fell. "I really am a fool," he mumbled. "Too many days spent listening to the storytellers in the bazaar. My poor dead father was right. No wonder I'm such a sorry excuse for a merchant! The others see me coming and give me poor goods, short prices, and no credit. If I protest, they cover their swindles with long, tearful tales of hungry children and aged parents whom they must support. Even when my common sense tells me they *must* be lying, I wind up believing them every time! Oh, I make it too easy for them, I do. Anyone can cheat a fool."

He was still tearing himself down when he noticed an eyelash-thin wisp of smoke coming out of the lamp's spout. It started off blue, turned orange, then seemed to lose interest in the whole matter of colors and was just a drab, common gray. He took fright and dropped the lamp, but the smoke kept pouring out. Thicker and thicker it grew, until the whole room was filled with a dull haze.

The young man felt panic rising in his chest. He

could hardly see in this magically summoned fog, but he was willing to bet that the genie could. (There *had* to be a genie, even if it hadn't materialized yet. As the old saying taught, "Where there's smoke, there are monsters.") If humans had learned the trick of deceiving unfriendly genies, why couldn't genies have learned a trick or two of their own over the years? All this smoke made a perfect ambush. He looked around for the doorway and couldn't find it.

"Help!" he cried. "Someone help me!"

"You're going to have to be more specific than that, you know," said a very cranky voice. " 'Help me' isn't much of a wish, Anyhow, it doesn't count; I haven't offered you anything, yet. O Master." This last was added as an afterthought, with no respect at all.

"Where—?" The young man coughed violently. "Where are you? I can't see a—"

The smoke vanished. The young man found himself eye-to-eye with a being who did not look like any sort of monster. Tall and wide-shouldered, with curly golden-brown hair and bronzed skin, the only thing frightening about him was the ugly sneer twisting his fine-boned face. Apart from the small fortune in jewels sewn to this creature's saffron belt, trimming his blue brocade vest, and pinning the white ostrich plume to his purple turban, the genie could pass for a human being of about his newly made master's age.

It was almost disappointing.

"Are you—are you the Slave of the Lamp?" the young man faltered.

"No, I'm the Giant of the Unclean Dishcloth. Of course I'm the Slave of the Lamp! And who are you?"

The young man knitted his brows. He had heard of genies being eager to please, or sly, or crafty, or downright evil. He had never heard of one being this rude.

Still, nasty or not, the being had come out of the

lamp and must possess great magical powers. Better to be polite. He bowed. "O Slave, I am called Haroun ben Hasan, son of Hasan ben Mustapha, a great merchant of this city."

"Great?" There was a positively spiteful tone to the genie's voice now. He looked around the room. It was clean enough, but mostly bare. The cushions were badly worn, the carpet was ragged, the low wooden tables tilted at crazy angles on chipped and broken legs. The genie took it all in, then said,"If this is how the sons of great merchants live, I would hate to see the houses of the poor."

Haroun's black eyes smoldered with anger. "My father *was* a great merchant! His caravans never failed to bring back treasures from the East. Once, this house was filled with music, guests, servants, poetry—"

"I know, I know, and then your evil uncle came along and stole everything. Or the sultan took it. Or maybe the grand vizier felt grabby. I'm not interested. You're wasting your time and mine, crying after what's over and done with, when you could be putting your life back into halfway decent shape. Well? What are you waiting for?"

"Waiting—?"

Khalid made rapid, encouraging motions with his hands. "Come on, hurry it up. You don't *look* like a man who's never read a book in his life. You know what I'm here for or you wouldn't have called me the Slave of the Lamp. Slave—ugh! I hate the word. My name is Khalid. Use it."

"You mean I'm supposed to—you're here to—I can have you grant my wishes?"

"Yes, three of them; if you can make them before we both keel over from old age."

"Heaven be thanked!" Haroun clasped his hands

together. "I know *exactly* what I want. First, I wish for—"

"Hold it." Khalid held up a delaying finger. "First I have to go through the usual enchanted gibberish binding my magic to your wishes or it's not official and we'll have to waste *more* time while you start all over again. Let's see, how does it go . . . ? Oh, yes. Ahem: Hail O Master name your wish for I will grant it yes three wishes I will grant you if these terms please you then by them I am your slave." He rattled off his speech so swiftly that it seemed like one continuous word. "All right, that's out of the way. Go! And put wings on it, I have better places to be."

"I wish for wealth . . ."

"Granted. I mean, hearkening and obedience." A bag of gold the size of a yearling lion cub fell from the ceiling, nearly smashing Haroun's foot.

"I wish you'd be more careful," Haroun snapped, then clapped his hand over his mouth.

"Too late." Khalid's smile was meaner than a hungry hyena's. The bag of gold jerked itself back up to the ceiling and floated down as carefully as possible.

"I don't think that was fair," Haroun protested.

"I don't have to be fair, I just have to be your slave until you've used up your three wishes. Stop dawdling and try wishing for something useful this time."

"But it *isn't* fair. What I said was just a figure of speech. I shouldn't be punished for a slip of the tongue."

Khalid had a sympathetic nature, but his botched first mission had turned it sour. Ordinarily he would have agreed with Haroun and allowed him to take back the second, wasted wish. He was a generous soul.

However, all he could think of at the moment was what might be happening back in the genie homeland. Time among mortals and time among genies was different. Sometimes days passed back home that were minutes here, and sometimes a single day among the genies turned out to be a mortal century. Where were his classmates? Had Master Ishmael forgotten his promise and told them of Khalid's blunder? Had Gamal managed to sniff out the truth? Would Tamar still gaze at him as if his smallest magic trick were the cleverest thing she had ever seen? Alone in Master Ishmael's lamp this time, he had had plenty of time to miss the companionship of his classmates (Gamal excepted) and to notice how the memory that kept returning more than all the rest was a vision of Tamar's face, smiling at him.

He realized that he missed her most of all.

I have to finish this job and get back home, he thought furiously. *I have to speak to Tamar, to tell her my side of what happened, before someone else poisons her mind against me. Why, she might even* laugh *at me! I couldn't stand that. Once I'm back, successful, that first assignment will be nothing more than a joke.*

His impatience to be on his way made Khalid even more irritable. "Whining won't change anything," he told Haroun. "Rules are rules. You know, instead of complaining to me about your own thoughtlessness, you ought to be grateful. I *could* have taken advantage of you when you made your first wish. All you asked for was wealth. You never said how much. Wise wishing is a skill few mortals possess. You have to be spe–ci–fic. I could have given you one gold coin. To a man in your position, that would still be wealth. I think I've been more than kind to you; kinder than you deserve." He folded his arms across his chest and looked haughty.

Haroun looked down at the huge sack of gold. "You're right, I suppose." He sounded glum. "I'm sorry."

"Don't mention it. Next time, think before you speak." Some time passed. Khalid tapped his foot. "You don't need to think *that* long. If you can't think of a third wish, I can make some standard suggestions. We have a nice deal on marriages to the sultan's daughter. Or how about a flying carpet? A palace with invisible servants? A stable of white horses? A palace with invisible servants and a stable full of white horses attached?"

Haroun did not look tempted by any of these. Khalid tried a new tack. "You're a merchant, right? Well, how'd you like a year's supply of whatever kind of bric-a-brac you mortals merch?"

Haroun licked his lip. "I've decided—"

"Good! Come, out with it. What do you want? Speak up!"

"I want . . . I want . . ."

"Yes, yes, yes—?"

"More wishes. As many wishes as there are stars in the heavens and grains of sand on the shore and hairs on all the heads of all the generations of men who have ever been born, and who live now, and who ever will be born, until the end of time." He paused for breath, then added, "Specific enough for you?"

This time the silence was all Khalid's creation.

Finally he said, "Gah."

"What happened to 'hearkening and obedience'?" Haroun wanted to know.

"You can't *do* that!" Khalid exploded.

"Why not? I just did."

"No, I mean you *can't*! It's illegal. You agreed to the terms. Three wishes, no more, and you can't use any of them to wish for more wishes. You *promised*—"

"You never said anything about that, about not wishing for more wishes. Why, it's so simple, I'm surprised no one in the old tales ever thought of it."

Haroun straightened his shoulders, pleased with himself.

"I did, too, say something about it! The *However* clause is standard procedure. If it weren't, every genie alive would still be serving his first master. You mortals are such hogs! And no exceptions to the rule, believe me. Even King Solomon couldn't hold on to the genies that served him after they'd done his bidding three times."

"I wish," said Haroun, "you could hear yourself."

"I can hear myself just fine, and I—"

"Not now. *Then.*"

And suddenly Khalid felt a tugging in his chest as his inborn magic stirred. Without his consent, his lips formed the words. "Hearkening and obedience," and the shabby room dissolved into a vision of the same room some minutes earlier. Horror-struck, Khalid saw his own face, bored and arrogant. Here was no honest genie, eager to perform the work of wish-granting for which he had been born. Here was only Khalid the Proud, Khalid the Vain, Khalid whose only care was protecting his own false image as the smartest, the most talented, the best.

He recalled his selfishness and the impatience that gave it birth. He saw that same impatience make him race through the magical words that bound him as Haroun's slave. He heard the words, but more important were the words he did *not* hear.

"The *However* clause!" he cried as the vision vanished. "I forgot the *However* clause!"

It was Haroun's turn to smile. "Careless of you."

Khalid groveled before him and grasped his knees. "O Master! O kind, benevolent, wise Master, you won't make me grant you all those wishes, will you? It wouldn't be fair."

"I don't have to be fair," said Haroun.

"But my forgetting the *However* clause—that was

only an accident; a slip of the tongue! Surely I shouldn't be punished for that?"

"Whining won't change anything," Haroun said, enjoying himself more than he'd done in years. "Rules are rules." He patted Khalid on the head, knocking his turban over one eye. "Next time"—he drew out the words on purpose—"*think* before you speak."

Khalid did think. He thought of his past vanity, of Master Ishmael's high hopes, of Gamal's black envy, of the awful, dismal situation into which he'd gotten himself.

He thought of Tamar.

When he had thought enough, he opened his mouth. He didn't speak; he screamed.

"There, there," said Haroun. "Don't make such a fuss. In fact, I *wish* you wouldn't." Against his will, Khalid's screams evaporated. "Much better." Haroun picked up the lantern.

"This is going to be *fun*."

CHAPTER FOUR

There was a party in the palace that night. There was always a party in the palace.

Rose petals drifted down from the ceiling just as the acrobats finished their famous fifteen-man pyramid in the middle of the feasting hall. The guests applauded wildly and threw handfuls of silver and pearls from the little gold pots their host had provided so thoughtfully. The sight of so much wealth was too much for the men on the bottom row of the pyramid. They lunged forward to gather up as much as they could grab, only to be knocked flat by their fellow performers as the whole carefully balanced arrangement came tumbling down.

The guests applauded louder, laughing. Heartily ashamed of what their greed had done, the acrobats hauled themselves up off each other and slouched out of the hall. A stony-faced servant whose uniform was made from cloth-of-gold gave each of them a small scarlet leather pouch filled with coins as they left. Other servants scurried across the pearl-strewn floor with brooms, sweeping up a fortune that would later be thrown from the highest balcony of the palace to the beggars waiting at the gate below.

In the midst of all this wealth and luxury, the master of the house sat on a gilded throne shaped like a lotus flower. Those guests lucky enough to have been given places near him were beginning to feel the first pangs of hunger. The banquet that came before the entertainment was lavish—the leftovers alone would feed the sultan's harem for a week—but these guests had not eaten a single bite. The roasted peacocks with all their feathers replaced and their toenails painted gold, the broiled doves in plum sauce, the giant carp stuffed with honeyed locusts, all passed them by untasted. The wines of a hundred legendary vineyards were poured into their jeweled goblets, and they left these unsipped.

Those who sat beside the master might feel uncomfortable for an evening, but they would rather starve than risk the alternative. Was it worth taking a mouthful of the most delicious meal ever cooked if the master decided to ask you something *right then*? There you would be, your mouth crammed with a big chunk of coconut cake with apricot glaze, and the master would be staring at you, waiting for a reply.

What if he didn't want to wait? What if waiting made him *angry*? What if the question he had just asked you was something to do with one of his legendary gifts?

My friend, would it please you to have a palace of your own? Oh, nothing fancy. Just a small one, on the shores of a mountain lake, a place to spend the summers. Would you like that?

He had done it before, giving presents so magnificent that some of his guests had fainted when he described them. He was likely to do it again, at any time. It was worth going without dinner when you wanted to keep your mouth ready to say "I accept with thanks, O my lord Haroun ben Hasan!"

This night, though, Lord Haroun did not seem to be his usual, generous self. The most he had given to his guests was a fine silk carpet apiece and pots of costly perfumes to take home to their wives. The guests nearest him noticed how solemn he looked. They did their best to cheer him up, making jokes and singing comical songs for his amusement. Nothing worked. He looked almost as gloomy as that gold-clad servant of his, the one rewarding the entertainers.

Lord Haroun was not amused by the entertainers nor by the songs and jokes of his guests. He stared out over the entire feasting hall and saw nothing. His own dinner, served to him on gem-studded plates, was uneaten. He stroked the brown-striped cat in his lap and fed it the best bits from his platter.

"Well, Boabdil, what do you think?" he asked the animal. "Is this fine? Are you happy?" The cat snorted and dug his claws into his human's satin robes. "Ouch! A little easier there, my friend. If you don't want to answer, I know I can't force you. I only wish—"

The feasting hall froze. The flames of the scented torches stopped burning. The dancing girls stayed where they were, caught in mid-leap. The guests were turned to stone where they sat. Here a goblet hovered an inch away from a thirsty mouth and there a piece of half-chewed food waited to be swallowed.

Only the grim servant in his cloth-of-gold moved. Slowly, wearily, he crossed the floor, weaving his way between the motionless dancing girls. When he reached the foot of Lord Haroun's lotus throne he bowed and said:

"*Now* what?"

Haroun made a face. "I thought we went over this before, Khalid. That is *not* the way to speak to your Master."

"If it isn't, you only have to *wish* for me to speak to you any way you want," the genie replied. "Why don't you?"

"I don't see why I should waste good wishes on something you can learn to do for yourself perfectly well." Haroun pursed his lips. "You are just like Boabdil;

you spend all of your free time looking for new ways to annoy me."

"What free time?" Khalid shot back.

"Oh, never mind." Haroun leaned his cheek on one hand and gestured with the other at the petrified banquet hall. "Look at them," he commanded. "Just look. One hundred fifty of my best friends. How many of them do you think know who I am?"

"The fame of Lord Haroun ben Hasan is greater than that of all the kings, all the princes, all the sultans, all the warriors, all the—"

"Enough!" Haroun cut off Khalid's monotonous recitation. "You know what I mean: How many of them *really* know me? How many would still be my friends if, by some miracle, I awoke tomorrow without the riches your magic has given me and without you to bring me more?"

The genie brightened. "An *excellent* idea, O Master! We ought to try it at once. Now if you'll just be good enough to put that into the form of a wish—"

"You'd like that, wouldn't you?" Haroun gave a dry laugh. "I think that rather than wishing for your magic to abandon me, I shall wish for it to abandon *them* instead. In fact, I *wish* this whole stupid party were over, that my so-called friends were back in their own homes, and that we three were—what was the name of that other palace you conjured up for me? The pinkish one on that quiet street? It had a very pretty garden full of peach trees—"

"The Palace of Eternal Bliss, O Master," Khalid said with a sigh.

"Yes, that's the one. I wish for you to take us there after you've cleared all *this* away." He waved at the frozen banquet.

"Hearkening"—each word was trailed by a sigh—"and obedience."

The frozen torches flickered back to life, but only

for a moment. The guests moved again, but not for long. The genie clapped his hands together once, and the lights went out. There was a short explosion of panic-stricken screams from the guests that ended the instant Khalid clapped his hands together a second time. Now total silence matched the total darkness.

"Well?" Haroun's voice came out of the dark. "What's taking you so long? We are waiting."

"Try holding your breath while you wait," Khalid growled, but not loudly enough for his Master to hear. Slowly, reluctantly, he brought his hands together a third time.

The echo of the clap still lingered in Haroun's ears when he and Boabdil found themselves transported to the palace of his wish. They were in the Garden of the Five Tigers, lying on fat silk pillows under the prettiest of the peach trees. Pink and golden fruit hung heavy from the branches. If Haroun wanted to taste the sweetest peaches the world had ever known, he had only to reach up his hand and pick them from where he lay.

Instead he said, "I wish I had a nice peach in my hand right now."

A sigh came from behind the tree trunk. "Hearkening and obedience."

Haroun looked at the peach that had appeared in his hand. He turned it over and around, studying it from every angle. If he had the eyes of a hawk, he would not be able to find any fault with it. In shape, in color, in fragrance, it was entirely perfect. No doubt the first bite he took would prove that its flavor was perfect too.

He did not bother biting it. "You've put the peach in my *left* hand. Khalid," he said. "You know I only use my *right* hand to eat fruit."

Khalid came slouching around the tree to scowl down at his Master. "Your wish didn't say anything about that. You just wished for the peach to be *in your hand.*"

"Yes, but you *know*—"

"I don't know anything!" Khalid bellowed. "Free beings *know* things; slaves just do as they're told. If you want me to show some independent thought, I'll have to *be* independent, and you don't want that, do you?"

Haroun put the peach aside and rubbed his upper lip thoughtfully. "I'm not a fool yet, Khalid. It's not that I don't want you to be free. I have nothing against independence. It's just that when you give most slaves their freedom, they tend to run away with it. That's the part I wouldn't like. I'd miss you."

Khalid plopped himself down in the dewy grass under the peach tree and gave his Master a hard stare. "Maybe if you had some other friends, you wouldn't miss me so much."

Haroun laughed. "I just tried having some other friends, remember? It didn't work." He scratched Boabdil behind the ears. The cat twitched his whiskers at him, sprang up, and stalked away. Haroun called and called after the beast, but Boabdil kept walking until he reached one of the five life-sized onyx tigers that gave this garden its name. Purring, Boabdil leaped into a loop of the sleeping tiger's tail and went to sleep himself.

"You see?" Haroun demanded, gesturing after the cat. "*That's* independence for you! By my own wish, I commanded you to make that ungrateful animal talk. That way, I thought, I would never lack for a companion. Has he said a single word to me? Does he even appear to understand human speech?"

Khalid gazed after the cat with longing. "There are some things which magic may not change; not even the magic of the world's most powerful genie, and I am certainly not that."

"I wish you were," Haroun said. He was not joking.

"Hearkening," Khalid replied, "but no obedience. It is not possible."

"Why not? Just use your magic—"

"Don't you have ears, O Master? There are always walls, in this world. Some we learn how to go around, or over, or under. Some we learn how to knock down. Some we learn to build doors through. But some things cannot be forced; some things cannot be changed. Eventually we find the wall that stops us, no matter whether we are mortal or magical."

"Very poetical." Haroun knitted his brows. "It still doesn't explain why you can't make a cat speak."

"I made him speak the minute you desired it, O Master," Khalid responded. "What I cannot do is make him want to speak to *you*."

"What? And why not?"

"Because like all cats, he is an excellent judge of character, and from watching your behavior ever since you got me for your slave, he has come to the conclusion that you are seven kinds of jackass and three sorts of idiot. O Master," he added, trying not to smile.

Haroun's stormy face grew darker. "I don't believe it. I *refuse* to believe it. You are using my poor, innocent cat as an excuse for your haphazard magic. The best genies can use their powers to do anything! I know; I've read the old tales."

"Have you? I cannot remember the last time I saw you pick up a book, O Master."

"I've been—I've been busy." Haroun shifted uncomfortably. The truth is often itchier than a swarm of red ants. "And anyway, it's none of your business!" he lashed out.

"No? Then what is my business, O Master? I'm sure you'll tell me."

"I'm still waiting for that peach! In the *proper* hand, this time."

Khalid did nothing. He did it in a way guaranteed to enrage Haroun.

"Well?" the young man snapped. "Where is it? I *said* I was waiting."

"So am I." The genie had come to treasure every tiny chance he got to slip little burrs into his Master's cushiony life.

Haroun gritted his teeth. "Very well. I *wish* I had a nice, plump, delicious, edible peach from one of these trees in my *right* hand now."

"Hearkening and obedience." The peach appeared.

Haroun sniffed it. He was always extra careful about Khalid's gifts immediately after one of these Master/genie discussions. Bickering gave him an appetite, and once he had wished for a fine quail dinner. The dinner Khalid produced, like the peach, was perfect. It even *smelled* perfect. Haroun had picked up one of the birds and taken a tremendous bite . . .

. . . of the most perfect wooden quail he'd ever tasted.

It didn't matter how real this peach smelled; Haroun had learned that lesson from the wooden quail. Very cautiously, he set his teeth to the velvet skin and took a tentative nibble. Sweet juice filled his mouth.

"Will that be all, O Master?"

"Mmmm?" Haroun was so happy with the delectable peach that Khalid had to repeat the question. "Oh, yes, yes, that's all for now. You may go."

"Ahem."

"I mean, I *wish* you would go away—"

"Hearkening and—"

"—to whichever room of *this palace* you like!" Haroun winked. "You don't escape me that easily. Nor will you escape until my wishes run out or else I decide I've had enough of wishing."

"Until you've had enough?" Khalid groaned. "Why not just say *until the world's end* and be honest about it?" He did not whisk himself out of the Garden of the Five Tigers, but straggled off into the palace, dragging his feet.

Haroun shook his head. "Tsk. To hear him carry on, you'd think I was one of those really greedy people. Of course I'll have enough of wishing someday. Only not just yet. In fact"—he pulled himself up straighter on his pillows and looked self-righteous—"he ought to appreciate me more. If I freed him, he'd only fall into the hands of another person, and *that* one would probably be greedy enough for twelve misers and a tax collector. I'm doing him a favor, keeping him here serving me. Is he thankful? No more than that miserable cat of mine."

Still licking peach juice from his fingers, Haroun continued to marvel over the ingratitude of cats and genies. He did not see Boabdil rouse himself, leap down from the sleeping tiger statue, and run into the palace.

Far above the Garden of the Five Tigers, the ungrateful cat sat on a windowsill and spoke to the equally ungrateful genie: "No luck."

Khalid slumped into a chair beside the arched window and closed his eyes. "I had hoped"—

—"that I would be the key to free you?" Boabdil switched his tail. "You expect too much. I'm just a cat."

"But I was kind to you! In all the old tales, when the hero is kind to an animal, that animal always finds a way to pay him back when he's in trouble."

"I think you've spent too many hours with your eyes in a book and not enough reading the world. My human does that, too. I'm surprise the two of you don't get along better; you have much foolishness in common." He paced the windowsill, tail high. "Tales or no tales, I don't know why you come to me for ideas of how to get you out of this fix."

"Cats are wise."

"Wise enough not to get ourselves into predicaments like yours in the first place. Therefore we have no experience with getting *out* of them." Boabdil settled down in the sunniest spot on the sill and closed his eyes. "I'm going to nap now. Scat!"

Shoulders bent with all the misery in the world, Khalid rose to go. He lingered awhile to gaze enviously at the cat on the windowsill. A full belly, a clean coat, and another living soul to care for him: that was happiness. It didn't require palaces or performers, gold platters or gemmed goblets. Food, comfort, love: Why couldn't Haroun learn that simple lesson and be content?

"He never will," Khalid said softly to himself. "He will continue to crack his brain and my back trying to come up with the perfect wish to bring him happiness. We shall grow old together, until he dies with ten thousand times ten thousand unused wishes still owing him. And in all that time, my classmates will have served hundreds of masters. They will learn, they will grow, they will become the respected elders of our people, they will teach a new generation of genies!"

Tears blurred his sight. He had a vision of his old, beloved classroom full of strange, young faces. He saw himself come in—a worn and weary self who came to tell Master Ishmael that after so-and-so many mortal years, he had *finally* fulfilled his first mission.

Master Ishmael was not there. Gamal had taken his teacher's place. The other genie's lip curled in scorn when he saw Khalid standing alone in the doorway. *What? Forgotten how to materialize? And you used to be so* good *at it, Khalid!* Every word cut like a dagger.

But that was not the worst of it. She was there,

too: Tamar. She sat on her familiar carpet and looked just as beautiful as the last time he'd seen her. He tried to make her look at him. She saw him, but it was the same way she saw a wall, or a door, or a table; there was no recognition.

Then he realized that she was at the head of the class, too, her carpet floating beside Gamal's. Gamal reached out and took her hand. *Too late, Khalid,* he sneered. *Too bad.*

Khalid saw himself rushing up the aisle, jostling the carpets to either side. *Tamar! Tamar!* He called her name again and again; she did not hear. *Tamar!* He was shouting now. *Tamar, you have to hear me! Tamar!*

"Tamar!"

Khalid was at the window without knowing how he'd gotten there, leaning out over the street. His fingernails dug into the soft pink plaster on the outside of the palace wall.

"Hey! Be careful!" Boabdil leaped up, fur bristling, and jumped for the safety of the room. "You almost knocked me overboard," he accused Khalid.

Khalid ignored him. In the street below, a face was turned up toward the palace, toward this very window. It was a face that was dear to Khalid—dear too late, he'd thought—a face that was first bewildered, then astonished, then lit up with the loveliest of smiles. She was dressed in the plain garb of a common mortal woman, a market basket on one arm. Already it was half-full of a variety of fruits from a merchant's stall.

"Tamar!"

"Ten thousand devils seize your tongue, you impudent rogue!" cried the merchant, shaking his fist at Khalid. "I will not have you bothering my customers! This is a respectable woman—even if she is robbing me blind by the minute. How dare you shout at her?"

Tamar was giggling. "Good merchant," she said,

"it's all right. That is an old friend of mine." Tilting her head and waving, she shouted back, "Khalid!"

The merchant was aghast. "Such behavior! For a woman to act so is scandalous, scandalous. If you do not care about your reputation, think of mine! Be gone! Be gone before you cause me to lose all of my customers!"

Tamar became suddenly serious. "Is that what you desire, Merchant?" she asked.

He crossed his arms. "I do."

"Is it what you want?"

"It is."

"But is it—is it what you *wish*?"

"Yes and indeed and truly!"

She pressed her hands together. "Hearkening and obedience." She vanished, leaving him to gape at the place on the street she had left empty and the market basket she had left him full of coins.

CHAPTER FIVE

Tamar hugged her knees to her chest and giggled. "Just look at that poor man, Khalid," she said in a whisper, peering cautiously out of the window. "Look, but don't let him see you looking. Did you ever see such an expression? Misery is spelled out across his face in letters a foot high. Now he realizes that the shameless woman he was so angry with is really a shameless genie. A genie that granted him one wish, out of the kindness of her heart, and he wasted it on wishing her away! Yet see. Now he counts the basketful of coins I left him and knows that in spite of his wasted wish, he has come out of this pretty well. He's starting to smile. No, no! Now he's remembering the wasted wish and back comes the long face. Oh, aren't mortals funny?"

"Hilarious," Khalid did his best to share in Tamar's amusement, but he felt more like sympathizing with the bamboozled merchant. He knew how badly it hurt to be hooked on the wrong end of magic.

Tamar continued to spy on the merchant from her comfortable perch. The window she had chosen for her pryings had a wide sill, well padded to make a snug seat. "Do you think he'll ever decide whether to be happy or sad?"

"I expect he'll either make up his mind one way or the other, or else he'll break his neck trying to skip with joy and kick himself at the same time." Seated cross-legged in mid-air, Khalid made an impatient gesture and a refreshment tray materialized before him. Another flick of his fingers and the brass teapot lifted itself to pour steaming hot mint tea into a pair of earless, leather-wrapped cups.

Something disturbing in Khalid's voice made Tamar suddenly lose interest in her merchant. Concerned, she asked, "Is everything well with you, Khalid?"

"Oh, very well." He wiggled one finger, and the little silver dish of honey tilted a thin, gold stream into his cup and hers. The tea stirred itself without benefit of spoon, churning up a thick froth of rainbow bubbles on the surface of each cup. He floated one across to her. "And you?"

"I can't complain." She took her cup and sipped it. "I've earned a lamp of my own at last, and I can't say I'm not glad. Do you know how cramped you get in one of those enchanted rings? That was my first assignment: a ring. From there I worked my way up to a magic bracelet, then an emerald-studded belt, then a brass bottle, and just when I'd given up all hope, the Council of Elders said I was ready for the real thing. At last! It's a very nice lamp." A coy note came into her voice, "Perhaps you'd like to come up and see it sometime?"

Khalid's throat tightened. The joy he'd first felt at seeing Tamar again had evaporated. Having her there only increased his pain.

Look at her, he thought. Listen to her, chirping merrily away about all her different assignments, all the mortals she's served. She hasn't any idea about the awful mess I've gotten myself into. She doesn't know that she's visiting a prisoner.

With all his heart he yearned to seize Tamar's hand, to leap with her out the window, to fly away to wherever she desired—even to that pretty little lamp of hers, the one she spoke of so proudly! He knew that he could not; that maybe he could never.

She mustn't know, he decided firmly. *She wouldn't laugh at me—not Tamar—but she'd feel sorry. I don't want her pity. Better to send her away from here thinking I'm still the self-centered snob I always was in class. Better to have her remember me as a braggart than as a fool.*

Very deliberately, he yawned in Tamar's face. "Maybe someday I will pop by that little lamp of yours. If I haven't got anything better to do. I'm a very busy genie."

"I know."

His brows went up sharply in alarm.

"I mean," she added, "that's what everyone back home assumed when you didn't come back for graduation. We were all so proud of you!"

Khalid breathed easier. Relieved, he could not keep from teasing, "All?"

Tamar shrugged prettily. "I can work the seven hundred and seventy-seven greater magics, but when it comes to Gamal, even I don't expect miracles." A look of distaste flitted over her face. "When I was still in that enchanted ring, he had the nerve to barge in and suggest we share it as a married pair. The idea! It wasn't even an engagement ring."

Khalid tried his utmost to appear indifferent to what Tamar was telling him, but his flesh went cold at the thought of Gamal anywhere near Tamar. "Master Ishmael put him in his place when you told him about that incident, I'm sure," he drawled.

"Master Ishmael is gone."

It was no use trying to pretend disinterest. Khalid was not that good an actor. "Gone? Gone how? Where?"

"No one knows." Tamar's eyes grew shiny with tears. "It was shortly after you left us. The Council of Elders summoned him and he never came back. We had a new teacher the next day, a scrawny old thing with breath like a dead goat and no more common sense than a clay jug. He thought he was magic's gift to the world, though, and Gamal was right there to agree with him all the way. I knew Gamal was a bully, but I never imagined he could be such a weasel-faced flatterer, too." She turned grim. "Flattery pays. Our noble teacher saw to it that Gamal was assigned to a lamp right away. No rings or bracelets or brass bottles for his pet, oh no!"

"With a lamp of his own, at least he won't trouble you any further," Khalid said, trying to sound casual about it.

"You think so?" Tamar's sparkling eyes darkened. "Ha! Beggars have fleas that are easier to get rid of then Gamal. He cheats, did you know that? Mortals are fair game for trickery, but all in the spirit of fun. He treats his as cruelly as he can without attracting the unfavorable attention of the Council of Elders."

"How do you know this?"

"He brags about it!" Tamar took short, angry sips from her cup. "Every time he finishes with one master, he rushes off to find me and crow over how badly he fooled the poor, idiotic mortal. Oh, Khalid, our purpose in this life is to share our magical powers with mortals. The more mortals masters we serve, the greater our own ability to work magic grows!"

"Practice makes perfect, as Master Ishmael used to say," Khalid recited dully. His own tea lay untasted in his hand. "And by giving, we receive."

The ancient lessons hung heavy in his heart. Serving only one master, he had gained experience, but not ability. A genie's magic was like the never-empty wine jug in the old story: the more it was passed around, the more wine flowed freely back into it. Yet if it only sat untouched in a corner, the sun and the air itself would cause the wine within to evaporate until one day its selfish owner came to find it truly empty once and for all.

"But that's it, Khalid; Gamal doesn't give. Not really. He always finds the means to grant his master's wish so that the result is unbearable. If a man asks for wealth, he receives stone coins the size of millstones. Wealth, yes, from an island over the edge of the world! If a woman asks for beauty all men may admire, Gamal transforms her—into the swiftest and sleekest of racehorses!"

"Sneaky," Khalid said, pretending to be shocked. Actually he was busy making mental notes to apply Gamal's methods to Lord Haroun.

Then Tamar said, "In all the time you have been gone, with all the masters you must have served, I know that you never once behaved so wickedly as Gamal."

Khalid's mental notes puffed themselves up like a balloon and popped. He felt his cheeks turn hot with a guilty blush. "Of course not," he mumbled. "Never."

"Oh, let's forget about Gamal!" Tamar made a graceful gesture that beckoned the teapot over to refill her cup. Another wiggle of her slim fingers caused an almond cake to float from the platter into her waiting hand. "It's news of your life that I'm famished for, Khalid. The adventures you must have had by now! The grand variety of human masters you must have served! Were any of them kings or princes? Did you ever appear to a poor beggar boy and make him into a great lord, with a beautiful princess for a wife? Have you ever met a mortal poet, or taught new tales to a storyteller?"

Khalid made himself chuckle, although his heart wasn't in it. "Why don't you ask me whether I ever obeyed the beautiful princess?"

Tamar did not find this thought at all funny. Her

sweet mouth pulled itself tight as a drawstring purse. "Really, Khalid, even I know that beautiful princesses are kept locked away in their fathers' palaces. How would one of them ever get her hands on a filthy old lamp?"

"Well, my lamp could have been found in the street by a beggar girl, and she might've wished to become a beautiful princess." Khalid was beginning to enjoy this.

Tamar wasn't. "Then she would be a fool! Who would want to wish for a life you spend shut up all day, even if you are shut up in a palace?"

"Then she could wish for me to stay and keep her company," Khalid suggested, his faint, teasing smile now genuine.

"Ohhh!" With an impatient sound, Tamar leaped to her feet and brushed cake crumbs from her robes. "You are the most infuriating genie I ever knew! Next you'll be telling me that old story about how the beauty of mortal women is so much more wonderful than the beauty of female genies because you know it must fade away one day. Well? Why not say it?"

He studied her as she stood there, eyes bright, chin raised, defying him, and his heart ached. He could not tease her any longer. Instead he rose from his invisible seat and took her hands in his own. "I can't say it," he said.

"Why not?"

"Because it would be the last of too many lies."

He would have said more, but just then there was a terrible racket from the hallway. The cat Boabdil came bounding into the room, every wisp of fur on his back standing straight up, his tail puffed out like a feather duster. "Brace yourself," he announced. "Here he comes with another bee in his turban—no, a whole swarm of them!" He was followed a moment later by Haroun.

Khalid's Master was a sight to behold. His gorgeous silken clothing was torn in a score of places and he was covered head to foot with white plaster dust, gray-green smears of mildew, and yards of cobwebs. He was coughing badly with every step he took. At the sight of him, Tamar veiled herself and drew back into the darkest corner of the window seat.

In his hands, Haroun held a gigantic book. It was so large, his knees buckled under the weight of it. It was as big as the back of the king's second-best throne, and as thick as the cushion on the seat of that same piece of royal furniture. Its cover was fine old leather, dyed red and bound with an iron spine, corners, and a heavy latch. There were still a few glimmering flakes of gold clinging to the binding to show that the heavier metal had once been richly gilded.

"Khalid!" Haroun called, squirming as he tried to wipe himself clean of dust on his shoulders. "Khalid, I have found it! I've found the answer to what I most want in the world!" He coughed some more and sneezed seven times in a row. "Khalid, I—oh, bother. I wish I could see clearly."

"Hearkening and obedience."

The dust and dirt peeled away from Haroun's body like a white sheet and blew out the window.

"That's better. Now I wish you'd bring me a table, so I could put this thing down." Haroun was so overcome with the burden of the book that he did not notice Tamar there, at first.

"Hearkening and obedience," Khalid repeated, his voice flat. A suitable table appeared. He kept his eyes fixed on it, even though it was a common table like a thousand others. He did not want to look at Tamar. He knew that she could count up to three, and any moment now . . .

"That's better." Haroun let the book drop with a loud thud. He cleared his throat a few more times before saying, "This dust is terrible! I wish I had a nice, cool drink of pomegranate juice."

"In which hand, O Master?" Khalid stalled uselessly.

"Oh, any one you like; I don't care! And if you'll stop those silly little games about fulfilling my wishes to the letter, I promise not to act like a spoiled infant over which of my hands you put things in. This"—he smacked the book, sending up further clouds of dust—"has made me realize what is truly important for my happiness; and it's not having peaches pop up in one hand instead of the other. Well, Khalid? Why are you waiting? I did say I wish . . ."

"Hearkening"—even though Khalid was not looking at her, he knew that behind his back, Tamar's eyes were growing wide with horror and realization—"and obedience."

A silver goblet of ice-cold pomegranate juice appeared in Haroun's hand, its sweet-tart aroma so tempting the parched young man smacked his lips in anticipation. Just as he raised it to his lips, Tamar cried:

"Name of ten thousand demons, what kind of crazy mortal is this?" Her exclamation startled Haroun badly. Juice spritzed everywhere. "Three wishes!" the female genie went on. "Three wishes tossed away on the most trivial of desires—to clear off some dust, to fetch a table, to bring him a drink—and yet he stands there, sipping pomegranate juice as if magic were as common to him as old rags. Oh, my poor Khalid"—she ran to his side and threw her arms around his neck—"how awful for you to serve a madman! How happy you must be that at least it was over quickly. Come with me, now, and we'll see if we can't put your lamp in the path of a sane master this time."

Khalid stayed where he was, eyes on the floor. Tamar might as well have hugged a post. Haroun was still sputtering, his face and clothing dripping with the scarlet juice. "I wish—" Haroun began. "I wish only in a manner of speaking that you would ask my permission before you have visitors, Khalid. And I really wish I were dry and had fresh clothes on."

This time, Khalid's "Hearkening and obedience" was said as if it were something shameful. In the beat of a moth's wing, Haroun was wearing a completely new set of gorgeous white silk robes trimmed with gold and turquoise. His face was also dry, and with the pomegranate juice cleared from his eys, he got his first good look at Tamar.

He forgot all about the pomegranate juice. He forgot all about the book. A slow smile stretched the corners of his lips until they seemed ready to touch his ears.

"Well, well, well. If you are the sort of guest who comes to see Khalid, forget what I said about no visitors." He made her his most elegant bow. "I am Lord Haroun ben Hasan, at your service, Fair One. And what sort of enchanted garden grew a flower so beautiful as you?"

Tamar was not smiling. "Four," she said.

Haroun cocked his head to one side. "I beg your pardon?"

"That was four wishes. I can count. And Khalid granted them all."

"Of course; why not? He's a genie. Genies do that sort of thing every day. My dear, haven't you heard any of the old stories?"

"Yes, but four wishes—!" Tamar was insistent that Haroun understand how improper it all was.

"Closer to four hundred," Khalid said, in a voice as cheerful as the bottom of a dry well. "Or four thousand. Not that it matters."

Tamar looked sharply from Haroun to Khalid and back. Her brow was heavily creased in thought.

"Either you are mad," she said, pointing at Haroun, "or you have lost your mind"—this time she pointed at Khalid—"or I have been working too hard and I need a vacation."

"Good idea," Khalid said. "Leave now."

"I won't hear of it!" Haroun continued to waste his most charming smiles on the female genie. "My rose, you are the answer to the very wish I was about to make. Behold."

Gently he steered her away from Khalid and over to the table where the massive book lay. taking care, on account of the dust, he opened it to a page marked with a wide piece of scarlet ribbon. "Before your friend Khalid and I began our—ahem—business arrangement, all that was left me in this world was a trunk filled with my father's dearest possessions."

"Were you a beggar boy, then?" Tamar asked.

"No, but I wasn't far from it. Oh, it was a lucky day for me when I found Khalid's lamp! Why, it seems like yesterday."

"Wasn't it?"

Haroun laughed. "If yesterday were almost a year ago, yes. However, this book is none of your friend Khalid's doing. It was my father's, and I found it just now, at the bottom of that trunk I mentioned. I was so bored, you see. It's not easy, deciding what to wish for next. At first I thought I'd ask him to make me Supreme Ruler of the World, but then I recalled we'd tried that for my birthday and I didn't like it. While I was wandering around the palace, trying to come up with an idea for a wish, I stumbled across my father's trunk. Perhaps I'd find something in it that would inspire me, I thought, and so I opened it, found this book, and now all my problems are about to be solved forever! Why, if this wish turns out as well as I hope, it might even mean that I won't need Khalid around anymore."

"But after three wishes he's not supposed to—"

Haroun did not hear her. He was running his finger across the old, old words on the page he had marked. "There is it! Can you read? It's so simple, really. Here I've been racing after happiness in a dozen different shapes, and the key to it lies in a single phrase."

Tamar bent forward to read the words Haroun's finger underlined. Khalid remained where he was, downcast, seemingly forgotten by the two of them. " '. . . for the garden of joy lies open to the man who finds the gate, and a wise man knows that the gate opens at the touch of love.' " She looked up at Haroun, and suddenly she knew why he was gazing at her with that empty-skulled grin.

"Yes," he said, clasping her hands. "The touch of love: to be adored forever by a suitably beautiful wife. That would make me happy, and so that is what I'll wish for."

"A princess, I suppose," Tamar said.

"Hmmm? No, no. I was going to wish for a princess, but Khalid might act up and bring me an ugly one. It's easier to wish for him to turn you into a princess after we're married."

Tamar did not try to pull her hands away; not yet. "Don't you think there's something you should ask me first, before you go wishing me turned into a princess?"

"Like what? Oh, do you mean you might not want to be a princess? Well, if you insist, I could live with that. I may even give you three of my wishes as a wedding present. Won't that be nice?"

"Wonderful." Tamar's eyes were hard and cold as marbles. Khalid remembered her temper from class, and he didn't like the approaching-thunderstorm sound of her voice.

He hurried over to lay his hands on her shoulders. "Tamar, whatever you're thinking of doing to him, don't! He's my Master! Unless he's the one who starts the fight, I must protect him against all magical attacks until he has used up the wishes I still owe him. Please, I don't want to fight you."

When Tamar turned her face toward Khalid, it looked as smooth and white as an egg, but the sight of it left him feeling as if this egg were about to crack wide open and hatch a fire-breathing dragon any minute. "I can wait," she said. "I'm perfectly willing to wait until he's used up all the wishes you owe him. And do you know why I'm willing to wait? I'll do it because right now, there isn't anything on this world or under it I want half so much as to give this clown a good, firm, healthy kick to the moon!"

Khalid turned pale. Meanwhile, Haroun tried to get Tamar to pay attention to him again. "My pearl," he said, "I think I'll have to wish you become a princess after all. Princesses never talk like that about their husbands. Khalid, listen carefully: I wish to marry this girl at once!"

"Hearkening . . ."

CHAPTER SIX

"Well, you don't need to sulk about it."

Tamar lay on her belly on a small yet elegant flying carpet, blue and red with silver tassels. Fortunately the ceilings in Haroun's palace were high enough to allow her to hover a good ten feet above his head. From the expression on his face, he looked ready to start throwing things at her any moment.

"It's not fair!" he shouted. "You're a genie, too!"

"What's not fair about that?" Tamar wanted to know. "It's an odd job, but somebody's got to do it." She caused a bowl of salted almonds to appear and dropped them onto Haroun's head, one by one.

Khalid was quick to materialize a parasol over his angry Master. The falling almonds made a gentle pit-a-pat sound, like rain. The cat Boabdil came in to see what all the yelling was about. He batted at the nuts with his paws.

"Tamar, please . . ." Khalid's eyes begged her to stop teasing the young mortal.

"No, I won't!" she replied to his unspoken request. "I think he's been awful, treating you like this, and he deserves whatever little annoyances I can dish out. You are a disgrace to mortals everywhere, Haroun! You ought to be ashamed of yourself. You don't have to be so greedy. Most people are more than happy to have three wishes granted; even one! I admit, Khalid made a mistake, but why couldn't you just take fifty wishes—or a hundred, if you had to have them—and then let him go?" Small lightnings flashed from her eyes. "You are worse than Gamal."

She made a beehive grow from the roof and filled it with furious bees, then changed the falling almonds to honey drops.

"Tamar, he's not really that bad," Khalid protested. He summoned up a great wind that blew bees, hive, honey, and all out the window and over the city rooftops.

"You have to say that. He's your Master."

"Yes, but it's still the truth."

She remained unsatisfied. "Prove it!"

"I can't." Khalid looked down. "I just feel it."

"If he's so wonderful, why won't he set you free?"

Khalid opened his mouth to speak, then closed it when he didn't have an answer for her.

Tamar folded her arms. "I thought so."

"That's not fair, either," Haroun objected. "I am going to release Khalid . . . someday."

"When?" Tamar pressed the point.

Haroun looked like a small boy who has been caught stealing cake. "I said when. Someday. Someday when"—he gave the matter a lot of thought—"when I'm perfectly happy."

Tamar rolled over on her carpet with a loud moan. "Powers that be! Have I heard right? Oh, poor Khalid, if all your mortal master wants is not mere happiness, but perfect happiness, then you are doomed!" She turned over again and gave Haroun a piercing frown. "But if you are doomed, I shall see to it that you're not the only one."

Haroun licked his lips nervously. "Does she mean me?" he asked his genie. Khalid just shrugged. This was not a good enough reply for Haroun's liking. He grew angry.

"You'd better not try anything!" he shouted at Tamar. "In fact, I *wish* you would never do anything to harm me."

There was a silence in the room. Scowling in earnest now, Haroun turned to Khalid and demanded, "*Well?* Isn't this the time for you to say 'Hearkening and obedience'?"

"Master, I can say it until I am blue in the face, for all the good it will do. I can protect you if Tamar uses her magic to attack you directly—indeed, I *must* do so—but I cannot use my powers to block those of another genie. That is impossible. Your wish must remain ungranted."

"And I'm not fool enough to attack you directly," Tamar informed Haroun, a disconcerting half-smile playing about her lips. "But have you ever thought about how many times and places there are in a day for *little* things to go wrong?"

She half closed her eyes and began to count off the possibilities on her fingers: "Hot bathwater that suddenly turns to ice. Delicious foods that attract every insect in the city the moment before you try to take a bite. Fine carpets that hump up under your feet without warning and make you crash down flat on your face. Sweet dreams that are abruptly interrupted by nightmares of the most hideous terror. Why, I can think of one hundred thousand and seventy-three creative uses for fleas alone, right off the top of my head. Shall I go on?"

"Don't bother. I understand you." Haroun had gone from looking guilty to looking sullen. "Now you listen to *me*. For every pebble you place under my feet, I can make your friend Khalid move boulders. For every feast of mine you spoil, Khalid will be commanded to conjure up a hundred more. Do you want to make my life a series of burrs, fidgets, and itches, just to see how long it takes before I give in? Well,

I want to see how much magic a genie can spend on one Master before he uses himself up altogether and blows away!"

Tamar went white. "You wouldn't."

"Not if *you* won't." Haroun grinned, the winner.

"You are horrible! Unspeakable! Hateful!"

"And safe from you." He winked at her. It was the last straw.

"Ooooooohhhhhhhh!" With a terrible growl, Tamar vanished. Khalid stood staring mournfully at the empty air where she had floated.

"Snap out of that," Haroun ordered, nudging the genie with his elbow. "She's gone; think no more of her. I have work for you to do."

"Yes, Master." Boiled cabbage had more life to it than Khalid.

"Here, now! Perk up! I meant what I said about freeing you. You will be free once I say I've wished my last wish, won't you?"

"I suppose," Khalid remained glum.

Haroun really threw himself into trying to jolly up the disconsolate genie. "Well, so I shall! And it won't take forever, either. You see, thanks to that wonderful book my father left me, I know the one thing I need for perfect happiness."

"Yes. A bride. I'm sure that once you are married, you will be perfectly happy. Perfectly." The genie did not sound convinced, nor did he care what he sounded like. "I'll just go and fetch you one, then. What size?" If Khalid's lower lip had drooped any further, it would have swept the floor.

Haroun clicked his tongue. "No, no, no. You can't just order brides as if they were sugarplums. Love is somewhat different from shopping. I must have a bride worthy of me, certainly: young, beautiful, the daughter of a king! But she must love me—love me not because I am Lord Haroun, master of great wealth and commander of an actual genie, but because—can you guess why?" He gave Khalid a foxy look.

"I don't know." The genie slumped cross-legged to the floor and rested his face on one fist. "Why should she?"

"Because I am *me*, of course!"

"Oh. That." In a softer voice Khalid added, "I'll be stuck working for this one for a hundred years."

"I hope you don't mind?"

"Not at all. Plenty of room."

"Thank you. You're very kind."

"My pleasure." The cat Boabdil thought a friendly purr at the magical being who had entered his body. Although he could not smell her properly—she being inside him and all—he could use the far keener sense—the *hrrown*, or Nose of the Mind, as cats everywhere called it—to decide that she was acceptable. Not a cat, but almost as good.

"Did you hear what that idiot just said?" Tamar demanded.

"How could I not?" Boabdil sent her a feline chuckle. "You heard it with my own ears."

"Loved for himself! By a princess, no less! There's as much chance of that as of a cobra being loved for his winning smile."

"So you think it's impossible?" the cat asked.

"It would have to improve to be impossible!"

"Then I suggest you think of a way to improve it. Look." Boabdil cocked his head so that Tamar could see Khalid, crumpled up, his head cradled on his updrawn knees.

The cat felt her sob. "Oh, my poor darling!" The thought of her tears washed over Boabdil's mind like a cold, gray rain. He fluffed out his fur, irritated.

"Mewling like a hungry kitten won't help him.

Come along with me." Tail high and proud, the cat stalked from the room.

"Wait! Please, wait. What are you doing? Where are we going?" Tamar begged.

"Where?" The thought was as scornful as any cat worth his whiskers could make it. "Not to sea, certainly, nor into the desert. Where do you think we're going? We go to the king's palace, and we will not come back here without a royal bride!"

CHAPTER SEVEN

Very gently, trying to be a polite and thoughtful guest, Tamar made Boabdil lift his head so she could see the walls of the king's palace.

"It isn't much of a palace," she commented.

"He isn't much of a king," the cat replied.

Boabdil sniffed at the crumbly yellow stones of the palace's outer wall. The walls were extremely old, and many a young urchin of the streets had managed to scrawl his name or a nasty picture on them with charcoal.

"Disgraceful!" Tamar exclaimed.

"Perhaps the king does not have enough money or enough men to scrub his walls again," the cat suggested. "I must say, my human has more than one palace and he manages to keep all of them spotless, inside and out."

"Your human has help," Tamar said bitterly.

"Not for long," Boabdil smirked. "There's the gate. Let's go and find our princess."

He trotted off briskly. For Tamar, being inside the cat was even worse than being cramped up in her first enchanted ring. Whenever the car moved, she got a terrible shaking. The lurch she'd felt when Boabdil leaped from Haroun's palace window still made her stomach tremble. She could have made herself more comfortable, but she was afraid of bumping into the wrong things and doing some damage.

Everything is so dark in here! I guess this must be part of what makes cats so mysterious, she thought to herself. *Even they don't know why they do some things.*

As her eyes grew used to the shadows, she saw that Boabdil's mind was a neat and orderly collection of many lidded baskets. The two biggest she could see were labeled FOOD and COMFORT. There were others, almost as big, marked HOME, FREEDOM, HUNTING, LADY CATS, and THE MOON. She reached out to shift her weight carefully and felt something small under her hand. Picking it up and bringing it close to her eyes, she saw that it was a basket no bigger than a walnut. The label on it read: THE IMPORTANCE OF WHAT HUMANS THINK OF CATS.

The cat stopped without warning and Tamar fell against a stack of medium-sized baskets. "Oh, I'm sorry." she cried, hurrying to put them back in order. "I hope I haven't harmed anything."

"Think nothing of it," the cat answered. "You didn't even hurt my feelings."

"Where are we?"

"The great gate. Can you see all right?"

Tamar moved so that she could use Boabdil's eyes. Though the wall itself was not much, the gate was tremendous. Up and up it rose in a pointed arch. Blue and green and gold tiles decorated it in wavy patterns, until it looked like the entrance to a wonderful undersea land. The huge iron grille used to lock the gate in times of war was wide open. Tamar saw a moving forest of human legs rushing in and out before her. All at once a great cry rang out and the legs ran even faster, to get out of the way of a set of galloping hooves. The horse raced past, kicking up a dust cloud that made Boabdil sneeze and toss Tamar back and forth inside him.

"The way is open. We are in luck," the cat said. "What shall I do?"

"Go in. Follow the tracks of that horse. No one comes riding so fast unless he bears an important message, and all important messages go straight to the king. Once we find the king, it will be simple to find any spare daughters he may have hanging around the palace."

"If you say so." Obediently, Boabdil set off the way the horse had gone.

Tamar's theory proved right. They traced the horse to the royal stables. From there, the genie told the cat to use his magnificent gift of smell to follow the rider who had dismounted from the horse. The trail led up a wide flight of dirty white steps, down a towering hall lined with sick-looking potted palm trees, through a courtyard where all the fish in a scummy ornamental pond and half the rose-bushes surrounding it had died, and finally into a small, dingy, stale-smelling room. At every step Tamar advised Boabdil to hide wherever he could, and where he could not hide to walk close to the wall. It would not do to be discovered.

In this room, however, there was no choice. There was nowhere to hide, and the walls were all lined with heavy bookshelves,. Boabdil was clean, as all cats like to keep themselves, and his shiny fur stood out like a lighthouse beacon in contrast to the grubby surroundings.

"What shall I do?" he asked Tamar urgently.

"Pretend you're not here," she replied. "Cats can do that, can't they?"

"We are masters of invisibility when it suits us."

"Well, please have it suit you now. Maybe they won't notice you. Heaven knows, if these mortals notice anything they'd notice how dirty this place is. Look, do you see that one over there? The fat one with that lopsided gold circlet on his head?"

Boabdil squinted. "It doesn't look like gold."

"That's because it hasn't been polished since your grandfather was a kitten. He must be the king."

"He is, and there is our rider, speaking with him. I'm going closer." The cat padded up to the long, low, prettily inlaid table between the two men. On one side the king sat upon a heap of mouse-nibbled cushions; on the other the rider was pacing back and forth angrily, shedding the dust of his journey with every step.

"But surely he must realize that what he asks is impossible!" the king whined. "Go back and tell him so."

The rider—a tall man so sun-browned that his skin now matched his boots—stopped dead in his tracks. "Your Majesty, when I entered your service I told you I was loyal, but I never told you I was an idiot. He will only order me beheaded and send his armies after you anyway."

"Oh dear, oh dear!" The king wrung his hands. "Why will he not take no for an answer? Does he think I am lying? He is a king, the same as I. One king does not lie to another."

The rider stroked his beard, and a little stream of sand fell to the threadbare carpet. "He thinks that you are refusing him the princess's hand in marriage because you want him to pay you more for her. He also told me that he is not the kind of man who likes to bargain. Bargaining makes him touchy, and when he feels touchy the only thing that calms him down again is invading someone else's kingdom."

"He didn't happen to mention any one kingdom in particular, did he?" the king asked, shivering.

The rider let the questions pass. "He said that the

first price he offered you is more than fair for a wife, especially his twenty-fifth."

"Twenty-fifth or two hundredth, what is the use? We are doomed. No man was ever so unfortunate as I! Other kings have daughters and daughters and more daughters. I have heard of some so overrun with girl-children that they cannot take a step in their own palace without tripping over six or seven royal princesses. One king is supposed to have gone crazy from all that giggling under one roof. Oh, lucky man! Other kings sigh for sons. Sons!"

He uttered a short, cold laugh. "I have seventy-eight sons, all in good working order. What use are they? Only one can become king after I die, and the rest must go out seeking adventures and slaying giants and rescuing damsels and other such silly heroic stuff. But daughters—! Daughters can become brides. Daughters can marry other kings and make them behave politely to me."

The rider sat down on the low table and pulled off his boots. "This king was not speaking about you politely at all when I left." He turned one boot upside down and spilled out a tiny dune.

"Why should he?" The king propped his fat chin on his fatter hands and looked hopeless. "All I have is one daughter, but ten thousand demons live inside her. All that a daughter can do is get married, but this child of mine says she would sooner die!"

"Uh-oh," thought Boabdil.

"Hush," Tamar instructed him. "There may be more to it than what the king says."

"What more can there be? Only one princess, and she will not marry! Not even when her father's kingdom is in danger of being attacked!"

"Hush, I say. So far we know only what her father has said, and fathers seldom take the time to learn the whole story from their children. I am sure this king told his daughter to marry, she said she would sooner die, and he stalked away, complaining about how mean and cruel and ungrateful children are nowadays. But did he stop feeling sorry for himself long enough to ask her why she refused to marry? I think not. That question is for us."

"Us?" The cat's fur prickled up all down his spine.

"Yes, Boabdil. Now you and I must find our princess."

"But how?" the cat asked. "Grimy and shabby as this palace may be, it's still big! How shall we find—?"

"YOW!"

Tamar's eyes were almost split by Boabdil's enraged cry. Her stomach fell, then leaped up in a most upsetting way as she and the cat together were jerked high into the air without a word of warning. The outer world spun dizzily as she saw first the floor dropping away beneath them, then the walls swinging around, and finally the dark, laughing face of the king's rider staring into Boabdil's eyes.

"Well, my fine fellow, and what wind blew you here?" Rough fingers rubbed Boabdil's ears in a friendly manner. Tamar felt the cat go limp as he began to purr.

"Boabdil, keep your eyes open!" she commanded.

"I can't help it," the cat replied. "I always close my eyes when I purr, and I always purr when something feels this nice." The rumbling noise wrapped the genie like a big, warm, woolly blanket.

Through the din of Boabdil's purr, Tamar heard the rider say, "Maybe your royal daughter can be made to see reason."

"Ha!" the king replied. He was beginning to enjoy his misery. "On the day that wicked child understands I only want what's best for her, cats like that walking mud pie will grow wings."

Boabdil's eyes flew wide for a single, angry instant.

"Mud pie!" He stared hard at the king, and Tamar could see the fat little man turn white under the cat's furious scowl. Then the rider resumed scratching Boabdil's ears and the cat fell back into bliss.

"Your Extremely Elevated Highness is not afraid of cats?" the rider asked casually.

"No, no." The king swallowed so loudly that Tamar could hear it even over the sound of Boabdil's pleasure. "I just don't like them, that's all. Horrid, mean, cruel, cunning, unpredictable, selfish, ungrateful things!"

"Is that what you think, my lord?" The rider sounded amused. "True, this is the first cat I have seen in the palace. I always wondered why."

"I have given strict order to my guards and servants that they are to chase away any of the nasty pests," the king replied, speaking like a man who knows he is always right.

"I see. Which explains . . . you know, Majesty, if you would only bend your rule a bit and allow cats in the royal kitchens, you might be able to hang onto good cooks longer."

"How so?" His Majesty was skeptical.

"There is just something about reaching into the flour bin and scooping out a handful of mice that makes cooks suddenly decide to take their talents elsewhere." When the king merely snorted, the rider went on: "And the princess . . . does she share Your Altitude's opinion of cats?"

The king snorted again. He was very good at it. "I am a firm believer in the theory that children grow up learning from all the living creatures that surround them. Reason enough for me to forbid her to own one of the terrible beasts, even though she has begged for a kitten time after time! She is quite cunning enough as it is, and so selfish—so very selfish that she will not—will not—not even when her own dear father is in danger of being invaded—" He broke down into loud, blubbery sobs full of self-pity.

"Hmmm," said the rider. He stopped petting Boabdil. The cat opened his eyes and uttered a small, annoyed mew. This gave Tamar the chance to observe the thoughtful way the rider was staring at Boabdil. The genie knew a clever mortal when she saw one.

She knew, but that didn't mean she liked it.

CHAPTER EIGHT

The princess Nur hugged and kissed and talked baby talk to Boabdil fifteen minutes straight before she had a sudden second thought. She put the cat down in his basket, sat up tall among her velvet cushions, and narrowed her eyes at the rider.

"What is the catch?" she demanded.

The rider tried to look innocent. "Catch, Your Gracious Highness? I do not know what you mean."

"I think you do know," she said, and gave him a hard look. The rider was tall and strong and hard as leather from his long years of serving Princess Nur's father. Princess Nur was small and pale and a little plump from spending most of her life indoors in her father's palace, whether she liked it or not. Still, she had a way of frowning that made the man turn all cold and shaky inside. It was not easy to look Princess Nur in the eye and lie.

"Flower of Royal Loveliness, if this poor gift should happen to soften your heart just a little and make you more willing to obey your noble father's wishes, would we have to call that a catch?" the rider wheedled.

"Yes, we would." Princess Nur was firm. "My noble father never gives anything to anyone unless he expects to get something better back." She tickled Boabdil's ears lovingly and gazed at the cat with deep yearning, but she said, "I will not marry, and it will take more than a cat to change my mind. Take him away."

"No!" Tamar protested. "She mustn't send us away! Everything will be ruined."

"Don't be afraid," Boabdil advised the genie. "Hear how sadly she said that? She doesn't mean it, and the fellow who brought us here knows it. He's too smart to give up easily."

"But this princess sounds like a mortal who knows what she wants. I do not think he can change her mind."

"Perhaps not. But he understands how to make her change it for herself. Listen!"

They both pricked up Boabdil's ears just in time to hear the rider say, "Very well, Your Highness. I shall take the miserable beast by the scruff of his neck and toss him out of the palace this very instant." He looked at the princess. She did not seem to care. "From a high window," he added. She said and did nothing to contradict him.

He sighed deeply, preparing to use every trick in the book. "What a pity that it is so late in the day. This is the hour when the city streets are the most crowded. If the poor animal is not trampled by a horse or an ox, he might live long enough to be chased to death by the packs of stray dogs that roam the alleys at night. A homeless cat leads a hard life. Still, the clever ones sometimes manage to survive for, oh, a couple of weeks."

The princess's eyes grew wide as she listened to the rider tell of the many dangers waiting for Boabdil in the world outside the palace walls. He saw this, and kept talking. "You should have seen what this creature looked like when your noble father found him, Highness. The poor thing was nothing but bones and fur. 'Take him to the royal kitchens and feed him well!' your noble father said. 'He shall be a special gift for my most beloved daughter.' But if you do not like the cat, I suppose he must go. Come here, you unlucky beggar. You and I have an appointment with a high window." He reached for Boabdil.

Princess Nur gave a loud squawk and threw herself between the king's rider and the cat. "If you dare to touch one whisker of my precious pet's head, your own head will pay for it!" She cuddled Boabdil so close to her chest that the cat squirmed and snarled. "You may tell my father that just because I have accepted his gift does not mean that I will accept his command to marry."

"Certainly not, Your Highness." The rider smiled and bowed as he backed away from the princess. Only when he was at the door of her room did he add, "Sometime I really must tell you about what happens to cats when a war comes." The guards outside the princess's room slammed and bolted the door as soon as the rider was gone.

Princess Nur sat holding Boabdil tightly for longer than the cat could stand it. "I do not believe him," she murmured into the cat's thick fur. "We will not have a war if I do not marry that awful king, and I will not let anything bad happen to you even if we do have a war. Which we will not." Boabdil dug his claws into her arm. It hurt only a little, but it surprised her enough to make her release him. He leaped to the carpet and washed himself vigorously.

"What are you doing, you foolish cat?" Tamar demanded. "You know that she has to stroke you for my plan to work. Get back into her arms this minute!"

"Stroke me, not strangle me." Boabdil kept on licking his pelt. "Don't be so impatient. She will do it soon enough. I know humans. They expect us to ignore them."

The cat was right. Princess Nur fussed over her scratch marks for a few moments, then forgot all about them and started making silly sounds at Boabdil, trying to lure him near. He made her wait, and only when he seemed satisfied with how his fur looked did he walk casually back to her.

Almost at once, she began to stroke him, starting at the head and going all the way to the base of the tail. Boabdil purred, while inside his mind Tamar forced herself to wait until the princess had patted the cat three times. Wishes came in threes, but mortals had somehow gotten the idea that everything else magical had to come in threes as well.

Keeping this in mind, Tamar waited for the third stroke before she used her powers.

It was a pretty spectacular show that Tamar put on for Princess Nur. Three times Boabdil's eyes flashed with green fire. Three times puffs of rainbow smoke burst from his ears. Three times his fur changed color—blue to red to silver—before it went back to its normal shade. Three times Tamar made the sound of thunderclaps roll from the cat's mouth before she herself sprang out right in front of the gasping princess.

"Hail, O my Master!" Tamar cried, kneeling at the princess's feet. "I am the Slave of the Cat."

"The what?" Nur repeated, coughing a little from all the smoke still lingering in the room. Boabdil stalked away, shaking his ears irritably.

"The Slave of the Cat," Tamar repeated. "I am a genie. Surely you have heard the stories?"

"Heard them? I have read them for myself," the princess replied. She waved her hand, and for the first time Tamar noticed that the walls of Princess Nur's room were lined with well-filled bookshelves. "I adore reading," Nur said. "Sometimes it is the only thing that saves me from dying of boredom. When you are a princess, all they ever expect you to do is wait around to be married, but they never have any good ideas for things to do while you wait."

Tamar laid a finger to her lips thoughtfully and decided to proceed with caution. Mortals who read were usually more crafty than those who did not, and a clever mortal was a dangerous mortal. She made sure that the next thing she said was, "So you know that as my master you cannot use any of your three wishes to wish for more wishes."

"I can't?" The princess looked disappointed.

"*Mmmm-hmmm*, Tamar thought. *Just as I suspected. She's smart enough to have thought of asking for that. Smart, but maybe greedy too. Most mortals are, and that's just what I'm hoping for.* To Nur she only said, "Sorry, those are the rules."

"Oh, dear." The princess's chin sank into her hands. "And there are so many more than three wishes I want to make! I want to be free of this palace, and I want to have a way to take care of myself in the world, and I don't want my father to send his soldiers after me to bring me back, and I really don't want to be a princess anymore, and—oh, pooh, I guess I really ought to wish that my father doesn't have to go to war just because I won't become that other king's twenty-somethingth wife, and I know I don't want to be forced to marry anyone I don't love, and—" She gave Tamar a pleading look. "Could you at least give me some advice on how I could fit all that into three wishes?"

Tamar smiled regretfully. "That would be against regulations. In fact, I should charge you one wish just for asking that. But I won't. I like you. I like you so much that . . ."

She paused and looked around the princess's room as if she expected a gang of bandits, armed to the teeth, to spring out from under the floor cushions at any moment. In a spy's most secret whisper she asked,

"Can I trust you, O Master? What I am about to offer you is not—not entirely—not at all legal. We magical folk do have our laws. If my fellow genies were to learn of the deal I am about to offer you, it would mean my doom!"

Tamar was very proud of the way she said "doom," making it sound hollow and echoing and chilling, all at the same time. She even threw in a minor roll of thunder to add to the effect of dread she hoped to create. She was sure that the princess would fall to her knees, swear to keep any secret Tamar asked, and beg to know what wonderful bargain the genie has to give.

Instead, Tamar was startled half out of her wits when Nur's response was a calm, "Oh, really? Then perhaps you shouldn't do it at all. Now if you don't mind waiting, I just have to make my three choices."

"Choices?" Tamar echoed, helpless.

"For my wishes," Nur explained. "I cannot have everything I desire with only three wishes, so I must decide which three things I need most."

"But. But. But—but—but—but you can have everything you desire!" the genie exploded.

"No I cannot." Nur folded her hands. "You said so."

"But you can, I say! It would require just one little thing of you, a very small and simple thing—"

"Oh no." The princess wagged a finger at the genie. "You forgot that I have read the tales. You genies are a tricky lot. You would like nothing better than to fool me into squandering the three wishes I do have by promising me more. That will not work. Three wishes will have to be enough for me. I will not be greedy."

"Why not?" Tamar wailed. "You are a mortal! You are supposed to be greedy! Oh, this is awful. You have made a mess of all my plans. Why can you humans never do what we expect of you? Are you that cruel, or are you only stupid?" She sank down amid the princess's cushions and began to cry.

A jeweled finger tapping Tamar's shoulder roused her from her misery. "I may not know much of the world because I have spent my whole life inside a palace," Nur said, "but I think I know enough to say that you do not sound at all like the Slave of anything, let alone a cat. What are you, really, and what do you want from me?"

Tamar wiped her eyes on the back of her hand, then snapped her fingers. A gold-and-silver silk handkerchief appeared in midair. She blew her nose loudly, then said, "Well, I am indeed a genie."

"So I see," the princess remarked, smiling at the magical handkerchief. "A genie who has gone to a lot of trouble to make me her Master, am I right?"

Tamar nodded, then confessed, "I need your help."

"What help can you need from me?" Nur asked. "You have all the magic of the world at your command; I have twenty different ways to braid hair and paint fingernails. You can circle the world in a thought; I cannot set foot out of these rooms without fifty of my father's best guards to surround me. You have the power to move mountains; I do not have even the power to marry who and when I want, if I want to marry at all. What can I possibly do for you?"

"Well, for one thing," said Boabdil, coming back after having gotten the leftover smoke out of his ears and fur, "you can marry."

CHAPTER NINE

"Are you sure you would not rather change your mind about this, O Master?" Tamar wheedled. It was only the fourteenth time she had posed the question. She did not think Princess Nur had any right to glare at her like that.

"Yes, I am sure!" the princess snapped, and threw a dirty dishrag at the genie. Growling and grumbling, she plunged her hands back into the basin of soapy water and continued to scrub the dishes. From time to time she lifted one hand to push her hair out of her eyes.

Boabdil the cat came strolling into the kitchen as if he owned the entire palace. He thought he did. "Well, ladies, and how are we getting along today?" he asked pleasantly.

Princess Nur flicked a handful of soap bubbles at him and missed. The cat leaped backward, hissing. "It was only a friendly question," he said, then licked invisible foam from his fur.

"Do not pay attention to her." Tamar sounded more than a little bitter as she labored over a stack of plates that needed to be dried. "My wise Master has simply discovered that some wishes are harder to live with than others. Now we are waiting to see how long it takes before she also learns that what one wish bungles, another can make better."

"I thought you said that a new wish can never undo an old," Nur objected.

"That is partly true, O Master." The female genie made an elaborate gesture with her dish towel. "If you wish for a heap of gold and later wish it away, I can do that. In life it is a natural thing for gold to come and go easily. But if you wish for me to destroy your enemies and later on you decide they were not such bad folk after all, I cannot bring them back. Dead is dead and gone is gone. Not all of Solomon's magic can change what is universal law."

Boabdil listened keenly to all of this. "Does that mean that Princess Nur has to be a servant girl forever?"

"Not at all. Servant girls are always turning out to be princesses, in the old tales, so why cannot a princess be a servant girl? Besides, she is not really a servant; she just looks like one." Tamar spoke to the cat as if Princess Nur were a thousand miles away. She knew how easily some mortals became annoyed by people talking about them that way, so she did it on purpose. "My Master has wished—most foolishly, I think—to come into Lord Haroun's house in disguise. Instead of taking the very generous offer I made to her and being content, she had to make things complicated. Most mortals would jump at the chance to have a genie ready to grant their every wish—not just three, but every single wish they might ever desire! Would they ask questions? Would they make conditions?"

"Would they be greedy fools enough to marry a man they have never met just because someone else says it is a good idea?" Nur chimed in. "If I wanted that, I could have stayed in my father's palace and let him pick my husband."

"But if you marry the husband I have chosen for you, you will also get me!" Tamar insisted. "Me and all the wishes you could ever desire. All you would have to do is wish to marry Haroun ben Hasan. What could be simpler?"

"Sorrow is simple," Nur replied. "With happiness, there is always a catch."

Tamar rolled her eyes. "Master, far be it from me to lecture you. A genie is created to hearken and obey. I have stood by silently and watched you waste a perfectly good wish on this—this silly, romantic notion of yours to come into Lord Haroun's palace disguised as a common servant. Why? To see whether I am trying to marry you to some sort of monster? Well, you have seen him. Is he ugly?"

"He is quite handsome," the princess admitted.

"When he wandered through the kitchen and saw you working, did he speak to you rudely? Or did he behave as if you were just another thing he owns?"

Nur could not lie. "He spoke to me kindly and asked whether I was happy working here. He seems to have a good heart."

"Then what is stopping you from making that one small, easy, insignificant wish—to have him for your husband!—when making it will bring you so much more besides?" Tamar raised her hands to the heavens, tiny starbursts of white light sizzling at her fingertips.

A little smile tickled one corner of the princess's mouth. "Indeed, what is stopping me? I could use one wish to marry Lord Haroun, then use one of the countless wishes you promise me to unmarry him." She gave Tamar a sudden penetrating stare. "Couldn't I?"

Tamar opened her mouth, closed it, bit her bottom lip, and said nothing.

"I see." Princess Nur went back to scrubbing dishes.

Boabdil rubbed against the genie's ankles. "I think

you should tell her the whole story," he said. "She is too smart to settle for less than that."

"Too smart," Tamar echoed bitterly. "Master Ishmael never taught us that princesses could be smart; just beautiful."

"Your Master Ishmael should have spent less time in lamps," Princess Nur remarked. "This world is wide enough for a few smart princesses, too."

Tamar was on the point of leaping to her old teacher's defense when the whole kitchen began to shake and shimmer. Nur gasped, then cried out. "Oh! Oh! Oh! Oh!" in little puffs. Everything was changing. The plain, useful ovens with their black iron doors became bright blue enamel surrounded by pretty tiles shaped and colored like fish scales. All the cookware flashed away, coming back brand-new, pink and green porcelain pots and pans with gold and silver handles. Even the big basins in which Tamar and Nur were washing the dishes changed from plain tin to gorgeously painted ivory.

Then, as suddenly as they had begun, the changes stopped. Princess Nur clutched the edge of her dish basin. "What was that?" She looked down at her clothes—once the simple, dull brown dress of a common servant, now pale green satin robes richer than any she had owned while living in her father's palace—and added: "And what is all this?"

Boabdil peeked out from under the table. "I would guess that our friend Haroun ben Hasan has decided to redecorate his humble home."

The cat had scarcely finished speaking when Haroun himself stuck his head around the edge of the kitchen doorway. "Well, how do you like it?" he asked. For a man who commanded so much wealth and magical power, he sounded remarkably shy and uncertain when speaking to ladies.

Tamar and Nur both bowed low. The genie had

been wise enough to disguise herself so that Haroun would not be able to recognize her when she came back into his house. The face she had chosen was not so beautiful as her own—what mortal woman can be as lovely as a creature of magic?—but it was still beautiful. That face was, in fact, copied from a portrait that Tamar had seen hanging in the king's palace. She did not know it was the face of a great queen; she just "borrowed" it because it was the first mortal face she could think of.

This turned out to be a mistake, as she discovered shortly after she looked up and said, "Whatever changes you desire are certainly fine with your humble and obedient servants, O our Master."

Haroun ben Hasan stared at her so intently that he did not seem to hear when Princess Nur said, "We find these changes very attractive, my lord, even if we were not expecting them." Haroun said nothing, still gazing at Tamar.

The princess was irritated. She was not used to being ignored. Motioning to Boabdil, she whispered, "What is the matter with him?"

Seeing Haroun's distracted state, the cat did not even bother to lower his own voice when he replied, "Who can say? As a rule, he does not spend a lot of time in the kitchens. Perhaps he is confused by his surroundings."

"He does not look confused," said Nur.

"Then perhaps he is shy around new faces. You and my lady Tamar are very recent additions to the household staff. New servants are sometimes badly frightened by the effects of his wishes, you know. That is why he came down here in the first place, to see if you were all right."

"That is good of him. But my genie tells me he commands a genie of his own. Why does he need any other servants?"

Boabdil closed his eyes. "Lord Haroun is a kindly man at heart. He can see that granting wishes is sometimes tiring for his genie, and so he decided to hire a few mortal servants to take care of the everyday chores rather than exhaust Khalid—that is his genie's name—by wishing for his bed to be made or his dinner to be cooked or his treasures to be dusted. For these tasks he hires ordinary servants."

Only now, Haroun was obviously discovering that one of his new servants was not quite so ordinary. A great feeling of confusion seized his heart. He felt his head spin. He was sure that he was sweating. His lips were dry, and when he opened his mouth to speak, all he could manage to say was: "Ungkh."

Princess Nur saw how pale he was and became concerned. "Master, are you well?"

"Ungkh," Haroun assured her. He continued to stare at Tamar with a face like a chicken that has run headfirst into a brick wall. Abruptly he recovered himself enough to shout, "Khalid! Khalid! Come to me at once!"

There was a whistling and a rustling as if something very large were flying through the air. The new pots and pans clinked and chinked together, the oven doors rattled on their hinges, and Princess Nur's pile of freshly washed dishes shattered into a million pieces.

Apart from that, nothing happened.

Haroun scowled into the air. "Come here, to me, at once, and make yourself visible," he snarled.

The air between Princess Nur and Haroun ben Hasan shimmered. Khalid stood with hands pressed together and head bowed. "Why did you not say so, O Master?" he asked innocently. "I am here to serve."

"Of course you are," said Haroun in a way that left no doubt about who he thought was the biggest liar the magical world had ever spawned.

"How may I make your life ever more comfortable?" the genie inquired. "Oh, I know I have just transformed the furnishings of every single room in this miserably tiny palace, exchanged all of the horses in your stable for pure white camels, traded your old brown camels for a fresh crop of horses—all of them identical black stallions with matching red-and-gold saddles and harnesses—and given all of your servants brand new clothes to wear, but think nothing of it! Ask for something else! Ask for anything you like! Do not think for a second that I might get tired, or want a little time to myself. I would only waste it on silly things like resting or thinking or going off to be with my friends. But who needs friends with a Master like you? Go on, wish! Wish for the world!"

"If you want some time to yourself, Khalid, you only have to ask for it," Haroun muttered. He looked embarrassed. "I only wanted to talk to you. Come see me in the Chamber of Ten Thousand Pheasants when you have a moment to spare. I will be waiting." Head pulled into his shoulders like a tortoise, he shuffled off.

"Speak to him 'when you have a moment to spare'?" Tamar wondered aloud. "That does not sound like him at all."

"No, it does not," Khalid agreed, scratching his head. "I suppose I had better go and see what it is he wants. Your pardon, ladies." The genie bowed and vanished.

"Who was that?" Princess Nur asked, grabbing Tamar's sleeve urgently. If the female genie had paid more attention, she might have noticed that the princess was wearing the same stunned-chicken expression as Haroun ben Hasan. But when Khalid was near, Tamar seldom noticed anything but him.

"That was the reason why I have asked you—no, begged you—to be a nice, sensible Master and wish to marry Lord Haroun ben Hasan," Tamar replied. She related the whole sad tale of Khalid's captivity, ending by telling the princess about just what it would take to guarantee Haroun's perfect happiness.

"*Me?*" Princess Nur shrilled.

"Do you see any other spare princesses around?' Boabdil asked.

"No, oh no!" Nur protested. "It is impossible, unthinkable!"

"But why?" Tamar implored, clasping the princess's hands. "You have seen Lord Haroun, you have agreed he is neither ugly or unkind. Wish to marry him, and I know he will be a good husband. He will certainly be a grateful one. His heart's desire is to marry a royal lady. You mortals do not value the wishes you get from genies. You think you have magical gifts coming to you! Yet when one mortal grants the dearest wish another mortal yearns for—oh, the thanks! The lifetime of gratitude! To say nothing"—Tamar lowered her voice and looked sly—"of the lifetime of wishes I shall grant you. For all of this, why can you not wed Lord Haroun and free my poor Khalid?"

Princess Nur looked at the floor. "Because I love another."

Tamar's mouth fell open in shock. Her lips trembled with unasked questions; unasked because she was afraid she already knew the answer. Then she let out a shriek loud enough to split the heart of the desert and ran out of the kitchens.

The cat Boabdil looked up casually from washing his front paws. He cocked his head at Nur. "Let me guess: You love Khalid."

"My heart leads, and I must follow," the princess answered, spreading her hands helplessly.

"Of course." Boabdil bit off the words as short as

if they were a tender mouse tail. "You know you won't be able to wish Khalid free," he told her.

"No?"

"No. One genie's magic can not undo the work of another's. Not unless they have a full-scale battle, and that is something far too noisy and messy to happen often." He gave his left paw another lick. "I hate messes."

"Can I wish for Lord Haroun to free him, then? Or wish that Khalid become a mortal man? Or that I become a genie? I just know I would not mind being a prisoner forever if I could be with him." She made cow-eyes at the doorway through which Khalid had departed.

"No," the cat said. "Those wishes (lick) go against (lick, lick) the natural order of things."

"And I suppose a talking cat is natural?" the princess sneered.

"Well, people (lick) have often thought we *could* talk (lick) or *should* talk (lick) or *can* talk but are too clever to let mere humans in on the secret. We are certainly (lick, lick) smarter than some creatures who do chatter. Besides (lick), if it went against the natural order of things (lick, lick, gnaw claws) for me to speak, I would not (lick) be speaking now. The magic would have simply (lick) gone to waste."

"Falling in love is natural," said Nur in a terribly moony, drippy voice. "Perhaps I shall wish for Khalid to fall in love with me."

"Wonderful." Boabdil's word was dry as a sandstorm. "Then he will not be just a captive, but a lovesick captive, too. I cannot tell you how very, very much better that will make him feel!" He finished with his left paw and added: "Anyway, it wouldn't work."

"Love is natural!" the princess objected.

"But forced love is not," the cat countered. "If it

were, you could force yourself to love Lord Haroun as easily as you claim you love Khalid. It would be the better bargain. By the bye"—Boabdil looked honestly interested—"why do you love Khalid? It is rather sudden, I think."

"Why do I love—?" Nur seemed unable to believe the question. "Why, because he is—he is so handsome—"

"So is Lord Haroun."

"—and so kind—"

"How would you know? You have seen more of Lord Haroun's kindness."

"—and so well-spoken—"

"Yes, I think he must have said three whole sentences to you."

—"and so—so"—she clasped her hands "so sad, so hopeless, so beautifully, beautifully tragic!"

Boabdil made a face. "Well, at least now I see what sort of books they allow princesses to read. Soppy stuff and romantic nonsense. It is a miracle that you did not decide to marry the first beggar you found in the street outside your father's palace. You would have assumed he was a prince in disguise!" He stalked away, tail high, muttering to himself about princesses.

Alone in the kitchens, Princess Nur found a chair and sat down with a sigh. "I *do* love Khalid," she told the air. "And I *do* have a good reason for loving him. I know I just saw him now, but has no one in this place ever heard of love at first sight? And I know I do not love Lord Haroun. For one thing he is—he is—" She searched her mind for something about Haroun ben Hasan that made him impossible to love. She had no luck. "Well, there must be *something* wrong with him, or my genie would not be trying to force me to marry him. Oh, she is just like my father! 'You must marry this king! You must marry that prince! You have to marry the man I choose. You cannot choose a husband for yourself.' I am very tired of having all my choices made for me. For once, I have made the choice, and I choose to love Khalid!" She folded her arms across her chest, very pleased with herself.

And a very good choice it is, said the air.

Princess Nur jumped up. "Who is it? Who is there?"

A friend. The voice came from everywhere and nowhere. It echoed inside the ovens and tinkled amid the pieces of broken china on the floor. *A friend who only desires your perfect happiness.*

If Princess Nur was afraid, she did not let it show. She knew that Lord Haroun's palace was a place of magic. Unseen voices were to be expected. Bravely she said, "If you are my friend, show yourself! Only enemies skulk in shadow."

A sigh like a small sandstorm gusted through her hair. *So suspicious. Very well, my lady. If that is what you wish . . . Hearkening and obedience.*

There was a rumble like thunder; the floor shook beneath Nur's feet until she had to grab the edge of a table to stay upright. Invisible demons howled in her ears, and from the corner of her eye she thought she saw flaming skeletons dance all around the room. A lesser girl would have fallen to her knees, hidden her face, and sobbed. Princess Nur was not that courageous, but she was stubborn. Clearly the unseen being that was causing all these frightening sights and sounds wanted her to be badly scared. She refused to give it the satisfaction of seeing her shiver, shudder, or shake.

"Well?" she shouted over the howling demons—shouted so loudly, in fact, that the dancing skeletons paused in mid-prance to stare at her with smoking, empty eyesockets. "What is taking you so long to appear? If you cannot handle so simple a spell as making yourself visible, I do not think you have the power to give me the happiness you promise, 'friend.' "

The howling and the rumbling stopped, the fiery skeletons crumbled to ashes, the thunder died away. Princess Nur found herself gazing up at the biggest, ugliest, nastiest-looking creature she had ever seen.

"Who—*what* are you?" she asked.

"You may call me Gamal," the thing said. "I am a genie. Could you not tell?" In one clawed hand he held a brass lamp, but with the other he indicated his jeweled turban and rich, gauzy garments.

"You, a genie? But you do not look—" Princess Nur stopped herself. The only other genies she had met were Tamar and Khalid. She had no idea that such beautiful beings could have so repulsive a relative as this Gamal. It was not his face and body alone that made him so hideous, but the way every word he spoke sounded like a cruel taunt. His expression, too, made the princess recall one of the palace servants who was always spreading mean gossip and who only smiled when someone else got hurt. "That is, I mean, you are so much more impressive than any genie I ever saw," she managed to add. Ugly and awful he might be, but he was also magical. Magic could mean danger.

Her words seemed to please him. "So I am. You are wise, for a princess. It will be my pleasure to serve you."

"Oh, I do not think that will be necessary," Nur said quickly. She had no specific reason, but she just knew that the less she had to do with Gamal, the better off she would be. "That would be greedy of me. I already have a genie."

"I know." Gamal sounded bored.

"You do?"

"Of course. Your genie is a dear, close, personal

friend of mine. Oh, she is nowhere near as powerful as I am, but that is why I like to look out for her."

You mean spy on her, Nur thought. She decided to walk very carefully until she could get rid of Gamal.

"I am also a dear, dear friend of Khalid's," Gamal went on. "We three were in school together. Ah, happy schooldays! It breaks my heart to see what has happened to poor Khalid. I do not think he should have to suffer so long for one small mistake, do you?"

The moment Gamal mentioned Khalid's name, Princess Nur forgot all about mistrusting him. She thought that he sounded sincere when he spoke of how sorry he was for his old schoolmate's plight. A few fat tears trickled down the ugly genie's face and vanished. Nur's common sense vanished with them.

"Oh yes, I do think it is awful!" she cried. "If you are his friend, can you not do something to free him?"

"Alas," was all that Gamal said, and two more tears slithered from his eyes.

"Hmph! Then a fat lot of good your promises are." Nur folded her arms and stuck out her lower lip. "You offer me perfect happiness, yet you say you cannot free Khalid!"

"Does your happiness really depend on whether he is free or not?" Gamal spoke persuasively. "You would be happy to be a prisoner yourself if only you would be with him; you said so. That is what you want: To be with Khalid forever. Am I wrong, my lady?"

Somehow, hearing her words repeated by Gamal, Princess Nur no longer thought the idea sounded quite so good. "It would be nicer if we were both free," she said.

"Oh, so it would! But how can that be, dear lady?" Gamal's smile was extremely oily. "Khalid will not be free until his Master is happy. His Master will not be happy until he has married a princess. You are the only princess around, and if you marry Lord Haroun, you cannot have Khalid too. Suck a sticky, sticky problem." He held up one claw. "How lucky you are that sticky problems are my specialty. I do so want to help you."

Princess Nur decided that, monster or no monster, she was going to get a straight answer out of Gamal, and so she asked him point-blank: "Khalid is your old friend, not I; why help me at all? Why not just help him?"

"Clever girl," Gamal purred. "Too clever," he growled under his breath. In a warmer tone he said, "Khalid is much too proud to accept my help. You see, he was not—not exactly one of the best students in our class. Now I, on the other hand, was—"

"I am sure you were," said Nur, eager to cut short Gamal's boasting. "Very well, I believe you. I must, for you are my only hope. What must we do?"

"We can do nothing until you do something first."

"What?"

"What mortals do best: Make a wish."

The princess was skeptical. Gamal had won her over with the tears he had shed for his "dear friend" Khalid, but a small voice in the back of Nur's head had begun to whisper, *Cannot a creature who is able to make gold appear out of thin air make tears appear as well?* "And if I make it, you will grant it?" she demanded.

Gamal smiled at her as if she were a child. "Fair one, how could I? You yourself admit that you already have a genie serving you. She must grant the wish you make. Those are the rules. The Council whose word governs all genies and other magical beings would have my head if I gave you any wishes at all."

"I was given three," said Nur. "I used the first to have my genie take me from my father's palace in such a way that no one would notice I was gone or worry about me. I used the second to have her disguise us both so that we could enter Lord Haroun's palace as servants because—well, the reason does not concern you. I have only one wish remaining. Why should I squander it on your say-so?"

"But that is the beautiful thing!" Gamal laughed. "It will not be squandered, for I shall tell you *exactly* how to word it so that it brings you everything you desire. Who knows how to get the most out of wishes better than a genie? Yes, wish for just what I tell you and I swear by all King Solomon's power that you will have your perfect happiness."

Nur raised one eyebrow. "That is a big promise."

"I am a big genie," Gamal replied. "And I am your friend. I risk much by making you this offer. We are not supposed to help humans make their wishes; those are the rules. If the Council found out, I would be in trouble. Oh, they are most terribly strict, the Council, and the punishments they give are horrible!" He turned the lower portion of his body into smoke so that he could come down to Nur's eye level and say, "The risk is mine, the gain all yours—and Khalid's! Will you do it?"

"I do not know." Princess Nur did not like having Gamal's eyes so close to hers. It was like peering into two huge yellow bonfires. "I need time to think."

Gamal's lips twitched impatiently, but immediately he turned his scowl into a smile. "Take all the time you like," he said. "Behold! I shall even give you a little gift just to show you that you can trust me." He reached into the folds of his robe and brought out a plain ring. It was not gold or silver, but dull iron. Nur did not think it was much of a gift from a creature who could make all the riches of the world appear as easily as blinking.

Gamal seemed to read her thoughts. "No, it is not much to look at," he said. "But I promise you, that ring contains great power. It was dipped in the Fountain of Eternal Love."

"I have heard of the Fountain of Eternal Youth," Nur admitted, studying the ring. "Never the Fountain of Eternal Love." She gave Gamal a hard stare. "If I put this on, it will not make me fall in love with whoever gives it to me, will it?"

"Perish the thought!" Gamal's smile grew a little tighter. "No one can force love, even by magic. But if you are able to make someone say that he loves you, then give him this ring to wear, his love will never fade; it will be eternal, like the stars that dance in the heavens." He laid the ring on his palm and held it out to her. "Will you do me the honor of accepting this gift and thinking about the other offer I have made?"

Nur hesitated, then took the ring from Gamal's palm as if it were red hot. It looked huge, yet when she slipped it on her finger it shrank to fit perfectly. A strange golden glow appeared to pulse from the ring for a few moments, and for an instant Nur thought she heard a plaintive voice crying in her ear, *Free! Set me free!*, but then both the voice and the glow vanished. She dared to look Gamal in the eye and said, "Thank you." She did not sound at all sure about it.

Gamal acted as if she had given him an hour's worth of the most sincere thanks in the world. Bowing until his great forehead nearly touched the floor, he begged her to take all the time she wanted to think over his offer of help. "When you have made up your mind and want to call me back, you have only to summon me by name. Farewell, dear lady, and may you have everything your heart ever wishes." So saying, he was gone.

Princess Nur stood where she was for a time, thinking about what had just happened. She could not take her eyes off the iron ring. There was something about it that made her skin itch; her brain itched too.

"Maybe I ought to speak to my genie about this Gamal and his gift," she said, thinking out loud. "Genies are famous for playing tricks on humans, and I still do not trust him." She pondered awhile, then added, "No. No, I think I will keep this as my own secret. If Gamal is telling the truth, this ring is more valuable than gold. And how do I know that I can trust my genie any more than I can trust Gamal? She, too, loves Khalid. If I ask her about this ring, she might lie, and tell me it is worthless, just to take it for herself to use on him!" Nur sighed. "That is the problem with genies: Sometimes they are as bad as people."

We are not! the ring chirped indignantly, but Princess Nur had gone back to washing dishes and did not hear. She plunged her hands into the water and could not notice when a tiny trail of bubbles gurgled up out of the iron ring to mingle with the soapy foam already in the basin.

CHAPTER TEN

In the Chamber of Ten Thousand Pheasants, Khalid listened to what his Master had to say and tried to keep a straight face. Laughing at his Master would be very rude and not the sort of behavior expected of a professional genie. Besides, Lord Haroun was being extremely kind to him all of a sudden, even to the point of telling the genie to lie back on one of the green damask-covered couches and help himself to a cup of sherbet. If Khalid laughed at his Master now, it would probably mean back to work, several dozen new wishes to fulfill, and no more sherbet.

It was very good sherbet—lime and pecan, Khalid's favorite flavor. The genie served himself a second helping and asked, "So, when did you decide that your new servant is really a princess in disguise!"

"I did not *decide* anything," Haroun replied. "She is what she is!"

There was no arguing with that. Khalid licked his ivory spoon and tapped it on the edge of the frosty silver cup. "What I meant, O Master, is how can you tell she is a princess? Even in the best houses of this city, no one has a princess washing the dirty dishes."

Haroun rolled his eyes as if asking the sky to witness what a thickheaded genie he was saddled with. "Well, of course no *normal* princess lives in someone else's palace and washes dirty dishes!"

"I see," said Khalid. "We have an *abnormal* princess."

Haroun made a sound like a tiger who had just backed into a bramble bush. "What we have is an *enchanted* princess! I would think that you of all beings would recognize magic when it shares the same roof. Oh, this is the opportunity of a lifetime! Princesses are *always* going and getting themselves enchanted. You know how it is: if you turn your back on them for an instant, half of them are frogs and the other half are washing dishes."

"What good luck that we do not have one of the froggier kind, then." Khalid leaned forward, holding out his dish. "May I please have some more sherbet?"

Haroun was so absorbed by his great good fortune that he served Khalid with his own hands. "This is wonderful, wonderful!" he exclaimed excitedly. "Some evil magician has placed the lady under a spell. Perhaps it is the Grand Vizier himself who is responsible. It is usually the Grand Vizier in these cases. He wanted to marry her, but she refused him because she did not love him, so he had an evil magician turn her into a common household servant. The spell is powerful, but it can be broken by—by—" Haroun searched the air for an answer and could not find one. He turned to Khalid. "How *can* this spell be broken?"

"How should I know?" the genie replied, his mouth full of lime-pecan sherbet.

A glob of sherbet, catapulted from Lord Haroun's spoon, caught Khalid right between the eyes. "What do you mean, 'How should I know?' you miserable, worthless puff of smoke?" Haroun jumped up from his couch, face red with rage. "You are a *genie*! Genies are supposed to know all about spells and enchantments."

"I can tell you this much," Khalid said, wiping the

sherbet out of his eyes. "You can never break a spell by throwing a tantrum. A window, yes; a spell, no."

"Oh." Haroun's shoulders sagged. "I apologize. But oh, my friend, if you only knew how upset I am!" He folded his hands over his heart. "The moment I saw her face, I knew her for what she was and I adored her on the spot. That face, so full of royal beauty! None but a true princess could have a face like that."

Khalid thought of all the pictures of princesses that Master Ishmael had shown the class when they were studying *King Solomon and His Friends 101: The Special Requirements of Royal Wishes*. Some of the regal ladies had been fat, some thin, some dark, some fair, some lovely as the dawn, some difficult to tell apart from their pet monkeys. (In his heart, Khalid still blamed the odder-looking princesses for how he had mistaken the cat Boabdil for a human being; for one thing, the cat had been prettier than some of them, more graceful than most, less hairy than others.) If there was such a thing as one specific type of face that said "Pay No Attention to the Dirty Dishes; I am Really a Princess," Khalid had missed it.

Still, if his master wanted to believe that one of the new servants was an enchanted princess, he was not going to say a word.

On second thought, he *would* say a word, several. Here was a chance too good to let escape. "O my Master," he said, floating up from his couch and gliding over to the lovestruck mortal. "Your words overjoy my heart. Not every man is wise enough to recognize a true princess when she has been so well disguised by the spells of an evil Grand Vizier."

"An evil magician," Haroun corrected. "The evil magician's spells are *bought* by the evil Grand Vizier."

"Just so. As I was saying, I have known for a long time that your wisdom is greater than that of King Solomon himself. If anyone can break the spell, it is you. That is why I have brought this unlucky princess into your home."

"You, Khalid? You are the one who brought her here?" Haroun's eyes were wide. "But I thought old Yazid was in charge of hiring new workers."

Khalid put on a mysterious smile. "To please a good, dear, generous Master, I thought that this once I could do a better job of hiring than old Yazid. It was . . . a little surprise for you."

"Oh, best of genies, I see your plan now! How clever you are! You have brought the enchanted princess here so that I can break the spell on her and she will fall in love with me for myself alone. My heart's desire will be fulfilled!"

"Mine also," Khalid murmured. Aloud he said, "And when you have your heart's desire, O Master, then do I dare to hope that you will remember your promise to me?"

"Never doubt it!" Haroun cried. "As soon as my princess admits she loves me, I will grant you your freedom. What is more, here and now I *wish* that as soon as the princess says, 'I love you, Lord Haroun,' my very next words will be 'I wish that Khalid be set free.' Can you ask for more?"

"Indeed not," said the genie. "Hearkening and obedience." The air between them shimmered momentarily as Haroun's wish was officially inscribed in the invisible books where such things are recorded.

Haroun rubbed his hands together. "Now I shall go to her and speak of love. Oh, not at once—such things must be done step by step. We shall start by discussing the weather."

"An excellent idea, O my Master," said Khalid. "We have been having so much weather lately."

Lost in his dream of romance, Haroun went on without hearing the genie's words. "It shall be just as it happens in the tales—no, better! I shall not let her know that I know her true identity, not right away. Nor do I want her to love me just because I will be the one to break her spell. By the way, Khalid, I do not suppose I could simply wish for the spell to be broken?"

Khalid shook his head. "We genies cannot use our wishes against one another or against the spells of mortal magicians. That would be cheating. However, I believe there are only so many different ways of breaking such spells, according to the stories."

"Yes, yes; a kiss is the usual method. I think I can handle that."

"But . . . suppose it is not?" Khalid suggested. "I have heard some tales in which a kiss only serves to make the spell that much tighter. Why, there was even one story in which an ill-timed kiss made the enchanted princess fall in love with the *next* man she met, leaving the first suitor to die horribly, of a broken heart."

"Horribly?" Haroun's chin quivered.

"Oh, most horribly; no doubt about that. They say his bleached bones still lie in the desert."

Trying to sound as if he treated the whole tale lightly, Haroun said, "There are no stories where the man finds the princess in the middle of the desert!"

Khalid smirked. "I know that. He went into the desert afterward, to forget his broken heart. His camel ate him."

"Camels do *not* eat—"

"It was a special case, and a very excitable camel." The genie sounded so sure of himself that Haroun had to believe he was speaking the truth. "With respect, O my Master, I have been alive so much longer than you that I might have changed your great-great-great-great-great-grandfather's diapers. Not that I would have wanted to. I have forgotten more stories than you will ever hear, each and every one of them about enchanted princesses and how to break the spells that hold them. It was wrong of me, before, to pretend ignorance. I only wanted to finish my sherbet in peace. The truth of things is, when it comes to enchanted princesses, I have all the answers."

"You do?" Haroun's voice rose hopefully. "Then—then you must know how to break the spell on this one! Tell me at once! I order, I command, I *wish* you would!"

"Hearkening and obedience, Master," said Khalid; and he floated back to his couch and said nothing else for a long, long time.

"Well?" Haroun demanded after the genie had finished off two additional dishes of sherbet. "I await!"

"So you do," said Khalid, not at all concerned. "I have heard your wish. I am fulfilling it even as we speak."

"What you are doing," said Haroun testily, "is sitting on *my* couch in *my* palace eating all of *my* lime-pecan sherbet. You are supposed to be telling me how to break the spell on my beloved princess."

"Yes," said Khalid. "So I shall. As soon as I remember it." He nibbled the tip of his ivory spoon, gazed at the painted ceiling of the Chamber of Ten Thousand Pheasants, and hummed an irritating little tune.

Lord Haroun began to curse.

"Oh my Master, why use such language? You are only making my task harder." Khalid set down his sherbet dish and spoon. "I have the answer you seek, but memory is like a merchant's caravan: every treasure, from greatest to smallest, is tucked away in its proper place. There it waits for the merchant to recall precisely where he packed it—is it in this saddlebag or in that chest? Is it locked in that steel strongbox or wrapped in a handkerchief and stuffed in his pocket? He can find it, but not right away; not if *some* people are standing over him, yelling for him to hurry up all the time."

"Wise merchants make a note of where things are packed," said Haroun, a nasty, sharp edge to his voice.

To Haroun's surprise, Khalid rose like a whirlwind from his couch and swept his Master up in a joyful embrace. "Ah! The powers witness that I spoke the truth when I called my Master wiser than King Solomon himself," the genie exclaimed. "A note! Yes, of course, that is it! Oh, the princess is as good as restored already! Invite the wedding guests, call the musicians, order the bridal feast, for you shall have your royal bride before you know it!" Still carrying Haroun, Khalid summoned up a cloud of blue-green smoke that engulfed them both.

"Where are we?" Haroun asked, coughing, when the smoke cleared and Khalid finally set him down.

"Need you ask, O my Master?" The genie gestured at the walls of the room in which they now stood. From floor to ceiling there were nothing but well-packed bookshelves, and the floor itself was a maze of towering bookcases. By the windows stood a table, a reading lamp, and a single comfortable chair. Khalid promptly selected a book from one of the shelves and plopped himself down.

"What are you doing?" Haroun stood before his genie with arms crossed and foot tapping.

Khalid looked up from the book in his lap and smiled mildly. "I am obeying your wish, O my Master. I am seeking the way to break your princess's spell. This library contains all the tales of enchanted princesses that ever were told. These books, like the packing notes the wise merchant makes, shall jog my memory. It will not take me too long—I read quickly—*provided that I am not disturbed!* Now, may I get back to my work?"

"Oh." Haroun looked guilty. "Certainly, certainly.

Do not let me interfere, O most excellent of servants. I apologize for having bothered you with foolish questions." He started to back out of the library. "Uh—you did say this would not take very long?"

"Not if I am left in peace," Khalid replied. "Do not worry, O my Master; I shall call you at once when I have found the answer. Or if I need anything." He wiggled his fingers, and a small silvery bell shaped like a lily flower appeared on the table. "I will ring for you. In the meanwhile, did you not say something about going to talk with your princess?"

"Oh, yes. I almost forgot. How silly of me. Yes, I was just going to talk to her about—about—"

"The weather," the genie reminded him.

"Yes, yes, yes, that is right, the weather." Haroun nearly tripped over his own feet as he left the room. The last Khalid heard of him, his Master was practicing saying things like, "It is never the heat, but the humidity; do you not agree?" and "Personally I do not think the rain will hurt the rhubarb."

Very pleased with himself, Khalid settled back in his chair with a good book. "This is perfect," he said to himself. "At last I can have some time off. A week will do, or two. Then I shall find out more about the servant girl with whom my Master seems to have fallen in love. At least he is no longer in love with Tamar."

At the thought of her, he turned from his book and gazed out the window. There was a pretty little garden, one of many within the palace walls. Flowering persimmon trees perfumed the air. White gazelles wandered between rows of gardenia bushes and ate most of the blossoms. Parrots perched amid the fronds of tall palms and had screaming contests to see who could make the gazelles jump the highest. It was all very beautiful and impressive, but Khalid saw none of it.

A vision of Tamar's face hovered over the little garden, her beauty making everything else dull by comparison. Her smile went straight to his heart. It hurt so badly that he had to look away and force himself to think of other things.

"*Could* this servant girl be an enchanted princess?" he wondered. A triumphant smile lit his face. "Ha! That does not matter. If she *is* a princess, a kiss will break the spell—it always does, in spite of what I told my Master—and he can marry her. He is not so bad for a mortal, so why would she not marry him? Then I will be free. And if she is *not* a princess —Khalid's smile grew brighter—"if she is not a princess, that does not matter either, for I shall use my magic to turn her *into* a princess! I know she will not object—what servant would be unhappy to trade a tub of dirty dishes for a lifetime of luxury?—and my Master will be none the wiser. Not even the Council will be able to find any rule of magic against this! He wished for a princess, a princess he shall have! And I—I shall have my freedom."

Chuckling merrily, Khalid began to page through his book. He was looking forward to his well-earned two-weeks' vacation.

CHAPTER ELEVEN

"Two weeks," Khalid groaned as he hung by his heels from the kitchen ceiling. "Two miserable weeks straight from the lowest pit of eternal torment! Ay, me, not even the Council themselves could come up with a punishment as devilish as these past two weeks have been!"

The cat Boabdil, who was racing through the kitchens in hot pursuit of a plump mouse, heard the voice from on high and stopped in his tracks. Looking up, he saw only the bunches of fresh herbs that were drying from the rafters. He twitched his whiskers, first in puzzlement, then as he let his most excellent nose sift through the various layers of scent until he discovered . . .

"Oh, it's you, Khalid," he said, addressing a fat bunch of dusty green thyme. "What are you doing up there dressed like a salad?"

"Hiding," the thyme replied.

"Mmmmm." Boabdil did not have to ask the obvious question. He knew from whom Khalid was hiding. The whole household knew, including old Yazid, and he never noticed anything except a late dinner. "She is still after you, is she?"

"Day and night." The thyme shuddered, losing a handful of leaves. Then Khalid gave up on his disguise and returned himself to his original shape. Still upside-down, he told the cat of his misery.

"I was so hopeful, at first! By using my wits alone I have bought myself a little time free of my Master's constant wishes. How was I to know that *she* would hear of it? One day of freedom I had—two at the most!—before she learned that I was working in the library. Two scant days of pleasure, being able to come and go as I liked, given all the books I cared to read—I was always very fond of books, Boabdil—allowed to help myself to anything I desired to eat or drink. My Master was so eager for me to get on with my task that he said I could have a servant of my very own to take care of my wishes! *My* wishes!"

"And of course, knowing what you know of wishes, you told your Master to let the servant have a little freedom, too?" Boabdil purred maliciously.

Khalid scowled at him, but upside-down it looked like a twisted smile. "This servant did not want any freedom, once she knew whom she must serve. The moment she set eyes on me, she began to—to—" The memory made his face go pasty.

"—recite poetry," Boabdil finished the sentence for him. "We know. We all heard her."

"*Love* poetry!" Khalid made a little gagging sound. "Romantic verses written by the masters of the art, no less. She also sang songs of love. Did you know that she can play the lute all by herself?"

"I have never heard of anyone playing the lute in teams," the cat murmured.

Khalid did not hear the barb. "Where does a common servant pick up such things?"

The cat's whiskers curved up into an unnatural grin. "A *common* servant does not. What does that lead you to believe, my friend? Think, now."

Khalid thought. All the possibilities streamed through his brain until— "Oh, no. No!" He did a somersault down from the ceiling and landed on his knees before the cat. "Tell me it is not so, Boabdil! Tell me that she is not—that she cannot be—that it is her companion who is truly—"

"The enchanted princess?" Boabdil preened himself with one paw. "No. Neither one of them is that."

Khalid toppled forward like a felled tree. The cat had to leap nimbly out of the way to avoid being crushed. As he circled the sobbing genie, Boabdil added, "If it is any consolation, she *is* a princess. Not exactly enchanted—I suppose it does not count if she had the spell put on herself, without the benefit of a wicked magician and an evil Grand Vizier—but she is still a princess for all that."

"She?" Khalid lifted his head from the floor. "You mean, the one who has been after me is the princess?"

"She is."

"And the other—the one my master has been courting for these past two weeks is—?"

"Not a princess. She is actually—"

Khalid did not wait to hear the rest. "Oh, what does it matter who or what that one is? She can still serve my purposes. I will go to her at once, Boabdil, and make her a very generous offer: Wed my Master, say nothing of her true identity, and once he has freed me, I shall transform her into as good a princess as ever was, enchanted or not. Ha!" He sat up and folded his arms in triumph. "I should have thought of this sooner. What could be simpler?"

Cats cannot snicker, but Boabdil managed to come close. "I could not recommend that course of action, my friend. You would not like the results."

"And why not?" This time Khalid's scowl worked properly. "Who are you to tell me how to use my magic? You are only a cat!"

"Only a cat," Boabdil slowly repeated the phrase in

a way that made it sound more magnificent and awe-inspiring than the hundred empty titles of a king. "But a cat who has known enough genies to also know that outside of a battle of magics, one genie's spells cannot change the effects of another's."

"Another genie's spells?" Khalid was definitely at sea. "The servant girl my Master loves is *not* a princess but *is* enchanted? What genie would want to enchant a servant girl?"

"Does the name Tamar ring any bells?" Boabdil was enjoying himself. It was the nature of cats to play with their prey, teasing the mice they caught with the illusion of possible escape. Some of the mice did get away, but the best part of the game was the playing, not the winning. Now Boabdil had discovered that the game of cat-and-mouse played just as well when it was cat-and-genie.

"Tamar!" The shocked look on Khalid's face was very satisfying. "*She* has enchanted the girl?"

Boabdil decided that it was time to let his prey go. "She *is* the girl, O my friend."

The sound of Khalid's cry was loud enough to bring old Yazid into the kitchen to ask whether dinner was ready yet. All he found there was his master's cat sitting beside a very crumpled bunch of thyme. The old man left, grumbling.

Once old Yazid had gone. Khalid returned to his proper shape. "Tamar! Oh, how can it be she? It was bad enough when my Master fell in love with her while she was herself, but to have him love her in disguise as well—!" The genie looked like a shipwrecked sailor whom the waves have battered badly."Why has she come back?"

"That should be obvious." Boabdil put on a superior air, superior even for a cat. "She is trying to free you by bringing your master the one thing he desires: a princess." The cat's whiskers drooped a bit as he added, "Alas, her plan does not seem to have worked out in quite the way she had hoped."

A tear rolled down Khalid's cheek. "Now I shall never be free."

Boabdil leaped into the genie's lap, then onto his shoulder. He purred as loudly as he could, to give comfort, and dabbed the tear away with one velvet paw. "Do not despair, my friend. Hope must never die."

"Why should I hope?" Khalid asked in a hollow voice. "What have I to hope for?"

Boabdil snorted. "More than most poor mortals! If you would only stop feeling sorry for yourself, you might be able to see that. Fool, you are loved! How many beings—mortal or magical—are lucky enough to say the same? Tamar loves you, and may my nose lose its cunning if you do not love her, too." The cat tilted his head to one side. "You *do* love her, do you not?"

"With all my heart," the genie sighed.

"Well, then!" Boabdil was pleased. "Two hearts with one desire, two creatures of great magic with one goal—what can stop you? Unless it be your own foolishness. Go to her, my friend. Tell her what is in your heart. Save your pride for another day. After all she has done for you, you owe her that much honesty."

For the first time in nearly two weeks, Khalid looked truly cheerful. "Boabdil, you are right. I shall do as you say, tell Tamar of my love, and see if together we cannot at last break the chain of wishes that binds me to Lord Haroun's service. Ah, to think I—greatest student in Master Ishamael's class—should have to learn wisdom from a cat!"

"Where better?" Boabdil purred. He butted Khalid's cheek. Just then, Princess Nur peeped around the side of one of the big kitchen doors. She was carrying a lute and she stared at Khalid with a terrible yearning in her eyes.

"Uh-oh," said the genie.

Boabdil butted him again. "Do not dare to vanish. Tamar is not the only one to whom you owe honesty. To live without hope is cruel, but it is crueler to allow anyone to live with false hope."

Khalid's eyes met Nur's; he swallowed hard. Setting the cat down on the floor, he stood up and approached the girl. She was quick to bow and ask if she could fetch him anything. He shook his head.

"Then perhaps you would not object if I were to entertain you?" she offered, showing him the lute. "A simple song, to pass the time?" Her fingers brushed the strings in the opening notes of yet another love song.

Khalid laid his hand over the lute strings, making them silent. "I have something to tell you," he said.

Lord Haroun was wandering aimlessly through the palace, trying to think of a rhyme for his latest love poem when he heard the sound of sobbing. It was coming from the smallest of the gardens where herbs and vegetables grew for use in the palace kitchens. Here no gazelles or peacocks walked, no fountains played, no rare and exotic flowers bloomed. There were no benches, and very little shade.

Benches or no benches, someone was sitting in the kitchen garden and crying. Haroun recognized the new servant girl at once. She was seated on the lip of the well that stood in the center of the garden, a lute at her feet. For a moment he hesitated—some people did not like company when they wept—but then his generous heart encouraged him to go into the garden and see what was wrong. *Perhaps it will get my mind off my own troubles*, he reasoned.

He did his best to act as if coming into the garden

were his own idea. Humming a bright tune, he made a great business of examining every other bush, shrub, or row of radishes he passed. He pinched leaves, plucked stems, and uprooted nearly half the lettuces before turning to the weeping girl and exclaiming, "Oh! Excuse me. I did not see you sitting there."

"Did you not?" Nur sniffled. "Then either you are blind, or you think I am stupid." She kicked the lute.

"I *beg* your pardon!" Haroun felt as if she had kicked him in the chest instead.

"Beg away." She gave the lute another kick. It rolled over in the dust, strings jangling. "You might make a better beggar than you do an actor. I am the biggest thing in this garden, and you did not see me? Take that tale to another marketplace!" She looked away from him and twisted the strange dark ring on her finger.

Haroun sat down beside her. "I was only trying to see if there was anything I could do to help you. You sounded so miserable." He took a deep breath and let it out slowly. "Is there?"

Nur kept twisting the ring. "What help do I need? I am rich. I have great men—kings!—begging to marry me. I have the powers of magical beings at my command."

"Have you been sitting out in this strong sun long?" Haroun inquired.

Nur's eyes snapped as she jerked her gaze up to meet his. "I am *not* crazy!"

"No, certainly not, not at all, not a bit." Haroun tried to calm her down. He had not bargained for hearing such words from a common servant when he had first come into the garden. "If you say so."

To his relief, the anger left her face. She began to laugh, although it was not a very jolly sound. "If I say so . . . But what am I saying? I forget who I am, now." Seeing how oddly Haroun was looking at her, she swiftly added, "I ask your forgiveness, O my Master. The poets and the storytellers all agree that a broken heart often makes us act a little mad. I should not trouble you with my problems."

"Oh, I do not mind," Haroun replied, somewhat shyly. "A broken heart, you say?"

"Well . . . I suppose it *ought* to be broken. My pride hurts, at any rate." Her brow wrinkled, and unexpectedly she demanded, "Have you ever thought you were in love?"

"Oh, yes, many ti—! That is, I understand what you mean." Haroun put on a solemn face and tried to seem older than he was. This was difficult, since now that he looked at her, he realized that the girl was about his age. "I assume that the boy you love does not love you?"

"Worse! He loves another. *Really* loves her, not just *thinks* he loves her. Do you understand that, as well?" Nur studied Haroun closely.

"Yes—that is—I mean—no." Haroun felt uncomfortable under Nur's steady gaze. There was something disturbing in this servant girl's eyes. It was the first time Haroun had really looked at her. How different this was from his enchanted princess! Oh, the enchanted princess had lovely eyes, true, but whenever Haroun spoke to her, they wandered. They were smiling eyes, eyes that looked back at him very prettily and politely, but there was nothing there behind them. It was like gazing into the eyes of one of his tame gazelles: beautiful, but boring.

Nur laughed again, and Haroun thought it was a very nice sound. He wondered how much nicer it might be if the girl were truly happy. "No, why should you understand? When you love, you love; there is no doubt in your heart or your mind about it, is there?"

Haroun said nothing. He was thinking about the servant girl's words. *Do I really love my enchanted princess?* He regarded Nur with new eyes. "Why did you love—*think* you loved him?" he asked.

Nur considered this. "Well, he is handsome. . . ." She let her eyes rest on Haroun's face. "But many men are handsome. And kind . . . as are other men, too; not that I have met so many men in my life. In fact, he was the first I ever met without someone at my back telling me I *ought* to love him."

The way the hero in all the old stories must always love a princess if he wants to live happily ever after, though Haroun. Out loud he said, "Have you ever thought that what you loved was not him, but finally being free of all those *ought-to's*?"

Nur's mouth opened slightly in stunned admiration. "By all that is sacred, I think you have hit it, O my Master. Has anyone ever told you how wise you are?"

Haroun's chest puffed out, though he tried to act modest. "Oh, I am not so wise as all that, my dear." *What a smart girl!* he thought. "For example, if you can keep a secret I will tell you that I, too, have not made so many wise choices when it comes to love."

"You mean—my fellow servant?" Nur asked the question for form's sake. Lord Haroun's courtship of Tamar was the talk of the servants' quarters second only to Nur's pursuit of Khalid. "She is beautiful." Nur could not help sounding bitter when she said that.

"Beauty is not everything," Haroun replied, and surprised himself by meaning it. "It is too soon lost to age and time. If beauty is the only thing that makes you want to marry a person, what will you have left in the years after that beauty fade away?" A thought struck him like a thunderbolt, and he spoke it aloud: "Happily ever after is a very long time to be miserable."

This time Nur's laugh came from the heart, warming them both. "You are honest as well as wise, O my Master. I am grateful for honesty, even if it sometimes has sharp teeth. Let me return the favor and be honest with you, too. Do you see this ring?" She stuck out her right hand. The iron band was dull, but still seemed to glow in the garden sunlight.

Haroun studied the ring, holding Nur's hand to do so. He found this to be a very pleasing sensation and for a moment forgot why he was doing it. "It is—it is a very unusual piece of jewelry," he said. "A family gift?"

"A gift of magic," Nur confided. "I did not lie, you see, when I told you that magical beings serve me."

Haroun used all this concentration to keep his hand from shaking. It was a very upsetting to hear this charming girl speak crazily again. "My dear—what *is* your name?"

"Nur."

"My dear Nur, how can you expect anyone to believe that? I am not saying it is impossible for you to have a little magic of your own—it is a free country for such things to happen, even to servants—but if you do have any magic at your command, why have you not—? Why are you still—?"

"Why am I working as a servant in this house?" Nur finished the question for him. Her fingers curled around his as she tilted her hand, the better to contemplate the iron ring. "Wish in haste, repent at leisure; and I have only one wish to my name."

"Really?" Haroun beamed at the thought of someone with but a single wish. "You are quite right, then; you must be extremely careful. How thrilling! How to wish for *just* what you want? How to make sure your genie does not trick you into wasting that wish? How exciting for you!"

"I think it is awful," Nur said. "I would rather be in your shoes, O my Master, with all the wishes I want."

"No, you do not." Haroun's face drooped with envy. "You just think you would like that. It is terribly dull, really. There is never any challenge. If I waste one wish, there are a dozen more where that came from—a hundred more! Wishes are not special for me anymore, and if magic becomes as common as radishes, what is the use of it?"

A sly look came into Nur's eyes. "If that is how you feel, O my Master, why do you not use one wish to rid yourself of all the rest?"

"What? Are you mad?" Haroun was scandalized. "Throw away wishes? Anyone who heard of it would think I was insane. How would I live, afterward? I am used to having everything I desire given to me at once. I am afraid I could never go back to things the way they were." Sadly, he let Nur's hand drop. "You could not understand."

"Oh, could I not?" Her brows rose. "You might be surprised. Before I came to work here, I was—Well, what I was then is unimportant. What matters is I too know that I could never go back to things the way they were. And yet, as unhappy as I was then, there are times I think I could go back to that life . . . if I did not have to go back alone."

Haroun saw the way she looked at him when she said that. He grasped both her hands before he knew what he was doing. "You know, if you think you cannot decide what to use your one wish for, you might try wishing to be a princess. Being a princess has all sorts of advantages. You would be rich and have pretty clothes and live in a palace and—"

"I do not wish to be a princess," Nur said firmly.

"Oh." Haroun was downcast. "It was just a thought. Not a very good one. You do not look as if you would be comfortable, being a princess. I suppose it is something you have to be born to do right."

"Sometimes not even then," Nur remarked under her breath. More clearly she said, "Oh my Master, this ring I wear is also magical."

"I knew that," said Haroun. "It holds the genie who shall grant you your one wish, is it not so?"

"Oh, there is no genie in this old thing," Nur told him. The ring vibrated angrily on her finger, like an enraged bumblebee, but she did not notice. "But it does hold magic—the magic of eternal love." She repeated for him all that Gamal had told her about the ring, without mentioning how she had gotten it. She ended by saying, "My lord, you have been good to me. I know you love my friend—"

"Do you also then know that she does not love me?" Haroun asked. For some reason that thought did not make him as sorrowful as it might have. *If I want a princess so badly, I could have Khalid turn my girl into one*, he thought, eyes never leaving Nur's face.

"Hearts change," said Nur, pretending not to see the way he looked at her. "Perhaps hers will. You only have to have her say she loves you once, then give her this ring and she will love you always." She slipped it from her hand and pressed it into his. "There are all sorts of situations that might make a girl say she loves a boy."

Haroun's hand closed over Nur's. "Are there? Would you say—could you show me—can you—?"

"You are joking with me." Nur smiled at him fondly. "Now I must go. I have work to do." She tried to leave the garden, but he would not release her hand.

"Hearts change, you say. Could yours—?"

"Oh, I know I said it was broken, but do not worry about me; it will mend." Her eyes twinkled. "It may heal faster than I thought." With a twist of her wrist she was free of his grasp and gone.

Haroun was left to stare at the iron ring in his palm.

You look just like a carp when you do that, the ring sneered. Its tiny voice went unheard.

CHAPTER TWELVE

Princess Nur went skipping through the halls of Lord Haroun's palace. Her heart felt lighter than it had in weeks. She was very pleased with herself and wanted nothing more than to find Tamar and tell the genie that she was ready to make her final wish.

She was so absorbed in happy thoughts that she did not see that cat Boabdil cross her path until she tripped over him. Boabdil let out an ear-splitting screech, even though he was unhurt. Nur picked him up at once and hugged him, which was just what he had intended. He let her pour out a thousand sweet names and apologies before he purred to show her all was forgiven.

"Oh, dear cat, please pardon me, but I was not thinking," Nur implored.

"You were not looking, either," Boabdil pointed out. "What could possibly distract you so?" He gave her a side-long look. "Is it love?"

Nur promptly twirled the cat around and around the hall in a wild dance until he yowled. "Love? Yes, it is love, you darling cat! How very smart you are! How fine your fur! How glorious your whiskers! It is love, true love, and all the world is beautiful!"

"Put me down before I put my beautiful claws into your skin," Boabdil spat. When she did so, he ruffled up his fur at her. "So it is love. Even after Khalid told you he loves Tamar, you still insist on loving him? What a waste!"

"Love . . . Khalid?" Nur put her fingers to her lips and giggled.

"Where is the joke?" the cat asked, eyes flashing. There is nothing a cat hates worse than feeling as if he is on the wrong end of a cat-and-mouse match.

"This is a magical palace, cat," she said merrily. "A magical palace that has everything: not merely an enchanted princess—that's me, I suppose—and a pair of genies, but—can you keep the secret?—there is also a great and mighty wizard dwelling here."

"A wizard!" Boabdil hissed lightly. "That is all we need. Who let him in?"

"No one needed to," Nur replied. "He owns the palace, you see."

"Since when is Lord Haroun a wizard?" The cat switched his tail rapidly from side to side. "Since when is he anything but a silly, greedy boy with more toys than are good for him?" His golden eyes became suspicious slits. "Is *that* your riddle, lady? Is *he* the one you love?"

"Yes!" The word became a glad song on Nur's lips. "I was like the princess who slept for a hundred years, but now I am awake. In my dreams I thought I loved Khalid, but now, thanks to the wisdom of Lord Haroun, I know the truth."

"Wisdom?" Boabdil wiggled his ears. "Are you sure we are talking about the same Lord Haroun?"

"You do not know him," Nur said. "I did not know him either, until now. His wise words cleared my eyes; he let me see that I was being a stubborn child. I have spent so many years saying *no* to all the old kings my father wanted me to marry that saying *no* became a habit! Therefore, when Tamar asked me to have Haroun for my husband, I said *no* without thinking just because *no* is what I always say whenever I am asked to marry!" She folded her hands over her heart. "Dear cat, you must help me."

Boabdil gave the traditional feline reply: "If I feel like it. How?"

"You must help me decide how I can best use my last wish."

The cat flicked his ears forward, puzzled. "I thought that was settled. If you still love Lord Haroun—?"

"I do."

"Good. The way you mortals have been behaving, your hearts seem to flip over every few minutes, like griddle cakes. Then if you do love him, as you say, what is the problem? Wish to marry him, as my lady Tamar asked, and everything will be done and well done!"

Princess Nur shook her head. "I will not wish that wish."

"Why in the name of the great Moon Cat not?" Boabdil yowled, at the end of his patience.

"Because I think he loves me, too," Nur answered, her voice full of joy. "I could see it in his eyes; I could feel it in my heart. I will need no wish to make him marry me. Oh, Boabdil!" She knelt before the cat. "Can you imagine how happy he will be when he learns that his bride is a princess after all?"

"That will be quite a wedding present," the cat admitted. "But—what of the lifetime of wishes Tamar promised you if you wished for Haroun as a husband?"

A secret smile curved one corner of Nur's lips. "I think that it is time my dear Haroun learned that life may be lived quite comfortably without wishes. How can he learn that if I do not live the lesson myself? Let Tamar be free, Boabdil. Let Khalid, too, have his freedom at last. I will not open his prison only to lock her up in another one."

"You would do that for them?" For the first time

in the history of all cats everywhere, a sane and healthy animal stared at a person with honest admiration in his eyes. "Are you *sure* you are a real human being?" Boabdil inquired skeptically.

Princess Nur laughed. "Real enough to ask your help about what to do with my remaining wish, dear cat! I would like it to be a wedding gift to Haroun, since it is the last wish either one of us will ever have, but I do not know what he would most enjoy."

"Well, what do you think he will be giving you?" the cat asked.

Nur's smile held a secret. "A ring," she said. "A plain iron ring, and that is all I desire."

"Hmmmm. Iron, is it? I must say, either mortal brides' taste in wedding gifts has changed or you are— Well, I am no longer certain about exactly *what* you are, my lady. But I like it. I will help you. I shall spy upon Lord Haroun and see if I can pick up any hints. Will that do?"

"That will do nicely," Nur scratched him behind the ears. "And I will go back into the kitchens to wait."

"For me?"

"For him, for Haroun. From what Tamar tells me, he will be coming along shortly to talk to me about . . . the weather." She sauntered off, singing again. Boabdil watched her go, flicked the air with his tail, and trotted away in the opposite direction to do as he had been asked.

Nur was almost to the kitchens when she suddenly skipped headfirst into a wall of solid air. Nothing was there to bar her path, yet she could not go a single step further. "What is this?" she wondered aloud, patting the invisible barrier with her hands.

A friend, said a familiar voice. *A friend who has come back to this palace to see how you are doing.*

"If you are my friend, show yourself!" Nur demanded.

You know the rules. The voice seemed to mock her. *Have you forgotten? You only need to call me by name.*

"Very well, if you insist." Nur was annoyed. "Show yourself, Gamal!"

The monstrous genie stood before her without any showy magical trimmings to accompany his appearance. This time he was solid, with legs instead of a trail of smoke, and no taller than an ordinary man. "I am here, my lady." His smile was cold and evil.

Nur was brave without knowing how brave she was; it was just in her to recognize a bully when she saw one and not to be afraid of him. "I do not see why that was necessary," she said. "If you wanted to see me, why did you not simply come?"

"Rules, my lady, as I said." Gamal bowed too deeply for the gesture to be anything but a nasty joke. "Have you ever heard me speak of the Council, whose laws command all genies everywhere? They are the ones who are so insistent that we follow their rules. They are very quick to punish us when we do anything wrong—even if the error is made for the best of reasons—and they become especially angry when someone interferes with one of their judgments."

"They sound like my father's advisers," Princess Nur said. "You can tell them anything except *You are wrong.*"

"I rejoice to hear that you and I share the same opinion of those old goats." Gamal's smile widened, showing off his tusks too much.

"You did not come here just for us to take turns insulting our elders." Nur was growing distinctly impatient with Gamal. "What do you want?"

Gamal put on a pained expression. "You hurt my

feelings, my lady! I have only come back to fulfill my promise."

"The promise to help me make my last wish well?" Nur could not help beaming; she was too happy to hide her joy, even from Gamal. "If that is all, you may go. I already know what I shall use that wish for!"

"You do?" Gamal's black brows became a thundercloud above his yellow eyes. His keen sight narrowed on the princess's hands, and he saw . . . "Gone! The ring is gone! Then you have given it to him? Yes, you must have done it, or you would not be so happy. Oh, excellent!"

Nur tried to speak, but Gamal burst from his human-sized body into a towering pillar of sooty smoke that spun around her like a whirlwind. "He has the ring! He has it! Ha! Wonderful!" The genie's voice rumbled inside the spinning smoke with the might of an earthquake. Nur trembled in spite of herself and pressed her back against the wall while Gamal's wicked laughter made bits of the ceiling come tumbling down. "It is done, then! Soon it shall be over!"

The voice inside the whirlwind changed. Every word it spoke vibrated and glowed with great magic. "O Great Ones! O Wise Ones! O Ancient Ones, come at once to give your judgment and to punish the guilty one whom I have found!"

The walls of Lord Haroun's palace shook. A cold, wet wind blew through the rooms, smelling like old books left out in the rain. Nur's skin crept as if all the ants in the world were marching over it. She hugged herself tightly and wished she were not alone. Then, as if she had spoken that wish aloud, someone was standing beside her. She looked to her left and saw an old, old man. His hair was white, his skin was darker than the sun-browned skin of her father's best desert rider, and his eyes had the color and shine of rubies. Nur gasped. No human being could have such eyes. When he smiled, she saw that every tooth in his head was long and sharp as a dagger, and grassy green.

He was not the only one there. Four others stood behind him, each almost as old and hideous as he, each with cold, glittering red eyes. They were all dressed in silk and satin robes sewn with gold thread and dripping with precious jewels. Each one carried a lamp in his hands, but these were solid gold set with diamonds. Nur did not need anyone to tell her that she was about to meet the famous Council.

"Why have we been summoned?" the oldest-looking of the five ancient genies demanded. His voice creaked and cracked like a door on rusty hinges.

Gamal whisked away the dirty whirlwind and showed himself once more at human size. He knelt and touched his forehead to the floor. "O Great Ones, it was I, Gamal, who summoned you."

"Gamal . . . ?" The oldest genie scratched his head. "The name sounds familiar."

The youngest-looking of his companions tugged at his sleeve. "It was Gamal who called us before, when master Ishmael's prison was stolen."

"Ah, yes, that is it!" The oldest genie looked as pleased as if he had remembered it by himself. Turning to Gamal, he demanded, "And where is Master Ishmael's prison, Gamal? Return it to us at once!"

With his face still on the floor, Gamal replied, "O Ancient One, you speak as if it were I who stole the prison in the first place. Can you believe I would commit such a crime?" (Nur had a chilly, certain feeling in her stomach that it would take far less time to list the crimes Gamal would *not* commit, but she said nothing.) "Yet a crime *has* been committed, I admit. Allow me now the honor of bringing the guilty one before you for punishment!"

The oldest genie wrinkled his brow. "You know who the criminal is?"

"You will find him within the walls of this humble building, O Wise One." Gamal dared to raise his head a bit and smile a foxy smile. "Shall I name his name?"

"Are we, then, powerless?" The oldest genie glared at Gamal scornfully. "We need no more from you than you have already given us." He raised the hand in which he carried his gold lamp and in a voice to make the thunder flee he boomed, "LET THEM COME!"

Earlier Nur had wished for company, and now she had it. The magical command of the oldest member of the Council was enough to fetch every living, breathing creature in Lord Haroun's palace. Lord Haroun himself was there, and Boabdil the cat. Khalid and Tamar, still in her mortal disguise, appeared together, holding hands as if that was what they had been doing at the moment they were summoned. Three female and five male servants whom Nur had never seen before stared in terror at the five magnificent genies before dropping their brooms and dust-cloths and racing away, screaming.

"Let them run," Gamal said quickly, jumping to his feet. "You want none of them, O Great Ones. Nor him." He pointed at old Yazid, who stood leaning on a rake and blinking at the Council. "Go away, old man."

Old Yazid shook his rake at Gamal. "I will go when I am good and ready, you young puppy!" Gamal twitched one finger, and the floor between them swarmed with an army of fat, black, hairy spiders. "Now—now I am ready," the old fellow stammered, and ran after the other servants as if he were thirty years younger.

Gamal was so eager, he did not bother ordering anyone else out. He strode across the floor, growing bigger with every step, until by the time he reached Khalid his head brushed the ceiling. "Here he is, O Great Ones!" he shouted in triumph. "Here is the one you want, the thief, the one who stole my poor Master Ishmael's prison!"

"Thief?" Tamar cried, holding tight to Khalid. "You are crazy, Gamal. How can you say—?"

"Be silent," the oldest genie commanded. He did not even have to raise his voice. Tamar knew who he was and knew that it would only hurt Khalid to argue with any member of the Council. She bowed to him and said no more.

But Khalid had something to say for himself. "Master Ishmael in prison? My beloved teacher, punished? What for?" He was so appalled by this news that he did not bother to defend himself against Gamal's accusation.

The youngest member of the Council noticed this and came over to pat Khalid on the shoulder. "There, there. It is good to see such affection for a teacher. A very *good* teacher, I think he was, but he lacked judgment. We were sent a message telling us that he gave one of his students a lamp, right away, instead of making him work his way up from a magic ring or a brass bottle or an enchanted spicebox. We were also told that the results were . . ." He looked embarrassed. "Well, they were nothing for genies to be proud of."

By this time, Nur had gotten over her fear of the Council. They really did remind her of her father's advisers—old men who had held her on their laps since she was a child and who laughed at everything she said, even when she was being serious. She did not like them at all. "Tell me, O Great One," she spoke up boldly. "Who was it that told you about this—*mistake* of Master Ishmael's?"

"Who told . . . ?" The youngest Council member

thought about it. "Why, I believe the letter was not signed."

"I thought so," said Nur, giving Gamal a meaningful look. "And I also think that believing an unsigned letter of accusation is also nothing for genies to be proud of."

"Who are you, to tell us how we should think?" the oldest genie growled.

"No one! She is no one!" Haroun rushed to Nur's side and stood between her and the furious genie. "She is only Nur, one of my servants. Do not harm her! Good servants are so hard to find." He raised his right hand, as if that could stop the powers of five of the mightiest genies.

"THE PRISON!" The oldest genie's red eyes flashed. Sparks flew from them and landed on the iron ring, which Haroun had placed on the third finger on his right hand. Haroun let out a startled yelp as the ring flew from his finger and clattered to the floor. "He is the thief!"

"Thief? Me?" Haroun crossed his now-bare hands over his heart. "Why would I want to steal an imprisoned genie?"

"To free him, of course!" The oldest genie's eyes became hard red slits glowing like eternal fires. "What mortal does not possess the power to free a genie, even one whom we, the Council, have imprisoned?"

"To free him," said the next-youngest genie, "and then to claim his magic."

"To free him," said the next in line, "before his allotted time of punishment is over."

"To free him," said the third, "and by doing so to fly in the face of our judgment."

"Look at him!" The oldest genie's lip curled in scorn. "Look at that shocked expression he has put on like a badly made mask. Yet even if he were a good actor, there is no arguing with the fact that he had Master Ishmael's prison in his possession. There is no doubt or question: he is the thief."

"*He?*" Gamal's mouth fell open like a poorly latched trapdoor.

"Why are you so surprised?" asked the youngest member of the Council, who often noticed things his elders did not. "I thought you said you knew who it was."

"Yes, but—I thought—he is not supposed to be—"

"ENOUGH!" The oldest genie threw his arms wide and shot up from human size until he shattered the ceiling of the hall. Without thinking, Tamar and Khalid threw a spell of shielding over Nur and Haroun, an umbrella of white light that protected the two humans from tumbling bricks and falling plaster. Boabdil the cat looked after himself, diving under the robes of the oldest genie.

That ancient creature was so furious that he did not notice or care if a cat was sharing his clothing. Rage made his face turn crimson. He leveled a huge finger at Haroun, and his words fell like lead. "I know your name without anyone to tell it to me, Haroun ben Hasan. Why does it not surprise me to learn that it was you who stole Master Ishmael's prison? It is not enough for you to hold one genie captive—you must have two! O mortal man, your greed is a legend among us. Your name is taught in the schoolrooms as a lesson with which to frighten young genies and as a constant reminder to all of us that mortal men are never to be trusted."

"Now just one moment—" Haroun protested.

"One moment will not be enough for you to think about your greed. Take several!" The oldest genie's hands shot purple and crimson stars. One struck Haroun on the forehead and he began to dissolve into smoke from the feet up, as if he himself were a genie returning to his lamp. Nur grabbed his hands, only to have them trickle away between her fingers as the unhappy young man was drawn into the center of the iron ring on the floor. He vanished with a little sigh.

Princess Nur wasted no time on tears. "What have you done to him?" she shrieked, her face white as bone. She faced the Council in a truly royal rage. "Speak, you herd of old goats! *What have you done?*"

She did not wait for an answer. Teeth clenched, hands balled into fists, she threw herself to her knees before Tamar. "Hear my last wish well, O my good friend and servant!" she cried. "Grant it, and then take your freedom. *I wish that I might never part from Haroun ben Hasan, no matter the peril, no matter the price!*"

"But—but—" Tamar tried to bring Nur to her feet. "But you know nothing of where he has gone or when—*if*—he shall ever emerge. Would you not rather—?"

"I would rather be with one I love, even in a prison of iron, than without him in the palace of a king. Grant my wish, O genie." Nur looked steadily into Tamar's eyes. "Grant it now."

Tamar saw she had no choice. Tears flowed from her eyes, but she managed to say what was expected of her: "Hearkening and obedience."

Tamar's magic was not as showy as the oldest genie's. There were no bright stars or any sound of thunder. The wish simply *happened*. The genies watched as Princess Nur dwindled into a wisp of smoke that poured itself into the iron ring. Her expression never changed: calm and sure of her decision, she went to join Haroun ben Hasan with a serene and joyful smile.

CHAPTER THIRTEEN

"Well, my boy, how does it feel to be free at last?" the youngest genie of the Council asked, patting Khalid on the back.

"Not as good as I thought it would." Khalid did not look at him. He was still staring at the iron ring. So was Tamar. He could see her shoulders shaking, and he knew without seeing the tears that she was crying.

"Free?" Gamal could not keep the indignation out of his voice. "What do you mean, he is free?"

The oldest genie explained it for him: "By attempting to get a second genie while he still had one working for him, Haroun ben Hasan forfeited his right to own any genie at all, now or ever." Looking smug, he added, "The closest he shall ever come to another genie is Master Ishmael, for Haroun ben Hasan is hereby condemned to share Master Ishmael's prison for as long as that genie remains in the iron ring."

"And for how long is that?" Khalid asked.

"Oh, a trifle," the youngest genie said happily. "His mistake was so small. Just a hundred years."

"Give or take a decade for good behavior," said the second-eldest.

"But that is terrible!" Khalid protested. "Nothing Lord Haroun has done was bad enough to deserve such a punishment."

"Do not tell the Council what is and is not a proper punishment," the oldest genie menaced, "or perhaps we will practice our judgments on you."

Khalid stood tall and fearlessly faced the ancient creature. "Even though you threaten me, still I will speak: Lord Haroun may have been greedy, but he was poor when he found me. It is frightening for a mortal to be poor. He saw me as his chance never to be poor again, and he took it. It was *my* responsibility to protect him from his fear, and it was *my* mistake that made Lord Haroun such a grasping man. Must he lose a century of freedom for that? You forget that mortals do not have the same lifespans we do. When he emerges from the ring, he shall crumble to dust! No, he should not suffer for my error; I should."

"O wisdom!" Gamal cried, clapping his hands and grinning with evil glee. "Heed him, O Great Ones! For once Khalid knows what he is talking about."

The Council did not hear Gamal, or else ignored him.

"Do not worry about the mortal Haroun ben Hasan," said the third-eldest genie.

"He will be the same age when he comes out of the ring as he was when he went in," said the fourth.

"And what of Nur, who is my Master?" asked Tamar, her face wet.

"Hmph!" The oldest genie snorted. "Silly creature. Never in all my eons as a genie have I ever heard a wish like the one *she* made. She will be the same, too, I suppose."

"She may and he might, but what of the world?" Khalid exclaimed. "Will that, also, be the same when they come out?"

"What a question! Of course not." The oldest genie shrugged. "What does it matter?"

"To you, nothing." Tamar's eyes were dry now, and stared hard at the leader of the Council. "But to a human being, much." Without another word, she snapped herself into a spear of smoke and plunged into the center of the iron ring.

"To you, nothing," Khalid repeated. "But to those who have lived with humans long enough to think of them as friends, it matters a great deal." He too turned to smoke and dived after Tamar.

The Council and Gamal gazed at the iron ring for a long while, too stunned to speak. Then the youngest genie said, "I wonder if we might not have made a little mistake, gentlemen. If this Haroun ben Hasan was so wicked a Master, why would Khalid speak so strongly in his defense? Why would he speak of humans as friends?"

"Because Khalid is a fool and has always been a fool," Gamal spat. He glared at the ring. "Who else but a fool would defend a human?"

The youngest genie looked at Gamal narrowly. "We never did find out who sent us that message about Master Ishmael, did we?" he remarked casually.

"Why do you stare at me like that?" Gamal demanded. "I will not stand for it!"

The oldest genie reached into one of his sleeves and drew out a much-folded piece of paper. "No, we did not," he said. "But by good luck, I have the message here with me. I never throw anything away." He seemed proud of the fact. "We could still cast the proper spells of discovery, if you think it is important."

"The mortal girl thought it was important," said the youngest genie.

"The mortal girl is a bigger fool than that empty-headed Haroun, and he is a worse fool than Khalid, and Tamar is the greatest fool of them all!" Gamal shrieked. He waved his hands and his own lamp appeared. Before any of the Council could do a thing, he lifted the lid of his lamp, grabbed up the iron ring, and dropped it inside. With a terrible laugh of victory and a blazing blast of orange flames, Gamal vanished.

The youngest genie reached for the lamp. A crackle of blue sparks burned his fingers badly. "How could I be so stupid?" he said, shaking them. "A genie's lamp is his castle. No other genie may enter it unless he is asked."

"Nor leave it unless a mortal frees him," the second-oldest genie added.

The other two genies just looked at each other and remarked, "Oh, dear."

"But the prison is in there!" the oldest Council member objected. "Khalid and Tamar are inside! They can get out of the ring whenever they like, because they are not being punished, but they cannot escape from Gamal's lamp. What does he mean to do with them?"

The hem of the ancient genie's robe rippled. Boabdil the cat stuck his nose out, sniffed the air for danger, then emerged and trotted over to the lamp. He sniffed this too before saying, "Well, I do not think he will invite them to a sherbet party." He sat down and looked at the Council. "O Wise Ones, when you make a mistake, it is a beauty."

Inside the iron ring, Khalid finally caught up with Tamar after what felt like hours. She was flying down the seemingly endless curved corridor when he grabbed the wispy end of her robes and forced her to stop. She looked so surprised to see him that he said, "Well? Did you think I would let you come after them alone?"

Tamar's smile lit up the dingy gray interior. "I am glad to have your help." She offered him her hand. "I think we two must be the only genies in the universe who believe human beings are worth looking after."

"Then we must stay together, so that we do not share such dangerous beliefs with other genies." Khalid's hand closed over hers, and for the first time in his life he looked truly happy. "With humans, it is only a matter of understanding them. I would even dare to say that they are not so different from us. Lord Haroun and I would often have some very interesting talks between wishes, and he did not *have* to hire human servants to help me around the palace. A good heart cannot hide itself forever."

"How true," Tamar agreed. "My Master, the Princess Nur, is also very easy to get along with." She looked around at their grim surroundings and shuddered. "I only hope that she will be as easy to find."

"I do not think that finding her will be that hard," Khalid said. "This is a ring, after all. It just goes around."

"And around and around and around," said Tamar. "If Nur and Haroun are going in the same direction as we are and they keep walking, we might not catch up with them."

"Then we shall not walk, my lady," Khalid floated up from the iron floor, taking Tamar with him. "We shall fly."

And fly they did. It was one of the most boring flights either one of them had ever known. The inside of the ring never changed. It was always the same dull gray all around them. Before long the two genies discovered a rule that human beings had known for ages: boredom makes time stretch itself out like a piece of taffy.

"How long have we been flying?" Tamar asked.

"Days," Khalid replied with a groan. "Months. Maybe years. Who knows?" He landed lightly and sat down on the hard, curved floor. "Perhaps we acted too hastily, Tamar. What can we do for Haroun and Nur if we do find them? He is condemned to remain in this prison for a hundred years and she, by her own wish, can never leave him. We cannot get them out of here."

"Why, we can—we can protect them," Tamar answered.

"Protect them from what?"

Tamar landed too, sat beside Khalid, and looked around. She saw only gray emptiness and more gray emptiness. "The Council did say this was a prison, and I thought they might have done something to the inside to discourage any genie from trying to break in and free Master Ishmael. You know: bottomless swamps, trackless deserts, hideous monsters."

"Such obstacles are not necessary. What genie would dare try to free Master Ishmael, knowing that the Council would find out about it sooner or later?" Khalid sighed. "A hideous monster would at least liven this place up a little."

Thank you very much, I am sure, but I happen to think the place looks quite lively enough the way I have it fixed up now! The voice boomed through the endless iron corridor, making the walls quiver. Tamar shrieked and threw herself into Khalid's arms.

"What is it? What is it?" she gasped, her eyes squeezed shut.

"How should I know?" he wailed, his eyes just as tightly closed as hers.

Really, my children, the voice spoke again, *I expected a kinder greeting than this. I have never meant anyone any harm. Look at me. I have missed you.*

Very cautiously Khalid and Tamar opened their eyes. The dull gray corridor was gone. Instead they found themselves seated on a thick, grassy lawn beside an ivory fountain. A little way off was a forest of slender, elegant trees where pheasants and red deer walked. Right where the grass met the forest was a silk tent, white with stripes of blue and gold. A simple blue banner with a silver cup on it flew from the top of the center pole.

From inside the tent, the voice called, *Come in! Come in! We are waiting for you.*

"Oh!" Tamar cried gladly. "I know that voice now!"

"So do I," Khalid exclaimed. The two of them ran a race to be the first into the tent and wound up tripping over each other at the entrance. As they lay sprawled on the fine carpet, they heard familiar laughter.

"Khalid, a man is known by the genie he keeps. I wish you would not embarrass me like that." Lord Haroun coughed, then added, "Oh, did I say *wish?* Sorry. Force of habit."

Khalid got up and helped Tamar to her feet. He saw his former Master seated on a chair fit to be a king's throne, with the Princess Nur on another one beside him. A copper table laden with all kinds of food and drink was set up before them, and behind them stood Master Ishmael.

"You see?" Khalid's old teacher said, gesturing to show off the tent and everything outside it. "I do not think that I have done such a bad job of making my prison a little bit more comfortable."

"Indeed it is so, Master Ishmael," said Khalid, admiring all the wonderful things the tent held. There were intricately embroidered hangings between the many tent poles, each telling part of King Solomon's story. The floor was covered with fat cushions and brilliantly colored carpets; in the very center, a tiny silver fountain shot a spray of rose perfume into the air. Yet in spite of all these marvels, the one object that attracted Khalid's attention was a plain, unadorned sword that hung by its hilt from a leather thong above the silver fountain. The thong itself was tied to thin air. "Is this—? Can this be—?" Khalid breathed, gazing at the sword.

"It is," Master Ishmael replied solemnly. "The very sword of Solomon himself. I was permitted to take it with me into my prison as a special favor of the Council."

Nur laughed. "If all prisons were like this one, we would be overrun with criminals."

Master Ishmael frowned at her. "Do not be deceived, my child. My humble magic powers have allowed me to create all that you see, yet they are not enough to let me see this place as anything but a prison. I know that I am not free. The strongest bars are those which stand around my heart."

"True," said Nur. "Yet I cannot ever think of this place as a prison, even though I must stay here for a hundred years." She reached out and took Haroun's hand. "Where he is, I am, I need no other freedom."

"Nor do I," said Haroun. He smiled at Master Ishmael and added, "Of course I do not mind having all this lime-and-pecan sherbet, too." He waved at the icy bowls on the copper table.

"Lime and pecan?" Khalid sprang for it, passed Tamar a chilled cup, and soon they were all seated on cushions around the table, smacking their lips over Master Ishmael's bounty. "This is very nice," Khalid remarked some time later, licking his spoon clean. "But still that does not change the fact that Tamar and I have come to get you all out of here."

"How?" Master Ishmael asked. "The Council—"

"I will make the Council see that you are not to be blamed for what happened," Khalid replied. "If they need a prisoner, I will tell them that they can have me."

"Tamar leaned near and put her arms around him. "And me. You shall not spend the century alone."

Oh, yes he shall!

A fierce wind tore through the entrance of the tent, ripping away part of the silk. Outside the red deer ran off, bellowing in terror as the lovely trees were torn up by the roots. The pheasants took to the air, only to have the magnificent feathers stripped from their bodies by the black blast. The grass withered and died.

Purple and green fire fell on the roof of the tent, burning it away. Solomon's sword swayed at the end of its tether. The gigantic face of Gamal peered down at them, yellow eyes cold with hate. *You are all my prisoners now,* he gloated. The words ached in their ears even though he never moved his lips. *This pitiful little prison now lies inside my own lamp. Even if the Council says that you are free, none of you may leave without my permission.*

Nur turned to Tamar and whispered, "Is this true?"

Tamar nodded grimly. "A genie is master of everything inside his own lamp. No magical creature can enter or escape it unless he allows, and even he cannot emerge from the lamp without a mortal to release him." her mouth looked hard. "Gamal must hate us very much for him to have followed us this far."

I heard that, Tamar, the ugly genie cried. *Hate you? No. There is only one I hate.* His face seemed to shoot flaming arrows into Khalid's heart. *I have hated too long, but that will end soon. Come out, Khalid, and fight me. I challenge you to a duel of magic. Once it is done and you are destroyed, you have my word that I will tell the Council to set the others free.*

"I am not afraid of you," Khalid said, getting to his feet. "And I do not think that I shall be the one who is destroyed." He started for the tattered doorway, but Tamar clung to him and made him stop.

"Do not go!" she exclaimed. "I do not trust his word any more than a snake's."

Harsh words. Gamal's voice boomed inside their heads, his nasty chuckling sounding like great waves battering the shore. *Why doubt me, Tamar?*

"Because the truth that will free these prisoners is the same truth that will make the Council lock you away in their place," she replied.

So it is. Yet I will not mind my prison as long as I have you to share it with me.

Tamar shook her head in disbelief. "You are insane."

I am not. It is your word, not mine, that shall free the prisoners. Gamal leered down at her. *Give your promise that you will stay with me for as long as the Council keeps me prisoner, and I will tell them the truth of who betrayed Master Ishmael, who stole the iron ring, and how it came to be on Haroun ben Hasan's hand.*

"You will tell them the truth without any promise from her!" Khalid shouted. "I will see to that." He shook himself free of Tamar's arms and strode out of the tent.

Gamal clicked his tongue, and a pitying smile twisted its way over his huge face. *This will not take long.* The face vanished. An instant later the whole tent rocked with the shock of a mighty explosion.

CHAPTER FOURTEEN

They rushed from the tent in time to see two towers of flame collide. One was the color of ashes and charred wood, the other flashing silver and spring-green. The air stank so terribly that the humans covered their noses and mouths with their hands and still choked and coughed horribly. Every bit of the artificial sunlight that Master Ishmael had conjured up to brighten his prison seemed to have been sucked away. In the dreadful gloom, the two genies battled.

The dark fire peeled itself away and changed into the shape of a dragon with eyes of bronze and talons as long as lances. It slashed at the green-and-silver flame with teeth and claws, then bathed it in a stream of poisonous smoke from its terrible mouth. The brighter fire shrank back, but only for a moment. Then it took a new shape too, standing tall against the gray sky as a griffon, with the strength of a lion in its body and the majestic power of an eagle in its head and wings. It leaped into the air and dived at the dragon, making the beast scream and cower with fear.

But when the griffon tried to soar away for a second attack, the dragon changed into a serpent and lashed itself around the griffon's hind legs, dragging it down. The griffon struggled for a moment, then appeared to melt away. It was a stream of green-and-silver water that slipped easily through the serpent's coils and soaked into the ground.

Gamal twisted this way and that, frustrated and enraged to have lost Khalid. His mouth gaped, showing icy fangs that dripped venom. His fury was so great that he looked ready to bite himself. Then his rage discovered a new target. His flat head swung slowly around and his lidless black eyes fixed themselves on the humans. With a loud hiss, he flung himself at Haroun and Nur.

Thick stalks of silver-and-green bamboo thrust themselves out of the earth between the snake and the mortals. Each stem was thicker than a man's leg and hard as iron. The snake hit the rustling wall head-first and reeled back, stunned. Shadows in the bamboo shifted, showing a fuzzy outline of Khalid's laughing face. A vine noose shot out of the thicket and tried to snare the giant serpent while he was still groggy.

Gamal was too quick for it. He kept his shape, but shrunk himself down to snakeling size and slithered through the noose. Quick as thought, he glided into the heart of the bamboo wall, curled himself around a single stem, and tried to sink his fangs into it.

The bamboo became a ghost; the snakeling's fangs snapped shut on nothing. Music filled the iron prison, music that made the curved walls and floor vibrate strongly. The snakeling could not see his enemy, and because snakes have no ears, Gamal could not hear the music that Khalid had become. He could not hear it, but before long he began to feel it. The vibrations grew more powerful. The many notes of the music became a single tone, like the chiming of a great brass bell. Nur and Haroun felt it, too, and even the genies Tamar and Master Ishmael had to cover their ears as the note droned on, louder and louder.

At first the vibration was only enough to make the

snakeling Gamal feel uneasy without knowing why. The floor under his belly hummed, and the humming spread into his body little by little. Gamal shook, and the swelling note seemed likely never to stop until it had shaken his fragile snakeling bones apart. He tried to change shape, but by the time he had noticed what was going on, he was trapped by the sound, his mind too full of panic to concentrate on working any magic. His small mouth hung open, his forked tongue drooped, and with a last, weak hiss, he toppled over, limp and motionless.

The note stopped. The iron ring no longer vibrated. Flakes of color fell from the air and became Khalid. Tamar ran to him with a happy cry.

"Well done," said Master Ishmael, bowing to his favorite student.

Nur squeezed Haroun's hand. "I am so glad that is over," she said.

Haroun was still staring at the body of the snakeling. Silently he made Nur release his hand, then went into the ruined tent. He returned an instant later with the sword of Solomon and marched right over to where Gamal lay. "My father did not leave me much money when he died," he said, "but he did leave me plenty of good advice. 'My son,' he would say, 'never trust a dead snake until you have cut off its head.' " He raised the sword.

A wise man, your father! The snakeling's body split apart and Gamal sprang forth. He snatched the sword of Solomon from Haroun's hands effortlessly and tossed it far away from him. Everyone could hear his words in their thoughts. *It will take more than a tune to destroy me, Khalid,* he gloated, *but I think it will take much less to get rid of this human creature.*

"Let him go, Gamal!" Khalid shouted. "The duel is done; I won fairly."

Gamal spoke aloud, saying: "Fine, if you win, he loses. There is still time to surrender."

"It is not fair!" Nur stamped her foot, fists clenched. "He *did* win! Why should he give in to you?"

"I never said he *had* to give in." Gamal grinned and moved his hands so that they could all see how close his talons lay to Haroun's neck. "Khalid has his choice to make; I have mine."

"You horrid liar!" Nur was so angry, she spoke her mind without stopping to think about whether it was wise to call Gamal names while he held Haroun hostage. "When you told me about all the rules you genies must obey, you lied like a camel-seller! Where are your famous rules now?"

"Rules are for fools," Gamal sneered. "Oh, I follow them, but only when those old Council crows are there to keep an eye on me. Otherwise I do what I like, and that bunch of doddering fossils never any the wiser."

"Ohhh, you—you—*you*—!" Nur's face was getting very red. She seethed like a boiling kettle as she searched for just the right words to tell Gamal how low and hateful and repulsive she thought he was. She was so angry that no name seemed terrible enough to call him, and the rage bottled up inside her made her feel ready to explode. Then, when she thought she would burst, the whisper of a thought crept into her mind:

My, my. Do you not just wish that the Council themselves were here to listen to what Gamal thinks of them?

"Yes!" Nur cried aloud. "Yes, I certainly *do* wish the Council were here and knew what you just said about them!"

"Hearkening and obedience," said Tamar.

A hand heavy with rage and authority fell on

Gamal's shoulder. Another closed around his wrist, making him free Haroun. Two more got behind him and shoved, while a slippered foot stuck itself out in front of him and made him trip. By the time a stunned Gamal picked himself off the floor, the five members of the Council were standing around him in a circle.

"Crows, eh?" The oldest genie's ruby eyes were colder and harder than usual.

"Doddering fossils, are we?" the youngest asked.

"Rules are for fools, you say?" The second-oldest tapped his foot.

"You only follow them when we are watching, do you?" The third-oldest smiled, but it was not a comforting smile.

"My dear colleague, why should he do otherwise?" the fourth-oldest pointed out. "We are never any the wiser. *Are* we?" His grin was even more frightening than his friend's.

"Gamal, your evil is at an end," the oldest Council member intoned. "We have discovered that it was you who accused Master Ishmael, and now we see that you did it not to serve justice, but only to serve yourself."

"What is more," the youngest genie chimed in, "you stole your old teacher's prison for some wicked reason. Of this we are sure, although how Haroun ben Hasan got it—"

"Gamal stole it and gave it to me!" Princess Nur declared.

All five members of the Council scowled at her. "Be quiet, human," said the oldest genie. "We do not need your help in taking care of our problems."

Still brave as ever, Nur replied, "If not for my wish, you never would have known Gamal's true opinion of you! He is a liar and a cheat." She told them of the false tales Gamal had told her about the iron ring and its powers. "Now I know that he hoped I would give it to Khalid, so that he would get the blame for stealing it."

"And so he would have," Gamal snarled, "if you humans were not so unreliable when it comes to love!"

"It may take us a while to make up our minds," Nur answered, "but once we decide, we do not need any magic rings to keep our love true." She stretched out her hand, and Haroun ran to take it. He stood proudly by her side as she said, "There is yet another crime to add to Gamal's list. When he first appeared, he tried to make me let *him* say how I would use my last wish. I can just imagine what sort of trick he would have played if I had been silly enough to let him do that!"

"One genie interfering with the wishes granted by another?" The oldest Council member frowned. "That is serious. Her last wish, too. Why, if she had wasted that, she would never have been able to wish to be with this fine young mortal forever, and then we might never have learned—"

"In the sacred names of magic and mathematics, hold!"

The iron ring shook. The youngest genie held up four fingers that shone like summer stars in the gloom. "Each genie learns to grant no more than three wishes to each mortal served. Accidents happen, but not frequently. Rules exist, and only *real* fools think they can get away without obeying them. This girl used her last wish to follow Haroun ben Hasan, yet she had a fourth wish granted to bring us here. Who did it? Who gave her a wish that was not hers to have?" His accusing stare went from Gamal, to Khalid, to Tamar, and there it stayed.

Tamar bowed her head. "Punish me for that," she said.

"So we will," the oldest genie said, "as soon as we are all out of here. You, too, Master Ishmael. The rest of your sentence is hereby forgiven. Gamal shall have this fine prison all to himself for a thousand years!"

"Give or take a century for good behavior," the youngest genie put in. "Let us be gone!" The Council joined hands while Tamar and Khalid took hold of Haroun and Nur, ready to fly from the iron prison.

Nothing happened.

Gamal snickered. "At least I will not lack company for those thousand years."

"What does this mean?" Haroun demanded.

"Alas, we forgot." The youngest genie hung his head. "Gamal threw the iron ring into his own lamp, and that is a prison no genie may escape unless a mortal summons him out."

"Well, then I suppose we must wait for someone to rub the lamp." Nur did not seem to be worried about it. "That should not take too long."

"Oh no?" Gamal showed all his teeth nastily. "Every mortal in Haroun ben Hasan's palace was scared away. Even now I will bet that they are telling the whole city that the palace is haunted, a place of great and evil magic. No one will dare to go inside. No one will find the lamp. No one will be brave enough to touch it, let alone rub it." He stretched out on the bare iron floor as if it were the softest couch. "We are all in here for a good long time."

"I doubt that," said a soft, rumbly voice from above. A sudden shaft of light fell over all the prisoners. They looked up, but the light was too dazzling for them to see anything.

"Oh!" Tamar exclaimed. "Oh, do you feel that?" Her hand tightened on Nur's.

"What is it? What is it?" the princess demanded.

All the genies except Gamal had their eyes closed and their faces tilted up into the light.

"It is—it feels like—ah, do not ask me to describe it!" Khalid gasped. "No human could ever understand."

"The lamp!" the oldest genie's voice lost all the hardness of age as if some very strange and wonderful force were making him as young as Khalid again. "Someone is rubbing the lamp!"

"No!" Gamal bellowed. "It is not possible!"

"Possible or not, it is happening," the youngest genie beamed. He began to rise. Higher and higher he went, until he was pulled through the iron roof of the ring. One by one the others followed, first the Council, then Tamar, then Nur, then Khalid, and finally—

"Wait a moment!" Haroun let go of Khalid and scurried away. He came running back with the sword of Solomon just in time to grab the genie's hand and be lifted up.

"No, no, *no*!" Gamal lay alone in the circle of light and pounded the floor with fists and feet. "This cannot be! Nobody was left in the palace! Nobody could possibly rub the lamp and set them free!"

"Be careful whom you call a nobody," said the cat Boabdil, and used his nose to slam down the lid of Gamal's lamp, leaving the wicked genie in darkness.

CHAPTER FIFTEEN

The oldest genie brushed imaginary wrinkles out of his robe and cleared his throat importantly. The first thing that the Council had done once they were out of Gamal's lamp was to confer about Tamar's punishment for granting extra wishes. Now they were ready, and Tamar waited nervously to hear what they had to say.

Khalid refused to leave her side. "Whatever they decide to do to you, they will have to do to me, too," he promised.

"They will not do anything to her," Haroun declared, raising the sword of Solomon. "I will not allow it. If she had not granted Nur's fourth wish, they never would have known about Gamal."

The oldest genie glowered at him. "Put that down. If you want to scare a genie, you need the right kind of magic. The only spell on that old thing is one that will make you win any fight against other humans. I would not advise trying it out on us."

"Oh," said Haroun. He let the sword fall slowly to his side.

"And now, Tamar, hear the decision of the Council!" The oldest genie's words filled Lord Haroun's palace like the pounding hoofbeats of a herd of warhorses. Tamar fell to her knees and hid her face.

Khalid knelt beside her, his expression a mixture of helplessness, anger, and love.

"I *wish* you would not shout like that," said the cat Boabdil. "In fact, I *wish* you would not say anything at all until I give you permission."

The oldest genie opened his mouth. Nothing came out.

"Oh, good," said Boabdil. "It worked even without him saying 'Hearkening and obedience.' But of course, how could he say anything after what I wished? The best sort of magic is the kind that makes sense." He swished his tail and rubbed against the oldest genie's ankles. "I will save the last wish *you* owe me to allow you to speak again, never fear." He then faced the other genies. "Hmmm, four plus Master Ishmael plus Khalid plus—no, no, I cannot claim any from Tamar. . . . Well, that is still six genies at three wishes each or—" Boabdil closed one eye in concentration. "I *wish* I were better at mathematics."

"Hearkening and obedience!" the youngest genie blurted out, then looked as stunned as if a stranger had just borrowed his mouth.

"Eighteen!" Boabdil exclaimed, overjoyed at his new talent. "Take away the one wish you just granted," he added, addressing the youngest Council member. "Still, seventeen wishes are nothing for any cat worth his fur to sneeze at."

"What has happened? What wishes? What has this small beast done? What does he mean by this?" Those Council members who could speak all spoke at once until the air was thick with unanswered questions.

"I *wish* you would pay attention!" Boabdil snapped at them, and instantly they did so. "Hmph. Only sixteen wishes left, but it was worth it. Now listen: I freed you from the lamp. Do I need to tell you what you owe me for that little favor?"

"Three wishes," said the second-oldest genie reluctantly.

"Apiece, it seems," said the third-oldest.

"But *only* three apiece!" the fourth-oldest pointed out.

"Certainly," Boabdil purred. "You did not even have to make that rule clear to me. All cats know that enough is enough. Greed is for humans and other creatures who were unlucky enough not to be born feline."

All the genies except Tamar bowed to the cat, and all the genies except Tamar and the silenced oldest Council member asked, "What is your wish, O Master?"

As usual it was the youngest who noticed things. "Tamar, you were freed from the lamp like the rest of us. Why do you not bow before our new Master?"

"She cannot," the cat replied for her.

"Why not? She was in the lamp with us!"

"Tsk. I thought you knew your own business better than that." Boabdil preened his whiskers. "Can any genie obey a new Master while she still serves the old?"

"The old? But she has already granted the mortal girl three wishes!" the youngest genie objected. "No, *four*!"

"And she shall grant more, if her Master desires," Boabdil said. "I *wish* that you would all know why."

"Hearkening and obedience!" cried Khalid. He flung his hands high, and the ceiling overhead became a swirl of clouds. A gentle wind blew the mists aside and everyone saw the faces of Princess Nur and Tamar in a vision out of the past.

. . . *and if you will have Lord Haroun ben Hasan for your husband,* Tamar's image was saying, *then I shall grant you all the wishes you may ever desire. I swear it by the wisdom of King Solomon, by the skill of my own magic, and by the power of the great Council.*

The vision disappeared. "I am now down to fifteen wishes," said the cat. "I hope that I will not have to use any more of them to make you understand."

"So Tamar did promise this girl extra wishes from the start. A promise is a promise," the second-oldest genie admitted.

"But the girl did not marry Lord Haroun ben Hasan," the third-oldest genie objected.

"She *did* wish to be with him forever, though," said the fourth-oldest. "I think that ought to count for something."

"Of course it counts!" The youngest genie smacked his open palm with a fist. "If it did not count, then Tamar would never have been able to grant the girl's fourth wish at all! We should have seen that for ourselves. Magic always knows what it is doing."

"Better than you do," Boabdil murmured. Holding his tail like a bright banner, he announced, "Let us settle this so that everyone is satisfied, even if it does bring me down to fourteen wishes. I *wish* that Nur and Haroun might be married, but only if that is what they wish, too."

"Who invited all these odd people?" the king wondered, staring at the huge crowd of rich and important people filling the largest room of his palace.

"Thirteen," murmured the drowsy cat who was curled up in Princess Nur's lap.

"Who decorated my palace so gaily?" Nur's father asked every one of his servants. They could only shrug.

"Twelve," came the sleepy purr.

"Who ordered this banquet?" the king asked the cooks. They had no idea.

"Eleven," said a voice no louder than velvet.

"Who scattered all these flowers everywhere? Who dressed my daughter in that gorgeous gown? And *who*"—the king's eyebrows came together in a look of deep bewilderment—"*who* is that richly dressed young man seated next to her?"

"Ten, nine, eight . . . No, no, that last one was none of my doing." Boabdil put one paw across his eyes and twisted himself onto his back so that Nur could stroke his stomach.

"Do not worry, Prince of a Thousand Graces," said the youngest genie, gliding up beside the king. "That excellent young man is her husband."

"Her husband?" The king scratched his head. "How did that happen?"

"Not quite in the usual way," the genie replied. "But so what? It has happened, and both of them are happy. That is what is important."

"Oh, fine." The king sank down onto a golden chair, miserable. "They can both be as happy as they like until we are all destroyed. That is just what will happen when a certain nasty old king I could name finds out that now he can never marry my daughter. What a temper he has! And what an army!"

Tamar appeared at the king's right hand. "Do you mean no one has told Your Majesty?"

"Told me what?"

"That the man your daughter has married is Lord Haroun ben Hasan, richest of the rich, kindest of the kind, and"—she paused for effect—"owner of the legendary sword of Solomon!"

Khalid drifted over from the banquet table. "No army however great, no king however bad-tempered can win against him," he added between mouthfuls of sherbet. "Your kingdom is safe forever."

"Really?" The king cheered up at once. He waddled over to the newlyweds and nearly smothered

Haroun in a big bear-hug. "Welcome to the family, my son!"

While Haroun struggled in his new father's embrace, Princess Nur motioned for Tamar to join her. The female genie and Khalid sat down beside the princess, whose lap was still occupied by the sleeping Boabdil.

"What do you desire, O my Master?" Tamar whispered to Nur, for fear of disturbing him.

"I have all that I could ever desire," the princess replied. "Now I wish to set you free."

"Free—?" Joy lit up Tamar's face, and Khalid's was a reflection of her happiness.

Before either one of them could speak their thanks, Boabdil began to snort and grumble. In his dreams he muttered, "—and I used one wish to bring us all to the royal palace, so that did leave eight. Oh, it *is* good to know mathematics! Then it was seven when I made all the fountains in the city run with free wine, six when I had the genies set out feasting tables in the streets for all the people, five when I ordered musicians for the palace, four when I thought the common folk should enjoy dancing and singing too, and three was when—three was when—was when—" He twitched and growled in his sleep, trying to remember.

"The other cats, dear one," Princess Nur breathed into one pointed ear.

"Ahhhhh, yes." Boabdil's tongue stretched out in a wide pink yawn and he waved his paws in the air. "I was left with two wishes after I filled every alley in this city with fresh meat for my friends and relatives." He fell into a deeper sleep and no longer spoke.

"Two wishes are still plenty for any cat to have left," said Khalid, daring to tickle the sleeping creature under his upturned chin.

"Yes, except he has only one left now," said Nur.

"He used the other to wish that all the dogs who think it is fun to chase cats are now ten miles outside the city walls."

"That is as good as saying he has none left," said the youngest genie. He and the other members of the council had come to gather around the sleeping cat. "He promised to use his last wish to give my friend here back his voice."

The oldest Council member nodded his head vigorously.

"He did give his word," said the second-oldest genie.

"But . . . is his promise to be trusted?" asked the third-oldest.

"Of course it is! It has to be." The fourth sounded decidedly stubborn about it. Then a small shadow of doubt crept into his mind. "After all, the beast has everything he needs—a home, food, humans to care for him. What more could an ordinary cat desire?"

Khalid decided not to remind a Council member that there was no such thing as an ordinary cat.

In Princess Nur's lap, Boabdil was talking in his sleep again. "I wonder . . . I wonder . . . I wonder what it would be like if cats were kings, if cats had wings, if people had to slink about in alleys and beg *us* to feed *them*, if dogs were small as mice, if mice came in different flavors, if cats could live among the stars, if the great Moon Cat could come down and visit me, if all the universe were ruled by cats, if—if—if—" He shifted onto his side and then spoke up as clearly as though he were fully awake: "I wish . . . I wish . . . I really, truly *wish*—!"

The princess gasped, the banquet hall fell silent, the genies froze, all magic held its breath, but the only thing that anyone heard was the unmistakable sound of one cat laughing.

CHAPTER SIXTEEN

On the day that Haroun ben Hasan married the Princess Nur, her favorite brother, Prince Masud, gave her a wedding gift: a young plum tree. He planted it for her in the royal palace gardens with his own hands. It was a thin, scraggly specimen of the plum tree and Prince Masud was not a very skilled gardener. Still, Princess Nur clapped her hands with joy when she saw it.

It was planted near the garden wall, between a flourishing pear and an ancient fig that still bore fruit. Flanked by two such perfect examples of hardiness and long life, the poor little plum tree looked even more pathetic. Tamar and Khalid, who had been honored guests at the wedding, floated together on a single carpet just above the bright green crown of the pear tree. Neither genie voiced a word of opinion about the prince's gift, but their eyes exchanged eloquent looks. The cat Boabdil, who had been underfoot all day, now rubbed himself against the new tree's skinny trunk and very nearly knocked it out of the earth.

"A plum tree . . ." the sultan muttered when he was dragged out to behold his eldest son's gift to the princess. "What a peculiar gift."

Prince Masud overheard his father's remark and

jovially replied, "Well, but after all, I am a very peculiar prince!"

"What? What?" The sultan sputtered like butter on a hot griddle. "How can you say such things? You are my eldest son! You are my heir! You must not speak so of yourself. It might give certain people the notion that you are not fit to rule this kingdom."

"But I am in no hurry at all to rule this kingdom," Prince Masud drawled.

"No hurry?" the sultan echoed, incredulous. "What nonsense! Do you say such things just to annoy me?"

"Since I can not rule this kingdom until after you die, Father, I thought my words would make you glad rather than annoy you," Prince Masud said with all the sincerity a man might express.

"Oh." The sultan was momentarily silenced. Then, harrumphing mightily, he wagged a finger in his son's face. "Be that as it may, never forget, you have seventy-seven brothers, any one of whom would be overjoyed to take your place as crown prince, even if it meant taking your life first. Never let any one of them know that you are so—so *casual* about inheriting my throne! An ambitious brother can seize upon any weakness of yours and use it to convince the nobles and the people that you would make a poor king."

Prince Masud laughed. "You speak about such things as if you knew them very, very well, O my father. By the way, didn't *you* used to have an older brother?"

The sultan blushed and looked most uncomfortable. "Have you been talking to your grandmother again?"

The prince threw one arm around the sultan's shoulders. "Father, I promise you this: Even if I am a peculiar prince, if I must rule someday, I assure you that I will never be a casual king."

The sultan was somewhat mollified. "Well . . . well

... Well, that's all right, then. But you'd still better keep an eye on your brothers."

Prince Masud shrugged.

Princess Nur came up to embrace her brother. "Dearest Masud, if Father insists about this so much, perhaps you ought to listen to him."

"Father also insisted about your marriage to that awful old king who wanted to make you his twenty-fifth wife."

Now it was Nur's turn to blush and look uncomfortable. "That was different," she mumbled, her cheeks aflame.

"It always is, when you're solving someone else's problems instead of your own," the cat purred. He arched his back and gave the itchy spot near his tail a really vigorous rubbing against the plum tree. This time the sapling teetered so badly that part of the root ball actually came tilting up out of the ground.

Khalid made the slightest of magical gestures and the imperiled plum tree was replanted, deep and secure. It still did not look at all well. "O Prince Masud, may you live ten thousand years, avoid your brothers, and keep away from dark, steep stairways!" the genie pronounced. "May you likewise live to tell me one thing: Truly I may claim that the ten thousand thousand mysteries of the Hidden World are as an open book to me, and yet your wedding gift to the princess leaves me as puzzled as it does your father. Why a plum tree?"

Prince Masud's wide, merry face assumed a look of immense gravity. He folded his arms and intoned, "O Genie whose wisdom is a thing of centuries, I can keep nothing from you. I did not choose my wedding gift to my only sister lightly. There is deep, dark reason behind this act—a reason best spoken of secretly, in whispers." His eyes shifted left, then right. "Dare I tell it?"

The genies, the sultan, the newlyweds And the cat all clustered around the prince, fervently urging him to speak.

"Very well." Again Prince Masud's eyes flashed left, then right, as if searching the shadows of the garden for lurking spies. His voice dropped even lower as he hissed, "The reason I gave my beloved sister a plum tree—*a plum tree I planted with my own hands by the light of the full moon, mind you!*—is that—is that—"

"Yes?" Haroun coaxed, making little encouraging motions with his hands. "Yes, yes, yes?"

"—is that Nur likes plums." And Prince Masud threw his head backed and laughed until he staggered into the plum tree and came near to uprooting it again.

There was no malice in the prince's laughter, and soon it grew contagious. Everyone laughed, even the cat. Only the sultan shook his head and went back into the palace, muttering dire predictions about the ambitions of Masud's seventy-odd brothers.

Haroun ben Hasan laughed loudest and longest of all. When he was at last able to speak, he wiped the tears of mirth from his eyes and announced, "Oh, I *like* you, Your Highness! You are a man after my own heart. I confess, when I married your dear sister, I was afraid that I would not feel at ease with her royal family, but you—! You have spirited off all my misgivings with a single jest."

"What jest?" Prince Masud put on a look of innocence. "Nur *does* like plums."

The princess gave her eldest brother a playful slap on the arm. "You are impossible, Masud!" she decreed. "And I like you better than any plum for it." She turned to her husband. "I am glad that you like Masud, but be warned: Do not expect my other brothers to be like him. They are all proud creatures who take their princely dignity very seriously."

"And are they also as ambitious as your father said?" the genie Tamar inquired.

Nur nodded her head. Taking her brother's hands, she told him, "Hearken to Father's words, Masud: Have a care with our brothers. There is not one of them who does not hunger for a kingly throne. They would take yours as soon as look at you."

"If they desire my throne so much, perhaps I should let them have it," the prince replied, only half-joking this time.

Nur was no longer in the mood for jokes. "And if one of our brothers did succeed in taking the throne from you, what then? Do you think he would let you live?"

The prince was very fond of shrugging away questions he did not care to answer.

"If that does not worry you, this should," Nur persisted. "Do you imagine that if one of our brothers takes the throne from you, our other brothers will be content to let him keep it? Each will say to himself, *If* that *crowned monkey could steal the kingdom from its rightful heir, why can't* I *steal it from him?* There will be war, Masud! And in such a war of brother against brother, our land and our people will suffer most of all."

Prince Masud sighed. "It is so. You are wise, my sister. You would make a finer ruler than any of your brothers, if you were a prince. Better for us all if you had been born a man."

"I do not agree with *that*," said Haroun.

The prince smiled. "I think I like you too, Haroun," he said. "They say that you are a man who loves the old tales, a man who is generous to all the singers and storytellers in the bazaar. And you know how to laugh. This is good. I can be honest with you—" he cast a look around at the genies and the cat "—and with your friends. There was indeed another reason why I gave my sister a plum tree for a present. I wish her marriage to be as strong as the tree, as pleasant as the sight of its blossoms, and as sweet as the taste of its fruit."

"Masud, you are a poet!" cried Nur, and she gave her brother another hug.

"Well," said Haroun ben Hasan, scratching his temple as he regarded the newly planted sapling. "It will be some time before we can enjoy the taste of this tree's fruit, but we can wait."

"And while we wait, you must come into my apartments and taste some delicious plum sherbet which my personal cook has just made. My *personal* cook—" he stressed "—who is very loyal, very, *very* well paid, and who allows no one to touch my food but himself." Prince Masud winked at his sister. "You see, my dear? I am not so careless of my welfare as you fear. I may not be eager to be sultan, but I am eager to stay alive. My dear wife has told me this very day that we are to have a child. I want to live if only to learn whether it shall be a son or a daughter. You of all people should know, O my sister, that I am never content until I see how a story ends."

The humans went back into the sultan's palace, but in spite of repeated invitations from Prince Masud, the genies and the cat chose to remain in the garden. Tamar floated down from the carpet and studied the plum tree.

"Prince Masud is a good man," she opined, "but a poor gardener. I do not think that anyone will ever taste the fruit of this tree."

"I believe you are right, my beloved," Khalid agreed. "It doesn't look like much, does it?"

"Instead of croaking over it like a pair of ravens,

why don't you two just use your magic to make sure it survives?" Boabdil demanded.

The genies just shook their heads. "There is just so much that magic can do," said Tamar. "It can not destroy the natural order of the world. Some things flourish, some things perish." She spread her hands. "It is beyond our power to intervene."

"Is it also beyond your power to *water* the poor thing?" Boabdil snapped.

"Oh!" Tamar's hand flew to her mouth. "I—I didn't think—Khalid! Khalid, help me tend this sapling."

"Hearkening and obedience," said the genie. A silver watering can appeared in his hand. "Though I do not know if this will help."

"It could not hurt!" Boabdil said cheerfully. He jumped aside to avoid being spattered with the water. The cat licked a few droplets from his fur, then settled down to watch the genies caring for the little plum tree. "Do you know what?" he announced. "I think this is what I like best about plum trees and people: You can never be quite sure of what you're going to get. And I do love surprises!"

"I will be surprised if this tree ever bears fruit," said Tamar.

"And I will be surprised if Prince Masud ever lives to be sultan," said Khalid.

"And *I* will be surprised if you two are ever quiet enough for me to enjoy a nap," said the cat. He lay down on the good, warm earth, curled his tail over his nose, and went to sleep.

The cat Boabdil yawned so wide that it was possible to count every single sharp, white tooth in his mouth. He stretched his legs and flexed his paws so that all his claws stuck out, then he rolled over, turned his sleek, plump belly to the sun, and tried to go back to sleep.

A delicate white blossom fell from the branches of the plum tree right onto the cat's nose. Immediately the cat flipped onto his feet and stood stiff-legged, fur bristling. He switched his tail sharply and looked left and right, but saw nothing.

LOOK DOWN.

Letters of silver smoke formed themselves in the air before the cat's eyes. The cat looked down and saw the fallen blossom that he had mistaken for an enemy.

"I meant to do that," the cat informed the air. "I was keeping in practice. A wise cat never lets himself become too secure. This world is a chancy place."

The silver letters shifted shape. HA, HA.

The cat puffed out his fur and sat with his paws very close together. "Are you laughing at *me?*" he demanded severely.

The smoke-writing shrank in on itself. NO, it said in very small letters indeed.

Boabdil relaxed somewhat. "Good," he announced. "I would hate to think you were making fun of me on my birthday."

NEVER, O MASTER, the letters now said.

Few creatures can look as smug as a cat, no matter how hard they may try. Even so, few cats could look as smug as Boabdil. The cat gave a happy sigh and lay down in the shade of the plum tree once more. "I *like* birthdays," he said. "Especially when they are mine. I wish I had always celebrated birthdays, but alas—" Now his sigh was wistful. "—who knows how many years I lived in the alleys and backstreets of this city without knowing about how delightful it is to have a birthday, much less to celebrate one? And alack—" His sigh was much deeper and more sorrowful this time. "—who knows how many years I may yet live to see more birthdays?"

OH, MANY YEARS, GOOD MASTER! MANY, MANY, MANY YEARS! the mysterious letters urged.

Boabdil grinned as only he could grin. "How very kind of you to say so. Even if we both know why you wish me such a long life. Well, that does not matter. I will take the gift of many, many, *many* years any way I can get it." He regarded the hazy writing steadily. "And I *will* get it, will I not, Master Basim?"

A sigh from an invisible mouth blew away the letters. The air shimmered into the shape of a venerable genie. In one hand he held a wax tablet, in the other a golden wand. He passed the wand over the face of the tablet and words appeared: MAY IT COME TO PASS THAT YOU GET EVERYTHING YOU DESERVE.

Boabdil chuckled when he read that. "You have not lost your spirit, Master Basim. That is good. After ten years, a lesser genie might have given up and resigned himself to a speechless existence."

Master Basim, eldest genie of the fabled Council, waved the golden wand across the wax tablet again: YOU PROMISED!

"I promised *what* I would do with my one remaining wish," said the cat. "I did not promise *when* I would do it."

The wand flashed a third time: IT HAS BEEN TEN YEARS! IS THAT NOT LONG ENOUGH FOR YOU TO TAUNT, TEASE, AND TOY WITH ME?

Boabdil closed his eyes, his whiskers curving up at a most provoking angle. "Spoken like one who has never seen a cat play with a mouse." He opened his eyes and sat up just in time to see the ancient genie's glower of pure, hot rage. "Oh, stop that. I was only joking. You are quite right: Ten years is long enough. If only they had not been such enjoyable years . . ." He tilted his head to the side and gazed back over fond memories. "Ah, the fine birthdays I have celebrated ere this! And I owe them all to you, Master

Basim. For anyone may receive a gift on his birthday, but how many can say they receive the gift of life?"

SOME OF US WOULD RATHER RECEIVE THE GIFT OF SPEECH, the genie wrote.

"And so you shall!" Boabdil cried. "I am feeling in a generous mood today; I cannot say why. Perhaps it is because of the baby."

THE PRINCESS AMINAH? Master Basim scribed across the tablet. His brow furrowed. NOT THAT I AM UNGRATEFUL, O MASTER, BUT IF THE THOUGHT OF A BABY'S BIRTH HAS THE POWER TO MAKE YOU HONOR YOUR PROMISE TO ME AT LAST, WHY DID IT TAKE TEN YEARS? THERE ARE ALWAYS BABIES BEING BORN, ESPECIALLY AROUND HERE! THESE MORTALS BREED LIKE MICE.

"Without being half as tasty," the cat concluded. "You do not understand: The princess Aminah is no ordinary baby. She is the child of my dear friends, Lord Haroun ben Hasan and Princess Nur."

YES, BUT IF ALL YOU WANTED WAS TO SEE THE BIRTH OF ONE OF THEIR CHILDREN, THEN WHY DIDN'T YOU—?

A howl of outrage shook the entire garden.

CHAPTER SEVENTEEN

A blizzard of blossoms plummeted from the branches of the plum tree, shaken loose by pure force of the racket now coming from the palace. Stunned by the hellish outburst, Master Basim dropped his golden wand before it had finished writing his latest message on the wax tablet.

Boabdil sprang to fur-fluffed attention, ready to fight or fly. "In the name of the ten thousand golden cats of Taprobane, what was *that?*" he demanded. In answer, more howls rolled through the garden, and the sound of shrieks, screams, bloodthirsty war cries, and the thunder of running feet coming nearer, nearer, ever nearer until—

"You take that back!"

"Make me!"

Two small boys clad in bright silks, satins, and brocades dashed into the garden. If it was a race they ran, the taller of the two was winning. His feet fairly skimmed the white pebbled path, and indeed so fast did he run that his delicately sewn slippers could not keep up the pace. They flew from his pelting feet as he galloped on.

It seemed as if he would outdistance even the famed winged horse of the ancient tales. What hope had his pursuer of overtaking him? A wise man would confess himself beaten and give up.

A wise man, yes; a determined boy, never. The smaller lad came on, his brown face flushed with the effort, his shorter legs pumping doggedly. Streaks of moisture gleamed on his cheeks, though whether these were the tracks of sweat or tears of frustration remained a mystery. And still for all his exertions, he found the breath to gasp, "Liar! Liar! How dare you say that about my father! I'll take all your lies and stuff them down your stupid throat!"

"You'll have to catch me first!" the taller boy threw back over his shoulder. And he laughed and laughed without even growing winded.

This was too much for the smaller boy. With an enormous concentration of effort he put on a sudden spurt of speed, drew nearer to his prey, and then with a final surge, launched himself into a flying tackle.

It was not a very good tackle—he hit the ground instead of the target—but it was good enough for him to hook the taller boy's ankle as he fell. The pair of them went down in a tumbling heap on the garden path, losing goodly measures of skin and clothing to the pebbles.

The dust settled. All was stillness in the garden.

"Them again," said Boabdil wearily.

Master Basim recovered his wand and wrote: THEY'RE NOT DEAD, ARE THEY?

Boabdil sniffed. "How can you be so old, with such an ill-deserved reputation for wisdom, and know so little about humans? Of course they are not dead! They are healthy mortal children. They have just had the wind knocked out of them, that is all."

The cat started over to investigate, but was detained by a tugging at his tail. He turned a poisonous look on Master Basim, whose hand still lingered at the furry tip. The venerable genie was holding out his tablet for the cat to read: I AM PLEASED TO SAY THAT IN ALL MY YEARS I HAVE MANAGED TO

HAVE *NO* CONTACT WITH YOUNG MORTALS. THE FULL-GROWN ONES ARE BAD ENOUGH.

"Is *this* why you dared to profane my tail?" Boabdil spat. "To have me read *that?*" He switched the offended appendage out of the genie's hand. "I have better things to do with my eyes than to waste them on your scribblings. Hear me now, O heedless meddler with a cat's chief glory! I command you to take an oath that you will not trouble me with any more of your piddling scrawls until my birthday is done."

THAT IS UNFAIR, the genie wrote.

Boabdil was in no mood for argument. "Obey me, or I will never restore your voice!"

YOU PROMISED, Master Basim repeated. AND YOU ALSO PROMISED IT WOULD BE TODAY! SO DO NOT TRY THAT OLD "BUT I DID NOT PROMISE *WHEN*" EXCUSE.

By now the cat's tail was lashing back and forth at a furious tempo. Boabdil knew what he wanted and saw no reason why this impertinent genie was making such a fuss over following orders. "Has no one told the ignorant creature that it is the will of heaven for cats to be given their own way in all things?" he muttered to himself. He looked down the garden path. The boys no longer lay there in a motionless tangle, but were sitting up, examining their cuts, scrapes, and bruises, each trying not to let the other catch him sniffling. It looked very interesting, and Boabdil intended to make further inquiries into the situation as soon as he got Master Basim sorted out.

"You are right, O Insistent One," he purred. "And I swear by the great Moon Cat that I will fulfill all my promises. I shall certainly wish your voice back today, as soon as my birthday is done, whether or not you decide to please me by honoring my oh-so-modest request concerning that obnoxious tablet of yours."

Master Basim beamed, and could not refrain from inscribing HA! on the aforementioned tablet.

"I have promised *what,*" Boabdil continued. "And I have promised *when.* But I have not—" his whiskers twitched "—promised *how.*"

The genie frowned. WHAT?

"Not 'what'; *how,*" Boabdil bantered. The cat appeared to sink deep into thought. "Have you never heard what a wonderful variety of voices there are in this world, my friend? Every creature has one. I could wish you to regain the power of speech accompanied by the sweet tones of the nightingale! Or the duck. You would regain your lost eloquence, only to have your every word resound with the donkey's bray, the dog's vulgar bark, or even the locust's chirr. So long as I also wish for you to regain the ability to talk, what does it matter if you squeak like a mouse or squeal like a pig? My promises will still be fulfilled." Boabdil's grin was insufferable.

Master Basim nibbled nervously on the ends of his fine white moustache. Then he held out his wand and tablet and, with a breath that was pure flame, reduced them both to ashes.

"Nor may you trouble me by inflicting your scribbles on the air," said the cat. "Your oath bans you from employing all manner of writing; agreed?"

Master Basim nodded his head heavily, shoulders slumped.

"Good." Boabdil glanced back at the boys. They were still seated on the ground, facing one another, their knees drawn up to their chins. If they could have conjured flames from their eyes as easily as Master Basim did from his mouth, both would have been seared away to smoldering piles of embers. "Perhaps now I may discover what all this is about," the cat remarked.

He walked nonchalantly down the garden path, tail

held high, until he was right between the two of them. Neither lad had so much as a blink to spare the cat. They continued to glare at one another, fists clenched, brows knit into grimaces of unstinting hatred. Boabdil sat down and cocked his head, considering the picture before him.

"Hafiz, what is the meaning of this?" he demanded of the smaller boy. "You and Rashid are friends! You have been inseparable comrades from the cradle. But lately, a civilized cat cannot put one paw before the other in this palace without tripping over another one of your brawls. What is the matter?"

He got no answer. He was not used to being ignored and he did not like it; it put him out of temper. Fortunately, he had learned a foolproof remedy for just such a case as this.

"OW!" Hafiz jerked his hand out of the cat's reach. "You bit me, Boabdil!"

"And I will bite you again, if that is what it takes to teach you manners." The cat was untroubled by Hafiz's accusing looks. "I asked a civil question; answer it!"

The taller boy snickered. "He is probably afraid to answer it unless he has the Sword of Solomon in his hands to protect him. He is just as big a coward as his father!"

Hafiz sprang into an almost feline crouch, ready to hurl himself on the other boy again. Before he could move, Boabdil leaped onto the taller boy's chest and hung on with all claws hooked deep into costly silk and brocade, ruining it utterly.

"Do not think that I will not bite you—harder—just because you are Prince Masud's only son, Rashid."

The boy gazed deep into the cat's cold green eyes, swallowed hard, but managed to correct him: "*Prince* Rashid."

"Do not bother me with silly things like royal

titles," the cat replied. "You all taste the same to me." He disengaged his claws carefully and jumped to the ground. "Now, tell me nicely: What is the problem here? I have known you boys since you were naked and helpless as newborn field mice. You have had your quarrels and I have seen you tussle with one another before this—kittens will be kittens—but these days your behavior is the talk of the palace. Never have I seen you fight with such venom!"

"What do you care if we fight?" Prince Rashid grumbled.

"I? I do not care at all about that," Boabdil answered. "I would be a disgrace to cats everywhere if I pretended that I cared a whisker about two humans pounding one another into the dirt. But if you fight so viciously today, your parents will hear of it. *They* will care. *They* will want to know what is the matter. And while they are trying to discover the source of the trouble between you, they will neglect other matters, much more important matters."

Hafiz grinned. "Like your birthday?"

Boabdil regarded the boy as if he were a perfect booby. "Of course. Is there anything more important in the world than celebrating *my* birth?"

Hafiz's smile vanished. "Do not worry about that, Boabdil. My father and mother have already prepared your gifts. They still pay attention to *you*."

"And my father has written a poem 'specially for your party," Prince Rashid said, just as gloomily. "At least he is sometimes willing to pick up a pen, even if he never chooses to pick up a sword."

"At least your father is home sometimes," Hafiz snapped at Rashid.

"At least your father does things besides laze about, linking words like girls link daisies!" Rashid snapped back.

The two boys fell into a mutual silence.

"This is not good," Boabdil pronounced. "Things are not as they should be."

"Things are the way they always have been," Prince Rashid moped. He was thin as well as tall, and in his tunic and trousers of fine green silk, with his legs drawn up to his chin that way, he looked like a large grasshopper. "Things are the way they always will be."

"Spoken like one who has seen nine summers and mistakes them for eternity," the cat opined.

Rashid did not pay any attention to Boabdil's wise words. "My father will go on living his life in the same dull way he has always lived it. He will write his songs and his poems, he will read his scrolls and books of old tales, and when Grandfather dies he will become the sultan. Then he will be able to buy even more scrolls and books of old tales, but nothing else will change. Perhaps things might have been different if Mother had not died but—" The boy wiped away a stray tear on the back of his hand and went on: "He will never be a fighter or a hero or a doer of great deeds. He will never go out to win kingdoms, like his brothers."

Hafiz was puzzled. "Why should he need to win a kingdom? He already has one! But his brothers did not. That is why my father had to take them out, one by one, and help them get lands of their own. Now each of your royal uncles has a kingdom and is happily married to the beautiful princess that goes with it." Hafiz was plumper than his companion, with a handsome round head atop his strong, round body. Clad all in iridescent satins, when he hunched over and rested his chin in his hands that way, he looked just like a little beetle. "Even though you are all out of uncles and Father has returned at last, I still never see him. First he only wanted to be with Mother, even when she grew so fat. And now that she is thin again, he gives all his attention to that horrible baby!

So does Mother. Why did they need *her?* I was good enough for them for nine years!"

Boabdil planted his forepaws together, closed his eyes and looked inscrutable and wise. "These are mysteries which will become clear to you after you have lived a few years more, Hafiz. There are some things which you are not now meant to understand."

"I understand that I *hate* Aminah." Hafiz's face hardened like a fist. "I hate her, I hate her, I hate her!"

"You are going to cry now, I suppose," Prince Rashid sneered. His own recent brush with tears was a memory easily forgotten. "Your parents have two babies, not one."

"You take that back."

"Make me."

And they were back at each other's throats once more. Hafiz flung himself onto Prince Rashid and the two boys went tumbling heels over head into the flower beds while Boabdil looked on and shook his head in exasperation.

"These two are like a very bad dream that keeps repeating itself. I can see that they need the firm paw of my great experience and wisdom to put an end to their squabbles."

The genie could not speak, but he could snort sarcastically enough. Boabdil chose to overlook this. He had other fish to fry: two small, extremely angry fish who were presently pummeling the life out of each other. The cat sprang into the midst of the free-for-all and dug his claws into whatever part of whichever boy was most handy. A few judicious nips besides and the lads were soon separated, nursing a half-dozen scratches and bite marks apiece.

"How dare you!" Prince Rashid complained. "I am the son of the next sultan!"

"Yes, how dare you!" echoed Hafiz. "I am the son of the next Grand Vizier!"

"Ha!" Prince Rashid barked, fixing the smaller boy with a withering look. "Your father is a commoner. The only reason he shall be my father's Grand Vizier is because he was so skillful at getting rid of all of my uncles."

"My father may be a commoner, but he is a hero!" Hafiz shot back. "*He* does not waste his life lolling around the palace! *He* has adventures!"

"Were you not complaining about that very thing only a short while ago?" the cat inquired.

"No." Hafiz was blessed with the same selective memory as Masud.

Even the cat could see that Hafiz's words stung Rashid to the heart. The young prince huffed and puffed himself up like a bladderfish, then spat: "It is easy to be a hero if you have the Sword of Solomon! Without it, your father would be no better than mine! At least *we* have royal blood. Without the Sword, he is nothing!" An afterthought struck him: "And without his pet genies he is *less* than nothing!" With that parting shot, he got to his feet and stalked out of the garden.

"Who put a burr under his tail?" Boabdil murmured, watching the young prince's irate departure. Then he glanced at Hafiz.

Tears were trembling on the boy's lashes. He hastily dashed them away, but more followed. Although Boabdil would have bitten anyone who said so, the cat was deeply troubled to see his old friend's son made so unhappy. He decided to apply an ancient, infallible remedy for sorrow, known to generations of cats: He began to rub his lithe, furry body against Hafiz's legs, purring louder than the roar of a sandstorm. It was an attention no human could resist.

Before long, Hafiz was scratching the cat's ears, his wounded feelings seemingly forgotten.

"Pay no attention to Rashid," Boabdil counselled between purrs. "It takes more than a sword to make a hero, even an enchanted sword! True, the Sword of Solomon guarantees victory to he who wields it, but only a hero would trouble to pick it up in the first place. Being a hero devours your life, as your noble father knows. It keeps a man busy, away from his home and family. If you slay an ogre, the crowd cheers your name . . . for an hour. Can this make up for the weeks and months of lonely solitude spent seeking out the ogre in the first place? Not even the magic of a genie can restore lost time."

"I wish I knew a genie who would grant me three wishes," Hafiz gritted.

"That is one wish gone right there," the cat said lightly. "If you are so careless with wishes, perhaps it is a good thing you do not have any to waste. Still, if you did have three wishes, tell me how you would use them. I might get some ideas." He gave Master Basim a teasing look. The old genie blanched and tightened his lips.

"First I would wish that my father had never been a hero. Then perhaps he would have spent more time paying attention to *me.*"

"A wish can not undo the past," Boabdil said sagely. "And a wish once made is a wish lost. Is that not so, Master Basim?"

The old genie used many elegant gestures to let Hafiz know that the cat was right.

"Well then, I would use my second wish to make Rashid admit he is wrong about my father!"

Boabdil chuckled. "That is a wish well spent! Without a genie's power, it would take the word of Solomon itself to make the young prince admit he was wrong. And your third wish?"

But Hafiz never said what his third wish would be. He had grown thoughtful on hearing the cat's words. Boabdil uttered an impatient hiss, but before he could rouse the boy from his reverie, the cat found himself snatched up into the air without warning, paws splaying out over empty space.

"Boabdil!" Hafiz shouted, terror in his eyes, as high overhead the cat dangled helplessly from the talons of a gigantic golden bird whose wings were fire and whose beak was a sword.

CHAPTER EIGHTEEN

"That was not funny," said Boabdil as he stepped from Khalid's outstretched palm onto the top of the garden wall.

The genie's laugh filled the garden as the rest of the great bird's shape melted away around him. "I thought it was, and Tamar agrees with me. Do you not, Tamar?"

From her place seated cross-legged on the wall beside Boabdil, Tamar giggled and said, "I do, but I think Master Basim has another opinion." Gracefully she inclined her head towards the elderly genie who was still staring red-faced and pop-eyed at Khalid.

The younger genie shook himself slightly, dislodging the last few golden feathers from his shoulders. "Come, come, Master Basim!" he cried. "Are we not taught that it is our duty as genies to play harmless tricks on mortals whenever we can?" He patted the cat's sleek head. "Boabdil and I are old friends. I would lay down my life before I would let anyone hurt—*hey!*"

The rock was small, but it was big enough to knock Khalid's turban over his eyes. Hafiz was bending over to pick up a second missile when Tamar vanished from the wall to reappear at the boy's side, her delicate hand closed tightly around his wrist.

"That will be enough of that, Hafiz," she said

sternly. "What would your father say if he could see you throwing stones at Khalid?"

"He wouldn't care." The boy let the rock drop back to the garden path and gave it a halfhearted kick. "He only cares about Aminah."

Tamar did not hear his words. Once she had disarmed Hafiz, she felt that her task was done and she could return to the wall. Hafiz watched her go and grumbled, "They are all alike, these grownups, mortal or genie. And it was *not* funny."

"Forgive me, Boabdil," Khalid was saying as he straightened his turban. "I could not resist. I am in such high spirts this day. My heart sings!"

"I hope it has a better voice than you do," the cat responded, still nursing his wounded dignity. "The last time you sang anywhere near the palace, the royal elephants stampeded and the royal camels gave sour milk for a month."

Khalid clicked his tongue. "Is this any way to speak to one who has brought you a birthday present?"

"Present?" The cat's ears pricked up. "An expensive one, I hope?"

"Oh, this is a present worth more than the ransom of a hundred generations of kings!" Khalid assured him. "This is a present of untold worth and beauty! This is—"

"—taking too long," the cat concluded. "Where is it? Give it to me!"

"Hearkening and obedience," the genie said, a twinkle in his eye. He waved one hand and there was a flash of bright light, red and blue and green.

Apart from that, nothing changed. Or so it seemed.

"If that was my birthday present, it was very pretty, but it was not expensive enough," said the cat with a small sniff of disdain.

"You are missing the point, O blind one," Khalid

said. He thrust his left hand under the cat's nose. "Behold!"

Boabdil considered the hand from several angles, then sniffed again. "No, thank you," he said. "I could not possibly eat another bite."

Khalid made an impatient sound. "Not the hand, the *wrist,*" he said. "See what I wear on my wrist, you impossible animal."

The cat frowned. All that he could see on the genie's wrist was a plain copper bracelet. It was not even new copper, but already sported the blue-green patina of time. It looked as if it had been made by the hands of an overeager child given a spool of wire and a vague idea of how to braid it.

"Is this supposed to please me?" Boabdil inquired. "Because if it is, you are—"

"—*Bound,*" said Khalid. And he said in such a way that no one could mistake how momentous that one word was meant to be.

In an instant, Tamar was off the wall and at his side, her arm linked with his, her own wrist extended for Boabdil's inspection. She wore a bracelet of the selfsame design as the one Khalid showed off so proudly. "Is it not wonderful, Boabdil?" she said. "Khalid and I have decided to become Bound to one another on your birthday. Truly it is written that such days are blessed. Much good fortune will come to all who witness it. That is why we have decided to make the formal announcement at your birthday dinner tonight."

"Bound . . ." The cat rolled the word from his tongue as if it were a morsel that might be very tasty or very nasty; for that reason alone he hesitated to bite down on it.

"It is the closest thing we genies have to marriage," Khalid explained.

"Marriage is as common among humans as fleas on

a dog's back," said Boabdil. He wrinkled up his nose in distaste at having to mention his kind's most despised enemy. "If being Bound is the same thing, why have I not heard more about it ere this? It is not as if I am unused to the society of genies." He turned to Master Basim and asked, "Are *you* Bound?"

The ancient genie had regained his calm after the fright Khalid's trick had dealt him. He had shown no reaction whatsoever when Khalid and Tamar announced that they were Bound. But at the cat's innocent question, his face went a ghastly white and he shuddered in every limb. Horrible gobbling sounds escaped his lips and flecks of foam starred his beard.

Tamar hastened to Master Basim's side and patted him gently on the back until he stopped shaking. "There, there," she cooed. "Do not think about it if it upsets you so." To the cat she said, "Being Bound is the closest thing we have to marriage, but it is not so close as that. For one thing, it is not very popular among us. When two genies agree to become Bound, the magic of that act gives each one complete control over the actions of the other."

"Except, of course, when one or the other of the Bound pair is serving a mortal master," Khalid put in. "Sometimes a disagreement between Bound partners can last for centuries, especially when both are stubborn."

Tamar had a mischievous smile. "That will never happen to us, will it, Beloved?"

"Oh no, never," Khalid said fervently.

Master Basim exchanged a knowing look with Boabdil.

Hafiz kicked at the bigger pebbles on the garden path. He was tired of all this grownup talk of marriage, no matter if the genies chose to call it by another name. He knew what marriage meant: It meant babies, sooner or later. He was tired of babies, too. He was also tired of being ignored. He was almost used to being overlooked by his parents, who made such a fuss over his worthless baby sister, but he did not want to put up with the same treatment from his friends.

Thinking of his friends made him think of Rashid, who had once been his best friend in all the world. What was it that Tamar had said about disagreements lasting centuries?

"*He* is the stubborn one, not I!" Hafiz growled fiercely to himself. "If only he would admit he is wrong about my father, I would forgive him and we could be friends again. He would not ignore me. *He* doesn't think Aminah is so wonderful, either!"

Tamar was saying, "—know, any genie can volunteer to be the Slave of the Lamp or the Slave of the ring or the Slave of Whatever as soon as the Council says he is no longer a student."

"It is usually Bound genies who volunteer the most readily," Khalid provided. "Especially those who are caught up in an argument with their partners. Being under the control of a mortal is so much easier than being deadlocked with your mate." He cast a sheepish glance at Master Basim. "Or so they say."

Master Basim reached into the folds of his robes and withdrew an exquisite jewelled frame for the inspection of all present. Within the golden wreath reposed the likeness of a formidable female genie. The muscles on her arms were almost as thick as the wealth of her blue-black hair, and the look of sheer pigheadedness in her eyes was almost as bright as her sharp-fanged smile. He sighed and put the portrait away.

Hafiz was not interested in pictures of genies. He was thinking about something that the cat Boabdil had said to him only a short while ago:

Without a genie's power, it would take the Sword

of Solomon itself to make the young prince admit he was wrong.

"Boabdil is right," Hafiz said under his breath. "Father has often told me that the cat is very wise. Although to be truthful, Father's exact words were 'That cat is too smart for his own good.' But no matter. I know wisdom when I hear it. The Sword of Solomon gives victory over all mortal foes to him who wields it. That means that if I wield the Sword of Solomon, it will grant me victory over Rashid. He will *have* to admit he was wrong! Then we can go back to being friends."

Well satisfied with his own flavor of logic, Hafiz started back for the palace. Tamar and Khalid were too busy telling Boabdil all about their plans for the future to notice the boy's going. The cat might have noticed, but he was too busy telling them exactly what they ought to serve at the banquet.

"What banquet?" Khalid asked. "This is not like a mortal wedding. We genies do not have a banquet when we are Bound."

"You should," the cat maintained. "In my opinion, nothing should be official unless there are plenty of overfed guests, including me. Especially me. Now if you will kindly stop interrupting, I will tell just how to cook the thirty different kinds of fish you must serve. Then we shall move on to the poultry."

Master Basim did not have much heart for listening to the younger genies speak so enthusiastically about becoming Bound.

The first five hundred years may be a golden pageant of delight, he thought, *but they are over soon enough.* Then *you will learn the true meaning of being Bound!*

His spirit was entirely devoted to such musings as these as he wandered away from the others, directly into the path of the hurrying Hafiz. The boy tried to jog around the venerable head of the Council, but the old genie was unaware of anything save his own bitterness and took an absentminded step to one side that put him squarely back in the boy's path. Hafiz tried dodging the other way, and again Master Basim blocked him on the very threshold of the palace door. Back and forth they danced, Master Basim all unaware, until at last Hafiz took a misstep and stumbled right into the old genie.

"Oh! I beg you to pardon me," the boy blurted, offering Master Basim a hand up from the doorstep. "I did not mean to—You see, you were in my—"

He sucked in his lower lip and fell silent. He realized that Master Basim was perhaps the most powerful of all the genies his family knew (and indeed he had often wondered whether many families were in the habit of knowing so many genies on a day-to-day basis). He knew he ought to show Master Basim not only respect, but a heavy helping of self-abasement too, since some day the ancient one would be free of Boabdil's power and might make a truly dangerous foe if mistreated now. Yet knowing all this, Hafiz simply could not bring himself to take all the blame for the accident. It had not been his fault entirely. He had tried to avoid the collision. The same pride that kept him and Rashid apart would not let him grovel before the head of the great and fearsome Council.

Master Basim could hear silence perhaps better than many mortals could hear words. He suspected what was going through the boy's mind and he did not find it at all acceptable. He was still too full of sour thoughts to let this slight pass. However, he was also still voiceless, and so he confined his anger to one deadly look blacker than a whole bank of thunderclouds.

It worked. Hafiz drew in a sharp, hissing breath under the genie's glare, yet still his pride stood guard over any words of humility he might have spoken. He knew he must do *something* to rescue the situation, but what?

In this moment of need, his father's face rose before his eyes and he heard Haroun ben Hasan say: *If your opponent knows that you dare not attack and cannot retreat, then stand your ground and at the first opportunity, distract him. Then run.*

Therefore, as Master Basim stood before him, brushing off his robes, Hafiz ben Haroun smiled his most winning smile and asked, "O Master Basim, may your wisdom flourish like yonder plum tree! Tell me, do you think that the Sword of Solomon has the power to grant me victory over Prince Rashid if we are merely having an argument, or would I need to pick a real fight with him first?"

Master Basim automatically opened his mouth to reply, but before he could recall his voiceless state, the boy Hafiz slapped his forehead in mock realization and exclaimed, "Ah! but how can you tell me anything when you cannot speak? Never mind. I shall find out for myself." With that, he ducked around Master Basim and disappeared into the palace.

Master Basim stood there with a mask of perplexity on his face. Then, by degrees, another expression replaced it. A dawning look of horror inched its way across his features. He dashed to where Boabdil was still chatting with Khalid and Tamar and reached for the cat's tail.

". . . roast the pheasant slowly over a—touch it and you will have the voice of a cockroach—charcoal fire, basting frequently with butter. . . ." The cat did not even pause for breath to issue his warning. Master Basim jerked his hand back. Tamar and Khalid tried not to laugh.

The ancient genie cast a nervous backward glance over his shoulder. The palace doorway had completely devoured Hafiz. Not even the sound of his retreating footsteps escaped. Master Basim reached out to touch the cat again—not the tail this time—then thought better of it. Boabdil did not like to be interrupted when he was holding forth on a subject dear to his heart, like food, and Master Basim did not wish to annoy the cat when he was so close to regaining his voice from the horrid, provoking beast.

He would only spare me if this were an emergency, Master Basim thought. *But it* is *an emergency. Or it is about to become one. That mortal brat intends to lay hands upon the Sword of Solomon, master of ten thousand magics! Anything from that great king's household runs the risk of being infected with a dozen spells. What disasters might befall if the assuredly enchanted blade were to fall into the hands of a human pup that can not even wipe its own nose? Aie! Yes, this is most certainly am emergency, but how am I to convince the cat of it without my voice? I cannot. Therefore I must handle this myself.*

With that thought, Master Basim wrapped darkness about him like a cloak and flew after Hafiz into the palace.

CHAPTER NINETEEN

Everyone in the palace knew where the Sword of Solomon hung when it was not in Haroun ben Hasan's keeping. It was said to dangle from a pair of golden chains in the Chamber of the Lions, the Grape Arbor, the Jade Peacock, and the Leaping Fish.

Everyone from the lowest kitchen boy to the sultan himself likewise knew of the Sword's legendary power: It granted its master inevitable victory over all mortal foes. There was no need to add that such a weapon did not care who wielded it. Prince or potscrubber, it was all the same to the Sword. Why, even if a woman's hand (O, unthinkable!) should close around its hilt, the Sword would obey her as readily as it would a man. What, then, was there to prevent some upstart wretch from seizing his chance along with the Sword and toppling the whole kingdom?

Simple: Everyone knew where the Sword of Solomon hung but only three people in all the palace knew how to find it. These three were the sultan, Haroun ben Hasan, and the Princess Nur.

Haroun deserved most of the credit for this state of affairs. "When I am away from home, the Sword never leaves my side," he told his wife. "But when I return, I do not wish to have the clumsy thing encumbering me all the time, especially since I cannot find a sheath that will hold it. On the other hand, neither do I wish to keep it in our apartments, a temptation to every petty thief who knows the Sword's fame and fancies himself a great conqueror."

"How do you propose to solve this puzzle, my beloved?" Nur asked. "You cannot have your cake and eat it too."

"A cake is a cake, but a sword is a horse of a different color," Haroun replied, giving his dear wife a kiss on the cheek. "Your father's palace is huge. Surely there must be at least one room among hundreds which is so small, so obscurely placed, so out-of-the-way that it is as good as invisible?"

The princess knit her brows in thought, then brightened. "The Chamber of the Lions, the Grape Arbor, the Jade Peacock, and the Leaping Fish!" she cried.

Her husband frowned. "That does not sound like the name of a small and insignificant room."

"On the contrary, my dear; it is one of the smallest and most insignificant rooms in the whole palace, barring the servants' quarters. It is one of the many throne rooms Father reserves for receiving ambassadors from foreign lands. The larger chambers are for receiving delegations from kingdoms that are larger than ours, or more dangerous—lands whose soldiers we could not hope to defeat in the days before you became our champion."

Haroun blushed. "Without the Sword of Solomon, I would not make a very great champion."

"A champion's worth lies in the heart, not in a piece of steel," Nur maintained.

"You speak thus because you love me," Haroun said. "Yet for all your faith, I would still sleep better knowing the Sword was secure. Are you certain—?"

"The greater the name, the smaller the room," his wife rejoined. "It is rather like the way Father names court positions. The Grand Vizier is far more powerful than the Third Assistant Auxiliary Examiner of Supplies for the Royal Cupbearers (Second Class). I assure you, there is no room with a greater name than the Chamber of the Lions, the Grape Arbor, the Jade Peacock, and the Leaping Fish. Most who hear the name think it means four separate rooms. Others hear it and think it is the start of a very bad joke. It is used to receive ambassadors from those realms so miniscule, so harmless, so helpless that even *we* do not fear them. The only reason no one bothers to conquer them is that they suffer from bad climate, atrocious food, or native music that sounds like a camel spitting up cactus. The room has not been used for years, and all the servants who used to attend Father when he sat upon the throne within are dead of old age. Shall I show it to you?"

"*You* know where it is, my dove?" Haroun was startled.

Nur shrugged. "I was born and raised in this palace, my father's only daughter. Until I reached the age for marriage, no one really knew what to do with me. I was left to my own devices most of the time, and whenever I could escape my rooms, I went exploring, adventuring—" She winked at him. "You know how I like adventures."

"And in your explorations, you found the room. I see." Haroun ben Hasan stroked his chin for a long time, then at last said, "It sounds the ideal hiding place for the Sword. Let us inform your father of our intentions."

The sultan was pleased with the plan, and so became one of only three human beings who knew how to find the place where the Sword of Solomon hung when it was not in Haroun ben Hasan's keeping.

Ah, no: one of only three *adult* human beings.

Hafiz ben Haroun ran through the sultan's palace with as much ease as the mice that had been born and raised in the cushions of the chief royal throne.

He knew every inch of the luminous marble floors, every thread in the silken carpets, every curve and curlicue of the airily carved stonework walls. Only Boabdil could claim to know the palace better, and Boabdil liked to lie about it. It was almost as if Hafiz had been born with a map of the palace clutched in his tiny brown hand.

Hafiz had been born in his father's own palace, of course, and a sumptuous one it was. But with Haroun ben Hasan away so much over the years, finding wives and kingdoms for his many brothers-in-law, the Princess Nur grew understandably lonely. There were the palace servants, but all of them were too much in awe of their royal mistress to offer her a friendly chat. True, there was always Boabdil, but Nur soon learned that cats have little use for conversations that do not center upon themselves.

Small wonder that she soon took her infant son and returned to her father's home for an extended visit. In the end, when Haroun finally married off the last of the superfluous princes, a happily reunited husband and wife agreed that it made no sense to keep up such an expensive separate household when they could dwell quite comfortably under the sultan's roof.

Besides, Nur argued, little Hafiz was so happy living near his dear friend and cousin, Prince Rashid! She could not foresee the quarrel ahead, nor that her firstborn child had inherited his mother's love for exploring, nor where that troublesome love might take him.

Therefore it was no miracle that Hafiz scampered through the maze of corridors straight to the room that housed the fabled Sword of Solomon as easily as a hound could track a fried rabbit.

The door to the Chamber of the Lions, the Grape Arbor, the Jade Peacock, and the Leaping Fish was partly hidden behind a tapestry. Few passers-by in the corridor even noticed it was there, and those who did catch a glimpse of it dismissed it as unworthy of further attention. It was not locked, relying entirely upon its shabby appearance for protection. So too does the humble oyster shell conceal the glory of the pearl.

Hafiz was in luck: The corridor was deserted. He did not need to wait for his chance, but slipped under the tapestry and through the door as quickly as he might. Once inside, he gazed about him with a contented sigh on his lips. Though all was dust and shadows in the so-very-minor throne room, a row of arrow slit windows set high on one wall admitted enough light for the boy's keen eyes to behold his coveted treasure: the Sword of Solomon!

There it hung, just out of a tall man's reach, above the throne itself. It was this same throne that gave the chamber its name, for its base was carved to resemble a brace of ferocious lions, its body made in the leafy semblance of a grape arbor, its back shaped like a peacock, and its armrests fashioned like leaping fish. It was said to be the gift of a mighty king, and it was easily the ugliest thing in the palace, including some of the princes.

Hafiz gazed up at the Sword. His smile turned over on itself. What was this? What had happened to the Sword? It was sheathed! A glorious, golden scabbard, intricately worked and heavily starred with all manner of smooth-cut gems hid the naked blade from sight.

"What witchery is this?" Hafiz murmured, all thought of his quarrel with Prince Rashid vanished. "The Sword of Solomon is *never* sheathed! No common scabbard can hold it. Someone has stolen the Sword and left this gewgaw in its place! I must tell Father." He turned as if to leave the chamber, then paused and looked back at the blade. "I'd better take you with me," he told it. "Just to make sure Father pays attention to me when I tell him."

With that, Hafiz marched up to the throne, placed the toe of one slipper in a lion's gaping mouth, and began his climb.

He had scaled the lion and was ascending the grape arbor when Master Basim slipped into the room, riding the back of a shadow. The ancient genie had chosen to keep himself invisible while he planned his course of action. He saw what the boy was up to and chewed his moustaches in a frenzy. *I must stop him!* he thought. He took a step forward, arms outstretched to sweep the boy from his course.

It was then that Hafiz, balanced on the back of a stone fish, spat generously into his hands. While Master Basim recoiled in fastidious dismay at the vulgar gesture, the boy rubbed his palms together vigorously and took a firm grasp on the first tier of the jade peacock's outfanned tail feathers.

Ugh! Master Basim thought, shuddering, as he watched Hafiz climb ever higher. He made no attempt to stop the lad now. He was a very prim and prissy sort of genie who abhorred messes of any kind. For this reason he disliked contact with mortal children intensely. The fact that he was ready to *touch* Hafiz in order to keep him from the Sword of Solomon was supreme proof of just how urgent the situation was.

Urgent or not, he could not bring himself to touch the boy now.

What am I to do? the genie moaned inwardly. *He must not lay hands upon the Sword of my late master, King Solomon of blessed memory. And yet—and yet—Oh, how can I prevent him? I cannot shout a command. Perhaps if I were to appear suddenly before his eyes in some hideous guise—? No, no. The shock might prove fatal. I can be* quite *hideous when I try.* He preened a little at that.

Meanwhile, Hafiz had scaled the peacock's fan almost to the top. Carefully he inched his way from the frozen plumage out across the bird's indrawn head until he crouched on the beak. The Sword dangled just out of reach, a tantalizing sight. Hafiz screwed up his courage, set his lips firmly, and slowly rose to his feet. The peacock's beak was scarcely wide enough to accommodate a child's foot, much less a boy's, although the throne itself bulked large in sheer repulsiveness. Even balanced on the beak as he was, Hafiz still could not reach the Sword. He would have to take at least one step forward, then lean out over the void if he meant to grasp it.

One step . . . As well ask him to walk on the face of the moon! It had taken nearly all Hafiz's resolve to stand up at such a height, but to take a step forward and then to stretch forth his body over empty space—! The throne was a towering monument to bad taste, and the sultan had never thought to ease the effect of so much ugliness by furnishing the chamber floor with soft carpets or plump pillows. The floor was naked slabs of stone, pure and unadorned and hard. One step might easily become one misstep, and one misstep would purchase Hafiz a hard landing indeed.

From his place in shadow, Master Basim observed Hafiz with an ever-waxing spark of hope in his heart. *He is afraid!* the genie exulted. *He has gone so far but can go no further. Ah, what luck! He will back down, and I will not need to touch him after all!*

Master Basim was almost right. Hafiz was afraid. He did not mind heights, but he minded falls. For an instant, Hafiz wished that Rashid were with him. The lithe prince was far better at playing the amateur tightrope walker than his chubbier companion. Besides, Rashid knew how to roll with a fall when he took one. All that Hafiz ever seemed to do was bounce and bruise.

"—and then he laughs at me," Hafiz gritted. His hands became angry fists, and the power of his rage kept him balanced perfectly upright on the peacock's beak. "He *laughs* at me!" the boy repeated, this time a shout that rang through the chamber.

Aghast, Master Basim saw the boy take the fateful step that brought the Sword of Solomon almost within his clutches. In his mind, the genie rushed forward a thousand times to pluck Hafiz from the peacock's beak and sweep him out of temptation's way. In reality, he stood rooted to the spot, choking on his own frustration, until he could bear it no more. Torn this way and that by *I must!* and *I cannot!*, Master Basim opened his mouth in a silent shriek and stamped the floor of the chamber with all his might.

The floor cracked, the stone shivering. The throne shook at its foundations, jiggling so hard that a webwork of fine cracks raced up the smoothly carved flanks and one of the lions lost a tooth. Master Basim stared as he saw his purpose achieved in spite of his compunctions: Hafiz tottered on the peacock's beak for an instant, arms windmilling the air, then plunged to the floor.

Oh, dear! was all Master Basim could think. *Someone really ought to catch— But I am the only one— Oh, dear. I hope he won't be* too *badly hurt.* The genie felt a pang of remorse. He took a step forward. Between the instant Hafiz lost his footing and the moment that Master Basim overcame his scruples there was plenty of time left before the boy would hit the ground. Genies can move with the speed of light, when it suits them. There is only one thing that moves faster than a determined genie:

A father who sees his child in danger.

"Hafiz! What were you thinking?" Haroun ben

Hasan staggered back under the weight of the boy and fetched up against one of the chamber walls. "You could have been hurt," he chided as he set him back on his feet.

"Oh, hello, Father," Hafiz responded rather sulkily.

Haroun straightened the lay of his clothes, which had been somewhat rumpled in the rescue, and scowled at his son. "Save your greetings. If I had not come into this room just now, you would have been badly injured. I want an answer: What are you doing here?"

"I wanted to surprise you," the boy replied a little too eagerly. He was not a liar, as a rule, but when he did bend the truth he did it enthusiastically.

"Surprise me?" Haroun echoed. "How? Not even I knew I would be coming here until a very short while ago."

"I wanted—I wanted to clean your sword for you," Hafiz said, the words almost tripping over one another as they spilled from his lips.

Haroun was unmoved, and crossed his arms over his chest to show it. "You know that it is forbidden for any to touch the Sword of Solomon save myself and, should he desire it (although he never does), the sultan. It is the chief treasure of our kingdom and our guarantee of freedom. So long as the Sword of Solomon is ours, no other nation can defeat us, however large or ruthless it may be. So what were you *really* doing—?"

Hafiz did not know it, but he had the mind of a born strategist. Having failed to disarm his father with a direct attack, he now turned to diversionary tactics. "Forbidden!" he exclaimed, scandalized. "Oh my father, then we have a great evil lurking in our midst. For see! The Sword—blessings be upon its keen blade—has been tampered with!"

"Is it so?" Haroun's eye flew to the hanging weapon

in its gorgeous scabbard, but noted nothing amiss. "How?"

"Some villain has sneaked into this room, into my august grandfather's very palace, and has—and has—" He paused for effect, struck a dramatic pose, and intoned: "—*sheathed it!*"

Haroun ben Hasan promptly burst into laughter so loud and hearty it set the Sword of Solomon jingling at the ends of its golden chains.

Hafiz gaped at his father until his expression knotted itself into a scowl. He did not like being laughed at. He would have preferred to be scolded. "How can you mock, O my father? You well know that the true Sword of Solomon can never be sheathed. Clearly yonder blade is an impostor."

Haroun ben Hasan's guffaws dwindled to mere hiccups of hilarity. Wiping tears of merriment from his eyes, he said, "There is nothing wrong with the Sword. All is as it should be. The Sword of Solomon can never be sheathed in any *common* scabbard, that is true. But there is no reason in the world why it may not be contained by the sheath that was made for it by the same unearthly hands that forged the Sword itself."

Hafiz's eyes went as big and round as an owl's. "But—but if that is the Sword's true scabbard, how did it come here? This is magic!"

His father chuckled and patted him on the shoulder. "Do you recall your uncle Najib?"

Hafiz nodded. "He was the last one of my uncles for whom you found a kingdom and a bride." *As if I could ever forget him!* the boy thought hotly. *It was shortly after you got rid of Uncle Najib that you came home to stay and Aminah happened!*

"Well, it was while he and I were off adventuring that we found it. It was buried deep in the sea, in the treasure chest of a sunken Tyrian sailing ship."

"Sunken treasure?" Hafiz's face was avid for the tale.

"Yes, and guarded by a sea serpent whose breath could melt a man's flesh from his bones," Haroun remarked casually. An afterthought bid him add: "Oh, and once we overcame the serpent, the skeletons of the drowned sailors rose up to do battle for the treasure, but we beat them. Nothing extraordinary about the whole affair, except for the moment when I saw the scabbard. As soon as I laid eyes on it, I knew it for what it was. How could I not? The Sword of Solomon itself fairly hummed with the power of recognition when it came within a stone's throw of it! Thus I claimed it for my own, leaving the rest of the treasure for your uncle."

Haroun strolled up to the throne and stepped onto the seat in order to reach the Sword. It came into his hands with no trouble at all. He then held it out for his son's inspection.

"A wonder, is it not?" He spoke with as much pride as if he himself had been the artificer who had created such a work of beauty.

"It is indeed a marvel," said Hafiz. His eyes wandered over the fantastically wrought patterns on the golden sheath. Here a willow tree grew, its leaves a galaxy of emeralds. There a dozen maidens danced, their eyes a twinkling lure of sapphires. Golden apples made from yellow diamonds weighed down the branches of an orchard guarded by a dragon whose fiery belly was the largest, most luminous ruby Hafiz had ever seen. A marvel indeed!

"A fitting home for such a magnificent weapon," said Haroun ben Hasan. "And yet it is the Sword itself that holds the true power. The sultan sent me to fetch it. He tells me we are to receive an ambassador this evening, and His Majesty wants the Sword in plain sight."

"An ambassador?" Hafiz echoed.

"Yes, and one who serves a mighty lord, or we would not need to have the Sword of Solomon on display, to make sure he minds his manners. One glimpse of the blade is always enough; everyone knows the legend. My son, you have no idea what a comfort it is to be able to show your enemies that they can never hope to conquer you, no matter how hard they try. It saves so much time and trouble and bloodshed." He grinned as his fingers closed on the familiar hilt and he drew the blade.

He *tried* to draw the blade. He could not.

His grin was gone.

CHAPTER TWENTY

The last of the servants scurried out of the second-best banquet hall in the sultan's palace, their work done. All was in readiness for the celebration of Boabdil's birthday. The long table groaned with all manner of food and drink, the platters and goblets sparkled, the divans were properly arranged, and the air was sweet with the scent of costly perfumes. Boabdil sat on a mound of cushions at the head of the table and looked over everything with an air of satisfaction. He was just settling himself into his downy nest to await the arrival of the first guests when Haroun ben Hasan came bursting in, followed closely by his son.

"Boabdil!" Haroun shouted, wig-wagging the Sword of Solomon. "Boabdil, you must give me your last remaining wish at once!"

The cat gave the man a long, cool look. "I doubt that," he said. "It is my wish, after all. I may want to use it for myself."

"How can you be so greedy?" Haroun demanded, shaking the sheathed sword under Boabdil's nose.

"Fine talk from a man who used one of his three wishes to wish for countless wishes more," the cat purred.

Haroun either did not hear the mocking words or chose to ignore them. "And after all I have done for you! I rescued you from the alleyways, took you into my home, gave you food when I had barely a morsel to spare for myself!"

The cat reclined languidly upon his cushions and regarded the man unperturbed. "But what have you done for me lately?" He opened his mouth wide in a pink, cavernous yawn and stretched his legs to the tips of his pearly claws.

"Ungrateful animal, this is an emergency! Do you not know what this is?" Again he shook the Sword in the cat's face.

"Beyond doubt I do," the cat replied. "It is a tool you humans use to improve one another. What has that to do with me?"

Haroun uttered an inarticulate gargle of anguish that rattled the goblets. "Nothing," he said when he was able to regain control of himself. "Nothing but your doom, and doom for us all if word of this ever reaches the ears of our enemies. The Sword of Solomon is worthless!"

Boabdil lifted his head just enough to sniff the glittering scabbard. "Oh, I would not say that. You could easily sell the sheath alone for a respectable sum in the bazaar."

"That is not what I mean and you know it." Haroun glowered first at the cat, then at his son, who was trying to suppress a fit of snickering at the shameless way Boabdil twitted his father. "If I only could separate the sheath from the Sword, I would sell it in an instant—nay, *give* it away, jewels or no! Through some strange enchantment, the Sword of Solomon has become trapped in its own scabbard. It resists all my efforts to draw it forth. If I cannot bare the blade, how can I wield it? And if I cannot wield it, how can I defeat our enemies? And if I cannot defeat our enemies—" he slumped onto the cushions beside the cat "—how can we stop them from defeating us?"

Boabdil patted Haroun's hand gently with one paw.

"There, there. Do not fear. I will save you . . . *again.*" The cat forced a sigh. "A true hero's work is never done."

Haroun's face kindled with joy. "May a thousand angels of the Most High keep your fur free from mange and fleas!" he exclaimed. "From the bottom of my heart, I thank you for wishing the Sword of Solomon free of its prison."

"For wishing what?" Boabdil's whiskers curved forward. "Do not be silly. I will not waste my one remaining wish on that!"

"What!" Without thinking, Haroun raised his empty hand as if to fend off the cat's reply. Unfortunately, the gesture looked as if he intended to strike the provoking beast.

A strong, dark hand materialized out of thin air and seized Haroun's in a grip unyielding as the grave. This apparition was followed almost at once by the remainder of Master Basim. The genie's face was a mask of rage capable of turning milk into maggots.

"You see," Boabdil said with the flicker of a smirk, "I have already promised my last wish to Master Basim."

The genie could not speak, but he bared his teeth and growled in Haroun's face in a manner that was most eloquent.

"Indeed, indeed," Haroun said swiftly, trying to free his hand and failing. He offered the angry genie a smile that was at once ingratiating and idiotic. "And a very good way to spend your last remaining wish it is!"

Master Basim let go of Haroun's hand. The man leaned the useless Sword of Solomon against the banquet table and chafed some feeling back into his wrist.

"Do not fear," Boabdil reassured him. "This is my birthday, a day meant for rejoicing, not for fear. I have given Master Basim my word that I will wish his voice restored as soon as my party is over. So it must be, for a promise is a promise. But among those guests I have invited to attend this great feast are some old friends of yours, the genies Tamar and Khalid. They come with joyous hearts, and a joyous heart is a generous heart. I am sure that they will be more than happy to use their magic to help you free the Sword . . . *after* my banquet." By the way he said it, the cat made it plain that he would not stand for anyone or anything interfering with his birthday party.

"Very well," Haroun grumbled. He reached for the Sword of Solomon.

It was gone. Instead of leaning against the table, where he had left it, it now reposed in Master Basim's hands. The old genie was studying the jewelled sheath, a puzzled look on his face. This was more than idle curiosity at work. Had Haroun been in a milder mood, he might have noticed that there was something very like a glint of apprehension in Master Basim's eyes, particularly when he examined the large golden dragon whose belly was an enormous, perfectly rounded ruby.

Haroun's mood was anything but mild. He snatched the Sword from the genie's hands with a waspish, "By your leave," and stalked out of the banquet hall.

Hafiz watched him go. "Father—?" But Haroun was too wrapped up in troubled thoughts for the safety of the kingdom to remember his son. The boy sank down onto a cushion and cradled his face in his hands, dejected.

A long, fluffy tail traced a ticklish path under his nose, rousing him from his melancholy. "Cheer up, Hafiz!" It was the cat's command. "This is too great a day for long faces."

"I wager that Father would not have forgotten me if I were Aminah," Hafiz muttered.

"Quite right," said the cat. "For then you would

have been a squalling, squirming burden in his arms. You probably would have wet on him as well. Come, come, cheer up for my sake."

Hafiz regarded him sourly.

"Cheer up or I'll bite you," the cat suggested.

Although it wanted several hours until sunset when Boabdil's banquet began, the servants had already lit the oil lamps in the hall. The soft murmur of many voices, all praising the food, the decor, and the generosity of their furry host, rose up on every hand. In a discreetly out-of-the-way niche, musicians called forth sweet and merry tunes from flutes, lutes, drums, and dainty finger cymbals to entertain the diners.

Attended by master Basim, Boabdil gazed down the length of the table to where Hafiz sat between his parents. "You see?" he remarked to the genie. "The lad is as merry as a spring lamb. And it is all my doing."

Master Basim suppressed a smirk, but he could not keep himself from pointing to a rapidly emptying plate of honeycake that lay within easy reach of Hafiz's hands. The boy's smile was as sticky as it was broad. The cat fluffed his fur in the same way a human might shrug.

"Well, I *ordered* the honeycake," he said.

It was a wonderful feast. There were over two dozen quests present, from the sultan's most highly placed advisors to the gardener's boy who had once rescued Boabdil from a stray dog. The sultan himself was also there, along with his heir, Prince Masud, and his royal grandson, Prince Rashid. The boy looked just as sulky as Hafiz when he first entered the room, but when he took his place at the table he found a plate full of honeycake awaiting him as well. It did not take long for the delicacy to work its special magic on both boys. Before long they were stealing shy, half-apologetic glances at one another. Only the fact that their seats were so distant, one from the other, prevented them from making up their quarrel then and there, before the honeycake crumbs were dry on their faces.

Boabdil's' whiskers swept up to either side of his mouth in a look of purest delight. Although he would never admit it out loud, he was pleased to see the boys on the brink of forgetting their differences. He was fond of them, in his own way.

He was even fonder of presents.

The cat's eyes strayed from the banquet table to rest contentedly on his birthday gifts. Each of his guests had brought him something in honor of the day: that went without saying. Moreover, those nobles who had not been invited to the feast, but who were wise enough to realize the cat's importance at court, had sent their own offerings.

The servants took the gifts as they arrived and heaped them up in the far corner of the room where they might be admired by all the guests and where Boabdil could keep his eye on gifts and guests both. There were diamond-encrusted collars, silk mice, golden pitchers of cream, string upon string of plump, exotic fishes, their skins smoked to a mouthwatering crisp, delicate porcelain feeding bowls the color of lilac buds, brought all the way from far Cathay—oh, scores of things! Even the gardener's boy had brought a healthy young catnip plant, flourishing in a broken soup bowl. Boabdil closed his eyes and rippled his fur in delight.

"I love birthdays," he thrummed.

Master Basim cleared his throat loudly, jerking the cat out of his reverie. The genie nodded down the table to where Haroun ben Hasan sat, arms folded, lips pursed, brow creased until he looked like a veritable gargoyle of grimness. He did not recline on his divan like the other diners, nor did he dine. There was something in his attitude to proclaim that no amount of honeycake would soothe his worries away.

"Yes, yes, I know," the cat told the genie. "But what can I do? Tamar and Khalid have not yet come. Much as I would like to set my old friend's mind at rest by freeing the Sword, I am powerless. I gave you my word to use the last wish on your behalf, and so I shall. So I must! We cats have a reputation for treachery which we do not deserve. We are taught from kittenhood that if we break our promises, the Great Moon Cat will come down from the sky to hunt us like so many miserable mice. Therefore I must wait until Khalid and Tamar arrive, to ask them this small favor. It can even be their birthday gift to me, if they insist." The cat flexed his claws. "I hope they do *not* insist."

Master Basim made some further noises in his throat, some so loud that more than a few guests looked up in alarm, thinking that the ceiling was crumbling in upon them. The cat switched his tail impatiently.

"No, I will not give you back your voice now!" he said. "I promised to return it to you after my party and that is when I shall do it, not an instant before. My party cannot be over until all my guests have come and I have received *all* my presents." He eyed the genie meaningfully when he said this.

Master Basim's face fell. Then he heaved a great sigh of resignation and held one hand out over the cat's head. From the genie's palm came tumbling a shower of silver sparkles. They fell upon the cat like snow, starring his pelt with brilliance for a moment before they melted into the fur. The guests could not help but witness this spectacular display. Their oohs and aahs and applause drowned out the musicians' best efforts.

Boabdil glowed. He arched his back under the silvery shower, tail standing up straight as a poplar, and the sound of his purrs was almost deafening. "Ahhhh! As much as I adore smoked fish and catnip, there is nothing like receiving an additional year of life to make for a *really* happy birthday." He rolled onto his back and waved his paws in the air as if he were a kitten. Then, quite suddenly, he flipped himself onto his feet and vaulted onto the genie's shoulder.

"You have pleased me, Master Basim," he said, giving the old genie's ear a friendly lick. "Now I am in the mood to please you. Oh, I know that I said I would wait until my party was done, but I have changed my mind. I feel generous." He leaned against the side of Master Basim's turban. His guests, rightly assuming that the magic was done, had gone back to eating.

"I am also in the mood to have everyone here see just how generous I can be," the cat added. "I want all of them to watch when I give you back your voice. Make them pay attention."

It was impossible to measure the joy that flooded the venerable genie's face. So eager was he to regain the power of speech that he obeyed the cat's demand with more zest than wisdom. Drawing himself up to a great height, he raised his hands and brought them together in a clap that sent lightning bolts arcing the length of the hall and sounded like the collision of stars.

This time the resounding boom *was* enough to shatter the ceiling. Guests squawked and rolled from their divans as flakes of plaster came pattering down on their heads. Haroun ben Hasan forgot all about the Sword of Solomon as he leaped to shelter his wife and son beneath his light silk cloak. The sultan's bodyguards lunged for the largest serving platter on the table, dumped its load of roast quail on the floor, and thrust it over the sultan's head to shield him from the falling debris. Unfortunately, they turned it upside-down and the sultan now sat beneath a slow, steady drizzle of gravy. He looked very thoughtful.

The ensuing silence might have been sliced with a sword. The only sound in all the banquet hall to disturb this monumental hush was the drip-drip-drip coming from the sultan and the low, desperate, half-strangled snufflings of two boys trying to suppress their laughter.

So great, so imposing was the silence that when the great doors of the banquet hall swung back on their hinges, the faint creak and squeak was enough to make every guest present draw in a startled breath that sounded very much like a gasp of awe.

"Why, thank you," said the young man who stood revealed in the doorway. "I know I am wonderful to behold, but really, you flatter me."

He was the sort of person who wore his vanity like a cloak, overlaying his every action. The sorry truth was, he was also a man who had much to be vain about. His sunbrowned face was extremely handsome, from the roots of his raven hair to the tip of his artfully trimmed beard. He wore silk, satin, and elaborately tooled riding leathers as if they were no more than an old cotton caftan he had thrown on without a second thought. A small fortune in gems and gold twinkled from his ear, his neck, his wrists, his fingertips, and his turban. Though his boots proclaimed him a skilled horseman, the dust of hard riding did not cling to his raiment. It would not dare.

He did not wait to be announced. Instead he strode into the hall as if he owned it, the sultan's old majordomo scuttling along in his wake like a paper sailboat trying to keep up with a royal treasure ship. The venerable servant, his snowy beard trailing almost to his knees, was a gnarled, bent bramble bush of a man.

He used his staff of office not for show alone, but to support a body which age had long since picked up and folded over double. In spite of his many years and the afflictions that went with them, his spirit was as hot and sharp as good mustard, and he did not like young whippersnappers who ignored the rules.

The young man who had just entered the banqueting hall without allowing the major-domo to do his proper job and announce him was the worst example of these. Therefore the aged servant made it a point to flip his staff of office forward with such skill that the gilded griffon topping the head caught itself neatly on the young man's voluminous trousers. The offending whippersnapper was brought up short in mid-stride and found himself tumbling right into the lap of Lord Reza, one of the sultan's fattest and fussiest counselors. Lord Reza uttered a yawp upon being so abruptly visited and leaped to his feet. Unfortunately, his girth prevented him from doing more than lurching forward, which tipped the unlucky young man right into the platter of stewed figs and apricots that the rotund nobleman had been so happily consuming only moments earlier.

A second silence descended upon the company. This one was less durable than the first, for the guests did not recognize the young man presently hauling himself upright, picking figs and apricots from his ruined clothes. It was safe to make fun of strangers, or so everyone believed. To prove this, they all broke into wild peals of laughter as the young man chased the last of the stewed fruit from his sleeves.

Not quite everyone behaved so rudely. The Princess Nur hastened to the young man's side, a clean napkin and a goblet full of water in her hands. Although Nur had always had plenty of servants to clean up after her and her children, she would never forget the days she spent disguised as a serving girl in Haroun ben Hasan's household. It was then that the princess first discovered that she liked to clean things for herself—dishes, rooms, laundry, or people, it made no difference. If she did it herself, she knew it would be done right.

Now she pounced on the gooey young man, damp cloth flying. He struggled to evade her attentions, but he squirmed in vain. The princess had had heaps of practice cleaning up unwilling victims in the days when her son Hafiz had first discovered mud puddles.

"Hold still!" she commanded, dabbing at his face. "Do you want to spend the rest of your life looking like a fruit salad?"

The young man huffed and snorted and finally seized the lady's wrists to make her stop. "Woman, do you know who I am?" he demanded.

"No," Nur replied in all honesty. "And I do not think it matters. Whoever you are, you need to be washed." She gave her hands an artful twist that broke the young man's hold on her wrists and resumed the attack.

He grabbed her wrists a second time. "Woman, I am Malak the Murderous. Men call me the Whirlwind of the Desert, the Destroyer of Mine Enemies, the Lord of Ten Thousand Legions of Unstoppable Fury! How dare you plish-plosh all over me like a mother cat?"

"The fool," Boabdil murmured.

Nur's face became a thundercloud. She dropped the goblet of water with precision, so that it landed on Malak's toe and soaked his trousers generously. "And I am Princess Nur," she said. "Men call me the only daughter of our great and all-powerful sultan, the wife of Haroun ben Hasan the Undefeated and the Undefeatable. How dare *you* speak to *me* thus?"

Malak looked stern. "You are *the* Princess Nur?" She nodded, her expression not softening one degree more than his. "The very same Princess Nur whose hand in marriage was requested by Lord Qaysir the Unconquerable ten years ago?"

"More or less," Nur replied. She was having trouble holding onto her scowl. Now she was puzzled.

Malak gave a gladsome cry, released her hands, and threw his arms around her instead. "Oh, my dear Princess Nur!" he exclaimed. "You have no idea how happy I am to have found you!"

Haroun ben Hasan shot like an arrow to his wife's side and tapped the effervescent young man briskly on the back. "I would like to have some idea of how happy you are," he said. "And why. I am Lord Haroun ben Hasan, thrice blessed to be the lady's husband."

Malak took a step away from Nur and faced Haroun, his smile growing ever wider. "But of course you are!" he said. "I may be the lord of more sand than is truly profitable, but even in the deepest reaches of the great desert we have heard of you. Your fame is as ever-living as the fabled phoenix! Oh, could I but sing for you a single one of the epics that our musicians have composed in your honor, it would move you to tears! Alas, such is the quality of my voice that any song I choose to sing reduces my audience to tears. Tell me, the Sword of Solomon to which you owe so much of your fame and all your power—" He dropped his voice like an assassin conferring with his partners. "—is it real?"

"As real as you," Haroun snapped. "Behold it!" He tossed his light cloak back over one shoulder and the Sword was revealed at his hip. "You have given us your name, which means nothing to my ears. Who *are* you and what has brought you here?"

"And why have you disturbed my birthday?" Boabdil clamored unnoticed.

"I?" Malak laid a hand to his chest. "Why, I am as

I said, Malak the Murderous, son of the late Qaysir the Unconquerable." He draped one arm around Haroun's shoulders. "And as soon as you give your consent, my friend, I am going to be your son-in-law."

CHAPTER TWENTY-ONE

"You must be mad!" cried the sultan.

"You must be insane!" the princess gasped.

"You must be going," said Boabdil.

Malak the Murderous shrugged off all the words of astonishment, disbelief, and outright shock that had greeted his announcement. "What is the problem?" he asked innocently. "I am a healthy young man, lord of a great realm—even if it is mostly desert. I wish to pass my kingdom on to my sons, but I have no wife. Well, just one at the moment; you can hardly count that. Under the circumstances, I think I have made a perfectly reasonable request: I wish to wed the Lady Aminah."

"The Lady Aminah is a mere baby!" the sultan boomed.

"Oh, that is all right." Malak dismissed the objection. "It is not a permanent affliction. In time they get over it. Even I was a baby once. When I was born, my mother did not think I would live."

"No?" Haroun studied the young man. "You look hale enough now."

"I was hale enough then. But I was also the son of one of my lord Qaysir's *secondary* wives. For some reason, the children of the secondary wives kept . . . *disappearing* in a most inexplicable fashion whenever Father's chief wife came to visit."

"You do not look as if you disappeared," Haroun remarked in a way that as good as said he wished Malak would practice disappearing at once.

The desert prince chuckled. "Lucky for me that Mother made the chief wife disappear first; and all her children with her. A remarkable woman, my mother. I am sure she will be charmed by Lady Aminah." He rubbed his hands together. "So! Shall we name the happy day of our betrothal?"

The Princess Nur named a day. Malak considered it.

"But when *will* the world end?" He shook his head. "No, no, too indefinite; I am afraid that will not do."

"It will have to do," Nur replied stiffly. "I will not allow you to wed my precious baby girl any sooner than seven days after the end of the world, and that is that."

"But why?" Malak spread his hands. "I am young!"

"Not young enough to wed an infant."

"I am handsome!"

"So handsome that you will be more in love with yourself than with my daughter."

"I have many great treasures which I shall lay at your daughter's feet!"

"The greatest treasure any man can give my child is the right to choose her husband for herself."

Malak furrowed his forehead. "To choose her husband for herself? What sort of nonsense is this? Next you will be telling me that she must be my only wife!"

"I admit it goes against our traditions. Nonetheless, considering what you yourself have just told us about how fatal things were between your father's chief wife and his secondary wives, I think one wife should be enough for any man." Nur folded her arms in a manner that suggested she was not interested in further debate.

Malak laughed freely and waved away the princess's

words as if they were gnats. "But such little household spats happen all the time, especially between wives! As long as a man has at least one son alive left after the dust settles, there is no real harm done. Now if you wish to know what *real* harm is, I will oblige you." His smile vanished and he eyed the Princess Nur with menace, his hand dropping to the sword at his belt.

Haroun ben Hasan took a step forward. He did not like Malak; he was liking him less by the moment. He did not care for people who came barging into birthday parties uninvited, demanding his daughter's hand in marriage and threatening his wife. Red rage was bubbling up inside him. It wanted only a little extra stoking for it to reach the boiling-over point. Alas, the flames that stoked his rage likewise devoured his judgement!

"What harm?" Nur challenged, unaware of her husband's mounting temper.

"If you do not give me Lady Aminah's hand, I will lead my desert hordes on a wild rampage of destruction and conquest. I will burn this palace down around your ears, I will slaughter anyone who stands in my way, and I will *take* the Lady Aminah for my own!" He drew his sword and brandished it thrice overhead.

"Not before I take your head!" Haroun yelled, his hand clenching the hilt of the fabled Sword of Solomon and yanking it forth.

Yanking it, at any rate.

A shocked hush—the third of the evening—fell over the banquet hall. Guests and servants together stared at the spectacle of the kingdom's unquestioned champion unable to bare the blade on which his reputation rested. Rage had goaded Haroun ben Hasan to heroic action, but rage had also burned away all memory of the fact that the Sword of Solomon would *not* draw from its scabbard.

Too late, Haroun realized what he had done. He uncurled his fingers from the Sword, pulled back his shoulders, and with all the dignity he could muster said, "I am going to give you one more chance to leave this kingdom quietly. *Then* I will take your head."

Malak resheathed his own blade casually and studied the situation. He pressed his fingers to his mouth, partly concealing a wicked grin. "With what?" he asked.

"With this." Haroun slapped the Sword in its scabbard. His voice only shook a very little with the effort of maintaining his composure.

Malak nibbled a knuckle as he shook his head. "Mmmmm. No. No, I do not think so."

"Fool! Do you know what you are saying?" Haroun blustered. "This is the legendary Sword of Solomon!"

"The legend is stuck," Malak replied.

"Nonsense!" Haroun ben Hasan spoke boldly, but a keen eye could almost discern the outline of the imaginary wall against which his back was pressed. "I have merely chosen not to kill you with it at this moment. You only drew your sword to make a point. It would be churlish to slay you for ill-thought eloquence. Besides, your death would upset your mother. It is for her sake I spare you. Be grateful for my generosity and begone!"

"I do not think so," Malak repeated. He cocked his head to one side and contemplated the Sword. "I am young, but I have already been blooded in combat. Sometimes after a battle a man neglects to clean his blade properly and it becomes wedged in its sheath. I know a stuck sword when I see one. You, my lord, have a stuck sword." He peered at it from another angle, then added, "It is clean, yet it is stuck. I do believe it is stuck in a magical manner, as befits a legendary blade. What a pity."

With three magnificent springs, Boabdil covered the distance between his end of the table and the spot where Haroun and Malak stood facing each other. "Then, O Rude Despoiler of Birthday Feasts, you doubtless also know that what is magically stuck may become magically *un*stuck. Perhaps in the same manner that your arrogant head shall become unstuck from your shoulders if you are not wise."

Malak's brows rose in wonderment. "*A talking cat? What marvel is this?*"

"My lord Haroun ben Hasan is master of a thousand marvels!" Boabdil lied glibly. "Or have you managed to overlook the fact that there is a genie of uncommon size and power attending him?" He switched his tail in Master Basim's direction. The genie obligingly swelled himself to titanic proportions, his turbanned head touching the roof of the banquet hall, his complexion turning coal black, his eyes shooting fire, and crimson foam dribbling from his fanged mouth.

Malak remained unnaturally calm in the face of all Master Basim's ferocity. "My mother used to tell me stories about genies. She said that not even the mighty King Solomon himself could break the rules of magic governing these awesome creatures. Then she told me the rules." He drummed his fingers lightly on the pommel of his own sword and said, "If yonder monster does indeed serve you, O my lord Haroun, use one of your wishes now to sever my head from my shoulders."

"I—I would rather not," Haroun huffed. "Your poor mother would be devastated by your loss."

"My poor mother would rather have me dead than hear that I fell for such a poor bluff as this. Either chop off my head—use your Sword or use your genie;

I am not choosy—or the next time you see me, it will be at the head of my army, ready to destroy this realm and take the Princess Aminah for my bride."

Boabdil looked up at Malak. "But in truth, neither the genie nor the Sword of Solomon is required to remove your head," he said amiably. "An ordinary blade will do the task just as well. My good friend, the sultan, is more than well supplied with men willing and able to put a short, sharp end to your demands for his beloved granddaughter's hand in marriage. After your barbaric behavior here at my birthday feast, what makes you think he will allow you to leave this palace alive to make good your threats?"

"This," Malak replied, yanking at one of the countless gold chains adorning his neck. A silver whistle flew out of his tunic to twinkle in his hand. He set it to his lips and blew three shrill blasts.

All at once the hall filled with the sound of approaching hoofbeats. They did not thunder, but thanks to the marble palace floors they more imitated a violent hailstorm. Hail or thunder, they burst over the birthday guests as a corps of some twenty-odd desert riders came barrelling into the great chamber, nearly trampling the poor old major-domo in the process.

Malak the Murderous stood triumphant, hands on hips, watching his mounted men rampage up and down the length of the hall, sending most of the diners diving for haven beneath their divans. The horsemen drew their swords and used them to skewer their choice of leftovers from the feast. Boabdil jumped onto Haroun's shoulder to save his skin. He arched his back and spewed out bloodcurdling curses in both Cat and Human.

Two of the riders made their horses wheel in a tight circle around the Princess Nur, mocking her helpless fury, until she extracted a long jewelled pin from her hair and jabbed one of the horses in the rump. The painfully startled beast snorted and lashed out behind with its hooves, causing both steeds to bolt out of their riders' control and engage in a personal set-to. The princess calmly got herself out of harm's way and looked around her for another horse's rump.

The banquet hall was more than generously provided with such. The desert riders were having such a good time trampling what morsels they did not gobble up that they did not dream themselves vulnerable to attack.

Nur's courageous act inspired the other diners. Their expressions of abject terror changed to looks of solemn purpose. By ones and twos they crawled out from beneath their divans, with repayment on their minds.

The first to take action was the gardener's boy. He had a good eye when it came to throwing stones at marauding crows. Now he applied that same talent to the riders. There were no stones to hand, but he supplied that lack from a bowl of pomegranates. Soon the tough-skinned fruits were sailing through the air, finding a target every time. They exploded into showers of bright red juice and seeds on contact with man or mount. More than one rider mistook the scarlet liquid trickling down his face for blood. Howls of pain and terror rattled the dishes and scared the horses. Several of them galloped out the way they had come in.

Boabdil launched himself into the tumult with claws outstretched. He became a living burr to sting the steeds into wild panic. Haroun ben Hasan used the sheathed Sword of Solomon like a club to swat horses and riders both until it was knocked from his hands and sent spinning to the far end of the hall. Master Basim popped himself in and out of sight right in front of the desert riders, wearing a face ugly enough to make three horses throw their men and to cause one exquisite black stallion to turn snowy white from muzzle to fetlocks.

The nobles, feeling their sultan's eye upon them, did what damage they could with the table cutlery. As for the sultan's own guards, they were the only ones present with any real weapons to hand. However, in view of the harm their weapons might do to innocents, given the close quarters and the confused struggles of horsemen and guests, they chose to defend their lord rather than to attack his enemies. Prince Masud himself made a stand with them, though to be truthful his posture looked more like a slouch than a stand.

"My men, let us away!" shouted Malak. He had boosted himself up behind one of his picked riders and now waved his sword high to rally them all. "We go, but we do not flee! We depart, but we shall return to wipe these brazen fools from the face of the earth!" This said, he clapped his heels to the horse's flanks.

It was not a wise move, for at that very instant the horse's original rider likewise gave the noble beast a pair of healthy kicks. The horse did not expect or appreciate so much encouragement. He let out an offended whinny and reared up, pawing the air. Still waving his sword about, Malak had only the most fragile of grips on his man. The horse's show of temper caused him to slip from its rump and land once more atop Lord Reza.

Lord Reza pummeled him viciously in the ribs with an ivory marmalade spoon before another of the desert riders could swoop in and scoop up his assaulted lord. Malak the Murderous made his exit from the banqueting hall slung across the front of his subject's saddle like a sack of couscous. Those riders who had been unhorsed vaulted up to ride double behind their more fortunate comrades and the whole herd of them stampeded away.

The last echo of retreating hoofbeats had barely faded from the air when there was a shimmer of rainbow light, a delicate chime of silver bells, and the genies Tamar and Khalid materialized before the dishevelled company.

"I apologize for our lateness," Khalid said graciously. "Did we miss anything?"

"Only the doom of my entire realm and all I hold dear!" the sultan cried. Distraught, he dashed from the chamber. He was swiftly followed by his guards, his nobles, his son, his daughter, her husband, the major-domo, the musicians, the servants, and the gardener's boy, all of them calling out vain words of comfort.

Tamar observed the wreckage of Boabdil's birthday feast. She gave her beloved a sharp nudge in the arm. "You see? I *told* you not to spend so much time fussing over your turban. We have missed dessert."

Boabdil came picking his way primly through the flotsam and jetsam of the riders' visit. "We had best go after them," he said. "Our friend, Haroun ben Hasan, is in dire need of your help, the sooner the better."

"At once!" Khalid exclaimed. He picked up the cat and swept from the hall in the form of a whirlwind, with Tamar and Master Basim following after.

"Wait!" Hafiz exclaimed, creeping out from beneath his divan. He trotted to the doorway. "You forgot something!"

Prince Rashid slowly crawled back into the light as well. "Baby," he sneered. (The honeycakes were only a distant memory.) "My father too has forgotten me here, but you do not hear me whimpering after him like a newborn puppy."

Hafiz stuck out his tongue at the young prince. "I

do not mean that my father forgot *me,*" he replied loftily.

"Oh?" Rashid could make even the smallest word sound like: *You are a liar.*

"What he forgot," Hafiz went on, "is *this.*"

By the perfumed flames of the oil lamps, the Sword of Solomon glittered in Hafiz ben Haroun's chubby hands.

CHAPTER TWENTY-TWO

"Let's me see that," Prince Rashid commanded, reaching for the Sword.

"No!" Hafiz hugged it protectively to his chest and turned away from his former playmate. "I must bring it back to Father."

"Why?" The young prince's lip curled. "He is too much of a coward to use it."

"What!" Hafiz went pale. "How can you say such things?"

"I will say it again: He is a coward. He was too great a coward to use the Sword to slay Malak the Murderous. He is afraid of Malak and his desert hordes, your father!"

Hafiz looked ready to spit horseshoe nails. "Fool! He did not use the Sword against the upstart Malak because he *could* not use it. It is stuck in this scabbard through some evil spell. You saw that for yourself—*everyone* saw it!"

"Bah! What a lame excuse. He only *pretended* that he could not draw the blade. Your father is a coward *and* a bad actor." Prince Rashid sounded convinced that his opinion was fact.

"My father is *not* a coward," Hafiz said through clenched teeth. "He has fought battles and won kingdoms for all of our uncles. Is this the work of a coward? Not like *your* father. There is a coward if ever there was one! All he does is stay at home and write poetry. Your father is a coward *and* a bad poet!"

"My father is *not* a bad poet!" Rashid shouted. "And anyway, you saw him stand with the guards, protecting Grandfather."

"Ho, ho! He stood with the guards so that the guards could protect him as well." Hafiz scored a point off his opponent with that. "*My* father needs no guards. My father knows how to fight on his own. My father is a hero!"

"Your father *was* a hero," Rashid shot back. Not even honeycake could save matters now. "People can change; my father says so in many of his finest poems. The poor farmer can become a king, the great king can become a beggar, and your father has become a coward! He is scared to be the great champion of our realm. He fears that one day he will meet a man who carries a blade of even greater magic than the Sword of Solomon. That was why he pretended that the Sword of Solomon is useless: He wants to give up."

"My father never gives up!" Hafiz's face was now the same shade as an infant eggplant. "If you do not believe your eyes, believe your hands: *You* try to draw the Sword!"

And Hafiz offered the Sword of Solomon to Prince Rashid.

The young prince weighed the blade across his palms before taking a steady grip on hilt and scabbard and trying to free the enchanted steel. The Sword would not budge. He pursed his lips and gave it another pull. Nothing happened. Hafiz folded his arms and smirked. Rashid set his jaw, wedged the bottom of the scabbard between his feet, and with all his might he tried pulling the Sword upward with both hands.

Hafiz fell over on the messy floor and rolled back and forth, his body shaking with laughter.

"This—this is a trick," Rashid panted. He pounded Sword and sheath fiercely against the edge of the feasting table. He broke off a chunk of expensive inlaid wood, but did not even loosen the Sword enough to make it rattle.

"It is not a trick," Hafiz replied, still chortling. "It is as you see: The Sword is stuck. Probably there is some unknown enchantment set upon the scabbard. Father will have Khalid and Tamar fix it and—"

"There is no enchantment!" Prince Rashid bellowed. "It is only a coward's trick. More likely this scabbard has some sort of hidden catch to hold the Sword until your father decides it is safe for him to draw it again."

Hafiz gave a weary sigh. "Rashid, you are as stubborn as a camel with a belly full of thistles. What will it take to prove to you that there is no trick at work here?"

"Nothing you can say will persuade me."

"Then what can I *do* to change your mind?"

For a time both boys were lost in thought, pondering this question. Then Rashid brightened. "I know!" He snapped his fingers. "Let us both at once try to pull the Sword free. If we combine our strength then there is no clasp, however cleverly made, that can hold fast against us. It will break and the Sword will be released."

Hafiz did not look hopeful. "My father is a very strong man. Do you really think that we are stronger than he?"

"Of course we are." Once more Prince Rashid had convinced himself. "We are two and he is only one. It makes sense."

"Yes, but—"

"—unless you are willing to admit that there is no

enchantment upon this blade and that your father was just pretending that the Sword could not be drawn?" Rashid lifted one eyebrow and gave Hafiz a penetrating look.

Hafiz sighed and shrugged. "Oh, very well. What harm can it do to try?"

Rashid laid the Sword on the tabletop. "You hold the sheath, I hold the hilt, and when I give the word, we pull."

They tried it that way. It was not a success.

They tried it several other ways with unsatisfactory results.

"*Now* do you believe that there is a wicked enchantment on the Sword?" Hafiz demanded, wiping sweat from his brow.

Prince Rashid did not answer. He was studying the Sword with rapt attention, contemplating every minute detail of the scabbard's elaborate decoration. Finally he said, "I am a fool."

"I am glad we agree on something," Hafiz commented.

"I am seven different kinds of fool!" Rashid smacked his fist into his open palm. "My father has told me a thousand poetic tales of high adventure and great deeds, and in every last one the hero *never* wins by brute strength, but by cleverness. While other men squander their powers trying to batter their way into a sealed fortress, the hero watches the comings and goings of ants to discover the secret passageway. While giants roar that they can drink the ocean dry, the hero eats an orange and convinces them that he has devoured the sun."

Hafiz glanced at the Sword, still lying unchanged on the tabletop. "I do not see how eating an orange will help us."

"We have been going about it all wrong, Hafiz. Do you think this scabbard was made so intricately only for the sake of beauty?" Hafiz did not know what to say to this, so Rashid continued: "All of those curls and twists and twinings! Any one might hide the secret catch that holds the Sword imprisoned."

Hafiz's eyes grew huge as Rashid's inspiration took hold of him as well. "And the gems!" he breathed. "Do you think that one of them might conceal it instead?" He had completely forgotten that he was not supposed to believe in the hidden catch.

Rashid spread his hands. "There is but one way to find out." With the first goodwill between them since their quarrel, the boys pounced on the Sword.

They were like little mice, their fingers prying and pawing into each nook and cranny in the scabbard's complex goldwork. They ran their hands over every sapphire chip, every cluster of emeralds. Nothing wiggled. Nothing clicked. Nothing let the Sword of Solomon go free.

Nothing . . .

"I give up," said Prince Rashid. He gave the Sword on the tabletop a venomous glare.

"So do I," Hafiz agreed. "There is such a thing as a secret that hides itself too well."

"They say that King Solomon was the wisest of men, but this is not very wise. What good is it to own a Sword that lets you defeat all your enemies if you can not get the stupid thing *out*? By the time King Solomon could remember how to draw this blade, his foes would have swarmed all over his kingdom!"

Hafiz leaned his elbows on the table and rested his chin in his hands. "If I were the magician who made this weapon for King Solomon, I would have hidden the catch, but in a place that was easy to recall. That big ruby, for instance."

"What big ruby?"

"The big ruby in the dragon's belly. But you said it wouldn't move."

Rashid frowned. "I never said that. I said the big *sapphire* would not move. I never touched that ruby. I thought you checked it."

Hafiz's frown mirrored Rashid's. "*I* never checked it. It is so large, so obvious, I thought you had examined it already."

"But I—" The words died on Rashid's lips. The boys stared at each other for three breaths, then both let loose a yelp of excitement and grabbed for the great ruby at precisely the same time.

And at precisely the same time their hands slid over the smooth surface of the gem in much the same manner as Haroun ben Hasan's hand had once slid over the smooth surface of a certain lamp.

The floor of the banqueting hall shook. A deep-throated rumbling rushed up from the very heart of the world. The last few bits of ornamental plaster shivered loose from the ceiling. The long table shuddered as a steaming crack zig-zagged its way from one end of the unfortunate piece of furniture to the other. It collapsed in a crash of broken dishes, crushed gold goblets, and splinters.

The Sword of Solomon did not fall. It floated in midair between the two dumbstruck boys. An eerie, bilious glow pulsed and sizzled all around the enchanted blade. It emanated entirely from the great dragon's-belly ruby. Shadows swirled beneath the surface of the jewel and from its depths came the sound of laughter that was more like the grinding of old bones.

Before their goggling eyes and gaping mouths, a slow, sinuous serpentine of charry smoke oozed from the golden dragon's maw. It spiralled upward, ever faster, until a gigantic shadow the color of despair loomed above the boys. Ashes blew from the formless hulk, flying full in the boys' faces, stinging their eyes shut and making them cough. Blindly they groped for a loose fold of their turbans through which they might breathe easier, but a fresh roar of evil laughter bowled the pair of them head over heels all the way to the chamber door. There they smacked into the doorposts and were still.

The laughter faded to muddy chuckles. Hafiz was the first to dare open his eyes. He promptly closed them again. "I must have knocked my head badly," he muttered. "If I were well, I could not possibly be seeing anything *that* ugly."

"Alas, my brother," came Prince Rashid's trembling voice. "If that is so, I must have broken my skull in half because I see it too."

Ugly. Such a small word, yet in ordinary circumstances more than enough to describe sights not pleasing to the eye. Yet in this case, *ugly* was far too small a word, and wholly inadequate to the task before it. If it were any consolation to the poor, overwhelmed word, its comrades *hideous*, *repulsive*, and *loathsome* also had to leave the field in defeat.

What the boys now saw before them was the creature that had made his entrance wrapped in that stinging shroud of ashes. His muscular body was the ghastly color of a dead chicken that has been plucked and then forgotten in the sun for seven days. All he wore was a filthy blue loincloth and a wide leather belt that displayed an uncomfortably large number of bloodflecked daggers, maces, clubs, morningstars, and one lonely scimitar big enough to slice the heads from an entire troop of cavalry at once. Most of these weapons were decorated with the bones of beasts and men. Tufts of greenish-black hair bristled from his skull like growths upon an untended grave. Eyes, nose, mouth, and every crease and wrinkle of his face looked as if they had been gouged out by some blind, vindictive god armed with a blunt trowel and a peculiar sense of humor.

He had fangs and talons too. Somehow, when taken along with the rest of him, fangs and talons were commonplace, almost comforting, familiar things. They were nowhere near as frightening as they would have been on another genie.

For he was a genie, of that there was no need for second opinions. Rashid knew it, whose father's poems often sang of such magical creatures. Hafiz knew it, who had grown up in the company of Khalid, Tamar, and the silent Master Basim. And knowing this, the boys likewise knew that they would have to tread very, very cautiously.

Hafiz cleared his throat. "H—Hail, O Genie," he faltered.

"*What do you want?*" the monster roared, glaring at him with eyes like two cauldrons of hellfire.

"I—"

Hafiz did not get the chance to finish his sentence. A titanic paw fell upon him, its yellow claws plucking him from the floor and dangling him by the neck of his tunic. "Never mind what you want," the genie boomed. "Unless it be your death, you will not get it from me."

"Let him go!" Prince Rashid jumped forward, a large chunk of shattered table in his hands. Boldly he drubbed the genie's toes, all the time repeating his demand for Hafiz's immediate release.

For his pains, he found himself dangling from the claw-tips of the genie's other hand. "One fat and one thin," the monster mused. The carrion reek of his breath in their faces turned the boys' complexions pasty. "Shall I eat you both to see who makes the louder crunch or shall I drop you both at once to see who makes the juicier splat?"

"You shall do nothing of the sort!" Thanks to an excellent education as a royal princeling, Rashid was able to maintain a look of stern dignity even when dangling from a terrible height at the end of a genie's claws.

"No?" The creature was amused. "Are you a prophet or a fool?"

"Neither," Rashid replied. "I am your Master!"

The genie laughed. "You are a fine liar! I enjoy a good lie. Tell me another and I will give you a head-start. You may try to run away and save yourself while I devour your companion. I, Azem, swear this!"

"I am no liar, and I know the rules that govern your kind," Rashid replied.

"So do I!" Hafiz piped up. "And if Rashid is your Master, you must give him three wishes. You do not dare try to harm him."

"That is so . . . *if*, as you say, he is my Master." Azem turned a baleful eye upon Hafiz. "On the other hand, there is nothing to prevent me from doing what I please with you."

"Unless *he* is your Master," Rashid spoke up.

"Eh?" The genie had eyebrows like a pair of hedgehogs. Now they looked as if they were riding a teeter-totter.

The longer he remained uneaten, the more confidence Hafiz gained. "Be reasonable, O Azem," he said. "We all know you were imprisoned in yonder great ruby adorning the Sword of Solomon."

Azem winced. "Speak not that hated name of power!"

"Nor can any of us here deny that *someone* freed you from it," Rashid put in at the monster's other ear. "Genies can never free themselves."

"Whoever freed you is your Master, and we are the only ones here," Hafiz concluded. "Therefore one of us is entitled to three wishes and I promise you, if it is I who am your Master, I shall use my first wish to protect my dearest friend Prince Rashid ben Masud by making you send yourself to the deepest pit of Eblis!"

"That is not a pleasant place," Azem remarked thoughtfully. "Not even for one such as I."

"Bear that in mind, then," said Rashid, "for if I am your Master, I too vow that I shall use my first wish in exactly the same way as my best friend in all the world, Hafiz ben Haroun."

Reluctantly, with many a black look and many a grumble and growl, Azem set the boys safely back on the floor. "Hail, O Master," he mumbled. "Name your wish, for I will grant it. Yes, three wishes and no more I will grant you. *However!* Not one of these . . . Mmph. How did it go again? It has been too long. Ah! Now I remember. *However!* Not one of these may ask for more wishes. If these terms please you then by them I am your slave." He hooked his thumbs into his belt and waited.

After a time of silence, the genie bellowed, "*Well?* Speak up! I have been a prisoner of that scabbard for centuries beyond your puny powers of reckoning. There is nothing I desire more than to discharge my obligations to you and be on my way. There is much that I would be doing in this world."

"Like—like what?" Hafiz asked.

Azem blew a typhoon of a snort from his hairy nostrils. "If you must know, I would like to see my family."

"*You* have a family?" Rashid had not yet studied diplomacy, so his question did not come out as politely as it might.

"Yes, *I* have a family!" The genie mimicked Rashid's disbelief nastily. "A son. His name is Gamal. I had great hopes for him. Naturally he could never hope to be as evil as I—some say I am half ifrit, you know," he said modestly.

"Half ifrit?" Rashid abruptly lost more than half his

boldness. "But—but an ifrit is a demonic spirit that obeys no rules save the rule of destruction!" His father's poems sang of genies and ifrits and what a mortal might expect from either, but said nothing about what to do when confronted with a half-and-half creature like Azem.

"That is so," Azem agreed. "Therefore you would do well to make your wishes quickly and send me on my way. In fact, you would do even better to give up your wishes before I decide that I am feeling more ifritish today and tear you to pieces where you stand."

"Y—yes, of course, sorry to have detained you. I wish—" Rashid began.

"He wishes nothing!" Hafiz snapped, stepping between his friend and the monster. The plump boy rested his hands on his hips and stared up into Azem's face unafraid. "Genies cheat," he announced "Or try to. It is nothing personal. It is their duty to attempt to trick their mortal masters into wasting wishes; tradition demands it. You can not fool me about such things: I know genies. My father was the master of a great genie, Khalid. What is more, no matter how evil your son Gamal was, he was no match for my father, the great hero, Haroun ben Hasan! I know your son's name well, for my father often told me how he and he alone defeated and imprisoned Gamal as easily as swatting a fly."

Rashid nudged Hafiz and whispered, "But I heard it was the cat Boab—"

Hafiz gave him back the nudge with interest. "Shush!" he hissed. "He wants us to fear him. I want him to fear *us*."

Rashid stole a peek at Azem's expression. "I do not think he looks afraid. I think he looks angry." He flashed the genie a sickly smile and babbled, "Certainly Lord Haroun would never have treated Gamal so badly if he had known he was *your* son, O Azem!"

Hafiz rolled his eyes. The information about Azem's ifrit blood had worked an awful transformation in the young prince. His courage was dribbling out of him like meal from a mouse-nibbled sack. "Do not apologize to him, you idiot," he snarled under his breath. "If you are his Master, it is he who should fear you!"

"But what if I am not his Master? Once he has granted you your wishes he will be free. Free to come back and—" Rashid groaned at the possibilities.

"Now you listen to me—" Hafiz began, poking his friend repeatedly in the center of his chest. He was going to give Rashid a good, sensible lecture, such as his mother used to give him in the days before Aminah took up all her time. Before he could do so, he noticed the strange look Rashid was giving him.

Or, to be precise, his finger.

"Why is your fingertip glowing red?" the prince asked.

"What? Where?"

"There, said Rashid, and pointed at the shining digit with a finger that was just as red, just as glowing.

The boys stared down at their transformed fingers, then at one another, then at Azem. The genie was doing his own share of staring too.

"Merciless Powers," he marvelled. "Can it be?" He threw back his head and yowled. Having relieved his feelings, he took a deep breath, cleared his throat, and said, "I hope you will not make me repeat my oath of service."

"Why would you need to repeat it?" asked Rashid.

"Because the evidence is plain to see for anyone with half an eye," the genie replied. "The taint of the jewel that held me clings too you both, which means—"

"—which means we *both* must have rubbed the great ruby at the same time, and we are *both* his

Masters, and we *both* get three wishes!" Hafiz shouted, overjoyed. He seized Rashid's hands and the two of them did a merry jig.

Azem opened his mouth, then closed it without saying a word. A thin half-smile tugged his face into an even more stomach-churning mask. Silent, he merely bowed low.

"If we are *both* his Masters, he can not harm either one of us!" Rashid cried.

"And all we need to do to stay safe forever is to never use our last wishes!" Hafiz was jubilant. He had begun to regret mentioning his father's role in defeating Azem's son.

"What are you going to wish for?"

"I don't know. You go first."

"No, you. Your family is used to genies. I want to see how it should be done. Go ahead," Rashid urged.

"My *parents* are the ones who know such things," Hafiz replied. "They never taught me how to get the most from your wishes. Maybe we should ask them." He bent over to pick up the Sword, which by now no longer hovered in midair but had fallen noiselessly amid the rubble of Boabdil's feast.

A huge hand fell between Hafiz and the Sword. Hafiz looked up to see Azem attempting an expression of kindness that did not suit him at all.

"Oh, my poor young Master!" The genie clucked his tongue. "So much bravery, such spirit, and yet you run like an infant to your mother's skirts for something as trifling as how to make a wish? Forgive me for saying so, but I never thought you were a coward."

"Who are you calling a coward?" Hafiz puffed up like Boabdil in a bad mood. "Do so again and I will wish you away to the deepest—!"

"—pit of Eblis," Azem finished for him. "I know.

Though by the time you have asked your mama's permission, you might have changed your mind."

"I will not ask my mother's permission to use my wishes!" Hafiz stamped his foot. "I can make my wishes myself. I just want to use them the very best way possible."

"An admirable ambition, Gracious Lord." Azem laid a hand to his bosom. "Pardon me for ever having doubted you."

"Yes, well . . . Well, all right, I forgive you." Hafiz allowed himself to be mollified. "Now do not rush me."

"Rush you? Ah, nay! All my desire is to help you." The genie made a deep reverence to the boy. "But if I might make a few suggestions?"

"Suggestions?" Hafiz did not trust this genie as far as he could throw him, which was not far at all.

"You need not take them. I offer them merely as a courtesy."

Rashid laid a hand on Hafiz's arm. "Let him speak. It can not hurt us to hear him out. He has the experience of centuries behind him."

"He might also have a dagger behind him, hungering for our backs," Hafiz returned. "But you are right; let us see what he has to say." He gave the genie a magnanimous wave and said, very grandly, "You may proceed."

Azem shrank himself to a size where he was able to prostrate himself at the boys' feet. "My lords are most gracious. Why not use your first wish to obtain the wealth of the ages? That is a very popular wish with your fellow mortals."

"No," said Rashid almost immediately. "We are already rich enough." Hafiz bobbed his head in agreement.

"Well, then, why not wish for power?" the genie suggested. "I could make each of you a great king, with vast empires to rule and numerous armies to send to their deaths. That would be fun."

This time it was Hafiz who shook his head and said, "Rashid is a prince. He shall be sultan someday. Why should he waste a wish getting what is already his to have?"

"And when I am sultan, I shall make Hafiz my Grand Vizier," Rashid stated. It was a promise he had made to his friend in the days before their quarrel. Now the quarrel was forgotten and the promise remembered. "That should be more than enough power for anyone."

"Certainly enough for me," Hafiz concluded. "No, no, we shall not waste our wishes thus."

Azem's brows darkened and the many bones decorating his belt rattled together in sinister cacaphony, but he kept his voice mild. "Such wisdom, so young," he breathed. "All right. Those mortals who already possess power and riches next most often wish for the love of beautiful women."

Almost at once the boys responded with horror: "*Girls?* Ugh!" From there they proceeded to explain to Azem that girls were silly, useless, giggly pests at best. They did not see the point to them.

The genie covered his eyes with one hand and sighed. "So young indeed," he muttered. He dropped the hand and said, "Since my suggestions come to naught with you, I will instead tell you the great secret to the making of the very best wishes, use it how you will. It is simple: Take your life-as-it-should-be and lay it over your life-as-it-is like a veil. Where the two do not match, where as-it-should-be lies draped across a gaping hole in as-it-is, *that* is where to fit your wishes!"

"Like—like patches on an old cloak?" Hafiz asked.

"Precisely."

Hafiz pondered Azem's words. "Very helpful," he admitted.

"Very helpful," Rashid echoed. He pressed his lips together hard. "Which is why I do not trust him. Ifrits are *never* helpful."

"I am only half an ifrit," Azem prompted. "And the sooner you make your wishes, the sooner I shall be free."

"I *still* do not trust him," Rashid maintained.

"Neither do I." Hafiz shrugged. "But it is not as if he is encouraging us to wish for anything dangerous. I will still have two wishes left to set things right." He closed his eyes and lost himself in thought.

"I do not know about this." Rashid shook his head. He distrusted Azem mightily, yet at the same time he was burning to use his own wishes. And there was good, sound advice behind Azem's words. If Rashid lay his own veil of life-as-it-should-be over his life-as-it-is, there was one particular hole that he would like to patch over more than any other.

My father is *a hero!* he thought. *He* is! *Or he would be, if he had the chance. I would give him that chance.* He glanced at Hafiz, still rapt in concentration. *I will see how his wish turns out. Only if it goes well will I make mine.*

Hafiz opened his eyes. "I have decided," he announced. "I know the one thing that would improve my life the most. I wish that my parents would come to their senses and pay attention to *me* again."

Azem clapped his hands together with a report like boulders plunging into the sea. "*Hearkening and obedience!*"

On a terrace overlooking one of the loveliest palace gardens, Boabdil sat on the marble railing and gazed up at the winking stars. "I do not know why everyone had to make such a fuss over that rude desert lord," he said. "I grant you, my birthday feast was much livelier than last year, thanks to him, but what if his horsemen had trampled my presents?"

"Mmmph," said Master Basim meaningfully. He pointed to his mouth.

"Haroun ben Hasan is a great man, with or without the Sword of Solomon," the cat went on. "Its loss is not so great a tragedy as he thinks. He can rally the sultan's troops and defeat Malak the Murderous in a fair fight. Moreover, he has but to send word to the sultan's many sons and they will come to their father's aid with the armies of their own realms. Malak and his scruffy horde will be squashed beneath them like bugs."

"Mmmph!" Master Basim repeated, a trifle louder.

"Oh, I know that the sultan's other sons dwell far from here, but if we ask Khalid and Tamar nicely to transport one or two spare armies here by magic, then—"

"*Mmmph!*" This time Master Basim caused a blast of lightning to play over his mouth while blazing scarlet arrows materialized from thin air to point at it from either side.

The cat lifted his chin and smiled. "There is no need to shout," he said. "I remember my promise." He cleared his throat and pronounced: "I wish that my dear friend, Master Basim, might have his voice restored to him exactly as it was before I wished it away."

There was a sound like the badly oiled hinges of a long-buried treasure room turning in screechy protest in their sockets. The ancient genie's lips slowly parted, and from the depths of his chest came the raspy words, "Heark—Heark—*Hearkening and obedience!* Yaaaaaheeeeeee!"

Boabdil calmly observed the genie's reaction to having his voice restored, then remarked, "Really, Master

Basim, turning cartwheels at your age? And not even a word of thanks for me. Tsk-tsk. What would the children think?"

Master Basim paused in mid-somersault. "The children," he murmured. The image of Hafiz trying to reach the Sword of Solomon winked through his mind. "The Sword . . . O Cat, we must hurry! There is a great evil endangering us all!"

"You too?" Boabdil licked one paw, unruffled. "I would think that a genie of your years would not be thrown into such a panic by the threats of a scrawny desert lordling like Malak. I have just explained that it matters not if we have the Sword of Solomon in our service or—"

Master Basim snatched the cat from the terrace railing and held him by the scruff of his neck at eye level. "Where is it?" he demanded. "Where is the Sword of Solomon?"

Boabdil took a swipe at the genie's nose and missed. "How would I know?" he growled. "Put me down."

Master Basim did not seem to hear the order. "We must find it," he said. "At once! Oh, a thousand curses on the day that ever unearthed that accursed thing!"

"Had I but known what gibberish you would spout, I would have postponed returning your voice to you until doomsday," Boabdil said evenly, despite his position.

"Doomsday may be upon us even as we speak," Master Basim returned. "Follow me!" And he dashed off with the cat still swinging by the loose folds of neck fur in his grasp.

"As soon as he comes back to his senses," Boabdil told the air, "I am going to bite him."

* * *

"Well?" Hafiz asked Rashid.

"Well what?" his friend replied, avoiding the boy's eyes.

"I made my first wish. Aren't you going to make yours?"

"I am thinking it over," Rashid said. It was not all a lie.

"Take all the time you need," Azem put in. He was stretched out on his belly, idly playing with the bits and pieces of the fallen ceiling, using his magic to put them back together like a gigantic jigsaw puzzle. "But a word of caution to you both, my young Masters: A genie is a prize to be most carefully guarded. So long as I owe you any wishes, I must cling to the object that has housed me all these centuries. Now if it should happen that *another* mortal finds that object and does what is needful to free me, our contract is instantly broken—nay, as shattered as this ceiling." His hairy-backed hand swept over the pieces of plaster before him. "And there is nothing any one of us may do to end that."

"*I* can do something about it," Rashid said. He picked up the Sword of Solomon, still sheathed, and declared, "I shall put this somewhere safe until I am ready to make my first wish. Then we need not worry about someone else finding it and I need not feel rushed." He turned on his heel and started from the hall.

"Wait!" cried Hafiz. "What if my father needs—?"

The question went unasked, for in that exact moment, Prince Rashid let out a small yelp of pain as the Sword of Solomon slipped from its scabbard as slickly as if someone had buttered the blade and fell, hilt first, on his foot.

With an explanation of surprise, Hafiz pounced on the freed Sword. "A miracle!" He picked it up in both hands and stared down the length of the glittering enchanted steel.

"With my compliments," Azem said.

"You freed the blade?" Hafiz knew enough of genies to know that they did not *give* mortals anything for free but difficulties, if they could help it. Khalid and Tamar were the exceptions that proved the rule.

Azem said nothing, but looked like the very spirit and image of unselfish generosity.

Before Hafiz could question him more closely, there came the sound of running feet and his parents dashed into the ruined banquet hall. So intent were they on Hafiz that they raced past Rashid, still holding the empty scabbard, as if he were invisible. The young prince took advantage of their distraction to stow the sheath under the mattress of an upended divan and sit on it.

Truly, so singleminded were Haroun and the Princess Nur that they hardly saw the naked Sword itself. They flung themselves upon their son with no regard for the keen blade. If Hafiz had not been nimble-minded enough to toss the Sword behind him, he might have been covered with his parents' blood rather than the storm of kisses now pelting down upon him.

"Oh my darling son! My dearest, dearest child!" Nur sobbed, hugging him close.

"Oh my beloved Hafiz, apple of my eye, hope of my house, ruler of my heart!" Haroun blubbered, fighting his wife for the right to embrace the boy.

"Have you seen proof enough of my powers?" Azem whispered in Rashid's ear.

The prince jerked like a hooked fish, taken completely by surprise. The genie had vanished from his place beside the shattered table and reappeared in doll-size on Rashid's shoulder, all in the time it took for Nur to cry out that first "Oh!"

"Well?" Azem persisted, taking hold of Rashid's earlobe. "Could your friend ask for more attention from his parents?"

"No, he could not." Rashid was better than satisfied with the quality of Azem's powers. "Therefore, O Azem, grant me my first wish as perfectly as you have granted his: I wish that my father, Prince Masud, might be the greatest, the most acclaimed, and the best beloved hero this realm has ever known!"

"Hearkening and obedience," the genie hissed in the prince's ear.

It might have been his imagination, but Prince Rashid was almost positive that he likewise heard the genie chuckle darkly, somewhere between the words *hearkening* and *obedience*. However, when he turned his head to see if there was any evidence of such unsuitable mirth on the genie's face, Azem was gone.

Haroun and Nur were still there, of course, and still showering their son with tears and kisses.

If Azem has fulfilled my first wish only half so well, Rashid thought, *I shall be more than pleased.*

"Oh my pet," my treasure, my gift!" Nur howled, forcing Hafiz's head to her bosom. Struggle as he might, Hafiz was trapped.

Of course, there is such a thing as fulfilling a wish too *well,* Rashid reflected. *Poor Hafiz looks half smothered.* His friend looked so ridiculous, buried in his parents' vigorous embraces, that Rashid could not help laughing out loud.

At once he felt their eyes upon him. They were unfriendly eyes. In all his short life, Rashid had never seen so much wrath directed at his own small self. It was a sobering experience. Usually the princess, his aunt, treated him with tenderness in all things. In fact, since he had no mother, she had done as much as he permitted her to supply the feminine attentions his life lacked.

Now she was glowering at him with the eyes of a tiger, and a tiger with absolutely no maternal inclinations whatsoever.

"*You*," Nur snarled. Rashid felt the little hairs on the back of his neck prickle. "There you are, you unspeakable boy!"

"Yes, *there* you are, you atrocious child!" Haroun put in. The two of them released a thoroughly bewildered Hafiz in order to point accusing fingers at Rashid.

"But—but Aunt Nur, what have I done?" Rashid stammered.

"How dare you ask that, you serpent?" Nur ground her teeth together loudly enough to set Rashid's own teeth on edge. "How dare you ask that after the way you have treated my own, my darling, my adored son Hafiz?"

"I—I—" Now Rashid was really nervous. He knew he had not been the best of friends with Hafiz of late, but that had all been mended. In the way of all children he believed that once a quarrel was settled, it was forgotten.

Clearly it was not forgotten by older, wiser grown-ups.

"Ah, if I but had the Sword of Solomon in my hands, I would make you pay for how you have mistreated my only son!" Haroun thundered, shaking his fist at Rashid.

"Mother, Father, what are you saying?" Hafiz peeped, very much jangled and jarred by this display of overwhelming love and unreasoning rage. "Rashid and I are friends again! There is no need to—"

"Friends " Nur echoed. She gave a bitter laugh. "Would a friend have treated you so? Oh, we know all about it, my precious one! Do not think that we were blind or deaf to how badly that—that silk-clad *ape* hurt your dear, dear feelings. Well, we shall not tolerate it any longer! From now on, if he says so much as one word to you that is not worthy of your perfect ears, he will have to answer to *us*!"

"Prince or no prince," Haroun added.

"But I do not want you to do that," Hafiz protested. "Rashid is my friend. If we have a fight, we can make it up between us."

"Not anymore." Haroun was smug as he patted his son on the back.

"You will never be without our complete attention and devotion again," Nur declared.

"You will never be out of our *sight* again," her husband corrected. "Where you go, we go."

"Always," Nur concluded, pulling Hafiz back into her bosom.

Hafiz was beginning to squirm. Azem had delivered far more than he had bargained for when he made that wish. Although he liked having his parents' attention, he thought it might be best for all of them if they would take a little of it elsewhere. Thus it was that he pushed himself free of his mother's suffocating hold and suggested, "You mean always, except when you are taking care of my dear sister Aminah. Don't you?"

"Oh, never mind about her." Nur made a dismissive gesture.

"Yes, never mind," Haroun repeated. "She is no longer our concern. She is gone."

"Vanished."

"Disappeared."

"We have no clue as to where she might be."

"We have searched the whole palace and the gardens too."

"Yes," said Nur, smiling brightly. "She is no longer here. She is—" The smile began to wobble. "She is—" One corner of it caved in completely. "She is—" The whole smile snapped into an expression of total grief, dismay, and realization. "*My baby is gone!*"

And Nur collapsed in tempests of tears just as Master Basim came striding into the room, a fresh bitemark on his thumb and a slightly ruffled Boabdil trotting at his heels.

CHAPTER TWENTY-THREE

In the palace of the sultan, pandemonium reigned. Torches flared. Servants ran. Guards trooped double-time through the halls. Women shrieked. Nobles hastened from room to room, chattering among themselves like monkeys gone mad. Every light that could be kindled blazed from walls and ceilings and the hands of uncountable search parties until the whole palace looked as if it were engulfed in flames.

And in spite of all this, parents still expected children to stay in their beds and sleep.

Hafiz ben Haroun hugged the corridor shadows and peered around the swollen belly of a towering blue-and-white porcelain vase. He had sneaked out of his bed, out of his room, and all the way from one wing of the palace to the other, but it looked as if this was as far as he was going to get without being stopped. The hallway was a swarm of gibbering adults, the door that was his goal lay beyond them. He sighed and crouched on the floor, wrapping his hooded cloak more closely around him. He had taken it from his father's chest and there was enough cloth to it to conceal three boys his size.

He only needed enough to conceal himself and the Sword.

"I must reach Rashid," Hafiz grumbled under his breath. "I *must*."

"Then get up and go to him," said the cat.

Hafiz startled, sending the hood of his cloak tumbling down over his eyes. He pulled it back and saw Boabdil sitting close beside him, all four paws in tight. "Where did you come from?"

"You speak as if I do not have the freedom to be anywhere I like," the cat replied. "On the contrary, it is the birthright of all cats. To tell you the truth, I grew tired of the uproar. It seems to be everywhere. All the palace is set on ear." He yawned, then added, "And it is all your fault."

"It is not!" Hafiz blushed; even while he denied the accusation, he knew it to be true. Or at least partly so. "I never wished for my sister to vanish."

"Wished?" The cat's ears perked up. "What is this talk of wishes?"

"*Wanted*," Hafiz corrected himself hastily. "I never *wanted* anything to happen to Aminah."

"I see." Boabdil looked wise. "For a moment there, I thought I caught a sniff of magic at work. But where would a mere kitten like you ever get his paws on magic?" He gave the boy a grin that was too sweet to come from any cat worthy of his whiskers. It was a grin that as good as said: *If you want to fool me, you are going to have to do better than that.*

Hafiz knew when he was beaten. He petted Boabdil's head, then said, "Look." He flicked away one corner of his cloak to show the cat the Sword beneath.

"How did you get that gewgaw free of its sheath?" Boabdil asked.

"If you can help me sneak into Rashid's rooms, I will tell you. We both will. It is his tale as well as mine," Hafiz replied.

"Nothing simpler." The cat stood up, arched his back, spread his forepaws one by one, then marched into the midst of the brouhaha in the hall and announced, "His Merciful Majesty the Sultan commands that all those servants loyal to the throne and devoted to keeping their heads on their shoulders report to my Lord Haroun ben Hasan at once!"

The stampede that followed came very near to trampling the messenger into a fuzzy blot on the carpet. In no time at all, the hallway leading to prince Rashid's rooms was clear.

"Now why did I not think of that?" Hafiz wondered aloud.

"It would have done you no good if you had thought of it," Boabdil told him. "Adults will sooner listen to a cat then to a child."

"I am not a child!" Hafiz stamped his foot. "I hold the Sword of Solomon!" He shook the blade for emphasis.

It went without saying that the son's posturings had as little effect on Boabdil as the father's. He was almost another cat entirely from the scrawny stray that had accidentally rubbed against Khalid's lamp in the alley. Years of good living had given him more sense of self-possession than a Roman emperor, and better table manners.

"You hold the Sword of Solomon only until some grownup tells you to put it down before you hurt yourself," the cat drawled. He turned his tail on the boy and walked gracefully down the hall, pausing only to glance back and inquire, "Did you want to see Prince Rashid or not?"

The way to the young prince's rooms was unguarded. They found Rashid's sleeping chamber with ease. Here at least was one room in all the palace where darkness ruled. Only the silvery veil of moonlight fell upon the shapes within.

"Halt! Who comes?" Rashid himself sat up suddenly from among his cushions and challenged them.

"It is I, Hafiz. Boabdil has come with me. Were you asleep?"

"Who can sleep? Father made me go to bed; that is the only reason I am here."

Hafiz edged his way closer to Rashid's bed, groping in the dark until he felt the downy mattress under his hand. He hopped onto the foot of the bed and repeated, "*Made* you go to bed? Your father? He never *makes* you do anything."

From the floor beside the prince's bed, Boabdil looked up to see a few tiny sparks fly as Rashid fumbled with flint and steel. At last a light struck and caught on the wick of the oil lamp at his elbow. Rashid's long face came into sight wearing a gloomy expression that made it look even longer.

"I know," he said. "But that was before."

"Before what?"

"Before I made my first wish." He flopped over onto his stomach and fished around beneath his pillows until he hauled out the sheath belonging to the Sword of Solomon. Bobadil jumped onto the bed to contemplate Sword and scabbard.

"Wish?" the cat asked pleasantly.

Hafiz sighed. "We might as well tell him, Rashid." So they did. When they were done, the cat made small clucking sounds of pity deep in his throat.

"That explains much. No, that explains all. No wonder the Sword would not come free. The enchantment upon the scabbard must demand that someone free the genie if they wish to free the Sword. It also explains why the Sword and the scabbard existed so far from one another for so long: The disadvantages of having to confront this . . . Azem outweigh the advantages of possessing the power of the blade."

Rashid sucked his lower lip in thought. "But the genie must obey the one who frees him. It is no disadvantage to find yourself the master of the Sword *and* armed with three wishes!"

"*How* much did you say you are enjoying your first wish, my prince?" Boabdil purred.

Rashid's face fell.

"I thought so," said the cat.

"I only wished for my father to be a hero!" the prince cried.

"And I only wished that my parents would pay attention to me," Hafiz chimed in.

"Well, this whole palace knows how well *your* wish turned out, Hafiz," Boabdil said. "But as for Prince Rashid's—"

The prince swung his legs out of bed and threw an extra robe over his nightshift. A brief pause while he twisted his turban into place and he was ready. "Follow me and I will show you," he said in the accents of the tomb. "And bring the Sword." For his part, he picked up the jewelled scabbard and used it to wave them into line after him.

Rashid led Boabdil and Hafiz out of his sleeping chamber through a small door that hid itself behind one of the prince's great wooden clothing chests. It led to a narrow passageway which in turn ended in a deserted room. Here too all was night, but for moonbeams playing over furnishings made for royalty, used by none. The ghosts of many sweet scents drifted through the air.

"This was my mother's chamber," Rashid said, his throat dry. "My father's rooms lie just beyond. Come."

Still using the scabbard as a baton, he motioned them to follow him to the huge double doors across the chamber floor. Threads of brightness outlined them clearly, and the three midnight wanderers were at least four arm's-lengths away when they heard the row from the other side.

Rashid crept right up to the doors and gently pulled the golden handles back no more than a finger-joint's width. Silently he invited Hafiz and Boabdil to spy through the crack.

Hafiz set his eye to the light. The first thing he saw was Rashid's father, Prince Masud. Ah, but not the Prince Masud he knew! Not the jovial, gentle, lazy man who preferred songs to swords and did not care who knew it. This Prince Masud did not loll upon his divan, nibbling grapes and pondering rhymes.

This Prince Masud was on his feet, swaggering back and forth before a terrified manservant who hung cringing from the fists of two brawny guardsmen. This Prince Masud paused every time he passed in front of the shaking servant, paused just long enough to give the pathetic fellow a resounding slap across the face. This Prince Masud drew his dagger and used it to feint at his captive's eyes just to watch him squirm, all the while demanding that the man confess that he knew the whereabouts of the Lady Aminah. This Prince Masud marched and preened and bellowed and hit the helpless and blustered and bullied and—

"O Merciful Powers!" Hafiz whispered, averting his gaze from the door. "What has happened to your father?"

"This is only the guess of an uneducated animal," Boabdil commented, "but I would say he has become a hero."

CHAPTER TWENTY-FOUR

"Give it to me!" Hafiz shouted, making a grab for the scabbard. He and Rashid were back in the young prince's sleeping chamber after a fast retreat from their spying post in the abandoned room. "I have to use my second wish! I have to bring my sister back!"

"I have to use mine first," Rashid argued, holding the sheath just out of his friend's reach. "If I do not put my father back the way he was, it will be the worse for us all."

"Ha! How? If Aminah is returned safe and sound, your father can stop bullying everyone into confessing that they stole her."

"No, Hafiz," said Boabdil. "Prince Rashid is right and you are wrong. Prince Masud has been transformed into a true hero. Even if your sister is found, it will make no difference to him. He will still want to discover the one to blame for her disappearance, and he will still want to punish the guilty one."

"But if Aminah is unharmed—"

"I say it will not make a fleabite of difference to Prince Masud," Boabdil maintained. "A hero is like a fire: Both must be fueled constantly if they are to blaze their brightest. A fire's fuel is wood, a hero's is glory. There is no glory in saying, 'Oh good, the baby is back safe. Now we can all have a dish of sherbet and relax.' On the other hand, think of the glory as

Prince Masud himself seizes the evildoer who stole the child, drags the wretch through the city streets to the scaffold, and personally gives him a lashing to make strong men faint and ladies cheer! Ah, the shouts of the crowd, praising the great dispenser of justice! If these are not fuel enough to stoke a hero's flame high, then I know nothing of the world."

"But it was Hafiz's wish that made his sister vanish," Rashid pointed out. "My father would never whip Hafiz."

"Mother would not let him," Hafiz put in.

"True," the cat agreed. "Which is why our hero would have to find someone else to blame for the baby's vanishment. And he will find that someone, never fear! Someone with no powerful mother to protect him. Someone small and meek and helpless and innocent. Fortunately for all heroes, it is never too hard to find someone like that."

"Oh." Hafiz rubbed his eyes sleepily. "In that case, I suppose you ought to make your wish first." He yawned.

Rashid's yawn mirrored Hafiz's. Outside, the sky was beginning to turn from black and silver to rich blue underlined with a pearly pink. "Yes, I will wish—" another yawn. "I will wish that my father—" a third yawn, louder and wider than the other two.

Boabdil jumped into the young prince's lap and reached up to bat him lightly on the cheek with one paw. "*I* will wish that you have the wisdom to go to sleep. Your head is a nest of swamp-fogs. If you summon up a genie, you had better have your wits about you. If it is a genie like Azem, you will need all your wits and a sackful of your neighbor's too."

"But my fa—" a further yawn. "My father has to be—"

"Your father not done any lasting harm yet. How many heroes can say the same?" The cat rubbed his head under Rashid's chin most seductively. "It will make no difference in the great scheme of things if he waits a few hours more to be set right. I will see to it that he hurts no one too badly while you get some sleep."

"All right," Rashid agreed, and stretched out on his bed without further to-do. The scabbard lay cradled in his arms as if it were a favored toy.

Boabdil trotted up to the head of the bed and stuck a cold, moist nose in Rashid's ear, wakening him. "*Now* what?"

"Now you stay awake at least long enough to hide the scabbard," the cat instructed. "And the Sword as well."

"He is right, my friend," Hafiz said. "It would be bad for us if someone else discovered the secret of the great dragon's-belly ruby. You would never get to wish your father back the way he was."

"Hmmm?" Rashid was fighting a losing battle against the weight of his eyelids.

"Besides, if the grownups discover that we have the Sword of Solomon *and* the scabbard, we will be in enough trouble for ten of us."

"Ohhhhh." Rashid nodded, or perhaps he was just trying to keep his head up. "Hide'm in my motherroom. No one nnnnevergo there. Unnerbed." He held out the scabbard. Hafiz no sooner took it from Rashid's hand than the prince collapsed back into his pillows and began to snore softly.

Hafiz tried to carry Sword and scabbard at once, but the Sword alone was almost more than he could manage. Boabdil observed his series of failed attempts to tote, drag, or shove the two parts of King Solomon's most famous weapon through the secret door. The cat's small body shook as if in the midst of an earthquake.

Hafiz noticed this and demanded, "What is the matter with you?"

"I am trying not to laugh," the cat responded. "Why do you not simply make *two* trips through the passageway? One to hide the Sword, one to hide the scabbard?"

"I was just about to do that," Hafiz said stiffly, and he did. He returned from the second trip, stood tall before the cat, and flung his borrowed cape across one shoulder before striding from Rashid's rooms with all his dignity upon him.

His dignity and the rest of him took a nasty tumble when he made a misstep in the hallway and tripped on the hem of the cloak.

Boabdil placed himself so that he must be the first thing Hafiz saw when he picked himself up again. "If you give me a saucer of cream, I will not tell a soul about this," he said.

The sun had climbed halfway to the peak of noon when a small, furry shape stole into a long-disused palace chamber and began nosing around eagerly under the bed.

"*Choo!*" The dust made Boabdil sneeze violently. Puffs of it clung to his eyebrows. He regarded what it had done to his usually spotless coat and curled his lip in a snarl of disgust.

"I think it suits you," said a familiar voice from atop the bed. Prince Rashid pulled himself to the edge and leered down at the cat. "Looking for something?" He gave him just a glimpse of the Sword, but a good long look at the scabbard.

"I was making sure that nothing had happened to it," the cat said, as if that were the truth from an angel's mouth.

"Such as someone else trying to make some wishes of his own?" The prince gave a good-natured chuckle.

"You have had more than your share of wishes already. You are greedy, Boabdil."

"I am a cat. I ask life for no more and no less than I deserve." He shook the worst of the dustballs from his fur. "Can you blame me for being what I am, O Prince?"

"No."

"Then learn from me: Do not blame Azem for being what he is either. Do not blame him, but do not trust him!"

"Never fear," Rashid assured him. "I am very careful in my dealings with the genie."

"Perhaps. But Azem is a creature with centuries of wickedness behind him, while you and Hafiz are so young that—"

"*Young* again!" Rashid's face closed. "I am sick of *young*! Why is it always the grownups who insist that you can not be wise unless you are also old and gray and tired and stodgy and—?"

"Forgive me," the cat mewed. "I did not know that you were born with the keys to all earthly knowledge clutched in your infant hand. Yet in view of this, I do not understand why it took your nursemaid so long to train you out of diapers."

"Did you come here just to steal wishes from the Sword and to insult me?" Rashid demanded.

Boabdil's whiskers swept up, then forward. "The wishes lie in the scabbard, not the Sword. But you know that as you know all things. I bow before your monumental knowledge." He did not.

Rashid leaned his chin in his hands. "Cat, what do you want from me?"

"I want to help you make your second wish. What harm would there be in saying 'I wish that my father be restored to his old self and that Boabdil the cat would get a bucketful of the finest new milk at the very same time'? Very efficient, such a wish; very economical."

Rashid laughed and tickled the cat behind his ears. "Very sloppy too. You tell me to be careful of Azem, yet your wish gives him every chance to do you harm! He might give you the milk by pouring it out of the bucket onto your head. He might drop the bucket straight down upon you from the top of the highest tower in the palace, squashing you flat. He might plunge you into a pail of milk the size of the western sea and watch you drown."

"Ahhhh, yes." The cat closed his eyes and purred. "But what a way to die!"

"No, I think I will make my second wish without any help from you," the young prince concluded. "I will keep it simple; that way Azem can not twist my words into something I do not want. In fact—" he held up the scabbard "—I think I will do it now." He rubbed his hand over the great dragon's-belly ruby before the cat could say another word.

This time Azem materialized without all the destructive fanfare that had accompanied his first appearance. He was man-sized, no more, and he wore the voluminous grab of one of Malak's desert raiders. This served to hide most of his ugliness, though by no means all. That was an impossibility.

"You summoned me, O Master?" he inquired, cleaning hefty chunks of soil from beneath his claws with the black blade of a bone-hilted dagger.

"Yes, O Azem. I want you to grant me another wish."

"Is that so?" The genie's wiry brows rose. "Then speak, and I shall serve you as my best I may."

"I am not happy with how my father behaves now that he is a hero," Rashid told Azem. "Therefore I wish—I wish—" He paused it concentration. He did not need the cat to tell him that it was vital to get the words exactly right. "I wish that my father were just as he was before I wished him to be a hero."

"Very good," said the genie. He wiggled his hand languidly. A few twinkles popped from his fingertips, but these fizzled to dead ash before they hit the ground. Boabdil cocked his head to one side, uttered a low, hunting growl, and pounced on them as they fell.

"Nice cat," said Azem. "May I eat him?"

"No, you may *not*!" Rashid was livid. "Is this how you fulfill my wish? 'Very good'? A few lame sparkles tossed into the air? Whatever happened to 'Hearkening and obedience'?"

Azem was still studying Boabdil with the eye of a housewife contemplating a leg of lamb at the butcher's stall. The cat lay on his back, revealing the wide, white luxury of his underbelly. "But see how nice and fat he is!" the genie protested. "All going to waste. My mother gave me a recipe that will transform the worthless beast into a feast fit for—"

"You had better transform yourself into a genie first!" Rashid shouted. He clung to the scabbard and shook it at Azem the way an old man might shake his cane at a pack of marauding dogs. It had about as much effect on the genie.

"My lord has a complaint?" Azem's mouth twitched. "Ah! No need to speak; I can divine it. Do you believe that because I only put on a halfhearted show of mystic fireworks that I treated your wish in a similarly halfhearted manner?"

"I—um—" Rashid felt suddenly thrust into the wrong. Where did it say that a genie needed to stage a showy display every time he fulfilled a wish? Perhaps flashes and flourishes were for younger genies who had less experience with magic, bright distractions to impress their masters and give themselves confidence. a creature of Azem's great age must feel quite at home among spells and enchantments after so many centuries. Curses and cantrips were like comfortable old slippers to him. He did not need to make a fuss every time he reached for them.

Rashid looked at Azem. Strange and wonderful to say, the genie actually looked as if he had had his feelings badly hurt by the boy's thoughtfulness. "I—I'm sorry," said the young prince.

"Why apologize?" The look of hurt melted away into a smile of all-consuming malice. "You were *right!*" And with that, Azem grew to three times the height of a man, swept Rashid from his feet with one hand, whipped a black whirlwind around them both, and vanished amid rumbling thunderheads and peals of gloating laughter.

"Show-off," said Boabdil.

CHAPTER TWENTY-FIVE

"I do not believe this," said the sultan. He rose from his throne and began to pace up and down the length of the Chamber of the Four Great Councillors. His servants trotted beside him, one waving an ostrich plume fan, the other bearing a cup of cool water.

They were trying to do their duty by looking after their lord's comfort, but his nervous wanderings made this very difficult. More than once since this meeting's start the ostrich plume fan had knocked Haroun ben Hasan's turban askew or had given Prince Masud a hearty thump on the back. Princess Nur and the Grand Vizier both were liberally sprinkled from the number of times the water-bearer had stumbled.

"Most Serene Majesty, we are doing all we can," the Grand Vizier soothed, trying to steer the sultan back to his seat.

"I still do not believe this," the sultan repeated, allowing the Grand Vizier to have his way. "*Two* of my adored grandchildren spirited away by a genie! No, I do not believe this at all." He sounded very old.

"Well, *I* do!" Prince Masud boomed. He drew his sword and slammed it down on the council table. "What is more, I say that the genie is not the one to blame. For one thing, he is not here. I see through your evil plot, O Traitor! Be warned, unless you turn from your wickedness I shall tear you apart with my bare hands!" He thrust out his arms as if he intended to put his words into action then and there.

"But Uncle Masud—" Hafiz protested, ducking behind his mother.

Nur slapped her brother's hands away with two short, sharp motions. "Sit down, Masud," she said.

"No, I shall not sit down!" Prince Masud planted one foot on his chair and pounded on his chest. "I shall not sit, I shall not rest, no razor shall touch my head, and no figs shall pass my lips until I have found my beloved son Rashid and my beloved niece Aminah, returned them safely home, and punished their kidnapper. Thus swears Masud the Mighty!"

"Masud, you sound silly. You do not even like figs. Be quiet," said his sister.

"Yes, Nur," Masud replied, abruptly tame. He sat down with his hands in his lap.

The sultan sighed. "There are times I am more worried about you, my son, than about the children. You have not been acting like yourself since yesterday."

"I am acting like Masud the Mighty, which is precisely who I am," Masud responded. "And I will trounce anyone who says otherwise!"

"Ah." The sultan, much agitated, turned from his son to his son-in-law. "Sometime before noon today he took a turn for the worse," he confided in Haroun. "I do not know what has come over him. He used to be such a dependable boy. Predictable. No matter whether calm or chaos ruled the palace, I always knew what my son Masud would do: He would write a poem. But now—"

"Poems?" Masud snarled. "*Poems*? What need have I of such stinking things as poems? Words are not for real men. We need action! Glory! Bloodshed! Where are the servants who were supposed to watch over Aminah? They have failed! They must be punished! I will peel their skins from their bodies as if they were bananas, and then I will slowly crush them in my hands as if they were—"

"—*mushy* bananas," Haroun finished for him. He was fed up with his brother-in-law's posturings; so was everyone else. "O Prince Masud, you have heard my son's confession. Our daughter Aminah was stolen away not by man, but by magic! The servants are not to blame."

"I will *make* them be to blame," Masud growled.

Under the table, Boabdil nudged Hafiz's knee and said, "Yes, he is a hero all right."

Just then Masud added, "That is, I will do it only if it meets with your approval, Lord Haroun. May I? Oh, please say that I may!" Without warning his face darkened and he bellowed, "Woe unto you if you do *not* say that I may!"

"Alas, my son, what demon spins you like a top?" the sultan beseeched Prince Masud. "One moment you are fierce, the next you are a field mouse."

"How dare you speak to me thus, old man?" Masud bawled in his father's face. "While you dither and fuss, I have taken action! I have summoned a fearsome host of our best soldiers to prepare for battle. I have made them swear an awesome oath upon the tombs of their ancestors that they will follow me down the very throat of Hell itself! I have even explained the situation to their wives. I shall lead them into the heart of the desert, my sword in my hand, and we shall not return until we have found my son and my niece!"

Nur sighed. "Masud, do you have any idea at all how big the heart of the desert is or where you should start looking for them?"

The prince's warlike grimace blew away like smoke. Meekly he said, "Why, no my dear sister. I really do not. Could you give me directions?"

"May Heaven save us, a curse has fallen upon this house!" the sultan wailed. "My son is mad!"

"Uncle Masud is not mad," Hafiz volunteered. "He is also a victim of the evil genie."

The sultan would not be comforted by Hafiz's words. This was mainly because he had not really been listening to a single word the boy had uttered since the meeting began. "First he is a poet, then he is a hero, and now he flies like a shuttlecock between fear and fearless! And all the while Malak the Murderous prepares his hordes for the invasion! Oh, what shall become of my kingdom?"

"But Grandfather, behold!" Hafiz cried, shoving the Sword of Solomon into the center of the council table. "You do not need to be afraid of Malak the Murderous or his hordes any longer. The Sword is free!"

The sultan shook his head, still paying his grandson no mind. "We are doomed."

"Aha!" Masud pounced on the Sword, snatching it from the table before Haroun could react. He waved it over his head with a grim look of satisfaction. "*Now* let them come! I, Masud the Mighty, will chop their limbs like firewood and stack up their heads like melons in the marketplace!" He lowered the sword and in a gentler tone added, "That is, unless you would rather have me stick their heads on lances in the royal gardens, Father?"

"Doomed," the sultan repeated.

"Highness, give me back the Sword of Solomon," Haroun said in a perfectly reasonable tone.

Prince Masud crossed his arms, the Sword still welded to his fist. "No."

"Masud, you are being silly again," Nur chided her brother. "My husband Haroun ben Hasan has always led Father's troops and he has always wielded the Sword of Solomon. Give it back to him."

Masud's grip on the blade only tightened. "I will not."

Boabdil bounded from his place beneath the council table onto Hafiz's lap and then onto the tabletop itself. Flaunting his tail like a banner, he strode up to the sultan and said, "He is not mad; he is just obnoxious. And he is that way because of the trickery of the evil genie Azem. I was there; I saw everything. The genie did not harm me because he thought I was an ordinary cat." Boabdil enjoyed a private chuckle over that. "As if there were such a thing! Humans and genies never learn. In any case, it was I who told young Hafiz ben Haroun to bring you this information, along with the Sword of Solomon and its accursed scabbard. You have repaid his efforts by acting as if he were invisible and you were deaf. Tell me, do all humans treat their little ones like this? Always?"

"I do not ignore my children!" the sultan responded indignantly.

'Your children are grown," the cat reminded him. "I think I can read the riddle now: When humans have children, they treat them as if they were not there, but when those children grow up, they treat them as if they were children." He licked his flank philosophically. "On the whole, I think I will stick with raising kittens." He trotted back to Hafiz's lap.

"I still do not understand how Azem was able to lay hands upon Rashid," Nur said. "Rashid was his Master, along with our Hafiz."

Haroun was equally at a loss. "Genies are not permitted to harm Masters. Moreover, they are bound to protect their Masters' lives with their own. The penalties for disobedience are severe."

"Maybe Azem is not afraid of the penalties for genies," Hafiz said. He only said it half aloud; no one was listening to him anyway.

To his surprise, his uncle Prince Masud asked, "What do you mean by that, boy?"

"Only—only that Azem is not a full-blooded genie. He is half ifrit."

At the mention of those dire beings, a little gasp of fear escaped the lips of all present.

"If he is of ifrit blood, no rules can control him!" the sultan cried. "Oh, doom! Doom!"

"No, Grandfather." Hafiz spoke out loud and clear. "I think he is as subject to the rules governing genies as Khalid or Tamar or Master Basim. If not, why was he captive in the great scabbard ruby for so many centuries?"

A shocked hush fell as the grownups realized that the boy had not only said something sensible, but that it was also an idea that had eluded all of them.

"Mystery on mystery." Haroun ben Hasan rubbed his chin. "How shall we unravel it? For so we must if we mean to find our children."

"Why not ask the genie himself?" Hafiz offered. He reached under the table and placed the scabbard in the very spot from which Prince Masud had snatched the Sword.

"A fine notion!" his father exclaimed, laying hold of the bewitched object. "Better than fine, it is the answer to all our woes. If I rub the great dragon's-belly ruby, your contract with Azem is at an end and I shall be his Master, with three wishes to make besides! I shall use two of them to make the genie bring back Aminah and Rashid, then I shall use the third one to command him to never trouble mortals again!"

"My friend, are you quite sure—?" Boabdil began. His words were either too late or ignored. Haroun ben Hasan fancied himself somewhat of an expert in the ways of genies, having been the master of one for more years and more wishes than was the common case. He had no fear at all as he picked up the scabbard and rubbed the great dragon's-belly ruby.

Azem's appearance this time made his first eruption look like a butterfly dancing into a rose garden. The ostrich plume fan burst into flames, the water boiled away to steam in the cup, the servants ran shrieking for their lives, and the council table shattered into pieces, none larger than a fingernail. The stench of sulfur mingled with the reek of week-old fish and butter gone bad. Everyone sprang to their feet as their stools crumbled into piles of sand from under them. Boabdil was spilled hissing from Hafiz's lap to the floor.

Out of a cloud the color of a corpse's skin came the genie's hand. It was the only portion of him visible, but it was enough. It seemed big enough to close over a full-grown man from head to foot and it proved this at once by closing around Haroun ben Hasan and giving him a mighty shaking.

"WHAT IS THE MEANING OF THIS?" Azem's voice roared forth. Flakes of paint blew away from the murals of the Four Great Councillors like peach blossom petals.

"Put him down!" Prince Masud shouted, taking a slice at the genie's hand with the Sword of Solomon to no effect. Masud studied the situation, then sat down. "Perhaps later."

Haroun had the breath half squeezed out of him, but he was no coward. Despite his predicament, he used the scabbard to lever the genie's titanic fingers apart far enough for him to take a good, deep breath and reply, "You heard the prince: put me down! I rubbed the ruby that holds you; I am your Master now."

Azem's jollity shook loose a further snowfall of paint from the murals. The image of Lord Zahid lost its head entirely (which was amusing, in its way, since

Lord Zahid had ultimately lost *his* head after an argument with the then-sultan over who should paint his image on the council chamber wall).

"O FOOLISH MORTAL! YOU KNOW NOTHING YET THINK YOU KNOW ALL! I AM NO COMMON GENIE; THEIR RULES ARE NOT MINE."

"You see?" The sultan appealed to the air. "I told you so. But no one ever listens to me unless I threaten to have them executed first."

With one additional belch of ghastly fumes, Azem manifested himself fully at only twice man-size, letting Haroun drop from the grasp of the gigantic hand as he did so. He lounged upon the rubble of the council table as if it were a divan arrayed with rose petal-stuffed cushions and showed his teeth to all.

"Wipe that jackal's smile from your mouth, Azem," Haroun said, brushing bits of table from his clothing. "You will not find this so funny when the Council lays hands on you."

"The Council laid hands on me centuries ago," Azem replied. "How do you think I wound up a prisoner in that stupid ruby?"

"What makes you think they will not do the same thing to you this time, for disobeying your Master?"

Azem covered a genteel yawn. "In the first place, what makes you think I ever disobeyed my Master? And in the second, why are you so sure that the Council will be able to punish me again? They are not all-powerful. My magic is a match for theirs."

"Then how did they manage to lock you into the ruby?" Hafiz asked.

Azem patted him on the head, a friendly gesture that squashed the boy's turban down over his eyes and left it smelling of mold and camel dung. "By themselves, they could not. But in those days, King Solomon ruled—he who of all mortals was master of a thousand magics! With his help they accomplished it." He showed still more teeth and added, "These days I feel that my powers are stronger than ever, and King Solomon is dead."

"Villain!" Nur cried. "What have you done with our children?" She would have thrown herself on the genie, fists ready to pummel him wildly, but Haroun held her back.

Azem turned hooded eyes upon her. "My lady, what is this? Your man accuses me of wickedness for *not* doing my job and you accuse me of the same thing for *doing* it! My poor head whirls with confusion!" He clasped his temples and moaned piteously.

"What a terrible actor!" Boabdil whispered to Hafiz. "I would bite him now, but I am afraid that I would never be able to get the foul taste out of my mouth."

"I would bite him myself, taste or no taste," Hafiz grumbled. "He speaks in riddles, like all grownups. My parents always do that when they are talking about something they wish to hide from me. They did it for months before my sister came along. I am sick of it!" He marched up to his father, all business, and grabbed the scabbard from his hand. (Haroun might have had a better hold on it, but he was preoccupied with trying to restrain his wife from making yet another foredoomed attack upon the evil genie.)

Scabbard in hand, Hafiz commanded, "O Azem, enough of your games! Explain yourself so that we may understand."

Azem's smile was no longer toothy, but it was as smug as ever. "Did I hear you *wish* for me to do so, O Master?" he asked.

"No." Hafiz lifted a very determined chin. "But you will do as I say, or I swear on the Sword of Solomon itself that I will *never* make another wish. And you know what that means."

Azem's smile crumpled. "Indeed I do." He did not sound pleased with the knowledge. "Until such time as my servitude is accomplished, I am bound to that blasted ruby. Very well, I shall speak plainly. It will do you no good anyway."

He wiggled one long-clawed index finger and the scabbard began to twirl in Hafiz's hands. The boy gasped and let it go. The enchanted object floated across the room to spin slowly over Azem's head, then faster. The gems caught the light and made it look as if the genie wore a twinkling halo gorgeous enough for an angel of the Most High.

"I have told you that I was imprisoned in that accursed ruby by King Solomon and the Council because—" Azem winked "—because they did not approve of my artistic soul. I do not see why: It was only a *small* village that I wiped from the face of the world, and the valley looked *so* much prettier without all those hovels cluttering up the place." He sighed. "At any rate, Solomon in his wisdom believed that a dead peasant was worth as much fuss as a dead noble, and so he summoned the Council to deal with me. He sat in judgment on my case, he helped pass sentence, he even provided my prison and the terms for my release. He said that I would not be free until I behaved like a proper genie. To do so, I must grant three wishes to the one who first rubbed the great ruby that contained me and set me loose upon the earth once more." Azem folded his arms. "Then he made sure that day would be long in coming by throwing my prison into the depths of the sea. I call that inconsiderate."

"He wanted you to have time enough to think about your wrongdoings," Haroun suggested.

"Oh, I have had plenty of time to think things over," Azem replied in a way that left no doubt that here was a creature who knew how to nurse a grudge.

"But if you must behave like a proper genie, why did you refuse to accept me as your Master when I rubbed the ruby?" Haroun asked.

"Ah!" Azem laid a knobbly finger beside his nose and nearly poked out his own eye with the talon protruding from his fingertip. "You must pay better attention to my words, O Mortal Fool. Did you not hear King Solomon's decree? I must grant three wishes to the one who *first* rubbed the stone!"

"That means me!" Hafiz exclaimed. "And Rashid. We rubbed the stone together and—and—and—" A thought struck him: a thought that robbed the color from his cheeks with its heartstopping revelation. "*Oh no!*"

Azem's sharkmouthed smile was back and it had brought a few extra teeth along to improve itself. "Oh yes!"

"What?" the sultan demanded. "What is it? Is it doom? Mercy upon us all, I am sure it must be doom!"

"Three wishes," Hafiz said, his voice flat. "That was all that King Solomon said Azem must grant to the first to rub his prison and set him free."

"Why, of course, my son." Haroun was puzzled by the boy's sudden despair. "That is always the way it works with genies: three wishes to the one who rubs—"

"Three wishes and *only* three wishes!" Hafiz groaned. "And three wishes *only* to the first to rub the ruby!"

For a heartbeat the grownups stood there, at a loss to explain why Hafiz was so distraught. Azem knew, but he was saying nothing. Then, like a thief tiptoeing into a treasure house, the answer came to Prince Masud.

"Three wishes *in all*, not three wishes *apiece*," he said softly. "*That* is what the boys received from his monster. Which means that my son had but one-and-a-half wishes to his name and never knew it! (May ten thousand blessings fall upon the head of my mathematics tutor.) Once he made them, he was fair prey for Azem."

"Why did you not tell the boys that they must share the three wishes between them?" Haroun accused Azem.

The genie shrugged. "They never asked."

"And what of Aminah?" Nur asked urgently.

Hafiz hung his head. "That was my fault, Mother," he said. "I wished that you and Father would pay more attention to me. Azem fulfilled that wish by making her disappear."

"Oh, I did not make her disappear," the genie corrected him. "I just removed her. She is alive and well; she is just not alive and well *here*."

"Fiend! Where is my daughter?" Nur picked up what was left of the ostrich plume fan and tried to beat the answer out of the genie's hide.

Azem snapped the sturdy pole between his thumb and forefinger, then lifted the princess by the belt fastening her robes and hung her on a wall hook reserved for oil lamps. "That would be telling," he said. "But I could bring her back as easily as I took her away, if . . ." He let his words trail off meaningfully, his eyes resting on Hafiz.

"Yes! Yes, I shall wish her back again!" Hafiz cried full of remorse. "I wish that my sister—"

Haroun ben Hasan clapped his hand over his son's mouth before the boy could utter another syllable. "No, Hafiz! Remember, this creature does not owe you another wish, merely half of one. Now we know what happened to Prince Masud: One wish from Prince Rashid to make him a hero, one wish to bring him back to his old self; except the second wish could only be fulfilled halfway!"

"What more could I do?" Azem traced patterns in the rubble of the shattered council table and tried to sound helpless. "Prince Rashid got exactly what he had coming. I am as honest with my Masters as the laws governing genies allow."

"*Genies.*" The sultan spoke the word so that it was laden with bitterness. "I am heartily sick of genies and their tricks. I will issue an edict banning all genies from my realm! Let them bother other kings. Woe unto any subject of mine who traffics with them: He had best use his third wish to travel far from my lands, for if he does not, I will make him wish he had never been born!"

"O Grandfather, do not say such things," Hafiz begged. "Not all genies are like Azem."

"True," Azem agreed. "I dress better than most of them." He fingered his necklace of lizard skulls fondly.

"I do not want to be bothered with details," said the sultan. "I only want my grandchildren back." He sailed from the room without another word, the Grand Vizier hurrying in his wake.

"Father, wait for me!" Prince Masud dashed after them, still clinging to the Sword. "I will slay any genie that dares show its face within our borders! If you want me to do that. Or if you would prefer . . ." His words faded with distance.

"A hero who hesitates is only half a hero," said Azem. He popped one of the lizard skulls from his necklace and ate it like a cherry. "Now, my sole remaining Master, what can I do for you?" He removed a second lizard skull and proffered it to Hafiz as if it were the most delectable sweetmeat money could buy.

"You can return my sister and my friend, safe and sound."

"Fine. Wish for it."

Haroun moved to stifle his son's words a second time, but there was no need. Hafiz pushed his father's hand aside and said, "What will I get if I wish for it with only half a wish left me? Will you return them only halfway here? Will you return one and keep the other?"

"I could always return half of him and half of her," Azem pointed out. "That would bring them back sound, but not safe. Or would that be safe, but not sound?" He bit off a two-inch chunk of talon as he pondered this.

"It will not matter—not now, not ever! As long as you are my servant, you must stay in the ruby. I will never make my last half-wish and you will never escape to torment anyone else. Never, never, *never*!" By the time he was finished, Hafiz's face was bright red and his parents were staring at him with a mixture of pride and concern.

Haroun ben Hasan placed his hands on his son's shoulders. "May my son's words reach the ears of the Most High. Rather than risk releasing a monster like you upon the world once more, we shall find our darling child Aminah and Prince Rashid by ourselves."

"If you can find them," Azem replied. "You would do better to let the boy figure out how to make the half-wish he has left. He is not as stupid as he looks; he might even come up with a clever way to use it so that I would be forced to do his bidding without trickery."

"Knave!" Nur spat. "You can no more live without trickery than without breath." She fidgeted valiantly but could not work her way off the lamp hook. "My son will never wish, and you will never be free."

Azem snickered. "What do you mortal mayflies know of 'never'? For a boy, a century lies between one birthday and the next! Eternity is the length of time that stretches before him until he can enjoy the privileges of being a man! And there are so many, many things that the young wish for while they wait to grow up. Tell me, do you really think that this son of yours can pass the rest of his life without once saying 'I wish . . . I wish . . .'?"

"I will take an oath nevermore to use those words!" Hafiz retorted.

"Then you will wish you had never sworn it." Azem was not the smallest bit annoyed by Hafiz's intentions, which was in itself extremely annoying to Hafiz. "Life is full of surprises, and your life has barely begun. What will happen when one of those surprises leaps out and startles you into saying 'I wish so-and-so' or 'I wish I never thus-and-such'? Accidents happen. O my callow Master, if you dream you can live even a twelvemonth without wishing the world would remake itself to suit you, you dream in vain. And when you waken from that dream, I will be waiting to hearken and obey."

With that, Azem twisted his body into a spiral of smoke and seeped back into the great dragon's-belly ruby.

CHAPTER TWENTY-SIX

The garden of the plum tree looked like a wizard had chosen it as the perfect place to do his washing. Instead of flapping on a line to dry, eight silken weavings of gorgeous hue floated in an ascending spiral pattern just above the treetops. There was magic at work, but not a wizard's magic. The bright weavings were flying carpets, each one bearing a genie, each genie wearing a look of the utmost solemnity. On the ground, Hafiz and his parents gazed up at Khalid, Tamar, Master Ishmael, Master Basim, and the rest of the Council. Boabdil sat on the garden wall, intently trying to unravel the dangling fringe of Master Ishmael's carpet, which formed the lowest rung of the ever-climbing stairway of the air.

"What do you mean, you cannot use your powers to tell us where the children are?" Nur demanded. She plucked a nice, big fruit from the plum tree and hefted it like a marksman gauging the target's distance.

Master Basim simply floated his carpet a little higher, out of plum-range. "Princess, our decision was not an easy one. We hate and fear Azem as much as you do, but—"

"I am not afraid of him," Nur said, fists clenched. "I will make him afraid of *me*."

"That is hardly likely," the ancient genie remarked.

"You do not know my wife very well, do you?" Haroun stated.

Nur spun to face Khalid and Tamar. Their carpets hovered close to one another, their hands clasped across the small gap separating them. "Not even you, my friends?" she appealed. "What harm could there be in granting us this small, this tiny, this insignificant shred of magic?"

Khalid and Tamar exchanged a guilty look but said nothing.

"Please, my friends, I beg of you!" Haroun joined his voice to Nur's. "It would not take much. All you would need to do would be to enter a lamp. Then I could rub it and you could grant us three wishes. I would use them at once to recover the children, to restore Prince Masud, and to deal with Azem as he deserves."

"O my friend Haroun ben Hasan, do not ask this of us!" Khalid cried. "It crushes my heart to deny your request, yet I must. As you love your children, forgive me, but I refuse you because I love mine."

"Yours?" Haroun echoed, perplexed. "But you have no children!"

Khalid gave Tamar a melting look. "Not . . . yet."

Tamar slipped her hand from her mate's and gently steered her carpet to place her on eye-level with the princess. "Dear Princess Nur," she said, fingering the bracelet that Bound her to Khalid. "You are wise among women. You know that the ways of genies are not the ways of your own kind. I ask you to hear and understand my words: when a pair of genies chooses to be Bound, it is often the dearest wish of their hearts to bring new enchantment into the world. It is the job of the Council to say whether or not they may do this."

Nur mulled over Tamar's strange revelation. "You mean—" She hesitated, wanting to be sure she had it right. "You mean you cannot have children unless the *Council* says you may?"

Tamar bowed her head. "It is so."

"Then it is also foolish!"

"To your eyes, perhaps," Tamar admitted. "But as I said, our ways are not your ways. Each new genie born into this world brings with it a new measure of magic. Were we to scatter children about as freely as you mortals do, soon magic would be as common as dirt and every mortal would be a second Solomon, with legions of genies to command."

"Why would that be a bad thing?" Hafiz wanted to know.

Tamar beckoned him to climb up beside her on her carpet. She stroked his cheek and said, "O dear child, can you not see the answer for yourself? Magic that is common ceases to be magical. It loses the virtues of enchantment. Alas, you mortals do not value what comes cheaply to your hand. You do not respect or fear a power that anyone can master; nay, not even if it were the power to destroy your world!"

"I do not ask for the power to destroy the world," Haroun said. "I only ask for three wishes."

"Three wishes which we cannot give," Khalid told him. "For Tamar and I have received the Council's permission to bring our own small magic into this world. While we await the birth, neither she nor I must be parted from each other, not even for an instant. If one of us steps into a lamp so that we might grant you the wishes you desire, it would snap the spell we now must weave so very, very carefully between us."

Hafiz looked grave. Tamar regarded the boy with maternal concern and inquired, "Are you angry with us for refusing to help?"

"Oh no." The boy was taken aback by the question. "I am happy for you and Khalid." He lowered his voice and whispered in Tamar's ear, "I was just thinking how much nicer this world would be if some grownups would ask permission before having babies all over the place."

The female genie laughed out loud.

Hafiz's parents had not heard their son's words, but in any case they were in no mood for jests. "Khalid and Tamar cannot help us with their magic," Haroun stated. "Very well; I understand their reasons. But what of you, Master Ishmael?"

Khalid's former teacher sighed, his moustaches trembling in the breeze. "I too am subject to the will of the Council."

"And the will of the Council is that you must deal with this by your own means," Master Basim pronounced. The four other Council members murmured their agreement.

Boabdil stopped worrying Master Ishmael's carpet fringe. He leaped from the garden wall onto Master Ishmael's carpet and from there continued to bound up and up the spiral, from carpet to carpet to carpet, until he landed on Master Basim's.

" 'The will of the Council!' " he said scornfully, switching his tail. "And where does compassion touch the will of the Council? In all the years you dwelled with us, Master Basim, I thought you had lost some of your pompousness. I was wrong. I should have saved my last wish and used it to help these good people. Then you could have dealt with being voiceless by *your* own means. 'The will of the Council . . .' Pah!" Having said his piece, he hopped back down to the garden wall by the same route he had used to ascend.

Master Basim flushed and fidgeted. The cat's curt words had wounded him. He did not like being reminded of the years he had spent in attendance on Boabdil, doing a dozen little tasks a day to keep the cat in a good mood. He wondered whether the cat would ever mention those days before his fellow Council members. The very possibility churned his bowels.

I would be the laughingstock of the Council instead of its head, he thought. *Most especially if the wicked beast ever spoke of the time he was bored, so I conjured up a whole circus of dancing mice for his amusement. That was bad enough, but when he said he would like to see how I would look if* I *were a mouse—!* The image of himself with beady red eyes and a long, pink thread of a tail came back to haunt him. In that furry form he had danced on a tightrope of silk floss with a wee paper parasol in his paw. He shuddered.

"O Wisest and Best of Cats, you wrong us. We of the Council do not make our decisions without good reasons behind them," he said, adopting a soothing tone. The cat continued to stare at him with a cold, cynical eye. "Have you not just heard your friends say that they understand and forgive Khalid and Tamar for refusing to grant them the wishes they seek? Why can you not find it in your most generous heart to forgive us for the same reason?"

"*You're* going to have a baby?" Boabdil's whiskers quivered. "There are some things that not even all the magic in the world can do!"

Master Basim's complexion turned several shades ruddier. "No, I am *not* going to have a baby," he huffed. "I said that the Council's *reason* for refusal was the same as Khalid's and Tamar's, not the *cause*."

"I fail to see the difference."

"Have you not been listening?" Master Basim had his carpet swoop lower, until it touched the garden wall and he could speak almost eye-to-eye with the cat. "From the time before time began, we genies were created with but two purposes: to offer mortals a taste of magic and to see to it that they never glut themselves on wonders."

"That is the reason why we never grant any one mortal more than three wishes," one of the other Council members said. "Not on purpose, anyway."

They all paused to give Khalid a look so heavy with meaning that the poor genie squirmed like a hooked fishworm.

"You mean like granting some mortal creature an additional year of life every year for ten years on his birthday?" Boabdil mewed.

"Never mind all that!" Master Basim blustered, waving his hands frantically. "And the rest of you, stop staring at Khalid. He was only a novice. Accidents happen. The next genie here who makes him feel ill at ease shall answer to me!"

Boabdil purred and closed his eyes.

"That is still why we only grant three wishes," a second Council member maintained. "And it is a good thing, too!"

"It is as Tamar said," another Council member spoke up. "Mortals do not value what comes easily to their hands, whether it be treasure or power or love. Alas, how dismal your little lives would be if marvels surrounded you!"

"Therefore," the youngest Council member concluded, "it is likewise our duty to keep magic magical. And that applies to enchanted objects as well as wishes. You, O Haroun ben Hasan, have been master of the Sword of Solomon. Was that not a wonder?"

"Beyond question, it was," Haroun responded. "But I do not see how—"

"Yet suppose that besides the Sword, you had also been master of *this*?" The youngest Council member gestured and a glorious black stallion adorned with the wings of a giant eagle appeared in the air beside his carpet. "Behold the Steed of Soudistan, whose voice shatters towers, whose hooves strike fire from the earth, and whose wings can carry a rider from one end of the earth to the other in an instant!" He gestured again and the Steed vanished.

"And suppose you had also been master of *this*?" the second Council member asked. He snapped his fingers and a golden tripod materialized on his carpet. Savory smoke rose from the bowl, its aroma making everyone's mouth water. "Behold the Brazier of Bilgai, whose power is to grant its owner any food his heart desires, cooked to perfection within moments!" A second snap and the Brazier went the way of the Steed.

"Behold now the Fountain of Faisal!" cried the third Council member, with a wave of his hand. A silver fountain formed itself out of a lone white cloud high overhead, its waters sprinkling the garden below with cool delight. "He who possesses it shall never thirst nor ever need to send his servants to fetch heavy buckets from the well. If he so desires, the Fountain will become many smaller versions of itself and bring fresh water to many chambers of his house at once."

No sooner had the Fountain been banished than the fourth genie of the Council caused a deep, gleaming porcelain basin to appear. It uttered a strange, gurgling, draining sound, but before its summoner could describe this wonder, Master Basim raised two fingers and it was gone.

"I believe that we have made our point," he told his colleagues.

"And I say you have not!" Nur said loudly. "You show us wonders, you claim that it would be a terrible thing if they were ours to command, but where is your proof? How would it harm us to be able to travel fast and far, or to have hot food and cool water without tedious labor, or to enjoy whatever benefits that strange porcelain basin might grant?"

"Proof, is it?" Master Basim thundered. "I will give you your proof!" He made a fist and when he opened it a disc of glass twinkled in his palm. "Behold the Glimmerglass of Gad! Hear its tale and be lessoned!" He balanced the shining circle of his fingertip and spoke reverently: "The Glimmerglass of Gad has the power to bring visions to him who gazes into its depths. If he desires to know what is happening anywhere upon the earth, or under it, he has but to ask this of the Glass and the vision will come."

"That is precisely what I wish to know!" Nur exclaimed. "Give me the Glimmerglass of Gad so that I may ask it where to find the children!" She jumped for the enchanted mirror, but Master Basim held it out of her reach.

"That is what you say *now*." No one could talk down to mortals like a genie, and no genie could do it like Master Basim. "Yet if I were to give it to you, it would be the same story as happened with King Solomon. The Glass was his, to begin with, a present from one of his mystic servants. At first the king used it to keep track of his ministers, his ambassadors, his soldiers, and the rest. Then one day, while visiting the royal harem, he heard one of his wives weeping bitterly. She was a lady who had come to him from faraway Kush, and she was homesick. King Solomon was as kind as he was wise, and to soothe the lady he gave her the Glimmerglass of Gad so that she might see the doings of her distant family."

"King Solomon was kind and wise, and he was only mortal," Haroun said. "Why do you refuse to follow his example? We only want *one* vision!"

"That is what the Kushite lady said, too." Master Basim and the Council nodded to one another with all-knowing smiles on their faces. "At first. But no sooner had she enjoyed the power of the Glass then she used all her wiles to persuade King Solomon to let her keep it. He was, as you say, only mortal; he consented. Before long, word of the Glass spread throughout the harem. The king's other wives came to him to demand their fair share of the Glass. They too had come to the king from faraway lands and they too missed their families. The king, being wise, consented again. He even worked out a schedule by which each lady might use the Glass fairly."

"Still I see nothing wrong with all this," Nur protested.

"Nor do I," Hafiz put in. "I think it would be great fun to see the doings of people in faraway lands."

"Ahhhh!" Master Basim levelled a finger at Hafiz, all the while still keeping the Glimmerglass of Gad balanced on the fingertip of his other hand. "Truth comes out of the mouths of babes."

"I am *not* a babe!" Hafiz objected. "If you do not let my parents use the Glass to find Rashid and Aminah, then I will summon Azem and use my last wish to have him tear you in half!"

Master's Basim's eyebrows dipped. "But you only have half a wish!"

"Then I will let Azem figure out how to rip you only halfway in half. And after he has done that, he will be free." Hafiz looked ready to put his threat into action.

"Do not do such a foolish thing, boy!" the ancient genie cried. "You know not what wickedness Azem will wreak upon the world once he is released from his prison. It was his intention to use his powers to conquer the genie homeland, to turn the rules of magic on ear, to let chaos rule!"

"If you do not want that to happen, then let my parents borrow the Glimmerglass of Gad." Master Basim's pleas did not make Hafiz back down at all.

The old genie shook his head. "Then come, chaos, for I shall never willingly give any mortal the use of the Glass. When King Solomon's wives had it, they soon became its slaves. Instead of each lady taking her turn to observe the doings in her homeland, all the wives would gather around and watch the visions of the Glass constantly. It did not matter if the Glass showed them a land and people they did not know: They watched. They watched the loves and the hates and the sinister plottings of strangers from a hundred different kingdoms. Often they missed their meals because it was the hour to watch the Glass. They watched the doings of these other lives so avidly that they forgot to live their own. Therefore King Solomon, being wise, took the Glimmerglass of Gad away from them and gave it to me. He charged me to keep it safe always, and by no means allow another mortal to touch it. I have kept faith with my lord Solomon all these centuries. I will not break faith now."

"Whoops!" Boabdil murmured, and pounced.

His leap was a thing of beauty. It was as if he had sprouted wings to rival those of the Steed of Soudistan. Straight and true as the marksman's arrow he flew through the air to knock the Glimmerglass of Gad from Master Basim's fingertips. The genie made a wild grab for the magical object, but he lacked the cat's speed and grace.

"Catch it! Catch it!" Boabdil shouted as the Glass tumbled earthwards.

Alas, he did not say which of the three mortals below should be the one to catch it. Nur looked at Haroun, Haroun looked at Hafiz, Hafiz looked at both his parents, and while each one opened his mouth to say, "*You* get it. No, *you*. No, he means *you*," the Glass struck the ground and went up in a fountain of glittering shards.

Shards and a winged woman taller than twice the height of the garden wall.

CHAPTER TWENTY-SEVEN

The last fragment of the broken Glimmerglass tinkled to rest in the grass; the winged woman stood blinking in the sunlight at genies and mortals alike. Then she stretched her arms up and yawned to reveal a mouthful of teeth that might give Azem pause, each one bearing the stain of fresh blood.

"Ah, but it is good to be out and about once more," she said with a contented little sigh. She reached out and yanked a flying carpet out from under its rider. As the Council member plummeted to the ground, to turn an innocent quince tree into a pancake, she used the carpet to dab sweat from her brow. "Upon my word as a demon, it was hot in that Glass."

Boabdil sprang away to take refuge between Hafiz's feet. "Next time I tell you to catch something, you *catch* it," he spat. His tail bristled with apprehension as he gazed at what the shattered Glass had released into the world.

"Who—who are you?" Hafiz faltered.

The giant female slowly unfolded her black wings. They were like the bat's leathery pinions, except that hers were lined with fire. Her eyes too were living flame. When she looked down to see who was addressing her, Hafiz trembled.

"I am called Rafiqa," she said. Her voice was oddly sweet. "I come in peace."

"*Rafiqa*?" All the genies pronounced that name as one, and as one they all dashed from the garden, either mounted on their carpets or afoot.

"Now that is strange," Rafiqa remarked. "I did not think my reputation was still so well remembered among genies. Among mortals, yes, but not genies."

"Then you are—you are not the Slave of the Glimmerglass?" Nur was feeling rather wobbly inside, but for Hafiz's sake she forced herself to stand firm.

Rafiqa's gruesome mouth opened and a maiden's silvery laugh pealed forth. "May the Most High witness my words, *no*! I am—I *was* the Captive of the Glass. There is a difference. To be the Slave of the Glass I would have to be a genie; I am not. I am, as I have already told you, a demon."

"You mean an ifrit?" Haroun asked.

Rafiqa was even more amused by this question. "When I was young, my mother used to make me devour at least one ifrit a day. She told me that they were very good for the complexion. Of course this did not please Father, who was an ifrit himself, but Mother soon took care of *him*." She chuckled over happy childhood memories.

"So your mother was a demon and your father was an ifrit." Boabdil chewed over this information before inquiring, "Then you have no genie blood in you at all?"

"Certainly I do, from time to time. But I find that what *really* tastes good is—Oh!" Her error made her blush prettily. "Oh, *I* see what you mean. How silly of me. Yes, I do think that one of Father's ancestors was a genie. In fact, I am sure of it. Otherwise I could never have been locked up in that Glass. Demons of true pedigree may be summoned, banished, or destroyed utterly, but never kept captive in magical trinkets like that."

"Was it King Solomon who imprisoned you?" Hafiz wanted to know.

Rafiqa shook her head. "No, that was the demon Yassif, my fifteenth husband."

"Why did he do it?"

The demon's wings rose and fell in her version of a shrug. "Oh, just because I ate my first fourteen husbands, he thought I was going to devour him too, some day. How ridiculous! The first fourteen tasted simply dreadful; I learn from my mistakes. I would have torn Yassif to shreds, if he annoyed me, but I never would have eaten him." She clicked her tongue over her bloodstained teeth. "I should have listened to Mother: 'Never marry a demon,' she said. Ifrits are much tastier, and a nice, tender genie is—"

While Rafiqa chattered on about the comparative flavors of various magical beings, Hafiz motioned for his parents to bend nearer so that he might whisper in their ears.

"Why do we not ask Rafiqa to help us?" he suggested.

Nur eyed the monstrous female askance. "Do you think she would? Or *could*?"

"She is a creature of great power," Haroun opined. "And she was the Captive of the Glass. It must have been her magic that made it work. She could use that magic to help us find the children."

"So she could." Nur nodded. "But why would she want to?"

"We freed her from her prison," Hafiz reminded her.

"What do you, mean, 'we'?" Boabdil asked pointedly. The cat turned his tail on Hafiz's family and faced the demon. "Hail, O Rafiqa! I am Boabdil, whose skill and boldness you may thank you for your newly won freedom. Pardon the ill manners of these, my servants, for not having introduced us."

Rafiqa's eyes squinted at the small beast now commanding her attention. "You are a cat!" A look of utmost bliss broke over her face. She dwindled to human size, snatched Boabdil to her bosom, and cradled him there. "I adore kittycats," she crooned.

"Hmph—well—*good.*" Boabdil twisted and writhed in Rafiqa's embrace. The fiery lining of her wings was much too close for his comfort. He could feel the ends of his whiskers frizzling off. "Now if you will just put me down, I will tell you what you must do for me and then we can—"

Rafiqa was startled. "I adore cats," she repeated. "I do not obey them."

"But it was I who freed you from the Glimmerglass of Gad!" Boabdil flexed his claws against the demon's bare arm, only to find that what looked like a woman's silky skin was really as tough as a hippopotamus' hide.

"So what?" Rafiqa asked reasonably.

Haroun knelt at her feet. "O Mighty One," he said, "we will not ask great or difficult tasks of you. All that we want is for you to use your powers of vision to help us find two lost children."

"Children?" Rafiqa's ears perked up, so much so that their pointed tips poked through the thick black braids coiled around her head.

"O Merciful One," said Nur, kneeling beside her husband, "if you will only do this one small thing for us, we shall reward you as best we may."

The demon beamed. "What talk is this of reward when you speak of children? Tell me your tale." They did so, taking it in turns to describe Azem's wicked schemes and the vanishment of Rashid and Aminah. When they were done, Rafiqa released Boabdil and dabbed with the border of her veil at the smoking black tears dribbling from her eyes. "Alack, the poor dears! And one of them no more than an infant!

Ohhhh, if I only had this Azem in my hands now, I would teach him to treat children thus!"

"We can arrange that," Boabdil said, looking up from licking his coat smooth again.

"No, no. The children must come first," said Rafiqa. "I will do better than show you where they are: I will take you there! This I promise."

"Ten thousand blessings fall upon you!" Nur exclaimed. She flung herself flat and kissed the demon's sandalled feet. Rafiqa had talons rather than toenails, yet her feet were as dainty as any palace lady's and they smelled of orange blossom. "By all means, take us there at once!"

Rafiqa tittered. "Oh, no," she said. "I have just been released from the Glimmerglass of Gad after over a thousand years of captivity. I am not going anywhere for anyone until I have had a nice, hot bath."

Haroun seized the demon's paws. "Then you shall have the finest bath in all the sultan's palace!" he vowed. "The waters shall be scented with the costliest oils, a dozen maidens shall make music for your delight, and the most exquisite balms and unguents shall be prepared for your annointing when you emerge."

"Yes, and afterwards you shall be dressed in the richest robes and the most priceless jewels in my possession," Nur added, scrambling to her feet. "Come, come with us. We shall present you to the sultan himself and to Prince Masud. Ah, this is truly a fortunate day!" Still rejoicing, they bore the demon between them into the palace.

Boabdil and Hafiz hurried after them, Hafiz still bearing the scabbard of the Sword of Solomon. The boy did not feel comfortable letting it out of his sight for an instant. Even though Azem was safely shut within the great dragon's-belly ruby for the moment,

Hafiz still felt as if the evil genie were forever peering over his shoulder, watching him, waiting for him to make a false move, and mocking him without mercy.

Therefore when an invisible hand laid hold of one end of the scabbard and tugged it hard, jerking Hafiz backwards off his feet at the very threshold of the palace, the first name that rose to his lips was "*Azem!*"

"Where? Where?" Boabdil bounced back into the garden, ready for a fight. All he saw was Hafiz, sitting in the middle of the garden path. "Tchah! What sort of witless jest is this? Do not toy with me—a banquet is being prepared! If I miss it, I shall not be pleased."

You would not be pleased to attend Rafiqa's banquet, came a familiar voice. The air shimmered; Khalid and Tamar appeared standing over Hafiz. They looked grim.

"A thousand pardons for having detained you thus," Khalid said, stooping beside the boy. "We had to speak with you and did not dare to let Rafiqa see us."

"Why not?" Hafiz got up and brushed himself off, but not quickly enough to prevent Tamar fussing over him as well. "I know she is a demon—mostly a demon—but she is not all bad."

"If you fall from a tower five hundred feet high, it is not all bad either; just the last foot kills you," said Tamar.

Hafiz snorted with derision. "If you would not have run away like rabbits, you might have heard that she will take us to find Aminah and Rashid. And she will not hear of a reward for her services! *She* is not afraid to use her magic to help us."

"Rafiqa is always willing to use her magic when it is a matter of finding children," said Khalid.

"Especially babies," said Tamar.

"That is why we had to come back."

"We had to warn you."

Hafiz's eyes flashed back and forth from one genie

to the other until he thought his neck would snap. "What are you talking about? What warning? Why are you so afraid of Rafiqa?"

A cloud passed over the sun, or so it seemed. The garden basked in light, save only the spots where Khalid and Tamar stood. Hafiz sucked in his breath as he lifted his eyes to see two impossibly huge hands materialize above the Bound genies' heads. Before he could so much as squeak, the hands plucked Khalid and Tamar from the ground and cupped themselves around the pair the way boys capture fireflies.

Rafiqa's face filled the sky.

"Do not speak ill of me before the child," she said. Although her appearance inspired fear, her voice remained gentle and low. "You know how I feel about children."

From within her cupped hands, Khalid and Tamar set up a wild squawking that was totally unintelligible to human ears.

Cat ears were another matter. Boabdil cocked his head, twitched his ears forward to listen, then told Hafiz, "Yes, they *do* know how she feels about children. She loves children—"

"Then why—?" Hafiz began.

"—broiled."

Hafiz gave a shout of dismay and broke for the palace, but the demon's hand fell between him and the doorway like a gate. At this size, she was quite able to hold the Bound genies captive with only one hand while she used the other to nab Hafiz. As he rose into the clouds in her grip, the demon allowed the rest of herself to become visible. Boabdil gaped at the sheer massiveness of her sandalled feet, which were the size of ox-carts.

Rafiqa lifted Hafiz to eye-level. "Now listen to me, Hafiz: I have slipped away from a delicious bath to be here for your instruction. You mustn't let these silly genies fill your head with fears like that," she cooed. "I would never eat you."

"No?" The boy toyed with hope.

"Certainly not!" the demon reassured him. "You are too old and tough. I only eat human infants. Now this Aminah sounds like the ideal tidbit."

"Oh, you would not like her at all!" Hafiz blurted. "She may be young, but she is not at all tender. And she *smells*."

"Do not presume to instruct your elders," Rafiqa stated. "I will be the judge of the child's tenderness just as soon as we find her and—what was his name? Ah!—and Rashid." She smacked her lips. "Is he an infant, too?"

"No, Prince Rashid is my age and—and—" Hafiz groped for some way to dissuade the demon from devouring his friend along with his sister "—and he is just as tough as I am!"

"*Prince* Rashid?" The demon laughed. "Oh, princes retain their tenderness much longer than ordinary mortals! I can see you know nothing about the matter."

"Khalid! Tamar!" Hafiz cried in desperation. "Why do you not use your powers to free yourselves from this monster? Run, haste, fly to my parents and tell them of her evil plans!"

By sheer determination, Tamar managed to pry Rafiqa's fingers apart just far enough for her to peek through the gap and reply, "Alas, she is more demon and ifrit than genie, with all the strength of their raw, wild magics! It would take a greater power than ours to defeat her!"

Hafiz heard the logic in Tamar's words, yet his fighting heart was not born to heed reason. Even though he understood that the savage magic of ifrits and demons can master the more civilized enchantments of genies, that did not stop him from pounding on the demon's fingers with the edge of the Sword of Solomon's scabbard. He knew he was helpless, he knew he had no chance of victory, but he also knew that he had to do *something*.

"Fiend! Ghoul! Liar!" he sobbed. "I will slay you before I let you harm my sister and my friend! I will flay the skin from your body, spill your blood across the seven deserts, and feed your flesh to the vultures! Jackals shall gnaw your bones and hyenas shall den in your skull!" It was a terrible litany of curses, and it would have been much more impressive if the poor boy had not been crying hysterically while he spat out the words.

Rafiqa's eyes widened. She uncurled her fingers a little way from Hafiz's body and peered at him. "What did you say?" The question got no answer; Hafiz was weeping too much for speech. "Did you say I was a *liar*?" A single smoldering tear trickled from her eye. It burned away three whole rosebeds when it hit the ground. "How can you call me a nasty name?"

Hafiz wiped his nose on his sleeve and sniffled. "Why should you care if I call you a liar? You are a demon; that is worse."

"It is *because* I am a demon—and proud to be counted as one despite my father's ifrit and genie blood—that your words hurt me so," Rafiqa returned haughtily. "We demons may deceive, but we pride ourselves on keeping our word. If we did not have a reputation for honor, who would deal with us at all? You mortals are fools, not *utter* fools. You like to think that when you make an agreement with a demon, you have at least *some* chance of coming out the winner in the bargain." She smirked. "Not that you ever do."

"You promised my parents you would find Aminah and Rashid," Hafiz accused. "You said you would take us to them!"

"So I did. So I shall. In fact, so I shall do at once!"

Before Hafiz could say another word, the demon tucked him safely into the bosom of her garment, did the same with the captive genies, and clapped her empty hands together. "Come, storm!" she shouted to the heavens. "Come, clouds of thunder, black and awesome in power! Bear me to the place on this earth or under it where we may find the children Aminah and Rashid!"

The sky darkened. Lightning flashed. The plum tree shook itself to bare branches as a mighty wind rushed headlong through the garden. Rafiqa spread her flaming wings to catch the blast. It lifted her from her feet and sent her sailing away to the east, howling with the hunger of a hundred famished souls.

In the midst of so much tumult, it was no wonder that she did not notice she had something in her sandal.

CHAPTER TWENTY-EIGHT

Sand still swirled in an impenetrable curtain around the demon Rafiqa as she reached into her bosom and set Hafiz, Khalid, and Tamar on the ground at her feet. Khalid embraced Tamar protectively and the female genie did the same to Hafiz. He, in turn, hugged the scabbard for dear life. All three of them shielded their eyes against the sand with sleeve or cloak or untucked end of a well-wrapped turban.

Rafiqa's voice came from above, dimly heard through the dying howl of the whirlwind: "Oh dear. The children are in *there*? This is very bad."

"What place could look *that* bad to a demon?" Khalid murmured.

"We will know soon enough," Tamar replied.

"I do not think I want to know," said Hafiz.

The gale's roar faded steadily all around them. Hafiz thought he felt a lightening of the air as the last of the sand settled. Still he did not unveil his eyes.

Then he felt something small and damp nudge his ankle. "You can look now," said a voice rumbly with purrs.

"Boabdil!" Hafiz let the end of his turban fall as he dropped to his knees before the cat. "How did you come here?"

"I borrowed a place inside the demon's sandal, just where the thong divides her great toe from the rest.

You know, she really *would* benefit from a bath." He licked his fur vigorously.

"It is all right now; the sandstorm is gone." Hafiz tugged at Khalid's trousers. "We are here."

"But where is 'here'?" Tamar wondered. The storm had died, but there was still nothing but sand to meet the eye in whatever direction it chose to look.

"Can you not tell?" Rafiqa asked. "Do you not feel it?"

Khalid and Tamar confessed themselves at a loss.

The demon made an impatient sound. "You genies have dwelled among mortals too long; it has blunted your senses. It is just over those dunes. You will have to feel it then: the power! The untold power of magical wards strong enough even to bar *me* from intrusion!"

"Where are we?" Hafiz demanded. "What power? Where are Rashid and Aminah? You promised—"

"Hush, you and your talk of promises!" Rafiqa snapped. "I want to find the children as much as you do."

"Yes, and we all know why," Tamar said darkly.

"You have no right to look at me like that, Genie," Rafiqa told Tamar. "I promised to find the children and I shall. What I do with them *after* they are found is another story."

"If my father were here, he would write you a different ending to that story!" Hafiz blustered.

"But your father is *not* here, little mouse." The demon bent low to chuck Hafiz under the chin, shrinking herself as she did so. "So do not squeak so loudly, lest you wake the lion."

Boabdil presented himself with a triumphant yowl. "Do not speak of mice to us, O Rafiqa! I have learned from long observation that he who underestimates the mouse often goes without his dinner."

"Cat!" the demon exclaimed with pleasure. "How did you come here?"

Boabdil closed his eyes and solemnly replied, "Magic. Fear me."

Rafiqa only laughed. She straightened up, regaining the greater part of her gigantic stature, though she was nowhere near as large as she had been when she brought her captives into the desert. "All cats partake of magic," she declared. "It is only enough to overcome the common sense of mortals. Since you have chosen to accompany us, then come along. When we find the children you will see for yourself that I am one lion who does not let her prey slip through the paws."

With that, she picked up the cat and set out across the dunes. Hafiz and the genies hastened to keep up with her. It was not easy for the boy. The demon's stride equaled five of his own and the sand made him flounder. Khalid and Tamar did what they could to help him along, but the Bound pair were preoccupied with their own plight. For the sake of the child they hoped to have, they would not unclasp their hands for anything short of the world's end. If they did offer the boy their free hands, it was an awkward gesture, not very much help at all.

At first Hafiz was exasperated by this. He took more than a few tumbles down the steep sides of windblown sandhills. A child of the city and the palace, he fast discovered that the worst part about travel is the way the sand has of getting into every gap in a person's garb and building new dunes where it lies. He kept his lips pressed tightly together, yet still his teeth crunched loudly every time they met.

He was on the point of making a stand and refusing to take another step when he caught up with Rafiqa and the rest. They were standing motionless atop a ripple-sided dune. At first he thought that they had paused to wait for him; then he saw their eyes were fixed on something that lay before them, not behind.

When he drew up to them, he saw what they did: The desert sand fell away at their feet, the gleaming grains blending into the deeper yellows and ochres of a sandstone outcrop. This is turn formed one slope of a bowl-shaped valley and at its bottom was—O impossible!—a meadow of breathtaking green. Fine horses grazed at ease, or ran for the pleasure of their own beauty running, or drank together in amity from the crystal waters of a lake that had no business being so very cool and blue in the heart of so very desolate a desert.

On the far shore of the lake was a cluster of crude tents, beyond the tents grew a grove of regal date palms, and in the midst of the grove stood a building that had even less business being in the midst of the desert than the lake.

Hafiz rubbed his eyes. He could not convince himself this was no dream. He who had been raised in a great palace had never seen anything half so grand as this building. It was not tall, but did not need height to make an impression. Its lines were clean and simple as those of a pyramid—in fact, it began as a pyramid. Rose-red stone lay in great slanting slabs against its flanks, rising to where the edifice changed shape, becoming a perfect cube of blue-veined marble topped at last by a disc of purest gold. Twin lions perched rampant atop the cube, holding the bright disc in their paws. They had been carved of porphyry and looked likelife enough so that Hafiz was amazed not to hear them roar.

"What is this place?" he breathed, feeling the magic seep up through his bones.

"This is the Tomb of Solomon," Khalid replied. His own words bore a great burden of awe. "This valley is holy to all creatures of magic."

"It is so," Tamar concurred. "I never thought to see it while I lived. Its location is a closely guarded secret; not even the Council can find it, though they unite their arts to try."

"Not even my folk—demon or ifrit—can find this place through magical means," Rafiqa said. "The spells at work here are too strong."

"Then how did we get here?" Hafiz asked.

The demon's bat wings rose and fell. "If I had told my powers to bring us to the Tomb of Solomon, we would still be standing in the palace garden. But since I asked to be brought to where those two dear, sweet, tender children are hidden—"

"Stop calling them *tender*!" Hafiz shouted.

Khalid frowned. "But whose tents, whose horses are those that profane this sacred spot?" he demanded.

"That I do not know," the demon replied. "This place may not be found through deliberate magic, but there is nothing in the warding spells to prevent its accidental discovery. Behold the golden disc which the lions bear! Its purpose is to cast mirages that will cause desert wanderers to turn their footsteps away from here. Yet mirages do not fare abroad by night; wanderers may. It is all in the lap of Fate, who finds this place and who does not."

"Then how did Azem find it?" Hafiz wondered aloud. "This is where your magic brought us when you asked it to bring us to Aminah and Rashid, so here it is that Azem must have brought them as well."

Rafiqa did not give the question much thought. "Fate has a very large lap," she said.

"I would hazard that Azem did not command his own magic to bring the children to the Tomb of Solomon, calling it so," Tamar suggested. "He more likely commanded it to bear them all to a place where none might hope to find them, naming no names."

Hafiz considered the sheath in his hands. "I could

ask him." He spoke so quietly that no one save the cat could heard him.

"And he will tell you to make your question into a wish," Boabdil reminded him, likewise speaking low. "How they came to be here is of no importance. How we shall save them from Rafiqa once we find them, *that* is important. And for that purpose it might pay to use your remaining wish."

"Half a wish," Hafiz prompted.

"We cats do not concern ourselves with fractions," Boabdil replied, setting his tail at a jaunty angle and starting down the slope.

"Hoi! Wait for me!" Rafiqa called after him.

To say that the arrival of the giant she-demon caused a stir among the beings already in the valley is to call a diamond a piece of rock. The horses, being beasts of inborn sagacity, got one whiff of her approach and stampeded across the meadow, up the far side of the valley, and out into the desert. They believed wholeheartedly that their chances for survival were better in the burning sands than anywhere near Rafiqa.

As for the humans, those who were in the open beheld the demon's coming and behaved much like their steeds, only without as much elegance of movement. They fled helter-skelter, taking no care if their flight happened to trample their comrades. A handful of them had taken the precaution of keeping their horses tethered to tentpoles. A wild struggle followed as riders tried to mount, men on foot tried to pull riders from the saddle, and the tethered horses themselves took a great whiff of demon-scent, panicked, and lashed out at anyone within hoof range.

By the time Rafiqa and the rest actually set foot within the bounds of the camp, all was pandemonium. Boabdil prudently got himself out of the way, making a great leap onto Hafiz's shoulder, then onto the boy's head, and from there onto Khalid's turban. The twin bumps which were the genie's horns provided him with an excellent paw-hold.

Rafiqa was neither pleased nor impressed by the uproar she had caused. Growing herself slightly larger, she plucked one of the men from his feet and barked, "Where are they?"

Her captive replied, "Where are who?" It was a sensible question.

Rafiqa did not see it that way and ate him, tough or not. She then scooped up a second man and repeated the question.

"N—Noble Lady, Almighty Creature, Being of Infinite Mercy and Kindness—"

Rafiqa was as impatient with flattery as she was with ignorance. She ate him, too.

She was about to serve a third unlucky fellow in the same way when Hafiz spoke up. "I know these people! See how they are dressed. These are the hordes of Malak the Murderous, who demanded to marry my sister!"

"And who ruined a very nice birthday party," Boabdil added.

The man in Rafiqa's clutches heard the name of Malak and almost turned himself inside-out, trying to bow low while dangling in midair. "Yes! Yes! It must be my lord Malak you want, O Fearsome One! Spare me and I will take you to him, do with him what you will. May his name be cursed from where the sun rises unto where it sets, he has brought us to our deaths."

"You are not exactly the mirror of loyalty, are you?" Rafiqa remarked, turning him this way and that.

The man, feeling his death was inevitable, abruptly lost all fear, for fear is the cradlemate of hope. "I, not loyal?" He spat at the demon's feet. The glob took a long time getting there. "That is all you know of loyalty! I owe my lord my life, in the normal course of things. I am willing to die for Malak in battle, for conquest, or defending what is already ours, but he has asked too much. I did not become a desert rider to face howling monsters!"

"I am not howling," Rafiqa said. "But I can make you howl, soon enough."

"Ha!" Knowing he was doomed, the fellow was determined to spend his last few breaths in defying the demon. "I do not doubt it. Yet I tell you, you are not the only monster in these parts. Ten thousand miseries upon Malak's head, where did he ever find *those* two?"

"Those two?" Tamar seized on the man's words and would have snatched him from Rafiqa's grasp if she could. "Children? Are they children? Oh, tell us at once where they are!"

"They *look* like children," the man replied. "Although I have never had to go to the trouble of seeing such creatures at close range before. I left those matters in the hands of my wives, which is wisdom. Ah, more than divine wisdom, if what I have suffered here be any indication of what it is like to tend those—those—" He broke off, shivering with unpleasant memories. "We had just left the great city, where my lord Malak had been so grossly ill-used and insulted. We were heading home to fetch the rest of my lord's troops for the promised attack when night fell and we happened upon this delectable spot. My lord Malak claimed it was a sign that we were blessed. We believed him." The man laughed bitterly.

Rafiqa gave him a shake that jerked the laughter from his lips. "You still have not told us where the children are."

"And if I do not tell you fast enough or in a manner to your liking, you will eat me, is that it?" The fellow had turned defiant.

"Tell us any way you like, but tell us," Rafiqa said. Her eyes swept the camp, which by this time was deserted. If she did not use her captive well, she would be hard put to find another for questioning. "I will not eat you; you have the word of a demon on it."

"That is more than generous of you, my—my lady." The man was suspicious, but went on. "If we were blessed, as my lord Malak claimed, then may all my enemies have such blessings! We had not camped here long before the sky turned black and a shape made of doom and despair descended from the clouds to the very pinnacle of yonder structure." He pointed to the Tomb of Solomon. "The shape slid down the eastern face of the building and rushed in at the one doorway. We trembled in fear, knowing that our lord Malak was within—no tent for *him*! Oh no! A few brave souls ventured inside, to stand by him in battle against the dark unknown, should that be needful." He sighed. "It was not. The dark shape came back into the open air and flew away, taking the clouds with it. It was shortly after that we heard the howling."

"Aminah!" Hafiz exclaimed. "She *does* howl."

"Not half so loudly as the second one, another gift of the darkness," the man grumped. "At least the first one stops that unbearable racket after feeding—sometimes. The other one—! I have heard my lord Malak in a temper; his curses can turn a field of full grown barley to burnt stubble. Well, believe me when I tell you that when the *other* monster has a fit of temper, he leaves my lord Malak three leagues behind and a horse short."

"That must be Rashid," Hafiz said. "I did not realize he knew so many useful curses." He sounded as if his friend had gained new stature in his eyes.

"The monsters are in there," the man concluded, pointing to the Tomb of Solomon. "So is my lord

Malak. Now eat me. At least if I am devoured, I may find some peace."

"I gave you my word as a demon that I would not eat you." Rafiqa set him down carefully. "Run along." She shooed him the way his comrades had bolted. He stood there in shock for an instant, then blinked at his good luck and raced off on the path churned up by countless pounding hooves and feet.

There were two guards who still held fast to their posts at the doorway to the Tomb of Solomon. Rafiqa had not noticed them earlier, for the entrance to the Tomb was at the end of a well-recessed passage. They tried to stand her off with their spears; it was like threatening an elephant with a splinter. She picked them up and popped them out of their armor, a pair of human pistachio nuts. She brought the first to within a handspan of her lips, then made a face, set him and his partner down, and ordered them to begone. They did not wait for a second warning.

"Rafiqa, why did you do that?" Khalid asked. "Can it be that you know the meaning of mercy?"

"No, but I do know the meaning of appetite. I do not want to fill up on grownups. I am saving room for something better." With this comforting observation, the demon ducked her head to pass beneath the lintel of the Tomb of Solomon.

CHAPTER TWENTY-NINE

"Do not blame me." Rafiqa crossed her arms. "I did not know it was a maze!"

Khalid and Tamar gave her a hard stare as they leaned against the cool stone wall of the Tomb. "*Everyone* knows that the Tomb of Solomon is a maze!" Khalid said. "It is one of the first lessons they teach us in the classroom! From the way you plunged into this place, we assumed you knew the pattern that would bring us to the inmost chamber."

"Well, I did not," the demon shot back. "You genies make me ill, always flaunting how *educated* you are! Tell me, did you also learn how to read in that precious classroom of yours?"

Khalid was smug. "Of course!"

"Then read *that*." The demon jabbed a claw at the lines and lines of exotic characters carved on the Tomb wall. "Maybe it is a set of directions for finding our way through the maze."

Rafiqa spread her wings wide, so that their fires gave light enough for even the most weak-eyed scribe to read by. Khalid gave her a superior look and bent to the task. He stayed silent a considerable while. The only movement he made was when he would occasionally wipe away the smoke smudges that Rafiqa's fires left on the stone. When he at last stood tall he no longer looked so superior.

"It is written in a tongue I do not know," he said.

"Nor I," said Tamar after she too had examined the carvings.

"Do not expect me to read it," Boabdil said. Hafiz only shook his head, silently confessing himself ignorant.

"May the Infernal Lords obliterate this place!" Rafiqa swore, slamming her fist into the wall. The stone did not crumble; it did not even crack under a blow capable of smashing a boulder to powder.

"It seems that the Infernal Lords have little power here," Boabdil observed. He climbed down from Khalid's turban. "If magic cannot guide us, we must use our wits. I say that we split up and search for the way to the heart of the maze singly."

"You must think I was born yesterday." Rafiqa's hands were on her hips. She had dwindled to human height in order to walk the passageways of the Tomb. "I am not going to let you out of my sight."

"How would we escape?" Boabdil reasoned with her. "We might find a way out of the Tomb, back into the green valley—and then? We do not know where the valley lies and we have no means to travel beyond its borders. The desert is a better jailer than you."

"These two would not have that problem." Rafiqa indicated Khalid and Tamar. "I will not have them escape to fly back to the palace and fetch help."

"Keep them under your eye, by all means." The cat's tone was silken. "But you will risk nothing letting the boy and me try our luck."

The demon thought this over. "You are right. Wait." She drew a golden thread from her veil. Unlike a mortal garment, it did not unravel, though the thread she pulled from it seemed to stretch on for leagues. An unnatural brightness shone from the enchanted strand, illuminating the passageway. When she at last reached the end of it, Rafiqa seized Hafiz's hand and wound the thread rapidly around his wrist. "There! Now even if you find nothing, you will at least be able to find us again; also, this shall provide you with enough light to see by." Pleased with her handiwork, she tied the other end of the shining thread to one of the many bracelets jangling at her ankle. "If you find the children first, tug on the thread and we shall come to you. If we find them first—" she licked her lips absentmindedly "—we will let you know."

"May Fortune favor us." Boabdil inclined his head to the demon, then sat up on his haunches to paw at a loop of the shining thread. "Come, Hafiz."

Hafiz jogged after the cat, who led him back down the same passageway they had so recently walked with Rafiqa and the genies. He felt the thread dribble from his wrist as they ran. Sometimes it tangled itself around the jewelled scabbard he carried, sometimes it worked its way into a snarl around his fingers. "Boabdil, wait!" he called.

"Just a little farther," the cat called back without breaking stride.

Hafiz was angry. It struck him that he had spent more of his time lately in running after someone or other. If it was not his parents or Rashid or the demon Rafiqa, it was this outrageous animal. He did not mind all this running, but he did not particularly enjoy it, either. Above all, he felt that if he had to run, he also had the right to know why, and where he was going, and if there was any hope that he might get there soon.

Accordingly he stopped dead, took aim, and launched the scabbard like a javelin. It was dark in the Tomb, but the clew of golden thread around his wrist gave light enough for what he had in mind. The scabbard flew down the corridor to land with a clatter ahead of the cat.

Boabdil jumped and whirled around. "Are you trying to kill me?" he hissed.

"No, I am trying to save Rashid and my sister. So are you, I imagine. I will not go another step until you tell me your scheme; I know I can help."

"Scheme? What scheme?" the cat asked, his eyes empty of guile.

"I know you, Boabdil. You would sooner be without your tail than without a scheme," Hafiz said.

The cat chuckled. "Yes, you do know me, and I do you a disservice by not letting you in on my plans. I only wanted to be sure we had put enough distance between ourselves and Rafiqa before I told you what I have in mind. Demons are a notoriously keen-eared breed." He harked in the direction Rafiqa and the genies had gone, then relaxed. "I think it is safe to speak."

Hafiz sat with his back to the Tomb wall, his knees drawn up to his chin. "Tell me then, O Boabdil, what is your plan? It must be very clever. Of course it will all depend on us being the first ones to find Rashid and Aminah, is this not so?"

"That goes without saying."

"Yes, yes, and since we know that Malak the Murderous lurks within this Tomb, it must be that where we find him, we will find them. He would never trust two such important hostages to his troops."

"You have read my mind precisely. I suppose I do not need to tell you how he knows they are important?" Boabdil drawled.

"He recognized their importance the moment he saw them! Else why would they arrive at his camp in such dramatic fashion?" Hafiz's finger scored an invisible point for himself on the air.

"Or Azem told him who they were when he brought them here." Boabdil had his practical side.

"So now it will be a simple thing to find them, for they all need to eat. Malak's men must bring their food to them in here. It is pleasant in the valley, but the air is even cooler within these walls."

"True; I have often said that when it comes to living well, there is nothing like a tomb." The cat gnawed a pesky dewclaw and said, "You astound me, Hafiz. You have seen my plan through almost to the end, yet I wager you will never guess what comes next. *Why* will it be so simple to find them?"

"Ho, ho! You will lose that wager. Because of the smoke!" He held up the glowing clew around his wrist and showed Boabdil the faint smudge marks that Rafiqa's wings had made in passing. "Where these signs are thickest, it means that people bearing torches have passed most often. Malak and his captives do not dine in the dark. Follow the smoke and we find my sister and my friend!"

"Splendid!" The cat patted Hafiz's foot. "There you have it." He did not tell Hafiz that nearly every word the boy had spoken came as a revelation to the cat, whose only plan thus far had been *Wait and see*. It was a good thing for the beast's pride that every one of his feline race was master of pretending that he already knew everything in the world worth knowing. "Now let us find the smudge trail and—"

"Just a moment." Hafiz did not stir. "What about the rest of your plan?"

"The rest of—? You—I have already told it to you."

"You have not yet told me what we shall do once we find them. *That* will be the hard part."

"Mmmmm, so it will," the cat allowed. He brightened. "Not so hard as all that. Once we find them, you will call up Azem, make your last wish and—"

"Half a wish," Hafiz said. "I wi—I would be happy if you would remember that."

"In the right hands, half a wish is better than one." Boabdil was quite cheerful. "The widest waste is still crossed pace by pace. By the time we find Aminah and Rashid, I will have figured out a way for you to use your last *half* wish so that Azem must give you the whole of your desires."

"And afterwards, he will be free," Hafiz mumbled.

Boabdil was not discouraged. "Pace by pace, my friend, pace by pace!" He set off down the passageway, and this time Hafiz followed.

By the light of the enchanted thread they soon found a track of soot on the Tomb wall that seemed especially thick. "Now our only problem is discovering which way leads *to* Malak and which leads *away*," Hafiz remarked.

"That way," Boabdil said without hesitation. He kinked his tail to the left.

"How did you know?"

"I do not. but if the left-hand way does not lead us to Malak, it will at least take us to the door of the Tomb. It is better to know the way *out* of trouble before you seek the way in."

Hafiz could not argue with that, so he permitted the cat to have his way. They followed the smudge on the wall through passages that sloped up and passages that sloped down. Once the narrow way opened up into a vast hall where sunlight spilled from windows too high up and too cunningly placed to be seen. Once they wove in and out among a forest of pillars, jade green as the bosom of the sea. Once they came across a room where a single goblet stood in lonely beauty upon a plain white pedestal. Sometimes they thought they heard the music of flutes and drums, sometimes the sound of distant voices singing, and once they fled from the groans of lost souls in pain.

A path that leads the wanderer through many wonders is still a tiring path. Hafiz's feet hurt, and the coil of golden thread around his wrist was growing thinner and thinner.

"Oh, Boabdil, what shall we do if we reach the end of this before we find either the way out of the Tomb or Malak's lair?" he whined. They were in another of the Tomb's narrower passageways and the looming walls made him feel small and scared.

"We shall answer that question when we must," the cat replied. "Look there! The smudge is thicker than before and my whiskers tell me that this corridor is about to blossom into a room where we may catch our breath. Do not give up; you will see that I am right."

"May it be so," said Hafiz.

No one was more pleased (or surprised) than the cat when his prophetic words came true. They had not gone much farther before the cramped corridor did open up into a large, square chamber. The walls of this place were covered with the same alien scrawl that had baffled Khalid and Tamar, but sharing those same overscribbled walls were row after row of perfectly painted cats. Statues of cats big and small crowded the chamber floor. Images of cats were picked out in mosaic on the domed ceiling. In the center of the room, on a bluestone platform, stood a wooden ark. Boabdil and Hafiz walked around it slowly. Each face of the box and the top as well was adorned with the likeness of a regal feline.

"So now we know that King Solomon was truly the wisest of men," Boabdil said. "He knew how to appreciate cats." He sat contemplating the chamber with pride.

"Time runs out for even the wisest of men," Hafiz said. "That is what Grandfather always says. Let us waste no more of it here." He checked the walls for the telltale trace of smoke.

"Hafiz, it will cost us nothing to admire this room a while longer," the cat wheedled, winding his way in and out between Hafiz's ankles in his most persuasive manner. Hafiz ignored him; Boabdil changed his tune. "Oh, very well," he said, planting all four feet solidly. "If you are in such a rush, you can go ahead without me*eeeeee*YOW!"

It was a mistake for Boabdil to stop rubbing Hafiz's legs in that way, without warning. The boy was distracted, searching the walls for the smudge trail. He was looking up, not down. He did not realize that his next step would land right on the cat's tail.

Which it did. Boabdil's shriek reverberated through the chamber.

The last echoes still haunted the upper reaches of the dome, mixed with Hafiz's gabbled words of apology, when they heard it: a harsh, dragging, scraping noise. Neither spoke; neither moved; both turned to stare in the direction of the nerve-grating sound.

The top of the wooden ark was moving.

"Oh, Boabdil—!" Hafiz whispered in an agony of terror.

The cat did not answer. His fur stood out all around him like a hedgehog's bristles, he growled low in his throat, and his eyes were fixed on the moving lid.

Bit by bit the heavy slab of wood crept crabwise to the side until, with a crash and a clatter, it fell to the floor. From within, a solitary apparition rose up, a tiny figure swathed in fine linen bandages. A pair of gold hoops was attached through the wrappings to the creature's ears, a pearl-studded collar of blue and green enamelwork encircled the elegant neck. Two forepaws, individually bandaged, rested themselves on the rim of the ark.

Twin green fires burned where the eyes should have been. A voice very like Boabdil's own emanated from the covered mouth: "*Who summons Yeshisha?*"

CHAPTER THIRTY

"There is one thing about the lap of Fate," said Boabdil. "Every time you climb into it, you do not get petted; you get thumped on the head."

"Oh, stop your complaining!" Rafiqa said, kneeling to tie the last knot in the golden collar around Boabdil's neck. "We would have found you sooner or later. As it was the two of you came running down that hallway as if the hosts of Eblis were at your heels." She stood up, the end of the leash in her hand.

"We were hoping it would be later," the cat returned, his face twisted into a grouchy expression that looked like it was there to stay. He tried scratching the collar off, but one touch was enough. He yowled in pain and licked his burning paw.

"Why did the golden thread not burn me when I had it wrapped around my wrist?" Hafiz wondered.

"Count your blessings." Boabdil hunkered down, all four paws tucked under him until he resembled a cushion.

"It did not burn you because you did not try to remove it," Rafiqa told Hafiz. Then, to Boabdil, "Let that be a lesson to you. Next time I tell you to stop, you stop. If I had not caught you as you raced past us, you would still be running."

"That is not a bad idea." Boabdil cast a nervous glance behind him and shivered.

"Why *were* you running so fast?" Tamar asked Hafiz. "Did you find the children? Were there guards? Did they attack you?"

Hafiz imitated Boabdil's backward-glance-and-shiver to the life. "You do not want to know what we found," he said. "It was awful. It was hideous. It was—"

"*It was ridiculous!*" A ghostly voice drifted out of the passageway, followed in short order by the small, bandaged and bejewelled figure that had put Hafiz and Boabdil to flight. It walked into the midst of the search party boldly, if a bit stiffly. Its tail was held erect and there was a tiny jasper scarab tied to the tip. With a few creaks and cracks, the creature seated itself at Rafiqa's feet, fiery green eyes glowing behind linen strips. "*They summoned me, and then they ran away. Now they insult me. You look like a demon with a little common sense: Does that sound right to you? Does it sound kind to me?*"

"Ohhhh, you poor dear!" Rafiqa took the creature to her bosom. "I might have guessed it was a mistake to let you two go off on your own," she said, glowering at Hafiz and Boabdil. "Now see what you have done!"

"What *we* have done?" Boabdil was incredulous. "We did nothing! We were seeking the children when suddenly, for no reason, we were attacked by that—that—whatever-it-is." He waved a paw at the thing in Rafiqa's arms.

"*I am not a whatever-it-is,*" came the reply. "*I am Yeshisha! In the days before days, when King Solomon ruled with wisdom and cats were born with better manners, I was his favorite pet. He received me from the hands of his Egyptian wife, Pharaoh's daughter. I am of the royal line of Bast, a sacred maiden of Her temple, a direct descendent of the great Mooncat! And you, my unworthy kitten, are a fool.*"

"You . . . are a cat?" Boabdil's whiskers quivered.

"*I* was *a cat.*" The green fires burned brighter. "*Oh, what a cat I was! The great King Solomon himself often came to me for advice.*'

"I thought Boabdil was the only cat capable of human speech," Hafiz said.

"*In these sorry times, perhaps he is.*" Yeshisha shook her head. "*Much has changed; the world is not what it was. I never thought I would see the day when a tomcat in the flower of his strength would summon me, then run away like a granary mouse.*"

Boabdil struck his haughtiest pose. "Royal Lady, if I have wronged you, you also wrong me by presuming I know what you are talking about. What is all this chitter-chat of summoning?"

"*You pronounced the Word of Power,*" Yeshisha told him. "*Do you not recall it?*" The mummified cat lifted her chin and uttered the exact caterwaul that had burst from Boabdil's mouth when Hafiz stepped on his tail. "*Like that.*"

Khalid frowned. "*That* is a Word of Power? 'Meow'?"

Yeshisha's eyes flamed with wrath. "*Do not mock our ways, O Genie! At least no one needed to rub the side of my coffin to summon me. Besides, your accent is atrocious.*"

"Your forgiveness, O Highborn!" Boabdil rolled on his back in a display of complete surrender. "The summoning was accidental. We did not know. I would sooner be chased by wild dogs than disturb your eternal rest."

"*Hmmmm. Maybe I was hasty, calling you rude and foolish.*" Yeshisha was mollified by Boabdil's graceful apology. She looked at Rafiqa and said, "*Put me down, O Demon.*"

Rafiqa scratched Yeshisha's swaddled ears, but obeyed. The mummified cat approached Boabdil, making those small, questioning motions with her nose that are the common coin of feline introduction. Boabdil did not flinch, but sniffed back.

"Your breath is sweet with spices, O Daughter of Bast," he purred. "And your coat is sleek with the fat of many slaughtered mice."

"*Flatterer!*" No cat can giggle, yet Yeshisha gave that impression of girlish pleasure at Boabdil's gallant words. "*There is no need to court my favor. I am at your service. To this purpose was I dedicated centuries ago, when King Solomon died. Oh, the mourning that there was on that dreadful day! My lady was wholly undone by grief. It was she who wrapped me in these very linens with her own hands and placed me in the Tomb with her departed husband.*"

"You mean—you mean you were buried *alive*?" Hafiz was stunned.

Yeshisha did not view the matter as at all shocking. "*When a great man died, it was the custom among my lady's people to send a few reliable servants into the Afterlife to wait upon him. It was said to be a great honor.*"

"Yes, by those who did the sending, not by those who were sent," Tamar remarked quietly.

The mummy twitched her tail, making the scarab at the tip clatter over the floor. "*If I did not mind, why should you? My lady was a great sorceress. She laid a spell upon me before wrapping me as you see. I felt no pain.*"

"But to be imprisoned—*entombed* all these centuries—!" Khalid protested.

Yeshisha was still indifferent to the reactions that her condition seemed to provoke in others. "*It is not as bad as you think. For the most part, I sleep. That is not a bad job for a cat. And my lady laid a generous supply of mummified mice in the coffin with me.*" She made a sound as if she were licking her chops, but of course it was impossible to see what she was doing under the bandages.

"Well, you may return to your sleep now," Rafiqa said. "We are all sorry to have disturbed you."

"I cannot." Yeshisha folded her paws demurely. *"The spell which sustains me also demands that I render help to any who summon me. Only after this condition is fulfilled may I return to my rest."*

"O Pearl of Enchantment and Delight, as I have told you, the summoning was accidental," Boabdil mewed.

"Nevertheless, it was spoken. Aye, and yours was the mouth that spoke of it. Therefore I will serve you. What will you have of me?"

"Ah me! More wishes?" Boabdil pretended that this was the worst news he had ever heard in his life. "Very well, for my first wish—

"Wishes? Do you take me for a common genie?" Yeshisha spat.

"Common?" Khalid and Tamar echoed as one.

"Then how may you serve me, if not by granting wishes?" Boabdil asked.

"I can serve you as I served others before you: by giving you the same sage advice I gave King Solomon."

"Oh." Boabdil was crestfallen. "I suppose that means you cannot get this insulting collar off my neck."

For her reply, Yeshisha extended one paw and made a slashing motion at Boabdil's throat. The collar fell to the floor, every filament of the golden thread severed. Boabdil stared in admiration and amazement as Yeshisha's claws retracted through tiny holes in her swaddlings.

"I would advise you *to know better than to try collaring a cat against his will,"* the mummy informed Rafiqa.

"Hmph!" The demon gathered up the shredded remains of her magic thread. "Is that all you can do? Give advice no one wanted and destroy things that do not belong to you?"

"*No.*" Yeshisha was unruffled by Rafiqa's sarcasm. "*There is one other service I may perform for the one who summons me.*"

"And what might that be?"

"*I can guide him through the Tomb of Solomon. That was the chief purpose for which my lady placed me here. It is a very large and complicated place, this Tomb. She did not want to get lost every time she came to pay her respects to her dead husband, and Pharaoh's daughter would never lower herself to ask directions from a mere human.*"

"You can guide us through the Tomb?" Hafiz repeated eagerly.

"*Have I not said so?*" The mummy approached him; Hafiz stood his ground and even called up courage enough to pat her head. He was surprised and charmed to hear her purr. "*I know this Tomb like the back of my paw. Waking or sleeping, nothing happens within these stone walls that I do not know or dream.*"

"Then you can tell us where to find my sister Aminah and my friend Rashid!" Hafiz cried.

"*Nothing is simpler.*" Yeshisha turned to Boabdil. "*You have only to ask it.*"

"How beautiful are your ears with gold, O Bast's Daughter." Boabdil rubbed his jowl against Yeshisha's. "Consider it asked."

"*There is the entrance to the heart of the Tomb of Solomon.*" Yeshisha indicated the open doorway with her scarab-tipped tail. "*And there you will find what you seek.*"

"Are you sure?" Hafiz squinted. "It looks so dark in there, and so quiet—"

An ear-piercing wail gave the lie to his last words.

"Aminah!" He started forward, but Khalid's hand fell upon his shoulder, holding him back.

"Shhhh!" the genie cautioned. "We do not know what else lies beyond that doorway."

"Nor do we care!" Rafiqa said. "What is there to fear? I am a demon! If there is anything on this earth or under it more fearsome than myself, I should like to see it!"

At this very moment, Aminah's crying was interrupted by a howling so eerie, so unnatural, that it made Rafiqa jump back with an involuntary squeak of dismay. "By all the Lords Infernal, what was that?"

"Aaaaaaiiiiiieeeeeeeee!" Another howl, as unnerving as the first, answered her.

"Ah, what a miracle!" Rafiqa said, forcing a smile. "I am no longer hungry; imagine that! I think I will be on my way." She turned to go, only to find Boabdil blocking her path.

"You promised to take us to the children," he growled.

"What is your complaint?" the demon replied. "I have kept my promise. The children are right through that doorway. Go ahead and get them."

"We do not *know* that they are there," the cat challenged. "Until we see them, alive, and well, your promise is unfulfilled."

"How would you like to spend eternity as a rug?" Rafiqa snarled. She lifted her foot, ready to put her threat into action.

Just then, the howling ceased. In the silence, it was possible to hear individual grains of sand tumbling across the Tomb floor. Hafiz counted forty-nine of them before he heard a strong young voice say:

"You can howl all you like; I am *not* going to change her diaper for you."

"Rashid!" Hafiz gasped in recognition. He ran to peer in through the open doorway.

There indeed was his friend, there was his sister, and there too was Malak the Murderous. Rashid was the image of immovability, arms folded, eyes shut, back turned on the desert lord and the sobbing infant in his arms.

"You said you would *try* it," Malak moaned. He did not look so murderous now; he looked at his wit's end. "You watched me do it once. You watched my men do it. If one of them were here I would have him do it, but I do not know what has become of them all. I will have the disloyal dogs beheaded for abandoning me like this! I will have you beheaded if you do not at least *try*."

Rashid closed his ears to the threat. "Then do so. I am a prince. Princes do not change diapers."

Malak uttered another one of those spine-raking howls. "*I* am a prince too, yet I changed her!"

"That is different." Rashid was unyielding. "She is your wife."

"Not yet." Malak held the baby at arm's length as the little one's face scrunched up for a fresh bout of angry tears. "Maybe never. *Definitely* never! Truly I swear that if I could lay hands on that ill-omened genie who brought her to me, I would give her back in an instant. Take her! For the love of the Most High, take her and I will—I will give you my finest horses! I will give you your weight in gold! I will let you hold the sword when we behead the men who *ought* to be here changing this brat!"

"Do not call my sister a brat!" Hafiz stormed into the room, waving the scabbard as if it were the Sword it no longer contained.

"Hafiz!" Rashid rushed to greet his friend as the rest of the rescue party entered the chamber.

"So this is the burial chamber of King Solomon," Khalid said, gazing all around him in wonder.

"No, this is what they call *the burial chamber,"* Yeshisha corrected him. *"The true resting place of the great king lies hidden beneath more layers of spells than anyone—mortal or not—can ever hope to penetrate."*

"There you are!" Rafiqa stood facing Malak. At first sight of her, the desert lord's face crumpled like a damp rag. "What do you mean by making such sounds, scaring innocent demons?"

"Mercy, in the name of heaven!" Malak whimpered, falling to his knees. They did not have the chance to touch the floor before Rafiqa snatched the baby from his arms.

"And what do you mean by making such a fuss over something like *this*?" she demanded. She swelled in size so that she could balance Aminah on the palm of one hand while with the other she expertly whipped off the infant's soiled diaper. She plucked a fresh one from the pile of rags she spied in one corner of the chamber and had the baby clean and sweet-smelling in the blink of an eye. Aminah crowed with pleasure at the novelty of it all and tried to suck Rafiqa's talon.

"*Men*," was all the demon said. While Rafiqa dealt with the baby, Hafiz and Rashid had been in earnest conference. Now both boys strode manfully up to the still-cowering Malak, holding the scabbard between them.

"Hear me, O Malak!" Hafiz pronounced, doing his best to sound imposing. "Behold this empty sheath and know that the Sword of Solomon is free once more. As you value your life, swear that you will no longer demand my sister's hand in marriage!"

"Yes, and swear also that you will never invade my grandfather's kingdom!" Rashid put in.

"Your sister? You may keep her! And as for the kingdom, keep that, too." Malak wiped cold sweat from his brow. "All I ask is a good horse and the open desert. Bad things happen to me between stone walls."

"Granted." Hafiz inclined his head in the way he had seen the sultan do when bestowing favors on his nobles. "But you will have to get the horse yourself," he added.

Malak did not stay to haggle over horses. He took to his heels and was gone before Yeshisha could offer to show him the way out.

"Now let us go home," Hafiz told his friend.

"How?" Rashid asked. "We do not even know where we are."

"Do not fear," Tamar told them. "Khalid and I may not be able to grant you wishes, but there is no law the Council ever made that forbids us from summoning our carpets and giving you a ride."

"That is a relief," Rashid said to Hafiz. "I thought you would need to use your last wish to get us home."

"Half wish," Hafiz reminded him.

"Half wish or whole, it would have released Azem forever. Praise the Maker of All Things, now that will never need to happen."

Hafiz felt a pang at his friend's words. Now he would have to spend the rest of his life keeping close watch over his tongue. Nevermore must the words *I wish* slip from his mouth. It would be hard, but he knew it was the way things had to be. He swallowed his true feelings and put on a smile. "No, Rashid, never."

"*I will lead you to the entrance of the Tomb now, if that is your desire,*" Yeshisha said to Boabdil. The living cat could have sworn that she sounded wistful. Before he could question her, she was heading out of the so-called burial chamber of Solomon, the rest of the rescue party filing after her.

Not *all* the rest of the rescue party.

"Wait for me!" Rafiqa called. "I do not want to blunder around inside this pile of old stones and bones."

"Hurry up, then," Khalid snapped. His hold on Tamar's hand tightened. "We must not keep this good news from the palace."

"I will not be long," the demon said. She took another rag from the pile of cloths which had served Aminah for diapers and spread it out on the floor. Seating herself tailor fashion, she laid Aminah on it and began to remove the baby's wrappings, one by one. Aminah cooed and gurgled, waving her naked limbs in delight.

Hafiz came to look over the demon's shoulder. "What are you doing?"

Rafiqa tucked a third cloth into the neck of her garment like a bib and smiled a bloodstained smile. "Guess."

CHAPTER THIRTY-ONE

"He guessed," said Boabdil, trotting behind Rafiqa as she stalked the corridors of Solomon's Tomb.

"I will find the wretched boy!" the demon roared. "He cannot have gone far. I would have stopped him at once, but he took me off guard. Who could know that he was able to move so fast? To make away with the infant *and* that awkward scabbard— I thought that because he was plump, he must also be slow and clumsy. Ah, I blame myself for underestimating him." Her fangs ground together. "It is an error I shall not make twice."

Tamar and Khalid ran after the irate demon, the female genie's free hand outstretched, trying to detain her in vain. "Rafiqa, Rafiqa, let them go!" she pleaded.

"Never!" The demon's roar shook the walls. "They are mine. I will haunt these halls until I find them."

"*I wish you would change your mind,*" Yeshisha remarked. "*I do not care for your company.*"

"You will never find them," Prince Rashid maintained. "My friend Hafiz is too clever for you."

"Ho! But I am not the only one who hunts them, little prince." The demon tapped Rashid's chin with the point of one claw. "I have a willing helper."

"Who?" Rashid darted a suspicious glance at the Bound genies.

Rafiqa chortled. "Oh, not them. My helper is a

friend of mine. Would you like to hear her name?" She brought her lips close enough to the prince's ear to make his hair prickle and hissed, "*Hunger.*"

Rashid gaped. While Rafiqa bellowed with laughter over his expression, Boabdil murmured, "The fiend speaks truth. When the infant feels the first pinch of hunger, she will cry and Rafiqa will track the sound. My poor Hafiz."

"*You are fond of the human?*" Yeshisha asked.

"I saw him born," Boabdil told her. "Their eyes are open from the start, did you know that?"

"*Then help him,*" the mummy said. "*If the demon has her ally, your friend needs his.*"

"I do not know which way he ran."

"*Your eyes do not know. Your nose does not share their ignorance.*"

"My nose!" If Boabdil had been human he would have clapped a hand to his brow. "May my whiskers go limp, I have dwelled among humans too long. All the time we wasted, following the trail of smoke smudges on the Tomb wall, when I might have simply sniffed out the hiding place of the children and Malak!"

"*But then you and I would have never met,*" Yeshisha purred. "*Do not stand there staring at me. Find them.*"

Boabdil did not need to be told twice. He stole into the shadows, his nose alert to catch the slightest hint of a scent belonging to Hafiz or Aminah. Yeshisha ran at his side, her bandaged paws whispering over the stone.

Boabdil's nose took them through a winding route that twisted and turned and finally climbed a flight of steps leading up to a bronze door. Boabdil leaned against it with both paws and tumbled out into the sunlight.

"Where are we?" he asked, blinking until his eyes became used to all the brightness.

"*Look up and know,*" Yeshisha replied.

He did so and saw one of the great lions from the roof of the Tomb looming above him. The bronze door through which they had come was the beast's toenail.

Then Boabdil heard the soft sound of weeping. He followed it around the back of the lion's paw and found Hafiz. The boy had his baby sister in his arms, the scabbard tucked under his knees, and tears flooding his face.

"Hush, hush!" Boabdil urged, dashing the tears from Hafiz's face with short, rough dabs of his tongue. "The demon will hear you."

"Oh, Boabdil, what does it matter?" Hafiz leaned his cheek against the cat's fur. Aminah giggled and tried to seize Boabdil's tail. "She will find us eventually, whether or not I keep still now. How can we escape her? Where can we go?"

"Khalid and Tamar will call their carpets to whisk you home," Boabdil told him. "I will tell them that you are on the roof of the Tomb and they will—"

"What of Rashid? Where is he?" Hafiz watched as Boabdil tried to come up with an answer that would reassure them both. It was no use; the cat and the boy both knew the truth of how things stood. "She has him," Hafiz said. "I cannot run away and leave him in her power. He is my friend."

"And Aminah is your sister!"

Hafiz held the baby close. "I cannot let her harm either one of them. If Rafiqa eats them, she will have to eat me too."

"*That will be my pleasure!*" The demon erupted onto the roof. In one hand she crushed the bronze door, in the other she held Rashid. Tamar and Khalid scrambled through the gaping hole, making ineffective grabs for the prince with their enjoined hands.

Boabdil whirled to face Yeshisha. "O Lady, you have said that even King Solomon sought your advice. Help us now! Give us wisdom! Tell us how we may all escape this fiend!"

Yeshisha's head drooped. "*Alas, wisdom is truth and truth is often bitter as a peach seed. Rafiqa is a demon. Even were you to flee from this place, what would keep her from coming after you? There is nothing we can do.*"

"There is something *I* can do," Hafiz said. His eyes had the steely glint of a battle-tried warrior's. He placed his sister in the shade of the lion's paw, picked up the scabbard, and rubbed the great dragon's-belly ruby.

"It is about time!" Azem boomed as he burst from the gem. His eyes took in the many faces, new and old, surrounding Hafiz. "Was such a large audience necessary to witness your last wish, O Master?"

"Half wish," said Boabdil before Hafiz could correct him.

"O Azem, I now know what I most desire," Hafiz said so gravely he looked like a miniature sage. "Above all things, I want Aminah and Rashid to be home, to be safe, to nevermore need fear the demon Rafiqa!"

"The demon Rafiqa?" Amen scratched his tufty skull. "Who is the demon Rafiqa?"

"I am the demon Rafiqa!" The fiend in question put down Rashid and took a menacing step towards Azem. When her foot touched the rooftop she shot up to the height of the lions. "Be warned, O Genie: Do not come between me and my prey."

Azem sized up Rafiqa, then laughed. A snap of his fingers and he stood as tall as the Tomb itself, lions and all. "Be careful whom you call 'genie,' O Insolent Female. I have eaten genies for breakfast."

"Then you have no taste as well as no brains," Rafiqa shot back. "Genies make poor eating, but I doubt a glutton like you would know that. Your uneducated tongue probably could not tell the difference between ambrosia and camel spit."

"Is there a difference?" This time Azem's puzzlement was intended to provoke. Rafiqa scowled and he guffawed triumphantly in her face.

"Get out of my sight, Gourdhead," the demon gritted. "Go now, while yet you may!"

"O woe, my dove, I cannot." Azem pressed his fist to his brow, all false regret. "Although I am no full-blooded genie, there is enough of that taint in my veins. I may not obey your gentle commands until I have fulfilled the final request of my Master. I am certain he will make it wisely." He leered at Hafiz.

The boy knelt on the rooftop of the Tomb, still holding the scabbard tightly in his hands. He licked dry lips, then said, "O Azem, you see that Rafiqa is your foe as well as ours. I beg of you, teach me how I may best use the half wish that is still mine to thwart her. Tell me what I must say to save Aminah and Rashid from her talons and send them safely home. Only this and I swear to you, I will be *your* servant; yes, your *slave*, even until the end of the world!"

"You *my* slave?" Azem doubled over with merriment. "What could you ever do for me, boy? Nothing! And that is just what I will tell and teach you: Nothing! Make your wish however you may and take your chances."

Hafiz squeezed the scabbard so hard that his palms would bear the impressions of its many images for days. "If I wish at all, you will be free. If I do not, you must remain the captive of the ruby. If you do not tell me what I ask, I will *never* make that wish!"

"That is an old threat, O Master." Azem's yawn blew down a row of date palms. "My answer is the same: I will never give a mortal something for nothing. I may lose my chance of freedom, but I will rejoice in my captivity knowing that you shall suffer more."

Rashid crouched beside Hafiz. "Use your wish to save yourself, my friend. Tell him you wish you were twice as safe as you need to be."

Boabdil rested his forepaws on Hafiz's shoulder. "Do not wish at all. If he loves captivity so much, let him have it," he rumbled.

"*Nay.*" Yeshisha spoke into Hafiz's other ear. "*Your enemy walks in ignorance. That which he claims he most desires is that which he least needs.*"

"So!" Rafiqa's teeth flashed in the sunlight. "It seems that you will do nothing to stop me after all, O Gourdhead."

"Not unless *he* wishes it so, no." Azem nodded at Hafiz.

"I do not care to listen to your whys and wherefores," Rafiqa said. "I only listen to my belly, and right now it is telling me that it is past time to dine." Water dripped from her jaws as she bent down, reaching under the lion's paw, seeking the baby.

"Stop!" Tamar dropped Khalid's hand and swooped beneath the lion to nab Aminah from beneath the demon's very claws. She gave a shrill whistle and her own flying carpet appeared within an easy leap of the Tomb roof. She sprang across the gap without hesitation and shot away into the sky.

Rafiqa's arm stretched out of all proportion to her body, her hand flying after Tamar. Her talons hooked into the carpet, anchoring it frozen in midair.

"Will you bring back my supper or shall I come and get it?" the demon growled. She began to drag the carpet back down.

Tamar leaned over the edge of the carpet, the infant cradled in her arms, and turned beseeching eyes to Azem. "Of us all, you are the only one who has the power to overcome Rafiqa! Do so and the Council will welcome you back among us as a hero."

"I do not need their welcome nor to be called your hero." Azem studied his scimitar-shaped nails. "When I come again among those pathetic wisps of magic, the Council, it shall be as their conquerer and their lord."

Khalid clapped his hands, bringing forth his own carpet. He soared to his mate's side, adding his pleas to hers: "Show kindness to these children now, great Azem, and I swear by the bracelet that marks us as Bound, Tamar and I both shall serve you!"

Azem merely stretched his arms heavenward, working out the kinks in his spine. "I need your service as little as I need the boy's. If he does not wish now and release me, another may come to do so after he is dead. That—" he eyed Rafiqa "—does not seem like too long to wait."

"Will you cut off your nose to spite your face?" Tamar gasped.

"Better. I will cut it off to spite *yours*." He studied the female genie. "A shame. It is a very pretty face." He reached out to touch it.

Khalid flew between Azem's gigantic hand and Tamar, ramming it away. Azem's lip curled. He flicked Khalid out of the sky with one twitch of his fingers, carpet and all. Tamar shrieked, though it was difficult to say whether it was for her fallen mate or because Rafiqa was still reeling her carpet earthward.

From the roof of the Tomb, Hafiz, Rashid, Boabdil, and Yeshisha watched as Tamar's carpet landed near Khalid's sprawled body. The female genie knelt beside her mate, Aminah kicking in her arms, and tried to shield both helpless ones as Azem and Rafiqa closed in on them from either side. Both monsters had cast off much of their supernatural size, though they still towered over their intended victims.

"One for me and one for you," Azem remarked jovially to the demon. "This is fair."

"I presume you want the big one," Rafiqa said.

"That was my plan."

"A bad plan, then; you cannot have her. Do you not see what she wears upon her wrist?" Rafiqa pointed at the simple copper bracelet, gloating. "She is Bound, you fool! That is one magic not even our powers can undo."

"Oh no? We shall see." Without warning, Azem jerked the bracelet from Tamar's wrist and held it high, ready to crush it in his mighty hand. "Let us see whether what is Bound cannot also be broken!"

"Do not do it, O Azem!" Tamar's prayer could have melted stone. "In my bracelet I hold Khalid's soul, as he holds mine in his! Spare it, in the name of all you love!"

"O Witless One, what a thing to say," Azem replied, his words honey dripping from a dagger's edge. "All that I have ever loved is me."

An idea may blossom as slowly as a flower or strike as suddenly as a snake.

"Azem!" Hafiz leaped to his feet, the scabbard's jewels twinkling in the sun. "Azem, as I am yet your Master, I command you to attend me!"

"Chirp, chirp, little cricket," Azem muttered. "Unless you have business with me, hold your peace." His fingers began to close around the bracelet.

"But I *do* have business with you," Hafiz shouted. "I have a wish—half a wish—to make. Then all things between us are paid."

"Is it so?" Azem lifted one eyebrow. "No more whining for advice? For teaching?"

"I want nothing from you but what you owe me."

"Very well." Azem made a great show of placing

Tamar's bracelet under his foot, where it could be as easily crushed as in his hand. He folded his arms and scornfully asked, "What is thy wish, O Master? For the safety of your sister? For the safety of your friend? For the safety of your own worthless skin? Speak! I stand ready to do as you say." He grinned wolfishly. "*Exactly* as you say."

"I will not wish for them nor for myself," Hafiz returned. (Had Azem not been so blinded by complacency, he might have noticed that the boy's grin was frighteningly like his own.) "No, this I wish for *you*, Azem; for you and for none other." He closed his eyes and intoned, "*I wish that you may have your freedom!*"

"You *wish* it? My freedom? But—But—But when you make your last wish I will have it anyway*ayyiii-ieeee*!" A scream of pain tore from Azem's throat. His body writhed and twisted itself into a coil, then whipped back into its original shape so abruptly that he was snapped from his feet. Tamar jumped to recover her bracelet. Azem did not mind the loss. He was too busy being torn this way and that by unseen hands. Gasping, panting, whimpering, at last he forced his mouth to form the words: "*Hearkening and obedience!*"

A shaft of light sliced through the air to strike the golden disc in the lions' paws. The reflected flash fanned out to engulf every being within the valley of the Tomb. It was over in the time it takes a mosquito to hiccup. When it was gone, the Tomb of King Solomon and all the land around it were deserted.

CHAPTER THIRTY-TWO

As if they shared a single throat, Prince Masud, Master Basim and Haroun ben Hasan all thundered, "Well? Speak! You have much to answer for."

"Very nice," said Boabdil. "Have you been practicing?"

The cat sat in the middle of the elaborately tiled floor of the Rose Chamber, the name by which all of the sultan's subjects, noble and commoner alike, knew and feared His Majesty's throne room of justice. It was so called on account of the many mosaic designs of blooming roses worked into the floor and the walls.

The throne of justice itself likewise resembled a single blossom of purest silver, the edges of its petals enamelled pink. This reposed upon a curved platform with some twenty shallow steps leading up to it, each hewn from priceless jade. To either side of the throne ran wrought iron shoots and brambles bearing lesser flowers. On the painted leaves of these the sultan's advisors and fellow judges perched uncomfortably, for no one ever said it was an easy thing to sit in judgment on one's fellow man.

It was from these lesser leaves that the command for speech had gone up in such perfect unison. The sultan looked to left and right, regarding the three speakers quizzically. "Perhaps you should take turns," he suggested. A murmur of agreement went up from the Bower, which was the curtained-off portion of the Rose Chamber reserved for female witnesses and visitors. The prince, the genie, and Hafiz's father exchanged a sheepish chuckle, then fell into floods of courtesy.

"You first, Master Basim."

"No, no, I am a genie; we have time. After *you*, Lord Haroun."

"I could hardly presume to speak before Prince Masud. Your Highness, will you—?"

Prince Masud seemed to be on the point of deferring to Master Basim when he was hit by another fit of half-heroics. All politeness melted from him, his chest swelled with self-importance, and he bellowed, "Of *course* I shall go first! The *idea* that anyone should ever come before me!" He turned a hawk's blazing eye to the unlucky subjects of the tribunal, three miserable creatures awaiting the judgment of sultan, genie, lord, and prince.

On the floor of the Rose Chamber, seated on three wobbly wooden stools, Hafiz ben Haroun, Prince Rashid, and Khalid all crouched with hands clasped and heads bent. The cat Boabdil sat beside Hafiz and rubbed himself against the boy's leg by way of reassurance. Laid out on the tiles before them all was the sheath belonging to the Sword of Solomon. The great dragon's-belly ruby that was its chief glory was no more than a gaping, charred, still-smoking crater.

The Sword itself reposed at Prince Masud's side. He stood up from his seat on an iron roseleaf and strode down the steps of the throne to confront the accused. He placed himself squarely in front of his son, spread his hands dramatically, and said, "What do you mean by disappearing like that, turning your grandfather's entire palace upside-down, and making me sally forth at the head of all our armies to search for you?"

"But Father, you never did have to sally forth, I am back unharmed, and Malak the Murderous is not going to invade us after all," Rashid replied.

"Oh." Prince Masud's face fell. "Never mind," he said curtly and stalked back to his seat.

"Is it your turn now?" the sultan asked Master Basim.

The genie did not await a second invitation, but sailed in upon Khalid like a tidal wave. "What do you mean by running off with your Bound mate, placing yourselves and your unborn child in danger, and battling monsters that not even all the Council put together could ever hope to defeat?"

"But Master Basim, we did not run off; we were snatched away by the demon Rafiqa!" Khalid protested.

"That is so!" Tamar's voice rang out from the Bower. "And as for the rest, am I worthy to bring a child into this world if I am unwilling to help those children already born, even if it means facing monsters to save them?"

Master Basim coughed into his beard. "Hrmph! Yes, well . . ." He retreated to his place and nodded to Haroun ben Hasan. "*You* try to make them see reason."

Haroun took a deep breath, clapped his hands to his knees and stood up. He tried to fix his son with a stern look as he descended the steps, but found himself unable to do so. He was too happy to have his children back, alive and well, to work up the proper level of fatherly anger. He did manage to wrestle a scowl onto his face, but it did not have the desired effect on Hafiz. Instead of cringing, the boy pressed his hand to his mouth, holding back laughter.

Haroun attempted to make his voice inspire the dread his face could not. "What do you mean by—?" he began, shaking a finger in Hafiz's face.

"Yes!" Nur called from behind the Bower's veils. "What do you mean by saving your sister's life?"

"What do you mean by rescuing Prince Rashid?" Tamar's question made the curtains of the Bower flap and ripple.

A small, tightly bandaged figure bounded out of the Bower to sit beside Boabdil. "*What do you mean by saving your sister* and *the prince* and *the genies* and *the kingdom* and *by defeating the demon Rafiqa and the evil Azem all at the same time? Yes, just what do you mean by* that, *eh?*" Yeshisha curled her tail around her paws and looked as pleased as it was possible to look with a face covered in linen.

Haroun stared at the cat-shaped apparition, then at his son. "You did all that?" His finger stopped shaking; it dropped to his side, vanquished.

"I think I did, Father," Hafiz replied.

"Could you—? Do you—? Would you mind telling me how?"

The boy shrugged. "I had a wish. I used it."

"Half a wish," Boabdil purred.

"May the All High have mercy upon us," said Haroun, clasping his hands together. "I, who in my day have had uncounted and uncountable wishes at my disposal, never accomplished so much with a single one of them!"

"And I, who have granted more wishes than I can number to more Masters than I can name have never heard of a mortal doing so much with a single wish, let alone half of one," said Master Basim. "Boy, how is this possible?"

Hafiz pressed his teeth to his lower lip. "I do not think I can explain it. It might be easier if I could show you, but I do not know how that would be possible."

Master Basim stood up. In his hand was the diamond-encrusted lamp that was both his mark of office as head of the Council and his temporary home whenever he chose to serve a mortal Master. "If you will swear not to take advantage of my kindness, I am willing to enter this lamp so that you may release me and I may use one of your wishes to satisfy the curiosity of all present."

Hafiz ben Haroun got up from his stool and bowed to the venerable genie, swearing by all things holy that he would do so. Master Basim hesitated, regarding the boy with an understandable measure of suspicion. Then his curiosity overcame every other emotion and he streamed into the lamp as a long trail of pale purple smoke.

"*Mine!*" Boabdil meowed happily, pouncing on the lamp.

He was quick, but Hafiz was quicker. The boy snatched the lamp from the cat's paws and hugged it close. "Boabdil! You heard me give Master Basim my word of honor! You ought to be ashamed."

The cat's whiskers quivered with mischief. "You can never blame a cat for trying."

Like his father, Hafiz tried to force himself to frown and, like his father, he failed. Fighting back a smile he told the cat, "Someone should teach you how to behave." Then he rubbed the lamp.

Master Basim's upper body emerged from the elegantly curving spout of the lamp balanced upon a column of the same pale purple smoke that had carried him inside. The Rose Chamber resounded with the old genie's deep, awe-inspiring tones as he hailed young Hafiz as his Master and offered him the standard three wishes (most definitely *not* forgetting the *However* clause). This formality done, Master Basim reassembled himself into fully visible form, legs included, and waited for Hafiz to speak.

"I wish . . ." The boy paused.

"Yes, yes, I know what you wish! You wish that I

would show us all a vision of how you saved so many lives and defeated such terrible monsters when all you had was a half wish to your name." The genie clapped his hands together lightly and rapidly, the way the sultan's major domo did when he wanted to make the lesser servants put a little speed into their chores. "Go on, go on, say it exactly the way I did and—"

"I wish Prince Masud was restored to being just the way he was before Rashid and I made any wishes!" Hafiz blurted.

Master Basim's jaw dropped. "You what?"

"You heard the boy!" Boabdil pranced in front of the genie, tail a banner. "He wishes that Prince Masud—"

"I heard him, I heard him. It is just that— Oh, never mind!" He snorted. "*Hearkening and obedience!*"

The sound of phantom trumpets shook the Rose Chamber, making the metal leaves and petals tremble on their stems. The smell of horses galloping in the first charge of battle washed over the room, mingled with the hot reek of freshly spilled blood. A ghostly army raced from out of nowhere, across the tiled floor, and up the steps of the throne. Swords waving, throats taut with their battle cry, they rushed straight for Prince Masud.

The Prince saw them coming and turned whiter than they. With one hand he covered his eyes, with the other he drew the Sword of Solomon and waved it in front of him as a blind man might use the staff that tells him where to set his feet. The gesture did not even slow the oncoming horde. With wild howls of glee they flung themselves upon the cowering prince's blade—

—and disappeared.

The Rose Chamber held silence. Princess Nur stuck her head out between the curtains of the Bower. "We could not see a thing," she announced, Aminah sleeping against her shoulder. "Did something happen?"

"You might say that, my dear," her husband answered, never taking his eyes from the still-shaking blade of the Sword. "You might."

Prince Masud slowly lowered his hand from his eyes and looked around. His eyes rested at last on the Sword of Solomon in his grasp. With every measure of his former elegance upon him, he crossed the floor to place the Sword in Haroun ben Hasan's hands.

"I thank you for the loan of it," he said. "It was an enlightening experience, but not one I think I would care to repeat. The Sword is yours, the pen is mine. When one is born to be a poet, the sharpest things one should ever have to face are the tongues of critics."

"*Father!*" Rashid leaped from his stool and ran into Prince Masud's arms. "Oh Father, you are yourself again!"

Father and son embraced with joy. Prince Masud cupped his son's chin in his hand and told him, "My child, perhaps now you realize that a ruler does better to pursue government, not glory."

"All I know is that you will stop acting like a bully and a fool," Rashid replied.

Prince Masud shrugged, a smile of self-mockery on his lips. "You may be half right."

"So something *did* happen!" Nur was not pleased to have missed it. She passed the sleeping baby to someone still within the Bower's curtains. "Hold this. *Carefully*." Hands free, she yanked down the filmy veils and kicked them aside. "That is better." She took back her baby from Tamar and resumed her seat.

Master Basim stamped his foot, his eyes shooting lightnings at Hafiz. "I see where you get your contrary spirit, young man," he said. "You swore that if I granted you a wish by which to show us your exploits, you would not take advantage of my kindness!"

"But you granted me *three* wishes, O Master Basim," Hafiz reminded him.

"I had to. It is the traditional number dictated by the law all genies must obey!"

"I know it, and thus I did not think you would mind if I used one of them to set things right between Rashid and his father. You would not want me to hold onto the two extra wishes forever, would you?" Hafiz's eyes were wide with innocent appeal.

Master Basim glanced from the boy to the cat at his feet. Boabdil, too, assumed an innocent expression. His was not at all convincing. "I see your point," the genie conceded.

"*Now* I wish that all here might know how my half wish worked so much good,"

"That is a good boy." Master Basim patted Hafiz on the head in the very same condescending manner that Azem had used. At least the older genie did not knock the boy's turban over his eyes. "Hearkening and obedience."

At the genie's words, a black wind blew through the Rose Chamber, snatching up the curtains Princess Nur had torn down and shredding them into rags, tatters, and threads. The gossamer scraps whirled into a pattern of dazzling color that held every eye transfixed until, from the center of the vortex, an all-too-familiar figure uncurled like a cobra readying to strike.

"Aiiiieee!" Tamar cried. "It is Azem!"

"Master Basim, why have you summoned our enemy into our midst?" Khalid implored, tugging at the ancient genie's sleeve. "You know that even together, we cannot defeat him."

Master Basim's beard and moustache trembled as he stared at the ever-growing presence of Azem. "I did not *intend* to summon him. I only called upon my powers to fulfill my Master's wish! I thought that they would bring us a vision, not a visitor."

"Ahhhhh!" Little fires licked from Azem's mouth as he breathed a great sigh and looked all around him. "It is very good to be here." His eye fell upon Hafiz. The boy stood gawping at the evil one, with the cat Boabdil nothing more than a pink, triangular nose poking out from beneath his young friend's robe. "*There* you are, O my late Master," Azem drawled, plucking the boy from the floor like a grape from the vine. "We need to have a little talk about the consequences of making unwise wishes, you and I."

"Let the boy go!" shouted Tamar. "He gave you the one thing which you have desired for centuries: Your freedom! How can you quarrel with him for having made such unselfish use of his last wish?"

Azem turned hooded eyes upon the female genie and merely said, "*Half* a wish."

"Half a—" Master Basim was perplexed. "But how is it possible to grant only half a wish for freedom? One is either free, or one is not. I do not see—"

"*AZEM!*" A fireball the size of the sultan's throne exploded from the ceiling. Like a dragon bursting full-grown from the egg, the demon Rafiqa flashed into sight. Her talons fell onto Azem's shoulder and dug in. "You put him down *right this instant*."

Azem stole a timorous backwards peep at the demon and whispered, "Yes, Beloved." He set Hafiz down gently and even straightened the wrinkles from the boy's robe.

"What do you think you are doing here, playing with these silly mortals, wasting time?" Rafiqa went on, her claws tightening in Azem's flesh. "I told you that I wanted a basket of candied plums from the market in Baghdad *at once*. You simply cannot get decent candied plums anywhere else," she confided to the onlookers.

"You speak only truth, my pearl," Azem soothed. "And may I be torn to pieces by the beak of the phoenix if I was not on my way to Baghdad. But before I might fetch you your candied plums, I was rudely yanked hither by the force of enchantment. I thought that as long as I was here, I might take care of some unfinished business that remains between myself and the boy." He nodded towards Hafiz.

"*What* unfinished business?" Rafiqa's eyes narrowed.

"Our friend Azem seems to have a complaint to lodge against Hafiz," Boabdil spoke up. "It is something about having his freedom."

"Freedom?" the demon echoed. "What complaint can he have about that? He is free. Nay, he is better than free!"

And she held out a wrist thick as a tree trunk for their inspection. Around it hung a bracelet that was the image of the two that Khalid and Tamar wore as a sing of being Bound.

"Well, well." Master Basim coughed and cleared his throat. "It would appear that congratulations to the happy couple are in order."

"*Half* the happy couple," said Azem. There was as much spine and spunk in his words as there was wine in watermelons. He held out both of his wrists for them to see. Neither one bore the bracelet that would signify that Rafiqa was as much Bound to him and subject to his will as he was Bound and subject to her.

"Oh, stop your whining!" Rafiqa snapped, smacking his hands aside. "I still want those candied plums. Move!"

Azem sighed from the depths of his broken spirit. "Yes, dear," he said. The pair of them vanished.

"I . . . see," said Master Basim, stroking his beard. He regarded Hafiz with respect and a goodly portion of dread. "You are obviously a mortal who knows how to get the most out of his wishes. I hope—I pray—I trust that you will use the wish remaining to you in a manner that will not cause me *too* much grief?"

"Master Basim, I—" Hafiz started to say.

"Hafiz makes no wish in haste!" Boabdil exclaimed, jumping into the conversation with all four paws, uninvited. "All wishes are the heart's dearest desires clothed in words. To speak them is to lay them out like a merchant's wares where any passing lout may trifle with them, laugh at them, shatter them past repair. For too long have you genies done your best to trick and trap unwitting mortals. You have made us worry more about the wording of our wishes than their worth. Who knows how many times a mortal's true wish was for a world of peace? And who can say how many times this wish went unasked, for fear of some genie interpreting it to mean a world without song or laughter or life? No, no, my friend Basim!" The cat's tail lashed violently. "Hafiz shall not use the last wish he may ever own *too* swiftly. He shall not use it until after he has had the benefit of my wisdom and good counsel. He shall not use it until—"

"Oh, be quiet, Boabdil!" Hafiz exclaimed impatiently. "You are always trying to mind everyone else's business. *Your* wisdom! *Your* good counsel! I wish that when someone *does* teach you how to behave they will also give you the benefit of *their* wisdom and good counsel!"

"And of *your* hasty tongue, O Monkey-chatter," the cat snarled.

It was too late. Master Basim spread his arms wide, exulting as he cried, "Hearkening and obedience!" He then collapsed into fits of laughter. When he was finally able to speak again, he said, "I do not know what form my magic shall give to the fulfillment of that wish, but I do know that after all these years I have at last had the better of you, O Cat!"

And the ancient genie bent over to tweak Boabdil's tail!

A golden paw with claws like tiny scimitars flashed across the imprudent genie's hand, leaving four red streaks in its wake. A melodious voice decreed, "That would be neither wise *nor* the right way to behave, O Master Basim!"

A gasp of pure wonder filled every mouth. Every head turned to behold a gloriously beautiful female cat in the pride and flower of her life standing in the midst of a puddle of castoff linen wrappings. Gold gleamed at her neck and ears, but the scarab that had been attached to the tip of her tail had fallen off with the bandages.

"Yeshisha?" Paw by paw, Boabdil stole near enough to sniff her. "It *is* you! But how—?"

The she-cat flared her whiskers. "In all the years I attended King Solomon, never did I find the tomcat whose wit and courage were worthy of me. Therefore when my lady placed her spell upon me, she did so with two intents: that I might serve as guide through the maze to the heart of the Tomb and that I might someday myself be guided through the maze of the centuries to the love of my heart." She rubbed her jowl against his. "I have found it."

"As have I." Boabdil licked her ears in bliss and purred words of wisdom that Solomon himself might have spoken: "Who could wish for more?"

To Read About Great Characters Having Incredible Adventures You Should Try ☛ ☛ ☛

BAEN

IF YOU LIKE . . .	YOU SHOULD TRY . . .
Arthurian Legend...	*The Winter Prince* by Elizabeth E. Wein
Computers...	Rick Cook's *Wizard's Bane* series
Cats...	Larry Niven's *Man-Kzin Wars* series
	Cats in Space ed. by Bill Fawcett
Horses...	*Hunting Party* and *Sporting Chance* by Elizabeth Moon
	Dun Lady's Jess by Doranna Durgin
Fantasy Role Playing Games...	*The Bard's Tale* ™ Novels by Mercedes Lackey et al.
	The Rose Sea by S.M. Stirling & Holly Lisle
	Harry Turtledove's *Werenight* and *Prince of the North*
Computer Games...	*The Bard's Tale* ™ Novels by Mercedes Lackey et al.
	The *Wing Commander* ™ Novels by Mercedes Lackey, William R. Forstchen, et al.